"The writers of the nineteen twenties and thirties brought to the short story an awareness of the complexity of modern life; they enriched it with a better understanding of psychology; and they endowed it with a sense of social values, putting into their work an ardent belief in the rights of the common man....

"The nineteen short stories printed in this book are first-rate examples of American storytelling, each one interesting in itself, all good enough for any country to feel proud of....Tempered by adversity, toughened by depression and war, and compelled to reappraise values that once seemed fixed, American authors have poured into their writing the very stuff of American life as it was lived during an era that is already passing away."

—from the Introduction

PHILIP VAN DOREN STERN is the author and editor of numerous works in the fields of literature and history during the past thirty years. He holds an honorary Doctorate of Literature from Rutgers University, and has contributed to many of the leading national magazines.

A POCKET BOOK OF MODERN AMERICAN SHORT STORIES

Edited and with an Introduction
by Philip Van Doren Stern

WSP WASHINGTON SQUARE PRESS   NEW YORK

A POCKET BOOK OF MODERN AMERICAN SHORT STORIES

A *Washington Square Press* edition

1st printing.......................October, 1943

29th printing....................February, 1970

Published by Washington Square Press,
a division of Simon & Schuster, Inc., 630 Fifth Avenue, New York, N.Y.

L

WASHINGTON SQUARE PRESS editions are distributed in the
U.S. by Simon & Schuster, Inc., 630 Fifth Avenue, New
York, N.Y. 10020 and in Canada by Simon & Schuster
of Canada, Ltd., Richmond Hill, Ontario, Canada.

ACKNOWLEDGMENTS

For permission to reprint copyrighted material, the
following acknowledgments are gratefully made:

BRANDT & BRANDT. The story "Johnny Pye and the Fool-Killer" by Stephen Vincent Benét. From *Tales Before Midnight*, published by Farrar and Rinehart, Inc., copyright, 1937, by Stephen Vincent Benét. "Silent Snow, Secret Snow" by Conrad Aiken from *Among the Lost People.*

COWARD-McCANN, INC. The story "The Romance of Rosy Ridge" by MacKinlay Kantor. Reprinted by special permission of Coward-McCann, Inc., copyright, 1937, by MacKinlay Kantor.

DOUBLEDAY & COMPANY, INC. The story "A Visit of Charity" by Eudora Welty. From *A Curtain of Green* by Eudora Welty, copyright, 1936, 1941, reprinted by permission of Doubleday & Company, Inc.; and from *Web of Green* by Eudora Welty, reprinted by permission of John Lane, The Bodley Head, Ltd. The story "Young Man Axelbrod" by Sinclair Lewis. From *Selected Short Stories of Sinclair Lewis* by Sinclair Lewis, copyright, 1917, 1945, reprinted by permission of Doubleday & Company, Inc.

DUELL, SLOAN & PEARCE, INC. The story "Country Full of Swedes" by Erskine Caldwell. From *Jackpot*, reprinted by permission of the publishers, Duell, Sloan & Pearce, Inc.

HARCOURT, BRACE AND WORLD, INC. The story "That Tree" by Katherine Anne Porter. From *Flowering Judas and Other Stories*, copyright, 1930, 1935, by Katherine Anne Porter, reprinted by permission of Harcourt, Brace and World, Inc.

MAXIM LIEBER. The story "The Happiest Man on Earth" by Albert Maltz. Originally published in *Harper's Magazine*, June, 1938, reprinted by permission of Maxim Lieber. The story "A Tree. A Rock. A Cloud" by Carson McCullers, reprinted by permission of Maxim Lieber, copyright, November, 1943, by *Harper's Bazaar*.

RANDOM HOUSE, INC. The stories "Going Home" from *Inhale and Exhale* by William Saroyan, and "That Evening Sun Go Down" by William Faulkner, reprinted by permission of Random House, Inc.

CHARLES SCRIBNER'S SONS. "Champion" is reprinted with the permission of Charles Scribner's Sons and Chatto & Windus, Ltd. from *Round Up* by Ring Lardner. Copyright, 1929, by Charles Scribner's Sons; renewal copyright, (c), 1957 by Ellis A. Lardner. "The Snows of Kilimanjaro" (Copyright, 1936, by Ernest Hemingway; renewal copyright, (c), 1961, by Mary Hemingway) is reprinted with the permission of Charles Scribner's Sons and Jonathan Cape, Ltd. from *The Short Stories of Ernest Hemingway.* "Babylon Revisited" (Copyright, 1931, by The Curtis Publishing Company; renewal copyright, (c), 1959, by Frances S. P. Lanahan) is reprinted with the permission of Charles Scribner's Sons from *Taps at Reveille* by F. Scott Fitzgerald, and with the permission of the Estate of F. Scott Fitzgerald.

SIMON & SCHUSTER, INC. The story "Profession: Housewife" by Sally Benson. Copyright, 1940, by *The New Yorker*, published by Simon & Schuster, Inc., in *Short Stories from The New Yorker*. The story "The Explorers" by Jerome Weidman. From *The Horse That Could Whistle "Dixie,"* copyright, 1939, by Jerome Weidman, published by Simon & Schuster, Inc.

JAMES THURBER. The story "The Night the Ghost Got In" by James Thurber. From *The New Yorker* Magazine and *My Life and Hard Times.*

THE VIKING PRESS, INC. The story "The Leader of the People" by John Steinbeck. From *The Long Valley*, copyright, 1938, by John Steinbeck, by permission of The Viking Press, Inc., New York, and William Heinemann, Ltd. The story "You Were Perfectly Fine" by Dorothy Parker. From *Here Lies*, copyright, 1930, 1933, 1939, by Dorothy Parker, by permission of The Viking Press, Inc., New York.

Contents

Introduction

DURING the period between the First and Second World Wars the American short story came of age. Many fine short stories had been written in this country before that time, but the writers of the nineteen twenties and thirties brought to the short story an awareness of the complexity of modern life; they enriched it with a better understanding of psychology; and they endowed it with a sense of social values, putting into their work an ardent belief in the rights of the common man.

During the years of the Long Armistice, insecurity, doubt, and the constant threat of war troubled the minds of all those who were sensitive to what was happening at home and abroad. European reflections of this uncertainty will be found in F. Scott Fitzgerald's "Babylon Revisited" and Ernest Hemingway's "The Snows of Kilimanjaro"—both containing fine portraits of the American expatriate; domestic aspects can be seen in Albert Maltz' ironically titled "The Happiest Man on Earth." John Steinbeck's "The Leader of the People" symbolizes the passing of the pioneers and their dream of boundless plenty; William Faulkner's tensely dramatic story, "That Evening Sun Go Down," is filled with the fear and violence of the era.

But even in a somber age writers spin romances, recount gay and joyous happenings, tell of the beauty and pity and wonder of man's everyday existence in this many-faceted world. Stephen Vincent Benét used romantic American folklore for some of his best tales; MacKinlay Kantor called upon the exciting events of our history for his material; James Thurber, Ring Lardner, and Dorothy Parker proved that the

vii

irrepressible humor which characterized American writing in Mark Twain's day is still a potent force in our literature—and they also showed that underneath their jesting lay the same deep feeling for humanity which made the great nineteenth-century humorist more than a teller of funny stories.

The nineteen short stories printed in this book are first-rate examples of American storytelling, each one interesting in itself, all good enough for any country to feel proud of having produced in the short space of twenty-odd years. Taken collectively they show a maturity which even the finest American work of the nineteenth century seldom possessed. They show that our writers have grown up. Tempered by adversity, toughened by depression and war, and compelled to reappraise values that once seemed fixed, American authors have poured into their writing the very stuff of American life as it was lived during an era that is already passing away.

For the America of the twenties and the thirties is now as much a part of our historic past as the America of the eighteen fifties or of the years just before the First World War. The stories in this book deal with our yesterdays—yesterdays that are still so close that even the youngest of us can remember them, yet they are gone forever as surely as the days of the pioneers. Here is the record of those yesterdays set down by artists who observed, who transmuted their experiences in the fire of imagination, and who then expressed in words what all of us may have felt.

This book is their joint product. They did not collaborate consciously to put it together, but the fact that they all lived at the same time in the same country gives it a certain unity. The reader, going from story to story, may say: "Why, yes, that's just how it was. I lived through that myself." And then perhaps for a moment he will recall old faces, hear again the old songs, and remember how the old scenes looked before this ruthless present marked *finis* to the days we all share as a common past.

PHILIP VAN DOREN STERN

A POCKET BOOK OF

MODERN AMERICAN

SHORT STORIES

STEPHEN VINCENT BENÉT

Johnny Pye and the Fool-Killer

You DON'T hear so much about the Fool-Killer these days, but when Johnny Pye was a boy there was a good deal of talk about him. Some said he was one kind of person, and some said another, but most people agreed that he came around fairly regular. Or, it seemed so to Johnny Pye. But then, Johnny was an adopted child, which is, maybe, why he took it so hard.

The miller and his wife had offered to raise him, after his own folks died, and that was a good deed on their part. But, as soon as he lost his baby teeth and started acting the way most boys act, they started to come down on him like thunder, which wasn't so good. They were good people, according to their lights, but their lights were terrible strict ones, and they believed that the harder you were on a youngster, the better and brighter he got. Well, that may work with some children, but it didn't with Johnny Pye.

He was sharp enough and willing enough—as sharp and willing as most boys in Martinsville. But, somehow or other, he never seemed to be able to do the right things or say the right words—at least when he was home. Treat a boy like a fool and he'll act like a fool, I say, but there's some folks need convincing. The miller and his wife thought the way to smarten Johnny was to treat him like a fool, and finally they got so he pretty much believed it himself.

And that was hard on him, for he had a boy's imagination, and maybe a little more than most. He could stand the beatings and he did. But what he couldn't stand was the way things went at the mill. I don't suppose the miller intended to do it. But, as long as Johnny Pye could remember, when-

I

ever he heard of the death of somebody he didn't like, he'd say, "Well, the Fool-Killer's come for so-and-so," and sort of smack his lips. It was, as you might say, a family joke, but the miller was a big man with a big red face, and it made a strong impression on Johnny Pye. Till, finally, he got a picture of the Fool-Killer, himself. He was a big man, too, in a checked shirt and corduroy trousers, and he went walking the ways of the world, with a hickory club that had a lump of lead in the end of it. I don't know how Johnny Pye got that picture so clear, but, to him, it was just as plain as the face of any human being in Martinsville. And, now and then, just to test it, he'd ask a grown-up person, kind of timidly, if that was the way the Fool-Killer looked. And, of course, they'd generally laugh and tell him it was. Then Johnny would wake up at night, in his room over the mill, and listen for the Fool-Killer's step on the road and wonder when he was coming. But he was brave enough not to tell anybody that.

Finally, though, things got a little more than he could bear. He'd done some boy's trick or other—let the stones grind a little fine, maybe, when the miller wanted the meal ground coarse—just carelessness, you know. But he'd gotten two whippings for it, one from the miller and one from his wife, and at the end of it, the miller had said, "Well, Johnny Pye, the Fool-Killer ought to be along for you most any day now. For I never did see a boy that was such a fool." Johnny looked to the miller's wife to see if she believed it, too, but she just shook her head and looked serious. So he went to bed that night, but he couldn't sleep, for every time a bough rustled or the mill wheel creaked, it seemed to him it must be the Fool-Killer. And, early next morning, before anybody was up, he packed such duds as he had in a bandanna handkerchief and ran away.

He didn't really expect to get away from the Fool-Killer very long—as far as he knew, the Fool-Killer got you wherever you went. But he thought he'd give him a run for his money, at least. And when he got on the road, it was a bright spring morning, and the first peace and quiet he'd had in some time. So his spirits rose, and he chunked a stone at a bullfrog as he went along, just to show he was Johnny Pye and still doing business.

He hadn't gone more than three or four miles out of Martinsville, when he heard a buggy coming up the road behind him. He knew the Fool-Killer didn't need a buggy to catch you, so he wasn't afraid of it, but he stepped to the side of the road to let it pass. But it stopped, instead, and a black-whiskered man with a stove-pipe hat looked out of it.

"Hello, bub," he said. "Is this the road for East Liberty?"

"My name's John Pye and I'm eleven years old," said Johnny, polite but firm, "and you take the next left fork for East Liberty. They say it's a pretty town—I've never been there myself." And he sighed a little, because he thought he'd like to see the world before the Fool-Killer caught up with him.

"H'm," said the man. "Stranger here, too, eh? And what brings a smart boy like you on the road so early in the morning?"

"Oh," said Johnny Pye, quite honestly, "I'm running away from the Fool-Killer. For the miller says I'm a fool and his wife says I'm a fool and almost everybody in Martinsville says I'm a fool except little Susie Marsh. And the miller says the Fool-Killer's after me—so I thought I'd run away before he came."

The black-whiskered man sat in his buggy and wheezed for a while. When he got his breath back, "Well, jump in, bub," he said. "The miller may say you're a fool, but I think you're a right smart boy to be running away from the Fool-Killer all by yourself. And I don't hold with small-town prejudices and I need a right smart boy, so I'll give you a lift on the road."

"But, will I be safe from the Fool-Killer, if I'm with you?" said Johnny. "For, otherwise, it don't signify."

"Safe?" said the black-whiskered man, and wheezed again. "Oh, you'll be safe as houses. You see, I'm a herb doctor—and some folks think, a little in the Fool-Killer's line of business, myself. And I'll teach you a trade worth two of milling. So jump in, bub."

"Sounds all right the way you say it," said Johnny, "but my name's Johnny Pye," and he jumped into the buggy. And they went rattling along toward East Liberty with the herb doctor talking and cutting jokes till Johnny thought he'd never met a pleasanter man. About half a mile from East Liberty, the doctor stopped at a spring.

"What are we stopping here for?" said Johnny Pye.

"Wait and see," said the doctor, and gave him a wink. Then he got a haircloth trunk full of empty bottles out of the back of the buggy and made Johnny fill them with spring water and label them. Then he added a pinch of pink powder to each bottle and shook them up and corked them and stowed them away.

"What's that?" said Johnny, very interested.

"That's Old Doctor Waldo's Unparalleled Universal Remedy," said the doctor, reading from the label. "Made from the purest snake oil and secret Indian herbs, it cures rheumatism, blind staggers, headache, malaria, five kinds of fits, and spots in front of the eyes. It will also remove oil or grease stains, clean knives and silver, polish brass, and is strongly recommended as a general tonic and blood purifier. Small size, one dollar—family bottle, two dollars and a half."

"But I don't see any snake oil in it," said Johnny, puzzled, "or any secret Indian herbs."

"That's because you're not a fool," said the doctor, with another wink. "The Fool-Killer wouldn't, either. But most folks will."

And, that very same night, Johnny saw. For the doctor made his pitch in East Liberty and he did it handsome. He took a couple of flaring oil torches and stuck them on the sides of the buggy; he put on a diamond stickpin and did card tricks and told funny stories till he had the crowd goggle-eyed. As for Johnny, he let him play on the tambourine. Then he started talking about Doctor Waldo's Universal Remedy, and, with Johnny to help him, the bottles went like hot cakes. Johnny helped the doctor count the money afterward, and it was a pile.

"Well," said Johnny, "I never saw money made easier. You've got a fine trade, doctor."

"It's cleverness does it," said the doctor, and slapped him on the back. "Now a fool's content to stay in one place and do one thing, but the Fool-Killer never caught up with a good pitchman yet."

"Well, it's certainly lucky I met up with you," said Johnny, "and, if it's cleverness does it, I'll learn the trade or bust."

So he stayed with the doctor quite a while—in fact, till he could make up the remedy and do the card tricks almost as good as the doctor himself. And Johnny admired the doctor and the doctor liked Johnny, for Johnny was a biddable boy. But one night they came into a town where things didn't go as they usually did. The crowd gathered as usual, and the doctor did his tricks. But, all the time, Johnny could see a sharp-faced little fellow going through the crowd and whispering to one man and another. Till, at last, right in the middle of the doctor's spiel, the sharp-faced fellow gave a shout of "That's him all right! I'd know them whiskers anywhere!" and, with that, the crowd growled once and began to tear slats out of the nearest fence. Well, the next thing Johnny knew, he and the doctor were being ridden out of town on a rail, with the doctor's long coattails flying at every jounce.

They didn't hurt Johnny particular—him only being a boy. But they warned 'em both never to show their faces in that town again, and then they heaved the doctor into a thistle patch and went their ways.

"Owoo!" said the doctor, "ouch!" as Johnny was helping him out of the thistle patch. "Go easy with those thistles! And why didn't you give me the office, you blame little fool?"

"Office?" said Johnny. "What office?"

"When that sharp-nosed man started snooping around," said the doctor. "I thought that infernal main street looked familiar—I was through there two years ago, selling solid gold watches for a dollar apiece."

"But the works to a solid gold watch would be worth more than that," said Johnny.

"There weren't any works," said the doctor, with a groan, "but there was a nice little beetle inside each case and it made the prettiest tick you ever heard."

"Well, that certainly was a clever idea," said Johnny. "I'd never have thought of that."

"Clever?" said the doctor. "Ouch—it was ruination! But who'd have thought the fools would bear a grudge for two years? And now we've lost the horse and buggy, too—not to speak of the bottles and the money. Well, there's lots more tricks to be played and we'll start again."

But, though he liked the doctor, Johnny began to feel dubious. For it occurred to him that, if all the doctor's cleverness got him was being ridden out of town on a rail, he couldn't be so far away from the Fool-Killer as he thought. And, sure enough, as he was going to sleep that night, he seemed to hear the Fool-Killer's footsteps coming after him —step, step, step. He pulled his jacket up over his ears, but he couldn't shut it out. So, when the doctor had got in the way of starting business over again, he and Johnny parted company. The doctor didn't bear any grudge; he shook hands with Johnny and told him to remember that cleverness was power. And Johnny went on with his running away. He got to a town, and there was a store with a sign in the window, BOY WANTED, so he went in.

There, sure enough, was the merchant, sitting at his desk, and a fine, important man he looked, in his black broadcloth suit. Johnny tried to tell him about the Fool-Killer, but the merchant wasn't interested in that. He just looked Johnny over and saw that he looked biddable and strong for his age. "But, remember, no fooling around, boy!" said the merchant sternly, after he'd hired him.

"No fooling around?" said Johnny, with the light of hope in his eyes.

"No," said the merchant, meaningly. "We've no room for fools in this business, I can tell you! You work hard, and you'll rise. But, if you've got any foolish notions, just knock them on the head and forget them."

Well, Johnny was glad enough to promise that, and he stayed with the merchant a year and a half. He swept out the store, and he put the shutters up and took them down; he ran errands and wrapped up packages and learned to keep busy twelve hours a day. And, being a biddable boy and an honest one, he rose, just like the merchant had said. The merchant raised his wages and let him begin to wait on customers and learn accounts. And then, one night, Johnny woke up in the middle of the night. And it seemed to him he heard, far away but getting nearer, the steps of the Fool-Killer after him—tramping, tramping.

He went to the merchant next day and said, "Sir, I'm sorry to tell you this, but I'll have to be moving on."

"Well, I'm sorry to hear that, Johnny," said the merchant, "for you've been a good boy. And, if it's a question of salary——"

"It isn't that," said Johnny, "but tell me one thing, sir, if you don't mind my asking. Supposing I did stay with you—where would I end?"

The merchant smiled. "That's a hard question to answer," he said, "and I'm not much given to compliments. But I started, myself, as a boy, sweeping out the store. And you're a bright youngster with lots of go-ahead. I don't see why, if you stuck to it, you shouldn't make the same kind of success that I have."

"And what's that?" said Johnny.

The merchant began to look irritated, but he kept his smile. "Well," he said, "I'm not a boastful man, but I'll tell you this. Ten years ago I was the richest man in town. Five years ago, I was the richest man in the county. And five years from now—well, I aim to be the richest man in the state."

His eyes kind of glittered as he said it, but Johnny was

looking at his face. It was sallow-skinned and pouchy, with the jaw as hard as a rock. And it came upon Johnny that moment that, though he'd known the merchant a year and a half, he'd never really seen him enjoy himself except when he was driving a bargain.

"Sorry, sir," he said, "but, if it's like that I'll certainly have to go. Because, you see, I'm running away from the Fool-Killer, and if I stayed here and got to be like you, he'd certainly catch up with me in no——"

"Why, you impertinent young cub!" roared the merchant, with his face gone red all of a sudden. "Get your money from the cashier!" and Johnny was on the road again before you could say "Jack Robinson." But, this time, he was used to it, and walked off whistling.

Well, after that, he hired out to quite a few different people, but I won't go into all of his adventures. He worked for an inventor for a while, and they split up because Johnny happened to ask him what would be the good of his patent, self-winding, perpetual-motion machine, once he did get it invented. And, while the inventor talked big about improving the human race and the beauties of science, it was plain he didn't know. So that night, Johnny heard the steps of the Fool-Killer, far off but coming closer, and, next morning, he went away. Then he stayed with a minister for a while, and he certainly hated to leave him, for the minister was a good man. But they got talking one evening and, as it chanced, Johnny asked him what happened to people who didn't believe in his particular religion. Well, the minister was broad-minded, but there's only one answer to that. He admitted they might be good folks—he even admitted they mightn't exactly go to hell—but he couldn't let them into heaven, no, not the best and the wisest of them, for there were the specifications laid down by creed and church, and, if you didn't fulfill them, you didn't.

So Johnny had to leave him, and, after that, he went with an old drunken fiddler for a while. He wasn't a good man, I guess, but he could play till the tears ran down your cheeks.

And, when he was playing his best, it seemed to Johnny that the Fool-Killer was very far away. For, in spite of his faults and his weaknesses, while he played, there was might in the man. But he died drunk in a ditch, one night, with Johnny to hold his head, and, while he left Johnny his fiddle, it didn't do Johnny much good. For, while Johnny could play a tune, he couldn't play like the fiddler—it wasn't in his fingers.

Then it chanced that Johnny took up with a company of soldiers. He was still too young to enlist, but they made a kind of pet of him, and everything went swimmingly for a while. For the captain was the bravest man Johnny had ever seen, and he had an answer for everything, out of regulations and the Articles of War. But then they went West to fight Indians and the same old trouble cropped up again. For, one night the captain said to him, "Johnny, we're going to fight the enemy tomorrow, but you'll stay in camp."

"Oh, I don't want to do that," said Johnny; "I want to be in on the fighting."

"It's an order," said the captain, grimly. Then he gave Johnny certain instructions and a letter to take to his wife.

"For the colonel's a copper-plated fool," he said, "and we're walking straight into an ambush."

"Why don't you tell him that?" said Johnny.

"I have," said the captain, "but he's the colonel."

"Colonel or no colonel," said Johnny, "if he's a fool, somebody ought to stop him."

"You can't do that, in an army," said the captain. "Orders are orders." But it turned out the captain was wrong about it, for, next day, before they could get moving, the Indians attacked, and got badly licked. When it was all over, "Well, it was a good fight," said the captain, professionally. "All the same, if they'd waited and laid an ambush, they'd have had our hair. But, as it was, they didn't stand a chance."

"But why didn't they lay an ambush?" said Johnny.

"Well," said the captain, "I guess they had their orders too. And now, how would you like to be a soldier?"

"Well, it's a nice outdoors life, but I'd like to think it over," said Johnny. For he knew the captain was brave and he knew the Indians had been brave—you couldn't find two braver sets of people. But, all the same when he thought the whole thing over, he seemed to hear steps in the sky. So he soldiered to the end of the campaign and then he left the Army, though the captain told him he was making a mistake.

By now, of course, he wasn't a boy any longer; he was getting to be a young man with a young man's thoughts and feelings. And, half the time, nowadays, he'd forget about the Fool-Killer except as a dream he'd had when he was a boy. He could even laugh at it now and then, and think what a fool he'd been to believe there was such a man.

But, all the same, the desire in him wasn't satisfied, and something kept driving him on. He'd have called it ambitiousness, now, but it came to the same thing. And with every new trade he tried, sooner or later would come the dream—the dream of the big man in the checked shirt and corduroy pants, walking the ways of the world with his hickory stick in one hand. It made him angry to have that dream, now, but it had a singular power over him. Till, finally, when he was turned twenty or so, he got scared.

"Fool-Killer, or no Fool-Killer," he said to himself, "I've got to ravel this matter out. For there must be some one thing a man could tie to, and be sure he wasn't a fool. I've tried cleverness and money and half a dozen other things, and they don't seem to be the answer. So now I'll try book learning and see what comes of that."

So he read all the books he could find, and whenever he'd seem to hear the steps of the Fool-Killer coming for the authors—and that was frequent—he'd try and shut his ears. But some books said one thing was best and some another, and he couldn't rightly decide.

"Well," he said to himself, when he'd read and read till his head felt as stuffed with book learning as a sausage with meat, "it's interesting, but it isn't exactly contemporaneous. So I think I'll go down to Washington and ask the wise men there. For it must take a lot of wisdom to run a country like the United States, and if there's people who can answer my questions, it's there they ought to be found."

So he packed his bag and off to Washington he went. He was modest, for a youngster, and he didn't intend to try and see the President right away. He thought probably a congressman was about his size. So he saw a congressman, and the congressman told him the thing to be was an upstanding young American and vote the Republican ticket—which sounded all right to Johnny Pye, but not exactly what he was after.

Then he went to a senator, and the senator told him to be an upstanding young American and vote the Democratic ticket—which sounded all right, too, but not what he was after, either. And, somehow, though both men had been impressive and affable, right in the middle of their speeches he'd seemed to hear steps—you know.

But a man has to eat, whatever else he does, and Johnny found he'd better buckle down and get himself a job. It happened to be with the first congressman he struck, for that one came from Martinsville, which is why Johnny went to him in the first place. And, in a little while, he forgot his search entirely and the Fool-Killer, too, for the congressman's niece came East to visit him, and she was the Susie Marsh that Johnny had sat next in school. She'd been pretty then, but she was prettier now, and as soon as Johnny Pye saw her, his heart gave a jump and a thump.

"And don't think we don't remember you in Martinsville, Johnny Pye," she said, when her uncle had explained who his new clerk was. "Why, the whole town'll be excited when I write home. We've heard all about your killing Indians and inventing perpetual motion and traveling around the country with a famous doctor and making a fortune in dry goods and—oh, it's a wonderful story!"

"Well," said Johnny, and coughed, "some of that's just a little bit exaggerated. But it's nice of you to be interested. So they don't think I'm a fool any more, in Martinsville?"

"I never thought you were a fool," said Susie with a little smile, and Johnny felt his heart give another bump.

"And I always knew you were pretty, but never how pretty till now," said Johnny, and coughed again. "But, speaking of old times, how's the miller and his wife? For I did leave them right sudden, and while there were faults on both sides, I must have been a trial to them too."

"They've gone the way of all flesh," said Susie Marsh, "and there's a new miller now. But he isn't very well-liked, to tell the truth, and he's letting the mill run down."

"That's a pity," said Johnny, "for it was a likely mill." Then he began to ask her more questions and she began to remember things too. Well, you know how the time can go when two youngsters get talking like that.

Johnny Pye never worked so hard in his life as he did that winter. And it wasn't the Fool-Killer he thought about— it was Susie Marsh. First he thought she loved him and then he was sure she didn't, and then he was betwixt and between, and all perplexed and confused. But, finally, it turned out all right and he had her promise, and Johnny Pye knew he was the happiest man in the world. And that night, he waked up in the night and heard the Fool-Killer coming after him— step, step, step.

He didn't sleep much after that, and he came down to breakfast hollow-eyed. But his uncle-to-be didn't notice that —he was rubbing his hands and smiling.

"Put on your best necktie, Johnny!" he said, very cheerful, "for I've got an appointment with the President today, and, just to show I approve of my niece's fiancé, I'm taking you along."

"The President!" said Johnny, all dumfounded.

"Yes," said Congressman Marsh, "you see, there's a little bill—well, we needn't go into that. But slick down your back hair, Johnny—we'll make Martinsville proud of us this day!"

Then a weight seemed to go from Johnny's shoulders and a load from his heart. He wrung Mr. Marsh's hand.

"Thank you, Uncle Eben!" he said. "I can't thank you

enough." For, at last, he knew he was going to look upon a man that was bound to be safe from the Fool-Killer—and it seemed to him if he could just once do that, all his troubles and searchings would be ended.

Well, it doesn't signify which President it was—you can take it from me that he was President and a fine-looking man. He'd just been elected, too, so he was lively as a trout, and the saddle galls he'd get from Congress hadn't even begun to show. Anyhow, there he was, and Johnny feasted his eyes on him. For if there was anybody in the country the Fool-Killer couldn't bother, it must be a man like this.

The President and the congressman talked politics for a while, and then it was Johnny's turn.

"Well, young man," said the President, affably, "and what can I do for you—for you look to me like a fine, upstanding young American."

The congressman cut in quick before Johnny could open his mouth. "Just a word of advice, Mr. President," he said. "Just a word in season. For my young friend's led an adventurous life, but now he's going to marry my niece and settle down. And what he needs most of all is a word of ripe wisdom from you."

"Well," said the President, looking at Johnny rather keenly, "if that's all he needs, a short horse is soon curried. I wish most of my callers wanted as little."

But, all the same, he drew Johnny out, as such men can, and before Johnny knew it, he was telling his life story.

"Well," said the President, at the end, "you certainly have been a rolling stone, young man. But there's nothing wrong in that. And, for one of your varied experience there's one obvious career. Politics!" he said, and slapped his fist in his hand.

"Well," said Johnny, scratching his head, "of course, since I've been in Washington, I've thought of that. But I don't know that I'm rightly fitted."

"You can write a speech," said Congressman Marsh, quite thoughtful, "for you've helped me with mine. You're a likable fellow too. And you were born poor and worked up—and you've even got a war-record—why, hell! Excuse me, Mr. President!—he's worth five hundred votes just as he stands!"

"I—I'm more than honored by you two gentlemen," said Johnny, abashed and flattered, "but supposing I did go into politics—where would I end up?"

The President looked sort of modest.

"The Presidency of the United States," said he, "is within the legitimate ambition of every American citizen. Provided he can get elected, of course."

"Oh," said Johnny, feeling dazzled, "I never thought of that. Well, that's a great thing. But it must be a great responsibility too."

"It is," said the President, looking just like his pictures on the campaign buttons.

"Why, it must be an awful responsibility!" said Johnny. "I can't hardly see how a mortal man can bear it. Tell me, Mr. President," he said, "may I ask you a question?"

"Certainly," said the President, looking prouder and more responsible and more and more like his picture on the campaign buttons every minute.

"Well," said Johnny, "it sounds like a fool question, but it's this: This is a great big country of ours, Mr. President, and it's got the most amazing lot of different people in it. How can any President satisfy all those people at one time? Can you yourself, Mr. President?"

The President looked a bit taken aback for a minute. But then he gave Johnny Pye a statesman's glance.

"With the help of God," he said, solemnly, "and in accordance with the principles of our great party, I intend——"

But Johnny didn't even hear the end of the sentence. For, even as the President was speaking, he heard a step outside in the corridor and he knew, somehow, it wasn't the step of a secretary or a guard. He was glad the President had said, "with the help of God" for that sort of softened the step. And when the President finished, Johnny bowed.

"Thank you, Mr. President," he said; "that's what I wanted to know. And now I'll go back to Martinsville, I guess."

"Go back to Martinsville?" said the President, surprised.

"Yes, sir," said Johnny. "For I don't think I'm cut out for politics."

"And is that all you have to say to the President of the United States?" said his uncle-to-be, in a fume.

But the President had been thinking, meanwhile, and he was a bigger man than the congressman.

"Wait a minute, congressman," he said. "This young man's honest, at least, and I like his looks. Moreover, of all the people who've come to see me in the last six months, he's the only one who hasn't wanted something—except the White House cat, and I guess she wanted something, too, because she meowed. You don't want to be President, young man—and, confidentially, I don't blame you. But how would you like to be postmaster at Martinsville?"

"Postmaster at Martinsville?" said Johnny. "But——"

"Oh, it's only a tenth-class post office," said the President, "but, for once in my life, I'll do something because I want to, and let Congress yell its head off. Come—is it yes or no?"

Johnny thought of all the places he'd been and all the trades he'd worked at. He thought, queerly enough, of the old drunk fiddler dead in the ditch, but he knew he couldn't be that. Mostly, though, he thought of Martinsville and Susie Marsh. And, though he'd just heard the Fool-Killer's step, he defied the Fool-Killer.

"Why, it's yes, of course, Mr. President," he said, "for then I can marry Susie."

"That's as good a reason as you'll find," said the President. "And now, I'll just write a note."

Well, he was as good as his word, and Johnny and his Susie were married and went back to live in Martinsville. And, as soon as Johnny learned the ways of postmastering, he found it as good a trade as most. There wasn't much mail in Martinsville, but, in between whiles, he ran the mill, and that was a good trade too. And all the time, he knew, at the back of his mind, that he hadn't quite settled accounts with the Fool-Killer. But he didn't much care about that, for he and Susie were happy. And after a while they had a child, and that was the most remarkable experience that had ever happened to any young couple, though the doctor said it was a perfectly normal baby.

One evening, when his son was about a year old, Johnny Pye took the river road, going home. It was a mite longer than the hill road, but it was the cool of the evening, and there's times when a man likes to walk by himself, fond as he may be of his wife and family.

He was thinking of the way things had turned out for him, and they seemed to him pretty astonishing and singular, as they do to most folks, when you think them over. In fact, he was thinking so hard that, before he knew it, he'd almost stumbled over an old scissors grinder who'd set up his grindstone and tools by the side of the road. The scissors grinder had his cart with him, but he'd turned the horse out to graze—and a lank, old, white horse it was, with every rib showing. And he was very busy, putting an edge on a scythe.

"Oh, sorry," said Johnny Pye. "I didn't know anybody was camping here. But you might come round to my house tomorrow—my wife's got some knives that need sharpening."

Then he stopped, for the old man gave him a long, keen look.

"Why, it's you, Johnny Pye," said the old man. "And how do you do, Johnny Pye! You've been a long time coming—in fact, now and then, I thought I'd have to fetch you. But you're here at last."

Johnny Pye was a grown man now, but he began to tremble.

"But it isn't you!" he said, wildly. "I mean you're not him! Why, I've known how he looks all my life! He's a big man, with a checked shirt, and he carries a hickory stick with a lump of lead in one end."

"Oh, no," said the scissors grinder, quite quiet. "You may have thought of me that way, but that's not the way I am."

And Johnny Pye heard the scythe go whet-whet-whet on the stone. The old man ran some water on it and looked at the edge. Then he shook his head as if the edge didn't quite satisfy him. "Well, Johnny, are you ready?" he said, after a while.

"Ready?" said Johnny, in a hoarse voice. "Of course I'm not ready."

"That's what they all say," said the old man, nodding his head, and the scythe went whet-whet on the stone.

Johnny wiped his brow and started to argue it out.

"You see, if you'd found me earlier," he said, "or later. I don't want to be unreasonable, but I've got a wife and a child."

"Most has wives and many has children," said the old man, grimly, and the scythe went whet-whet on the stone as he pushed the treadle. And a shower of sparks flew, very clear and bright, for the night had begun to fall.

"Oh, stop that damn racket and let a man think for a minute!" said Johnny, desperate. "I can't go, I tell you. I won't. It isn't time. It's——"

The old man stopped the grindstone and pointed with the scythe at Johnny Pye.

"Tell me one good reason," he said. "There's men would be missed in the world, but are you one of them? A clever man might be missed, but are you a clever man?"

"No," said Johnny, thinking of the herb doctor. "I had a chance to be clever, but I gave it up."

"One," said the old man, ticking off on his fingers. "Well, a rich man might be missed—by some. But you aren't rich, I take it."

"No," said Johnny, thinking of the merchant, "nor wanted to be."

"Two," said the old man. "Cleverness—riches—they're done. But there's still martial bravery and being a hero. There might be an argument to make, if you were one of those."

Johnny Pye shuddered a little, remembering the way

that battlefield had looked, out West, when the Indians were dead and the fight over.

"No," he said, "I've fought, but I'm not a hero."

"Well, then, there's religion," said the old man, sort of patient, "and science, and—but what's the use? We know what you did with those. I might feel a trifle of compunction if I had to deal with a President of the United States. But——"

"Oh, you know well enough I ain't President," said Johnny, with a groan. "Can't you get it over with and be done?"

"You're not putting up a very good case," said the old man, shaking his head. "I'm surprised at you, Johnny. Here you spend your youth running away from being a fool. And yet, what's the first thing you do, when you're man grown? Why, you marry a girl, settle down in your home town, and start raising children when you don't know how they'll turn out. You might have known I'd catch up with you, then—you just put yourself in my way."

"Fool I may be," said Johnny Pye in his agony, "and if you take it like that, I guess we're all fools. But Susie's my wife, and my child's my child. And, as for work in the world —well, somebody has to be postmaster, or folks wouldn't get the mail."

"Would it matter much if they didn't?" said the old man, pointing his scythe.

"Well, no, I don't suppose it would, considering what's on the post cards," said Johnny Pye. "But while it's my business to sort it, I'll sort it as well as I can."

The old man whetted his scythe so hard that a long shower of sparks flew out on the grass.

"Well," he said, "I've got my job, too, and I do it likewise. But I'll tell you what I'll do. You're coming my way, no doubt of it, but looking you over, you don't look quite ripe yet. So I'll let you off for a while. For that matter," said he, "if you'll answer one question of mine—how a man can be a human being and not be a fool—I'll let you off permanent. It'll be the first time in history," he said, "but you've got to do something on your own hook, once in a while. And now you can walk along, Johnny Pye."

With that he ground the scythe till the sparks flew out like the tail of a comet and Johnny Pye walked along. The air of the meadow had never seemed so sweet to him before.

All the same, even with his relief, he didn't quite forget, and sometimes Susie had to tell the children not to disturb father because he was thinking. But time went ahead, as it does, and pretty soon Johnny Pye found he was forty. He'd never expected to be forty, when he was young, and it kind of surprised him. But there it was, though he couldn't say he felt much different, except now and then when he stooped over. And he was a solid citizen of the town, well-liked and well-respected, with a growing family and a stake in the community, and when he thought those things over, they kind of surprised him too. But, pretty soon, it was as if things had always been that way.

It was after his eldest son had been drowned out fishing that Johnny Pye met the scissors grinder again. But this time, he was bitter and distracted, and, if he could have got to the old man, he'd have done him a mortal harm. But, somehow or other, when he tried to come to grips with him, it was like reaching for air and mist. He could see the sparks fly from the ground scythe, but he couldn't even touch the wheel.

"You coward!" said Johnny Pye. "Stand up and fight like a man!" But the old man just nodded his head and the wheel kept grinding and grinding.

"Why couldn't you have taken me?" said Johnny Pye, as if those words had never been said before. "What's the sense in all this? Why can't you take me now?"

Then he tried to wrench the scythe from the old man's hands, but he couldn't touch it. And then he fell down and lay on the grass for a while.

"Time passes," said the old man, nodding his head. "Time passes."

"It will never cure the grief I have for my son," said Johnny Pye.

"It will not," said the old man, nodding his head. "But time passes. Would you leave your wife a widow and your other children fatherless for the sake of your grief?"

"No, God help me!" said Johnny Pye. "That wouldn't be right for a man."

"Then go home to your house, Johnny Pye," said the old man. And Johnny Pye went, but there were lines in his face that hadn't been there before.

And time passed, like the flow of the river, and Johnny Pye's children married and had houses and children of their own. And Susie's hair grew white, and her back grew bent, and when Johnny Pye and his children followed her to her grave, folks said she'd died in the fullness of years, but that was hard for Johnny Pye to believe. Only folks didn't talk as plain as they used to, and the sun didn't heat as much, and sometimes, before dinner, he'd go to sleep in his chair.

And once, after Susie had died, the President of those days came through Martinsville and Johnny Pye shook hands with him and there was a piece in the paper about his shaking hands with two Presidents, fifty years apart. Johnny Pye cut out the clipping and kept it in his pocketbook. He liked this President all right, but, as he told people, he wasn't a patch on the other one fifty years ago. Well, you couldn't expect it—you didn't have Presidents these days, not to call them Presidents. All the same, he took a lot of satisfaction in the clipping.

He didn't get down to the river road much any more—it wasn't too long a walk, of course, but he just didn't often feel like it. But, one day, he slipped away from the granddaughter that was taking care of him, and went. It was kind of a steep road, really—he didn't remember its being so steep.

"Well," said the scissors grinder, "and good afternoon to you, Johnny Pye."

"You'll have to talk a little louder," said Johnny Pye. "My hearing's perfect, but folks don't speak as plain as they used to. Stranger in town?"

"Oh, so that's the way it is," said the scissors grinder.

"Yes, that's the way it is," said Johnny Pye. He knew he ought to be afraid of this fellow, now he'd put on his spectacles and got a good look at him, but for the life of him, he couldn't remember why.

"I know just who you are," he said, a little fretfully. "Never forgot a face in my life, and your name's right on the tip of my tongue——"

"Oh, don't bother about names," said the scissors grinder. "We're old acquaintances. And I asked you a question, years ago—do you remember that?"

"Yes," said Johnny Pye, "I remember." Then he began to laugh—a high, old man's laugh. "And of all the fool questions I ever was asked," he said, "that certainly took the cake."

"Oh?" said the scissors grinder.

"Uh-huh," said Johnny Pye. "For you asked me how a man could be a human being and yet not be a fool. And the answer is—when he's dead and gone and buried. Any fool would know that."

"That so?" said the scissors grinder.

"Of course," said Johnny Pye. "I ought to know. I'll be ninety-two next November, and I've shook hands with two Presidents. The first President I shook——"

"I'll be interested to hear about that," said the scissors grinder, "but we've got a little business, first. For, if all human beings are fools, how does the world get ahead?"

"Oh, there's lots of other things," said Johnny Pye, kind of impatient. "There's the brave and the wise and the clever—and they're apt to roll it ahead as much as an inch. But it's all mixed in together. For, Lord, it's only some fool kind of creature that would have crawled out of the sea to dry land in the first place—or got dropped from the Garden of Eden, if you like it better that way. You can't depend on the kind of folks people think they are—you've got to go by what they do. And I wouldn't give much for a man that some folks hadn't thought was a fool, in his time."

"Well," said the scissors grinder, "you've answered my

question—at least as well as you could, which is all you can expect of a man. So I'll keep my part of the bargain."

"And what was that?" said Johnny. "For, while it's all straight in my head, I don't quite recollect the details."

"Why," said the scissors grinder, rather testy, "I'm to let you go, you old fool! You'll never see me again till the Last Judgment. There'll be trouble in the office about it," said he, "but you've got to do what you like, once in a while."

"Phew!" said Johnny Pye. "That needs thinking over!" And he scratched his head.

"Why?" said the scissors grinder, a bit affronted. "It ain't often I offer a man eternal life."

"Well," said Johnny Pye, "I take it very kind, but, you see, it's this way." He thought for a moment. "No," he said, "you wouldn't understand. You can't have touched seventy yet, by your looks, and no young man would."

"Try me," said the scissors grinder.

"Well," said Johnny Pye. "It's this way," and he scratched his head again. "I'm not saying—if you'd made the offer forty years ago, or even twenty. But, well, now, let's just take one detail. Let's say 'teeth.' "

"Well, of course," said the scissors grinder, "naturally— I mean you could hardly expect me to do anything about that."

"I thought so," said Johnny Pye. "Well, you see, these are good, bought teeth, but I'm sort of tired of hearing them click. And spectacles, I suppose, the same?"

"I'm afraid so," said the scissors grinder. "I can't interfere with time, you know—that's not my department. And, frankly, you couldn't expect, at a hundred and eighty, let's say, to be quite the man you was at ninety. But still, you'd be a wonder!"

"Maybe so," said Johnny Pye, "but, you see—well, the truth is, I'm an old man now. You wouldn't think it to look at me, but it's so. And my friends—well, they're gone—and Susie and the boy—and somehow you don't get as close to the younger people, except the children. And to keep on just going and going till Judgment Day, with nobody around to talk to that had real horse sense—well, no, sir, it's a handsome offer but I just don't feel up to accepting it. It may not be patriotic of me, and I feel sorry for Martinsville. It'd do wonders for the climate and the chamber of commerce to have a leading citizen live till Judgment Day. But a man's got to do as he likes, at least once in his life." He stopped and looked at the scissors grinder. "I'll admit, I'd kind of like to beat out Ike Leavis," he said. "To hear him talk, you'd think nobody had ever pushed ninety before. But I suppose——"

"I'm afraid we can't issue a limited policy," said the scissors grinder.

"Well," said Johnny Pye, "I just thought of it. And Ike's all right." He waited a moment. "Tell me," he said, in a low voice. "Well, you know what I mean. Afterwards. I mean, if you're likely to see"—he coughed—"your friends again. I mean, if it's so—like some folks believe."

"I can't tell you that," said the scissors grinder. "I only go so far."

"Well, there's no harm in asking," said Johnny Pye, rather humbly. He peered into the darkness; a last shower of sparks flew from the scythe, then the whir of the wheel stopped.

"H'm," said Johnny Pye, testing the edge. "That's a well-ground scythe. But they used to grind 'em better in the old days." He listened and looked, for a moment, anxiously.

"Oh, Lordy!" he said. "There's Helen coming to look for me. She'll take me back to the house."

"Not this time," said the scissors grinder. "Yes, there isn't bad steel in that scythe. Well, let's go, Johnny Pye."

The Romance of Rosy Ridge

IT WAS good corn-growing weather that July night when the stranger first came along, making his music through the hollow all the way up to Rosy Ridge. Old Gill MacBean and his wife and the younguns were sitting out on the stoop when they heard the man coming.

Sairy MacBean and her daughter, Lissy Ann, had turkey-wing fans, and they felt kind of elegant, with nothing to do but sit there in the coolness of the hilltop and wave their fans, just as if they hadn't worked their arms off at the elbows all day long. The younguns had made a smudge in front of the step, partly to drive away the mosquitoes and partly to play Indian, and old Gill was just smoking his pipe and not thinking about anything much.

At usual times you couldn't hear any creatures but whip-poorwills in the dusk; it was only in the winter that you heard wolves, and panthers had been persecuted out of the country years agone. But this night the stranger sent his music on ahead of him, and it was hard for anyone to conclude just what kind of music it might be.

The younguns believed it might be a ghost, and they skedaddled up on the stoop behind the old folks—all except young Andrew; and he ran into the house for the pepper-box revolver that he kept hidden under his pillow.

Old Gill himself listened to the tune for a while; and then, without saying a word to anybody, he went and got the repeating rifle he had captured from a Yankee at Nashville. It wasn't customary for night riders to make that kind of a sound when they were coming after you, but in times like these you didn't dare take risk.

But Lissy Ann and her mother were both struck dumb by the beauty of the sounds—pretty much scared, too, but not scared enough to leave their chairs—and they sat there with their ears peeled, and finally Lissy Ann dropped her turkey-wing fan and let it lie forgotten at her feet.

Because the man who came up out of the dark woods was playing Gentle Annie in some kind of strange humming fashion none of the MacBeans had ever heard before. Lissy Ann said afterward it sounded like someone had captured a lot of grasshoppers and tree peepers, and katydids that were out ahead of their time, and had trained them to play the fiddle until they all played right smack together, as if one hand were drawing the bow across the strings. Still, it wasn't fiddling and it wasn't ballad singing, but something kind of between the two, and it got hold of your heart when you heard it. It bestirred all the sadness and prettiness that ever grew in those woods, in spring or high summer; and you thought of honeysuckle creeping wild, and morning-glories in the corn, and you thought, too, about how butternuts smelt in the fall, when the first frost browned their fuzz. The music changed from Gentle Annie into Billy Boy, and then on into Jack o' Diamonds. Gill MacBean walked down to the fence and leaned against a rail with the repeating rifle in the hollow of his arm. He made young Andrew stay well behind him, though this didn't sound like any night rider who had ever crossed the hills.

The stranger came up the road, walking slow in the dusk, and yet kind of pert on his feet. He made you think that he had walked twenty miles through the brush, and still had enough get-up-and-go to dance all night, if anybody invited him. He couldn't have missed seeing the house or sheds, or the way the family were staring at him, because the darkness wasn't yet thick enough for that. But he never made a break in his tune. He kept right on, brave and contented, and he quit Jack o' Diamonds when he first struck the rail fence, but he flowed right on into Arkansas Traveler, and that was the tune he was making when finally he stopped square in front of old Gill and said, "Howdy."

"Stranger," said old Gill, "that's a likely kind of noise you're making."

"I make the best there is," said the stranger, and young Andrew came out from behind his father, but still holding the pepper-box revolver.

And the stranger said, "Why do you folks come to welcome me with shooting irons? I have got no intention of harming a soul I meet along the way."

Old Gill told him, "There's people that ride through this country sometimes that have got worse intentions than yourn."

"But they don't come playing tunes, do they?"

"No," said Gill MacBean, "I ain't never heard them do that. Not yet. But they're liable to try anything once."

The rest of the family came down to the fence now, coming a little slow and fearful, but mighty sure that this man hadn't brought any harm with him. They all crowded close and looked him over, silent and wondering, and trying to figure what kind of instrument he had used to contrive such music, because he didn't seem to have a horn or a fiddle to his name. He just stood there and smiled, and at the first look Sairy MacBean thought he couldn't be much older than Andrew, although he was a mighty sight bigger. He was nowhere as big as old Gill, though, nor as big as the two boys who had been killed in the war. At the next look, they saw that surely he was a man grown, although there was a kind of fancy and a peculiar secret in his face that wouldn't make him more than a child in some ways, if he grew to be a hundred and ten.

He took off the old hat he wore, and he bowed to the womenfolks—a real courteous bow, good as any gentleman could have done. They saw now that he wore spectacles with brass rims. Nobody ever wore spectacles in those parts, except the parson and a few of the old folks, and some of the old folks wore them for pride. But this stranger had real spectacles with glass fronts in them, and if you peered close in the gloom, you could see his little dark squirrel eyes, pitying and good-natured, behind them. He sort of slid around inside his skin, and inside the woolsey coat he wore, with a manner that said he was lithe and quick-moving as a minnow.

The family looked to see what kind of pants he had, because pants meant a lot in Barbary County that year. The butternut and blue pants were pretty well divided, though I reckon the butternut had the edge. But the stranger's pants were such a funny faded color that nobody could tell what their dye was in the first place. They might have been Yankee breeches all soiled, and faded gray by the sun; or else they might have been the kind of pale gray breeches—not butternut—that the Confederates wore in the early days of the war, and that some of the officers hung on to for dress uniform, right up to the last gun.

"Stranger," old Gill MacBean said, and he set the butt of his rifle against the ground and put his hands around the barrel, "I make apology to you, because I came down here to the road thinking you might be a bushwhacker. Now I'll take my oath you ain't any such. But I surely wouldn't take my oath on where those breeches came from. Are you one of those that's inflicted with the oath, or one that's trying to inflict?"

The stranger laughed. He shook his head a little, and made a gay step into the road. He snapped his fingers at the younguns and began to recite a little poem—a singsong one, that might have been part of a play-party game. It was something about

> *Free as a ground hog, lazy as a possum,*
> *If I've had troubles I reckon I've lost 'em.*
> *Fit at Pea Ridge, fit in Tennessee!*
> *If that ain't fit, then don't ask me!*

The younguns jumped up and down in excitement, for this was just pie for them, and the old folks kind of smiled.

"At any rate," Gill MacBean told him, "you talk like the right color."

"They say there's no right nor wrong any more," the man told him, a bit guarded in his manner.

"Right will always be right," said old Gill. "I lost a brother at Wilson's Creek, and two boys in Arkansas. I'm still one of the meanest rebs in Missouri, but you don't talk like no Yankee that ever breathed."

And then Lissy Ann pulled at his elbow and whispered something to him, and so he spoke up to the stranger and said, "We'd admire to know just how you make that music of yourn."

The stranger told them in an amused whisper, but still as if he meant it: "It comes from a heart that would like to be carefree. It comes out of the berry bushes, and the mink holes down by the river, and the cleared land where folks grow potatoes. It's a variety of potato-bug music, among other things. I just comb it out of the air."

Then up comes his thin brown hand with a comb in it, and that's what he's made all this music with—just a comb with thin paper around it, like any boy would blow when he was playing circus out behind the stable. But the stranger has got some curious trick that no one else seemed ever to learn before—a way of hardening his lips against the paper and suddenly letting them grow soft again; and he uses his tongue and his teeth, too, as if he has to bite right into the heart of the tune, no matter how soft he plays it. That's the kind of music the stranger brought up to Rosy Ridge—just tin-comb-and-paper music, but he calculated it to charm anybody's soul away, and I reckon he succeeded before he was through.

"I sing for my supper," he informed the MacBean folks, "like minstrels bold in days of old," and with that he didn't go back into the Traveler song that he was humming with his comb, but he trilled sadly and easily into something none of them had ever heard before. It was a most important melody, and Lord knows you couldn't have danced to it, nor swung your partner's heels off the floor on any of the breaks;

and you couldn't have stomped, because it would have spoiled the music if you had. But they said—or at least Lissy Ann said—that it was the kind of tune you could die to; not the tune the old cat died on, nor the old dog, neither. But a song to make you make love, and perish happy, in the remarkable joy of doing it.

It was long-drawn-out, and there was firing and bugling in the middle; it ended up with an anguish that was so sweet you couldn't get your breath.

"Stranger," said Gill MacBean, when at last he had got his, "I'd like mighty well to know where you ever scared up that tunefulness. It don't seem decent, somehow—not strictly so. But I think you've confounded all the whippoorwills."

The man told them, kind of hesitating, "Well, maybe it hasn't never been played before in these parts. It comes all the way from Europe, and a man named Liszt made it up." And he smiled at the two hound pups sitting there eying him and looking like their hearts would break if he walked out of their sight. "I used to have a good foxhound," he said.

Gill MacBean found himself liking this stranger better than he had liked anybody for a long time. "Them two are good. That's Paul and Agrippa, and they're by Danger out of Yeary's old Jezebel. There used to be plenty of hilltopping around here. I reckon it can be revived again, though I don't admire to set down with my Yankee neighbors."

And the stranger wanted to know why he called the pups Paul and Agrippa.

"It's easy to see you don't know your Scriptures, young man, no matter how many tunes you know," Gill told him, "These was second and third born in the litter, and Paul came before Agrippa, didn't he? Leastways, that's what it says in the Bible."

"You haven't got Jesus and Pontius Pilate, then, somewhere around?" the stranger wanted to know. "Because I seem to have read that Jesus came before Pilate too."

But the family was plumb scandalized at that, and they shushed him up proper, and old Gill tapped his shoulder and said he reckoned the fried pork wasn't stone-cold yet. So they brought him into the house and told him they couldn't offer to let him sleep in the barn because the 'whackers had burnt it a month before, but they could and would let him sleep in the loft over the shed, where there was room beside young Andrew.

But the cat kind of got the stranger's tongue, as soon as the tallow dips were burning, and Sairy MacBean had set out the tin lamp she kept for company. Sure enough, the cat might catch anybody's tongue, when he looked at Lissy Ann, because she was growing more easy to look at every week of the world.

Finally, though, he said his name was Henry Bohun. And right away—this being the fashion—they called him Henry, and when they wanted to know what he had done before the war, before he became a comb-humming wanderer, he said promptly that he had been a schoolmaster. It was hard for the younguns to believe this, because he didn't look like any schoolmaster they had ever gone to. Still, he could use powerful words when he wanted to—the big, five-legged kind—and there was that song all the way from Europe, and he knew a lot more than that.

He entertained them in wonderful style, for a solid hour after he had eaten, and his pants did look pretty nigh gray in the candlelight, and the last thing he looked at before he went to the loft to sleep with young Andrew was Lissy Ann's face. I reckon any man, even one who wasn't a comb hummer, would do that; and he would forget all about the war and the bushwhackers and the hard, troublous times. He'd just see that strawberry-yellow hair and the clear blue eyes and the little freckles that were on her smooth round cheeks, and see her soft mouth smiling and hear her soft mouth murmuring something about what a pleasurable evening it was. And then he'd go off to the loft, and lie there unclad with the Missouri wind blowing in through the cracks, out of the forests and cornfields. And still he'd think about a face like hers, and see it when he slept.

I reckon it was the Yeary boys from the next place who first called him Comb-Hummin' Henry, because they stood in old Gill's oat field the next day and marveled at the music the stranger could make. Old Gill had a habit of trading work with the Yearys, and they came over to help him cut the stand of late oats which he had on the flat pasture behind his barn, or at least behind where the barn used to be before the 'whackers burnt it.

But when old Gill and Joe Yeary squatted down in the fence corner to have a pull at the jug, old Gill reckoned aloud that he didn't have much need of the Yearys. Comb-Hummin' Henry could bind up more oats than most young fellows. He seemed to have wire in his back and wire in his arms, and the wondrous thing about it was the way he kept singing little songs all the time he worked; though, naturally, he couldn't raise his comb to his lips and work too.

It was gray breeches in the Yeary family, and they still had a couple of extra boys circulating around somewhere who hadn't come home yet. Old Joe had begun to think that the boys were plumb dead and gone, but his wife had dreamt that they'd show up in good time. Old Joe hadn't been with the rebel army, because he was too lame, but both the youngest boys had got themselves chased around Arkansas for a spell. They talked big about it, but they weren't more than sixteen years old, and it was a caution to see how their eyes would bug out and their jaws hang open when Henry Bohun made some music for them, after the noon eating. He played two combs that time—his own tin one, and a nice white comb that he had loaned off of Sairy MacBean, and he had them both wrapped in the remarkable white paper that his pockets were full of. One had a high tone and one was deep and mournful, and he changed them about, in the same song, until you couldn't tell which he had at his mouth.

And he knew what to do for a sick ox, too, for Bum, the nigh ox, was down with the colic that day. Old Gill couldn't get the medicine down Bum's throat, but Comb-Hummin'

Henry mixed it up with bran mash, and they do say that Bum was a better ox from that day forth.

And he could make soft soap, because in the afternoon he went to help Sairy and Lissy Ann with the batch they were cooking. He fetched it off the fire, tender and sweet as butter, and he said it was all in talking to the spirits that roosted in the soap when it was stewing. Sairy didn't like such talk about spirits, because spirits reminded her of the bushwhackers and the way they came in their hoods, looking like so many ghosts. But she did say that such soap beat the nation, and a good half of Barbary County besides.

Comb-Hummin' Henry didn't hang around there to get praised. He just lit out for the oat field, and for an hour afterward you could see him heaving the big bundles, and tying straw around them so snug and tight that no wind in the world could blow them loose. And all the time he sang a song about the Arrow Rock jail, and how a man lived in it until he was hung.

Gill MacBean had worked a man or two, in the days before the war and the hard times following. But he had never worked a man like this, and, to tell the truth, he was kind of uneasy in his heart. Henry Bohun's breeches did look a mite bluish in the sunlight, when you were working side by side with him. Old Gill sought to try him out by cussing the Yankees in general, at first, and then certain Yankees he knew that were particularly ornery; then he slandered the new United States President, and all of Congress and the Constitution, too, for good measure; and he said he would refuse to be reconstructed until his dying breath; then he rounded off with some belittling remarks about the battle of Nashville and the Yankee from whom he had captured his repeating rifle; and he said that he'd keep that rifle till his dying breath. But Comb-Hummin' Henry just listened with a dreamy smile, though his bright shiny black squirrel's eyes were jumping quick and lively behind his spectacles.

And old Gill said, "One thing I've sworn, and I'll hold to it until the last bone rots out of my back. I won't have no

Yankee grandchildren. I keep my gun loaded for anybody who claims different."

That was when Henry quit smiling. "Mysterious things," he said, "do happen in this world."

"Like what?" Gill demanded.

"Like love, for one thing," said Comb-Hummin' Henry. "Your daughter is mighty pretty."

But Gill MacBean just hauled at his beard a couple of times, and he looked right over what Henry may have meant. I reckon the thought had sneaked around in his brain more than once that Henry was a Yankee, but he wasn't going to recognize it until he had to. I reckon nobody could hate Yankees as bad as old Gill said he hated them. "As soon as my brother got killed at Wilson's Creek," he said, "I up and left my wife and younguns and went to Springfield, and I became a private in Company I, Second Missouri Infantry, Little's Brigade, Price's Division, Army of the Trans-Mississippi. And I fought until Vicksburg, and then I joined the cavalry. I tell you direct and honest that I do hate a Yankee worse than poison, and we got all too many around here. Do you look what they did to my barn," and he showed Henry where the burnt parts of it were ugly and black.

Henry said, quiet and mild, "I have it in my mind that you talked about bushwhackers."

"Sure enough. Yankee bushwhackers! And they still ride these roads. It's not safe for a woman or child to go abroad without a man to bear them company," said old Gill Mac-Bean, and he sliced a mullein leaf clean down the center.

"Why, now," said Comb Hummin' Henry, "I have it in my mind that the Yearys told about Yankee barns that had been burnt, and Yankee people who had been robbed."

But Gill MacBean growled and said it was just a blind—a trick to throw dust in the eyes of everybody else, and make it look as if the wartime bushwhackers were still ranging around the neighborhood. He knew well enough, he said, that these 'whackers were just Yankee sympathizers who didn't have pity or sympathy in their hearts for anybody who came back from the army wearing gray pants. If a man had been a rebel, or his son or nephew had, they'd burn his barn quick as scat, and they'd even made bold to burn some houses.

These 'whackers lived somewhere close to hand, and they knew just when a man had sold his horse or his cow, and even if his children had scratched together some few dollars, trapping in the winter. They'd been that way all along, he declared; the war was over since spring, but the bushwhackers weren't over by a pretty sight. They robbed travelers on the highroad, and when they raided a farm they always made sure the man who owned it wasn't home. That was a regular Yankee trick, according to Gill MacBean, and he only hoped he'd live to give them a bellyful of hot lead from the repeater he captured at Nashville.

Well, there is no way to tell what Comb-Hummin' Henry might have said in answer, for about this time Lissy Ann came skimming out into the oat field with her skirts blowing behind her, and Henry Bohun stood up and took off his hat. He took out his comb, too, and had the paper around it before you could say "grandpappy," and he was humming a tune by the time Lissy Ann got to where the men were. It was a lively, sweet song that he gave her; the one some folks call Buffalo Gals and others call Louisiana Gals. It was a song about coming out at night and dancing by the light of the moon, and it looked like Lissy Ann was charmed to death by it.

"Pap," she said, when she could tear her eyes away from Comb-Hummin' Henry. "Pap, one of the Willhearts just rode by, and he says they're having a gathering down at Delight after supper. Mr. Callaway Baggett has got his new granary floor all laid, and it's going to be a play-party. Mam reckoned you'd better hang up your sickle and get some grease on your boots."

Nobody on Rosy Ridge, or all the way back to Lorn Widow Crossing, brought more enjoyment to a play-party than old Gill MacBean. "Why, daughter," he said, "one of my boots was sticking out from under the bed when I arose this morn-

ing, and I was certain it winked at me. But if they do Happy
Is the Miller, I'm bound to go through it barefooted. . . .
Henry Bohun, are you any great shakes at play-parties?"

"I never miss a fiddle bar or a smidgen of fried cake if I
can help it," said Comb-Hummin' Henry. He was smiling
down at Lissy Ann all the time he said it, and I know she was
beautiful with the low sun golden on her face, for I've seen
her that way many a time. The little bugs fiddled in the
grasses while the three people walked down towards the
house; and redbirds don't sing frequently in July, but I know
they were singing that evening, because Lissy Ann said so.

The whole family caught their snack on the fly, while they
ran around combing their hair and washing behind their ears;
and Henry Bohun shaved clean with a bright little razor that
he carried in his pocket. He helped young Andrew grease his
hair, too, and before it was dead dark, the whole biling of
them crowded aboard the wagon and headed down through
the hollow towards Delight, and Comb-Hummin' Henry made
Lorena go shivering up every little gully they passed. Old Gill
MacBean said that was one of his favorite tunes, and it looked
as if he was ready to forget the kind of bluish color he saw in
Henry's breeches, until he had to face the fact out in the
open, in the sight of God and the general public. And Paul
and Agrippa sat on the front stoop at home and howled a
mournful song of their own, because the whole family and
their new friend had gone away.

The town of Delight was well named that evening, for
there hadn't been a decent play-party anywhere along Agony
Creek since the news traipsed north that Kirby Smith had
surrendered. People came to the gathering sort of geeing and
hawing, as you might say; but in most cases the womenfolks
hung onto the reins, and the teams may have been fractious,
but they were kept well in the road.

There were gray breeches aplenty and blue breeches, too,
although, as usual, the grays had a little edge. There were
Lynches and Dessarks and Johnsons and Yearys on the one
side, and Odoms and Mercers and Willhearts and Billinses

on the other. But the green hill where Mr. Callaway Baggett's house and barns spread out was certainly neutral ground. Callaway Baggett himself was too old and fat and good-natured to go to war, no matter whose cat got singed. He had a lot of daughters, and some of them were married to National men and some of them to Claib Jackson men; and people used to whisper around that Callaway Baggett himself had letters written to him by young Francis Preston Blair.

But tonight it didn't make any difference; the Baggetts always lived in plenty and had plenty, and they were plumb willing to share it. Around the back part of the house opposite the big barn of stone and logs, there was a wide gallery built, and on that gallery there were sawbucks with boards across them. On those boards the Baggett women had laid out more piles of fried cakes and sugar cookies than anybody could eat, and more vinegar pies—rich ones, too, with hazelnuts in them—than the parson himself could eat in a month of Sundays. There was cornbread, too, and sides of cold pork, and crabapple pickles, and down around where the playing took place, alongside the new granary floor, people had some big brown jugs with cobs stuck in the top, though the cobs were out of the jugs a good share of the time. The young bucks mostly gathered down there, but there wasn't any angriness among them, because Cal Baggett wouldn't stand for that, and his sons by marriage were big men who could throw a steer over a corncrib without half trying.

And the music was of the best: they had Ninny Nat Tinley with his fiddle, and a banjo player, and a nigger man sitting on a bucket with bones in his hand.

Folks were kind of stiff and chilly when this unknown stranger climbed down over Gill MacBean's wagon wheel. Too many strangers had gone through those parts in the years just past, and had gone through in a mighty unkind way, to make people brim their hearts when they saw a new face close by them. But that was just pie for Comb-Hummin' Henry, because he liked to brim the hearts of those he met, and start from scratch doing it; and the Yeary boys had already talked his fame to everybody who would listen.

So the end of the first hour found Henry up on the board pile alongside Ninny Nat, and old Ninny Nat was gurgling and smacking his lips underneath his beard, because he hoped he'd die happy before he ever met another person who could tantalize a pocket comb like Henry Bohun. They went right down the list of tunes and around the corner, and there wasn't a one of them that Ninny Nat might strike up that Comb-Hummin' Henry didn't have dwelling ready in his mouth. This was potato-bug music for fair, as Henry had said, and when Lissy Ann looked at him—famous and contented and important beside the fiddler—it didn't seem possible to her that he could ever have played that heart-breaking melody which he played the night before—tho one he declared came all the way from Europe.

The young folks danced and swung on the shadowy side of the barn, because play-party games aren't really dancing, and good church people can go to play-parties, where I've seen them many a time. But there wasn't allowed any dancing, as such, at Mr. Callaway Baggett's. So, pretty soon, the most eager people came out of the shadows and stepped up on the granary floor, and then the games began. And the moon looked much amazed to see gray breeches and blue breeches stomping the smooth planks side by side, but there wasn't a single fist fight took place that night.

Gill MacBean was one of the leaders now, and he stood in the center of the ring and howled out the miller song:

> ". . . . *the wheel goes around,*
> *He's gaining on his pelf—*
> *One hand in the hopper*
> *And the other in the bag—*
> *Wheel goes around——*"

and when they came to "grab!" you can be mighty certain that old Gill came grabbing down on the prettiest girl present. But Sairy MacBean didn't object too loudly, for she reckoned to the other womenfolks that there wasn't any bigger boy in Barbary County than Gill MacBean, and heaven knew how he might have disported himself when he was gone with the rebel army.

Well, the fun went on, piled higher than pumpkins, and then, as happens all too frequently in the most pleasurable moments, some thing had to whistle sour. It wasn't Comb-Hummin' Henry; you can look in the book of records and see for yourself that it wasn't his fault. It may have been old Ninny Nat, for he was so innocent he scarcely knew that there had been a war, with folks who didn't come back from it, and other folks who did and who had raw feelings. The moon was high and white, and the whippoorwills had gone home disgusted, when all of a sudden the music swung into The Picnic.

If an entire company of Yankee cavalry hadn't squatted down in Delight for three mortal months, there were a lot of folks present who wouldn't have known the difference. And as for the men who had come creeping home in their worn-out butternut rags, many of them had been captured at one time or another, and they forgot, when they heard this eventful music, just how they might have played games to it when they were younguns.

From the far end of the granary floor a voice cried out, "Stop that damn Yankee quickstep!" and the musicians did stop, surprised wholly out of breath.

And then, from the other end of the floor, somebody else hollered, "Why do they have to stop it?" and a girl sort of yelped in fear and astonishment, and everybody seemed to freeze silent and unhappy in the moonlight.

Mr. Callaway Baggett came a-tumbling down the hill, and he panted his way through the crowd and got up, with a mighty puff, to where the fiddle and banjo people were, and to where Comb-Hummin' Henry sat, his comb in his hand.

"Unless I miscalculate," said Cal Baggett, "there is an open division of opinion concerning the melody just offered by the band. Shall we put it to a vote?"

A lot of folks yelled, "Yes," and more said, "No," and Callaway Baggett had to spread his hands and warn them to consider the matter calm and judicial. He said he was ready to hear evidence from both sides, and right away the evidence began to pour in. The people who had been National sympathizers swore that The Picnic was one of the best play-party tunes, and just as innocent as Oars on the Boat or London Bridge. But the butternut crowd all squalled their heads off at this, and they said that it was a guard mount used by half the Yankee regiments that they had met. They said they'd just as soon listen to Yankee Doodle and The Star-Spangled Banner, and some said they'd a blame sight rather.

"We'll ballot, ladies and gentlemen!" cried Mr. Callaway Baggett. "I demand that my guests be satisfied, and unprejudiced and elective in their choice." And so he began to marshal the guests to right and left. He ended up with two groups, one crowded on the nigh end of the floor and one on the far end, and when he counted noses, they were matched number by number.

There were a few scare-cats who hauled out and said they had to get home. They were afraid to register their votes, and they piled into their wagons or onto their mules, and talked about how they had to be in the fields early in the morning. But those who were earnest and bold and firmly sot in opinion stayed there, resolved to hold to their rights; and Mr. Callaway Baggett said that he approved them for their sincerity.

He said, "The musicians must vote and settle this dispute, for we're wasting a lot of God's best moonlight, and the fried cakes aren't half gone yet."

So the nigger who rattled the bones went scooting down to join his white folks at the far end, and folks agreed that that would count for half a vote. They couldn't persuade Ninny Nat to make up his mind, because he just laughed and didn't understand any of this racket; and the fellow who had been playing the banjo stepped down and registered himself as in favor of The Picnic.

Now Comb-Hummin' Henry was left high and dry. Lissy Ann MacBean, standing beside her pap, heard the old man draw in his breath and kind of groan.

"Stranger," Cal Baggett challenged Henry, "I can't make out the color of your breeches. I guess you'd better walk to one end or t'other."

Henry looked at him awhile, and his little spectacles caught the moonlight and the house lights and the flare from the fire in the yard, and the reflection made him look dangerous and spooklike.

"The war's over," he said, finally. "But I reckon The Picnic's a good tune, no matter who plays it or who dances to it, and we used to call it The Village Quickstep when I was in the Union Army." And then he walked to the nigh end of the platform with the Yankee sympathizers, and people stared at him and saluted his honesty.

Gill MacBean stared, too, and in spite of his disappointment, he must have respected Comb-Hummin' Henry—as a good man respects anybody who speaks his mind, firm and sane. Then he turned around to his daughter and said, "Lissy Ann, the moon's high, and it's a long way to Rosy Ridge. You and young Andrew hustle and see if you can scare up the younguns." Then he went over to the jugs and poured himself a stanch drink of corn liquor, and those near by him tell that he drank to the name of Claiborne Fox Jackson.

Well, they played The Picnic, but kind of half-hearted, and only two of the rebel folks danced to it. But when the tune had changed to Needle's Eye, Comb-Hummin' Henry put away his musical instrument and slid down from the pile of boards. He went hunting through the shadows and the white patches of moon glow, and sure enough he found Lissy Ann up on the hill by the gooseberry bushes, as if she had been waiting there for a purpose.

"Lissy Ann," he whispered to her, "I reckon I won't be riding back with you-all."

"I reckon you won't," said Lissy Ann, "and Paul and Agrippa are going to feel mighty bad about it."

He wanted to know if they were the only ones who would feel bad, but Lissy Ann, she began to fidget with her bonnet and say that she'd have to follow along towards the wagon. "Do you plan to go wandering again?" she asked Henry Bohun.

Henry said it all depended. He said that wandering was a kind of easy occupation, in spite of missing a meal every now and then, and sleeping out with the nighthawks. He told Lissy Ann that he had had to work hard all his life; that he had had to work hard on his father's farm, and that was right there in Missouri, a hundred miles away. And when he went to the academy, he had to keep humping to make both ends meet, and to study in his books; he chopped wood for the principal of the academy all winter long, and looked after cows and horses. And then he was a schoolmaster, he told Lissy Ann; and then war happened. He returned from the Union Army faint and sick, and schoolmastering came mighty hard. "Maybe sometime I'll tell you," he said, "just why I quit teaching the three R's and took up comb humming instead. It's a long story."

Lissy Ann MacBean said that she reckoned it was a long story, but she couldn't wait to hear it, because her father would be hitched up by now, and it sounded as if young Andrew was yelling for her.

"If I stay in these parts for a while," Henry Bohun asked her, "if I stay close at hand and don't go wandering too far away, do you reckon you'll find time to listen? It's a peculiar tale, and must be told only to someone who listens in sympathy."

Then she began to cry, or it sounded that way; she covered her face from the moonlight, and she went running away to the wagon. The story goes that Gill MacBean didn't utter speech all the way to his house on Rosy Ridge, and the music seemed to have fallen out of Henry Bohun's tunes, as if the teeth were broke clean out of his comb.

But he stayed to hand. He didn't go wandering the next day, for Mr. Callaway Baggett took him in that night, and the next day he went to work in Mr. Callaway Baggett's mill. But the millstones ground a most doleful melody, all the while on into September, and in another month Henry Bohun began to slack up in his work. He took to roving through the brush when he should have been toting wheat sacks up and down ladders, and only when he thought he was sole alone in the timberland did he give breath to the kind of music he loved to make, and then it was mortal sad.

How Mr. Callaway Baggett could prosper in this world seemed plumb miraculous to some people, for he was always quoting that a merciful man is merciful to his beast, and he never was a driver to any man that worked for him. Some millers would have sent Comb-Hummin' Henry packing up the road, the first time he didn't come willing to his toil, but Callaway Baggett never said a word to him. I reckon he hadn't agreed to pay Henry Bohun any great wages in hard money or paper money. Still, there was always a plate for him when Henry wanted to eat, and he slept comfortable in the Baggett barn. But most of the time, as the leaves got faded and crisp, Henry was walking the timberland all over that country.

Mean folks took joy in pestering him, and Barbary County was a fair land, but it had its share of the mean ones. There was Badger Dessark, for one, and the Lynch boys, and Roll Odom and Jack Billins. They were a wild and reckless lot, who didn't work more than the law allowed, and who used to get full of whiskey and go along the roads whooping until the windows rattled. If mischief of any kind was brought forth, you could guess quick as scat who had made it. And whenever they couldn't think of anything else to do, they'd put turpentine on a dog, and perform all manner of orneriness.

At the play-party in July, when Comb-Hummin' Henry first came to the neighborhood, the wild boys had kind of pulled in their horns, for they didn't want to bring the wrath of any of the Baggett folks down on them. Badger Dessark claimed to have fought in Forrest's cavalry, but some people believed it was just a forest cavalry, and a mighty irregular regiment at that. And Jack Billins was a bounty man for the Union, but just the same he and Badge Dessark and the others were thick as fleas.

Henry Bohun was their meat, because he was gentle and mild in his manner, and used big words sometimes, and knew the names of all the flowers that grew in the wilderness. But he never went hunting the way they did; he used to lie for hours beside the mill race, trying to tame the little shiners that swam there.

It is told how Badge Dessark and the Lynch boys came abreast of Comb-Hummin' Henry when he was walking back to the mill, one afternoon in fall. They pulled in their horses and sat still and grinned at him, and anyone could see that they were trying to think of some deviltry.

"What you got there in your pocket, Henry Bohun?" Badge Dessark wanted to know, and other parties who were passing by pulled up their teams, because it looked like trouble.

"It's a bird," said Henry. "A thrush."

"Oh," Badge Dessark said, "I reckoned it was a titmouse, because a titmouse would be just your kind of fare"—and the Lynch boys laughed heartily at that.

But Henry brought the thrush out of his pocket and showed them. "It got hurt one way or another," he explained, "and I found it fluttering in the brush. I reckoned I'd take it home until I could decide what to do with it."

"Sonny," said Badge Dessark, laughing deep inside his chest, "you've met just the man to decide for you," and he leaned down quick from his horse and jerked the bird out of Henry's hands, drawing out his .44 at the same time.

He heaved the thrush into the air and began to crack away at it while the bird flopped round and round, aiming hard to fly and not being able to do so. Not many people could hit a song bird on the wing, but Badge Dessark was a dead shot, and anyway the thrush was sorely crippled in its flight. So he put a chunk of lead through it that made the feathers scatter, and then he shoved his weapon back inside his shirt.

He said to Comb-Hummin' Henry, "Didn't I tell you I'd decide for you?"—and the Lynch boys nearly busted.

"Badge," said Henry Bohun, in a high, nervous voice that sounded as if he was ready to cry, "you've decided more than you know." He kicked the remainders of the dead bird into the weeds and started to walk past, but Dessark and the Lynches looked mighty solemn now, and they brought their horses together to block Henry's way, and demanded what he meant by such a speech.

Henry said, "I only meant this: I may be a kind of thrush myself, but something tells me I'll be bewitched into a catamount when the time is ripe. You're three against one, and any one of you is too big for me to whip, and you've got shooting irons, and I haven't got the price of a cartridge. Maybe I will have, one day."

Well, they rared around and called him names, and Badge Dessark demanded heaven to witness that he ought to shoot Comb-Hummin' Henry down like a dog. But he was the kind that shoots from behind a hedge, and usually when there isn't much sun or many people to see him.

So they let Henry go, and he traipsed slowly down to the mill and flung himself in the grass and lay there for a long time with his eyes shut; and he kept listening to the sound of the wheel, and the water sighing through the flume, as if he stood in need of good advice.

Long before sundown, he was on foot again, and he didn't tarry to take food with the Baggetts. He went off among the thick trees that seemed like his friends and relatives, and that he was happiest among. He followed Agony Creek for a mile or two, and then he struck off over the Spur, where he hadn't trod since the first night he walked into the lives of those neighbors who knew him.

It was close onto dark when he prowled through the hazel brush that grew around the MacBean place, and I reckon he was aware that old Gill MacBean had rode to Billingsgate that day, for Gill had to take the highway past Baggett's mill. There were just Sairy and Lissy Ann and Andrew and the younguns at home; Lissy Ann's pap was nowhere close by to chide her, when she first heard Comb-Hummin' Henry's music stealing through the blue dusk.

He was playing Gentle Annie, as he had that night when first he wandered out of the hollow, and after she had listened to him awhile, Lissy Ann walked to the stoop. The younguns wanted to follow her, because they were plumb excited at hearing Henry's tunefulness again, but their mother counseled them back; and young Andrew took a pattern after his father, and swore what he'd do with his pepper-box revolver if any Yankees came bothering around.

Sairy MacBean felt tender in her heart towards Lissy Ann, for it grieved her to see the girl pining the way she had pined since summer. It wasn't natural nor wise for a girl of her sort to look so droopy, and Sairy had cooked up the best tonic that Granny Yeary could recommend, but still it didn't seem to do any good. So, feeling generous towards Lissy Ann in her affliction, Sairy let her go out to the gate without a challenge, and the girl just stood there, waiting, while Henry Bohun hummed Gentle Annie amongst the hazel brush.

It might have been her very own tune, for it's certain fact that she was christened Annie—Melissa Ann MacBean—and her Great-Aunt Annie was the one who gave her the use of her name. And Lissy Ann's portion of this song must have been made up especially for her own sake: "Shall I never more behold thee . . . and the wild flowers are scattered o'er the plain?" I reckon she thought of the long story which Henry had desired to tell her, and maybe for the first time she saw the faith that he offered—by staying at hand instead of going away down the road, even when he wasn't allowed to court her properly. There were wild flowers all around, sure enough; though you couldn't call Rosy Ridge a plain.

Henry Bohun came closer and closer, until he was full in view, and Sairy MacBean felt something grab close and fearful around her heart. She came to the door with the younguns clustering behind, and she ordered Lissy Ann back into the house. Lissy Ann never heard her, and by that time she wouldn't have batted an eye if she had.

Henry Bohun grew bigger and more important in the shadows, and the song was still Gentle Annie, and the birds of the forest, and the coons, too, whickered about it. When he ceased his song, he was close enough to Lissy Ann to hear her speech, though all she did was to ask for a certain tune. "That one you played the first night," she said. "That tune the man made up out of his own heart, all the way off in Europe."

Well, he obliged her quickly enough, and by that time she was standing well beyond the fence. Her mother cried out, angered and bereaved at having her daughter charmed away before her eyes, though the frosty night was so deep and hazy now that Sairy could scarcely make out their figures. She cried, "Lissy Ann!" in terror, and then she thought to hunt for old Gill's rifle, but he had taken it away with him in prospect of meeting 'whackers along the road. And the family tells how young Andrew tore around and got his pepper-box revolver and snapped it a dozen times, aiming at the shape of Henry Bohun, but missing fire every occasion because there wasn't any life in the spring.

Then the night had swallowed the two of them. They had gone forth together into the brush that was so friendly to Comb-Hummin' Henry, and Sairy MacBean put her apron over her face and began to cry.

They call it Lovers' Walk nowadays, and it's a beautiful path that leads along the height of Rosy Ridge past the end of Gill MacBean's land and clean above the Yeary place, and on and on, far up to the wide wilderness where Uncle Davis Tinley built his cabin in the early days. It's a beautiful place to go meandering when you can see the violets, or the horse mint and wild geraniums in their season; and Sairy MacBean used to pick ladyslippers there when she was just a mite of a girl. This night Lissy Ann walked the path speechless and entranced, at her lover's side, and I reckon Comb-Hummin'

Henry must have had the eyes of a cat, for in more than one spot the bushes grew fair in front of them. But they didn't fall into any gullies, and their feet seemed to know the safest parts in which to plant themselves.

"It's nowhere near," Henry told her. "It's a forsaken place, but I walked there frequently when I was eating my heart out. There's an old chimney, too, and people have stabled horses there in recent days. But I reckon we won't be disturbed while I tell my story to you."

And when they got to that distant clearing, they sat close together in a bed of dry leaves, and he told her all the misery that had been in his soul early and late. He told her how he came back from the war to go to schoolmastering again, and how he couldn't stand the squeeze of the four walls, but needed to take his scholars out into the grass. People in the community thought he was crazy for doing it. He hankered, he said, to instruct the scholars that it was wickedness to kill unless one was sure he killed for the world's benefit; and that, he said, was the reason so many good people went to war. He grew weary oftentimes of setting up sums on the children's slates, because it was a sight more interesting and profitable if he split a daisy with his pocketknife and showed them how the Lord had put it together. And when the men in this community who set themselves up as the wisest ones banded together and drove him out for wasting the younguns' time and taking their parents' hard-earned money for it, he just put his comb in his pocket and paced away with a light heart.

But his spirit had grown forlorn and heavy, since he made his declaration at the Baggetts'. He swore there was no justice in a world where resentfulness locked him away from Lissy Ann. That misery had driven him nigh to distraction, but now he planned to make an end of it, and take Lissy Ann out along the highroads with him, if she was brave enough and willing to go.

She put her arms around his neck and laid her lips against his, and announced, by all that was holy to her, that she'd

take starvation and nighthawks at Henry Bohun's side before
she'd lie beneath her father's roof another night. There was
no ravishment nor sin nor such love-making, but a kind of
dark and secret comfort. And all night long Henry told her
what creatures made the sounds they heard, and what kind of
leaves were rustling loose in the groves; and he even made a
little fire, and saw Lissy Ann's face shining, confident and
pink, in the light of it. He hummed more tunes with his
comb, too, including the European one she fancied. Thus the
color of dawn came around them when they heard Paul and
Agrippa giving voice down the ridge, and old Gill coming,
too, driven mad with his rage and sadness, and toting his rifle
along.

Paul and Agrippa were by no means bloodhounds, nor
nigger dogs such as some people kept in the days before the
war; but they had good noses, and they knew the smell of
Lissy Ann's shoes, and maybe they were attracted by the
thought of Comb-Hummin' Henry mingling his footsteps with
hers. Whatever those two hounds thought, they were of as-
sistance to Gill MacBean in finding his daughter who had run
away, and the man who had lured her. They high-tailed it
straight across the clearing, to leap at the two and desire to
be fondled and made over. The lovers stood there scarcely
feeling the noses that touched them, as they watched Gill
MacBean coming past the towering chimney that showed
against the sky.

"This gun is for you, Henry Bohun," were the first words old
Gill said. "It's got your name on it! It's a repeating Henry rifle
that I captured from a Yankee at Nashville."

Lissy Ann hung close on Henry's shoulder, her two arms
hugging him hard, and she vowed that if a bullet found
Henry's heart, it would have to pass through hers on the way.
But Gill just laughed in his craziness, and tore her loose, and
Comb-Hummin' Henry stood there like he was stuffed and
let him do it.

"I don't aim to slay the daughter that I sired and raised

from the cradle," said Gill MacBean. "I do aim to punish her despoiler."

Henry said, "You ask your daughter if she has been betrayed."

"No," cried Lissy Ann. "I came with him of my own free will, and I intend to share his joys and sorrows, and wander wherever he goes."

"You'd wander," said her father, "with a pack of woods colts trailing after you. You'd be deplored by all people, and your name would be an abomination to those that once loved you"—and he dragged her back beside him. He cocked his rifle, though the girl fought hard to grab it loose from his hands.

She cried to Henry Bohun, "Pap's gone mad! For pity's sake, don't stand there like Ninny Nat and let yourself be killed in cold blood!"—and the hounds tangled and yapped underfoot.

Then Henry Bohun came forward like a wildcat off a limb, and when he sprang free from Gill, he had the gun in his clutch. "Down," he whispered. "Down, the two of you!"

But old MacBean went towering after him with the spit flying through his beard. "This has been a wicked night," he whooped, "and I aim to finish it with one just deed! The Yankee bushwhackers came down on old Granny Yeary and whipped her nigh to death, to make her tell where her money jar was hid. A Yankee stole my daughter from me," he bellowed, still raving and clawing for the gun, "and you'll find I'm strong enough to do punishment!"

Smack through the whirl of their wrestling and turmoil, Comb-Hummin' Henry thrashed out and fetched Gill Mac-Bean a clip with the butt of the gun. It staggered the old man, and he dropped down on one knee.

"Stay beside him, Lissy Ann," said Henry Bohun, "and lay flat against the ground!" For all along he had seen what they did not see, with their backs against the sunrise; and what he saw was men on horseback approaching from the east. They were the bushwhackers who had burnt Gill MacBean's barn and had done every sort of evil throughout Barbary County and into the hills that lay south of it. They stood up in their stirrups, now, and yelled as they came; and they looked like bad dreams a-riding, for they wore enormous hoods of black cloth such as they always wore, and fluttering black cloth to cover up their horses. Henry Bohun ran forward and got beside the ancient chimney of Uncle Davis Tinley's onetime cabin, and I reckon that was the first that Lissy Ann could recognize what Henry might have meant when he said there were marks of horses being stabled near by.

The riders shouted like all possessed, and the big leader who galloped ahead shouted loudest of all. "We know you, Comb-Hummin' Henry!" he called. "We haven't tasted blood yet in these parts, but we'll taste it quick enough if you don't lay down that rifle and fling up your hands for mercy!"

"I reckon you've tasted blood," said Henry, "for I hear you've whipped the back of a poor old woman, and I warn you, your deviltries will betray you! Dismount and give yourselves up, before I shoot."

He kept the chimney on his flank, and the riders spread out to circle their horses. "Knuckle under," they cried, "or we'll sacrifice you all, and the girl too!"

"Last warning," said Henry. "This is a Henry rifle, and it's in good hands."

Then they upped with their .44's, and rock splinters flew from the chimney, but Comb-Hummin' Henry fired calm, and he drilled the leader through his body. He shot him clean out of his stirrups, and the horse went bucking away. In another moment the smoke was so thick that you couldn't have told what was happening. Then it lifted a little, and now there were three 'whackers on the ground, and two who galloped for the timber as if wolves were after them. Comb-Hummin' Henry had his back against the chimney, and blood ran down from his ear, and his broken spectacles dangled loose. But he was white and proud, for all that; Gill MacBean's rifle was hot in his hands.

"Go look at that first one," he told Gill, when the old man

had clumb to his feet. "I warrant you'll find gray breeches." And so they did, for it was Badge Dessark, and he was as dead as a locust husk.

The next was blue breeches, or what should have been—the man was dressed in ordinary store clothes under his black cloth. He was Jack Billins, and henceforth the neighborhood could understand why Jack Billins had dwelt without toiling or spinning, apparently. The third man was dying when they lifted him up, and he was Luke Lynch, and his ghost dragged loose from its wickedness even while Lissy Ann was holding his handsome head and crying for the pity of it.

"When the other two are located," Comb-Hummin' Henry said, "I expect you'll find that blue breeches and gray breeches are mingled together."

And it turned out according to his prophecy, for the two were detected near Lorn Widow Crossing that day, and one was Roll Odom and the other was Sylvester Lynch.

Comb-Hummin' Henry demanded to know of Gill Mac-Bean whether he hadn't been sinful in his rage, and whether the evil weren't truly evil and the good truly good, no matter how they breeched themselves. But old Gill had no word to say, such was his weakness and bewilderment; so at last the three of them set out down the ridge to carry this news abroad, and Comb-Hummin' Henry and Lissy Ann waded in clouds to meet the sun, with Paul and Agrippa whining behind, and Gill walking with bowed head and carrying the Henry rifle.

Very soon thereafter the marriage was celebrated, just when folks wanted a taste of sweetness to take the shock and gall out of their mouths. They declared that it was one of the biggest weddings ever managed in those parts, with half an acre of dinner tables set out under the trees. It was a fruitful union and a loving one; I know, for I was born of it.

ERNEST HEMINGWAY

The Snows of Kilimanjaro

*Kilimanjaro is a snow-covered mountain 19,710 feet high,
and is said to be the highest mountain in Africa. Its western
summit is called by the Masai "Ngàje Ngài," the House of
God. Close to the western summit there is the dried and
frozen carcass of a leopard. No one has explained what the
leopard was seeking at that altitude.*

"THE MARVELLOUS thing is that it's painless," he said. "That's
how you know when it starts."

"Is it really?"

"Absolutely. I'm awfully sorry about the odor though. That
must bother you."

"Don't! Please don't."

"Look at them," he said. "Now is it sight or is it scent that
brings them like that?"

The cot the man lay on was in the wide shade of a mimosa
tree and as he looked out past the shade onto the glare of the
plain there were three of the big birds squatted obscenely,
while in the sky a dozen more sailed, making quick-moving
shadows as they passed.

"They've been there since the day the truck broke down,"
he said. "Today's the first time any have lit on the ground. I
watched the way they sailed very carefully at first in case I
ever wanted to use them in a story. That's funny now."

"I wish you wouldn't," she said.

"I'm only talking," he said. "It's much easier if I talk. But
I don't want to bother you."

"You know it doesn't bother me," she said. "It's that I've

gotten so very nervous not being able to do anything. I think we might make it as easy as we can until the plane comes."

"Or until the plane doesn't come."

"Please tell me what to do. There must be something I can do."

"You can take the leg off and that might stop it, though I doubt it. Or you can shoot me. You're a good shot now. I taught you to shoot, didn't I?"

"Please don't talk that way. Couldn't I read to you?"

"Read what?"

"Anything in the book bag that we haven't read."

"I can't listen to it," he said. "Talking is the easiest. We quarrel and that makes the time pass."

"I don't quarrel. I never want to quarrel. Let's not quarrel any more. No matter how nervous we get. Maybe they will be back with another truck today. Maybe the plane will come."

"I don't want to move," the man said. "There is no sense in moving now except to make it easier for you."

"That's cowardly."

"Can't you let a man die as comfortably as he can without calling him names? What's the use of slanging me?"

"You're not going to die."

"Don't be silly. I'm dying now. Ask those bastards." He looked over to where the huge, filthy birds sat, their naked heads sunk in the hunched feathers. A fourth planed down, to run quick-legged and then waddle slowly toward the others.

"They are around every camp. You never notice them. You can't die if you don't give up."

"Where did you read that? You're such a bloody fool."

"You might think about some one else."

"For Christ's sake," he said, "that's been my trade."

He lay then and was quiet for a while and looked across the heat shimmer of the plain to the edge of the bush. There were a few Tommies that showed minute and white against the yellow and, far off, he saw a herd of zebra, white against the green of the bush. This was a pleasant camp under big trees against a hill, with good water, and close by, a nearly dry water hole where sand grouse flighted in the mornings.

"Wouldn't you like me to read?" she asked. She was sitting on a canvas chair beside his cot. "There's a breeze coming up."

"No thanks."

"Maybe the truck will come."

"I don't give a damn about the truck."

"I do."

"You give a damn about so many things that I don't."

"Not so many, Harry."

"What about a drink?"

"It's supposed to be bad for you. It said in Black's to avoid all alcohol. You shouldn't drink."

"Molo!" he shouted.

"Yes Bwana."

"Bring whiskey-soda."

"Yes Bwana."

"You shouldn't," she said. "That's what I mean by giving up. It says it's bad for you. I know it's bad for you."

"No," he said. "It's good for me."

So now it was all over, he thought. So now he would never have a chance to finish it. So this was the way it ended in a bickering over a drink. Since the gangrene started in his right leg he had no pain and with the pain the horror had gone and all he felt now was a great tiredness and anger that this was the end of it. For this, that now was coming, he had very little curiosity. For years it had obsessed him; but now it meant nothing in itself. It was strange how easy being tired enough made it.

Now he would never write the things that he had saved to write until he knew enough to write them well. Well, he would not have to fail at trying to write them either. Maybe you could never write them, and that was why you put them off and delayed the starting. Well he would never know, now.

"I wish we'd never come," the woman said. She was looking at him holding the glass and biting her lip. "You never would have gotten anything like that in Paris. You always said you loved Paris. We could have stayed in Paris or gone anywhere. I'd have gone anywhere. I said I'd go anywhere you wanted. If you wanted to shoot we could have gone shooting in Hungary and been comfortable."

"Your bloody money," he said.

"That's not fair," she said. "It was always yours as much as mine. I left everything and I went wherever you wanted to go and I've done what you wanted to do. But I wish we'd never come here."

"You said you loved it."

"I did when you were all right. But now I hate it. I don't see why that had to happen to your leg. What have we done to have that happen to us?"

"I suppose what I did was to forget to put iodine on it when I first scratched it. Then I didn't pay any attention to it because I never infect. Then, later, when it got bad, it was probably using that weak carbolic solution when the other antiseptics ran out that paralyzed the minute blood vessels and started the gangrene." He looked at her, "What else?"

"I don't mean that."

"If we would have hired a good mechanic instead of a half baked kikuyu driver he would have checked the oil and never burned out that bearing in the truck."

"I don't mean that."

"If you hadn't left your own people, your goddamned Old Westbury, Saratoga, Palm Beach people to take me on "

"Why, I loved you. That's not fair. I love you now. I'll always love you. Don't you love me?"

"No," said the man. "I don't think so. I never have."

"Harry, what are you saying? You're out of your head."

"No. I haven't any head to go out of."

"Don't drink that," she said. "Darling, please don't drink that. We have to do everything we can."

"You do it," he said. "I'm tired."

Now in his mind he saw a railway station at Karagatch and

he was standing with his pack and that was the headlight of the Simplon-Orient cutting the dark now and he was leaving Thrace then after the retreat. That was one of the things he had saved to write, with, in the morning at breakfast, looking out the window and seeing snow on the mountains in Bulgaria and Nansen's Secretary asking the old man if it were snow and the old man looking at it and saying, No, that's not snow. It's too early for snow. And the Secretary repeating to the other girls, No, you see. It's not snow and them all saying, It's not snow we were mistaken. But it was the snow all right and he sent them on into it when he evolved exchange of populations. And it was snow they tramped along in until they died that winter.

It was snow too that fell all Christmas week that year up in the Gauertal, that year they lived in the woodcutter's house with the big square porcelain stove that filled half the room, and they slept on mattresses filled with beech leaves, the time the deserter came with his feet bloody in the snow. He said the police were right behind him and they gave him woolen socks and held the gendarmes talking until the tracks had drifted over.

In Schrunz, on Christmas day, the snow was so bright it hurt your eyes when you looked out from the weinstube and saw every one coming home from church. That was where they walked up the sleigh-smoothed urine-yellowed road along the river with the steep pine hills, skis heavy on the shoulder, and where they ran that great run down the glacier above the Madlener-haus, the snow as smooth to see as cake frosting and as light as powder and he remembered the noiseless rush the speed made as you dropped down like a bird.

They were snow-bound a week in the Madlener-haus that time in the blizzard playing cards in the smoke by the lantern light and the stakes were higher all the time as Herr Lent lost more. Finally he lost it all. Everything, the skischule money and all the season's profit and then his capital. He could see him with his long nose, picking up the cards and then opening, "Sans Voir." There was always gambling then. When there was no snow you gambled and when there was too much you gambled. He thought of all the time in his life he had spent gambling.

But he had never written a line of that, nor of that cold, bright Christmas day with the mountains showing across the plain that Barker had flown across the lines to bomb the Austrian officers' leave train, machine-gunning them as they scattered and ran. He remembered Barker afterwards coming into the mess and starting to tell about it. And how quiet it got and then somebody saying, "You bloody murderous bastard."

Those were the same Austrians they killed then that he skied with later. No not the same. Hans, that he skied with all that year had been in the Kaiser-Jägers and when they went hunting hares together up the little valley above the saw-mill they had talked of the fighting on Pasubio and of the attack on Pertica and Asalone and he had never written a word of that. Nor of Monte Corno, nor the Siete Commun, nor of Arsiedo.

How many winters had he lived in the Voralberg and the Arlberg? It was four and then he remembered the man who had the fox to sell when they had walked into Bludenz, that time to buy presents, and the cherry-pit taste of good kirsch, the fast-slipping rush of running powder-snow on crust, singing "Hi! Ho! said Rolly!" as you ran down the last stretch to the steep drop, taking it straight, then running the orchard in three turns and out across the ditch and onto the icy road behind the inn. Knocking your bindings loose, kicking the skis free and leaning them up against the wooden wall of the inn, the lamplight coming from the window, where inside, in the smoky, new-wine smelling warmth, they were playing the accordion.

"Where did we stay in Paris?" he asked the woman who was sitting by him in a canvas chair, now, in Africa.

"At the Crillon. You know that."

"Why do I know that?"

"That's where we always stayed."

"No. Not always."

"There and at the Pavillion Henri-Quatre in St. Germain. You said you loved it there."

"Love is a dunghill," said Harry. "And I'm the cock that gets on it to crow."

"If you have to go away," she said, "is it absolutely necessary to kill off everything you leave behind? I mean do you have to take away everything? Do you have to kill your horse, and your wife and burn your saddle and your armour?"

"Yes," he said. "Your damned money was my armour. My Swift and my Armour."

"Don't."

"All right. I'll stop that. I don't want to hurt you."

"It's a little bit late now."

"All right then. I'll go on hurting you. It's more amusing. The only thing I ever really liked to do with you I can't do now."

"No. That's not true. You liked to do many things and everything you wanted to do I did."

"Oh, for Christ sake stop bragging, will you?"

He looked at her and saw her crying.

"Listen," he said. "Do you think that it is fun to do this? I don't know why I'm doing it. It's trying to kill to keep yourself alive, I imagine. I was all right when we started talking. I didn't mean to start this, and now I'm crazy as a coot and being as cruel to you as I can be. Don't pay any attention, darling, to what I say. I love you, really. You know I love you. I've never loved any one else the way I love you."

He slipped into the familiar lie he made his bread and butter by.

"You're sweet to me."

"You bitch," he said. "You rich bitch. That's poetry. I'm full of poetry now. Rot and poetry. Rotten poetry."

"Stop it. Harry, why do you have to turn into a devil now?"

"I don't like to leave anything," the man said. "I don't like to leave things behind."

It was evening now and he had been asleep. The sun was gone behind the hill and there was a shadow all across the plain and the small animals were feeding close to camp; quick dropping heads and switching tails, he watched them keeping well out away from the bush now. The birds no longer waited on the ground. They were all perched heavily in a tree. There were many more of them. His personal boy was sitting by the bed.

"Memsahib's gone to shoot," the boy said. "Does Bwana want?"

"Nothing."

She had gone to kill a piece of meat and, knowing how he liked to watch the game, she had gone well away so she would not disturb this little pocket of the plain that he could see. She was always thoughtful, he thought. On anything she knew about, or had read, or that she had ever heard.

It was not her fault that when he went to her he was already over. How could a woman know that you meant nothing that you said; that you spoke only from habit and to be comfortable? After he no longer meant what he said, his lies were more successful with women than when he had told them the truth. It was not so much that he lied as that there was no truth to tell. He had had his life and it was over and then he went on living it again with different people and more money, with the best of the same places, and some new ones.

You kept from thinking and it was all marvellous. You were equipped with good insides so that you did not go to pieces that way, the way most of them had, and you made an attitude that you cared nothing for the work you used to do, now that you could no longer do it. But, in yourself, you said that you would write about these people; about the very rich; that you were really not of them but a spy in their country; that you would leave it and write of it and for once it would be written by some one who knew what he was writing of. But he would never do it, because each day of not writing, of comfort, of being that which he despised, dulled his ability and softened his will to work so that, finally, he did no work at all. The people he knew now were all much more comfortable when he did not work. Africa was where he had been happiest in the good time of his life, so he had come out here to start again. They had made this safari with the minimum of comfort. There was no hardship; but there was no luxury and he had thought that he could get back into training that way. That in some way he could work the fat off his soul the way a fighter went into the mountains to work and train in order to burn it out of his body.

She had liked it. She said she loved it. She loved anything that was exciting, that involved a change of scene, where there were new people and where things were pleasant. And he had felt the illusion of returning strength of will to work. Now if this was how it ended, and he knew it was, he must not turn like some snake biting itself because its back was broken. It wasn't this woman's fault. If it had not been she it would have been another. If he lived by a lie he should try to die by it. He heard a shot beyond the hill.

She shot very well this good, this rich bitch, this kindly caretaker and destroyer of his talent. Nonsense. He had destroyed his talent himself. Why should he blame this woman because she kept him well? He had destroyed his talent by not using it, by betrayals of himself and what he believed in, by drinking so much that he blunted the edge of his perceptions, by laziness, by sloth, and by snobbery, by pride, and by prejudice, by hook and by crook. What was this? A catalogue of old books? What was his talent anyway? It was a talent all right but instead of using it, he had traded on it. It was never what he had done, but always what he could do. And he had chosen to make his living with something else instead of a pen or a pencil. It was strange, too, wasn't it, that when he fell in love with another woman, that woman should always have more money than the last one? But when he no longer was in love, when he was only lying, as to this woman, now, who had the most money of all, who had all the money there was, who had had a husband and children, who had taken lovers and been dissatisfied with them, and who loved him dearly as a writer, as a man, as a companion and as a proud possession; it was strange that when he did not love her at all and was lying, that he should be able to give her more for her money than when he had really loved.

We must all be cut out for what we do, he thought. However you make your living is where your talent lies. He had sold vitality, in one form or another, all his life and when your affections are not too involved you give much better value for the money. He had found that out but he would never write that, now, either. No, he would not write that, although it was well worth writing.

Now she came in sight, walking across the open toward the camp. She was wearing jodhpurs and carrying her rifle. The two boys had a Tommie slung and they were coming along behind her. She was still a good-looking woman, he thought, and she had a pleasant body. She had a great talent and appreciation for the bed, she was not pretty, but he liked her face, she read enormously, liked to ride and shoot and, certainly, she drank too much. Her husband had died when she was still a comparatively young woman and for a while she had devoted herself to her two just-grown children, who did not need her and were embarrassed at having her about, to her stable of horses, to books and to bottles. She liked to read in the evening before dinner and she drank Scotch and soda while she read. By dinner she was fairly drunk and after a bottle of wine at dinner she was usually drunk enough to sleep.

That was before the lovers. After she had the lovers she did not drink so much because she did not have to be drunk to sleep. But the lovers bored her. She had been married to a man who had never bored her and these people bored her very much.

Then one of her two children was killed in a plane crash and after that was over she did not want the lovers, and drink being no anæsthetic she had to make another life. Suddenly, she had been acutely frightened of being alone. But she wanted some one that she respected with her.

It had begun very simply. She liked what he wrote and she had always envied the life he led. She thought he did exactly what he wanted to. The steps by which she had acquired him and the way in which she had finally fallen in love with him were all part of a regular progression in which she had built herself a new life and he had traded away what remained of his old life.

He had traded it for security, for comfort too, there was no denying that, and for what else? He did not know. She would have bought him anything he wanted. He knew that. She was a damned nice woman too. He would as soon be in bed with her as any one; rather with her, because she was richer, because she was very pleasant and appreciative and because she never made scenes. And now this life that she had built again was coming to a term because he had not used iodine two weeks ago when a thorn had scratched his knee as they moved forward trying to photograph a herd of waterbuck standing, their heads up, peering while their nostrils searched the air, their ears spread wide to hear the first noise that would send them rushing into the bush. They had bolted, too, before he got the picture.

Here she came now.

He turned his head on the cot to look toward her. "Hello," he said.

"I shot a Tommy ram," she told him. "He'll make you good broth and I'll have them mash some potatoes with the Klim. How do you feel?"

"Much better."

"Isn't that lovely? You know I thought perhaps you would. You were sleeping when I left."

"I had a good sleep. Did you walk far?"

"No. Just around behind the hill. I made quite a good shot on the Tommy."

"You shoot marvellously, you know."

"I love it. I've loved Africa. Really. If *you're* all right it's the most fun that I've ever had. You don't know the fun it's been to shoot with you. I've loved the country."

"I love it too."

"Darling, you don't know how marvellous it is to see you feeling better. I couldn't stand it when you felt that way. You won't talk to me like that again, will you? Promise me?"

"No," he said. "I don't remember what I said."

"You don't have to destroy me. Do you? I'm only a middle-aged woman who loves you and wants to do what you want to do. I've been destroyed two or three times already. You wouldn't want to destroy me again, would you?"

"I'd like to destroy you a few times in bed," he said.

"Yes. That's the good destruction. That's the way we're made to be destroyed. The plane will be here tomorrow."

"How do you know?"

"I'm sure. It's bound to come. The boys have the wood all ready and the grass to make the smudge. I went down and looked at it again today. There's plenty of room to land and we have the smudges ready at both ends."

"What makes you think it will come tomorrow?"

"I'm sure it will. It's overdue now. Then, in town, they will fix up your leg and then we will have some good destruction. Not that dreadful talking kind."

"Should we have a drink? The sun is down."

"Do you think you should?"

"I'm having one."

"We'll have one together. *Molo, letti dui whiskey-soda!*" she called.

"You'd better put on your mosquito boots," he told her.

"I'll wait till I bathe . . ."

While it grew dark they drank and just before it was dark and there was no longer enough light to shoot, a hyena crossed the open on his way around the hill.

"That bastard crosses there every night," the man said. "Every night for two weeks."

"He's the one makes the noise at night. I don't mind it. They're a filthy animal though."

Drinking together, with no pain now except the discomfort of lying in one position, the boys lighting a fire, its shadow jumping on the tents, he could feel the return of acquiescence in this life of pleasant surrender. She *was* very good to him. He had been cruel and unjust in the afternoon. She was a fine woman, marvellous really. And just then it occurred to him that he was going to die.

It came with a rush; not as a rush of water nor of wind; but of a sudden evil-smelling emptiness and the odd thing was that the hyena slipped lightly along the edge of it.

"What is it, Harry?" she asked him.

"Nothing," he said. "You had better move over to the other side. To windward."

"Did Molo change the dressing?"

"Yes. I'm just using the boric now."

"How do you feel?"

"A little wobbly."

"I'm going in to bathe," she said. "I'll be right out. I'll eat with you and then we'll put the cot in."

So, he said to himself, we did well to stop the quarrelling. He had never quarrelled much with this woman, while with the women that he loved he had quarrelled so much they had finally always, with the corrosion of the quarrelling, killed what they had together. He had loved too much, demanded too much, and he wore it all out.

He thought about alone in Constantinople that time, having quarrelled in Paris before he had gone out. He had whored the whole time and then, when that was over, and he had failed to kill this loneliness, but only made it worse, he had written her, the first one, the one who left him, a letter telling her how he had never been able to kill it. . . . How when he thought he saw her outside the Regence one time it made him go all faint and sick inside, and that he would follow a woman who looked like her in some way, along the Boulevard, afraid to see it was not she, afraid to lose the feeling it gave him. How every one he had slept with had only made him miss her more. How what she had done could never matter since he knew he could not cure himself of loving her. He wrote this letter at the Club, cold sober, and mailed it to New York asking her to write him at the office in Paris. That seemed safe. And that night missing her so much it made him feel hollow sick inside, he wandered up past Taxim's, picked a girl up and took her out to supper. He had gone to a place to dance with her afterward, she danced badly, and left her for a hot Armenian slut, that swung her belly against him so it almost scalded. He took her away from a British gunner subaltern after a row. The gunner asked him outside and they fought in the street on the cobbles in the dark. He'd hit him twice, hard, on the side of the jaw and when he didn't go down he knew he was in for a fight. The gunner hit him in the body then beside his eye. He swung with his left again and landed and the gunner fell on him and grabbed his coat and tore the sleeve off and he clubbed him twice behind the ear and then smashed him with his right as he pushed him away. When the gunner went down his head hit first and he ran with the girl because they heard the M. P.'s coming. They got into a taxi and drove out to Rimmily Hissa along the Bosphorus, and around, and back in the cool night and went to bed and she felt as over-ripe as she looked but smooth, rose-petal, syrupy, smooth-bellied, big-breasted and needed no pillow under her buttocks, and he left her before she was awake looking blousy enough in the first daylight and turned up at the Pera Palace with a black eye, carrying his coat because one sleeve was missing.

That same night he left for Anatolia and he remembered, later on that trip, riding all day through fields of the poppies that they raised for opium and how strange it made you feel, finally, and all the distances seemed wrong, to where they had made the attack with the newly arrived Constantine officers, that did not know a god-damned thing, and the artillery had fired into the troops and the British observer had cried like a child.

That was the day he'd first seen dead men wearing white ballet skirts and upturned shoes with pompons on them. The Turks had come steadily and lumpily and he had seen the skirted men running and the officers shooting into them and running then themselves and he and the British observer had run too until his lungs ached and his mouth was full of the taste of pennies and they stopped behind some rocks and there were the Turks coming as lumpily as ever. Later he had seen the things that he could never think of and later still he had seen much worse. So when he got back to Paris that time he could not talk about it or stand to have it mentioned. And there in the café as he passed was that American poet with a pile of saucers in front of him and a stupid look on his potato face talking about the Dada movement with a Roumanian who said his name was Tristan Tzara, who always wore a monocle and had a headache, and back at the apartment with his wife that now he loved again, the quarrel all over, the madness all over, glad to be home, the office sent his mail up to the flat. So then the letter in answer to the one he'd written came in on a platter one morning and when he saw the handwriting he went cold all over and tried to slip the letter underneath another. But his wife said. "Who is that letter from, dear?" and that was the end of the beginning of that.

He remembered the good times with them all, and the quarrels. They always picked the finest places to have the quarrels. And why had they always quarrelled when he was feeling best? He had never written any of that because at first, he never wanted to hurt any one and it seemed as though there was enough to write without it. But he had always thought that he would write it finally. There was so much to write. He had seen the world change; not just the events; although he had seen many of them and had watched the people, but he had seen the subtler

answer?

change and he could remember how the people were at different times. He had been in it and he had watched it and it was his duty to write of it; but now he never would.

"How do you feel?" she said. She had come out from the tent now after her bath.

"All right."

"Could you eat now?" He saw Molo behind her with the folding table and the other boy with the dishes.

"I want to write," he said.

"You ought to take some broth to keep your strength up."

"I'm going to die tonight," he said. "I don't need my strength up."

"Don't be melodramatic, Harry, please," she said.

"Why don't you use your nose? I'm rotted half way up my thigh now. What the hell should I fool with broth for? Molo bring whiskey-soda."

"Please take the broth," she said gently.

"All right."

The broth was too hot. He had to hold it in the cup until it cooled enough to take it and then he just got it down without gagging.

"You're a fine woman," he said. "Don't pay any attention to me."

She looked at him with her well-known, well-loved face from *Spur* and *Town and Country,* only a little the worse for drink, only a little the worse for bed, but *Town and Country* never showed those good breasts and those useful thighs and those lightly small-of-back-caressing hands, and as he looked and saw her well-known pleasant smile, he felt death come again. This time there was no rush. It was a puff, as of a wind that makes a candle flicker and the flame go tall.

"They can bring my net out later and hang it from the tree and build the fire up. I'm not going in the tent tonight. It's not worth moving. It's a clear night. There won't be any rain."

So this was how you died, in whispers that you did not hear. Well, there would be no more quarrelling. He could promise that. The one experience that he had never had he was not going to spoil now. He probably would. You spoiled everything. But perhaps he wouldn't.

"You can't take dictation, can you?"

"I never learned," she told him.

"That's all right."

There wasn't time, of course, although it seemed as though it telescoped so that you might put it all into one paragraph if you could get it right.

There was a log house, chinked white with mortar, on a hill above the lake. There was a bell on a pole by the door to call the people in to meals. Behind the house were fields and behind the fields was the timber. A line of lombardy poplars ran from the house to the dock. Other poplars ran along the point. A road went up to the hills along the edge of the timber and along that road he picked blackberries. Then that log house was burned down and all the guns that had been on deer foot racks above the open fireplace were burned and afterwards their barrels, with the lead melted in the magazines, and the stocks burned away, lay out on the heap of ashes that were used to make lye for the big iron soap kettles, and you asked Grandfather if you could have them to play with, and he said, no. You see they were his guns still and he never bought any others. Nor did he hunt any more. The house was rebuilt in the same place out of lumber now and painted white and from its porch you saw the poplars and the lake beyond; but there were never any more guns. The barrels of the guns that had hung on the deer feet on the wall of the log house lay out there on the heap of ashes and no one ever touched them.

In the Black Forest, after the war, we rented a trout stream and there were two ways to walk to it. One was down the valley from Triberg and around the valley road in the shade of the trees that bordered the white road, and then up a side road that went up through the hills past many small farms, with the big Schwarzwald houses, until that road crossed the stream. That was where our fishing began.

The other way was to climb steeply up to the edge of the woods and then go across the top of the hills through the pine woods, and then out to the edge of a meadow and down across this meadow to the bridge. There were birches along the stream and it was not big, but narrow, clear and fast, with pools where it had cut under the roots of the birches. At the Hotel in Triberg the proprietor had a fine season. It was very pleasant and we were all great friends. The next year came the inflation and the money he had made the year before was not enough to buy supplies to open the hotel and he hanged himself.

You could dictate that, but you could not dictate the Place Contrescarpe where the flower sellers dyed their flowers in the street and the dye ran over the paving where the autobus started and the old men and the women, always drunk on wine and bad marc; and the children with their noses running in the cold; the smell of dirty sweat and poverty and drunkenness at the Café des Amateurs and the whores at the Bal Musette they lived above. The Concièrge who entertained the trooper of the Garde Républicaine in her loge, his horse-hair-plumed helmet on a chair. The locataire across the hall whose husband was a bicycle racer and her joy that morning at the Crémerie when she had opened L'Auto and seen where he placed third in Paris-Tours, his first big race. She had blushed and laughed and then gone upstairs crying with the yellow sporting paper in her hand. The husband of the woman who ran the Bal Musette drove a taxi and when he, Harry, had to take an early plane the husband knocked upon the door to wake him and they each drank a glass of white wine at the zinc of the bar before they started. He knew his neighbors in that quarter then because they all were poor.

Around that Place there were two kinds: the drunkards and the sportifs. The drunkards killed their poverty that way; the sportifs took it out in exercise. They were the descendants of the Communards and it was no struggle for them to know their politics. They knew who had shot their fathers, their relatives, their brothers, and their friends when the Versailles troops came in and took the town after the Commune and executed any one they could catch with calloused hands, or who wore a cap, or carried any other sign he was a working man. And in that poverty, and in that quarter across the street from a Boucherie Chevaline and a wine co-operative he had written the start of all he was to do. There never was another part of Paris that he loved like that, the sprawling trees, the old white plastered houses painted brown below, the long green of the autobus in that round square, the purple flower dye upon the paving, the sudden drop down the hill of the rue Cardinal Lemoine to the River, and the other way the narrow crowded world of the rue Mouffetard. The street that ran up toward the Panthéon and the other that he always took with the bicycle, the only asphalted street in all that quarter, smooth under the tires, with the high narrow houses and the cheap tall hotel where Paul Verlaine had died. There were only two rooms in the apartments where they lived and he had a room on the top floor of that hotel that cost him sixty francs a month where he did his writing, and from it he could see the roofs and chimney pots and all the hills of Paris.

From the apartment you could only see the wood and coal man's place. He sold wine too, bad wine. The golden horse's head outside the Boucherie Chevaline where the carcasses hung yellow gold and red in the open window, and the green painted co-operative where they bought their wine; good wine and cheap. The rest was plaster walls and the windows of the neighbors. The neighbors who, at night, when some one lay drunk in the street, moaning and groaning in that typical French ivresse[1] that you were propaganded to believe did not exist, would open their windows and then the murmur of talk.

"Where is the policeman? When you don't want him the bugger is always there. He's sleeping with some concièrge. Get the Agent." Till some one threw a bucket of water from

[1] Drunkenness.

*a window and the moaning stopped. "What's that? Water.
Ah, that's intelligent." And the windows shutting. Marie, his
femme de ménage, protesting against the eight-hour day saying, "If a husband works until six he gets only a little drunk
on the way home and does not waste too much. If he works
only until five he is drunk every night and one has no money.
It is the wife of the working man who suffers from this short-
ening of hours."*

"Wouldn't you like some more broth?" the woman asked
him now.

"No, thank you very much. It is awfully good."

"Try just a little."

"I would like a whiskey-soda."

"It's not good for you."

"No. It's bad for me. Cole Porter wrote the words and the
music. This knowledge that you're going mad for me."

"You know I like you to drink."

"Oh yes. Only it's bad for me."

When she goes, he thought, I'll have all I want. Not all I
want but all there is. Ayee he was tired. Too tired. He was
going to sleep a little while. He lay still and death was not
there. It must have gone around another street. It went in
pairs, on bicycles, and moved absolutely silently on the pave-
ments.

*No, he had never written about Paris. Not the Paris that
he cared about. But what about the rest that he had never
written?*

*What about the ranch and the silvered gray of the sage
brush, the quick, clear water in the irrigation ditches, and
the heavy green of the alfalfa. The trail went up into the hills
and the cattle in the summer were shy as deer. The bawling
and the steady noise and slow moving mass raising a dust as
you brought them down in the fall. And behind the mountains, the clear sharpness of the peak in the evening light and,
riding down along the trail in the moonlight, bright across the
valley. Now he remembered coming down through the tim-*

ber in the dark holding the horse's tail when you could not
see and all the stories that he meant to write.

About the half-wit chore boy who was left at the ranch
that time and told not to let any one get any hay, and that
old bastard from the Forks who had beaten the boy when he
had worked for him stopping to get some feed. The boy re-
fusing and the old man saying he would beat him again. The
boy got the rifle from the kitchen and shot him when he tried
to come into the barn and when they came back to the ranch
he'd been dead a week, frozen in the corral, and the dogs had
eaten part of him. But what was left you packed on a sled
wrapped in a blanket and roped on and you got the boy to
help you haul it, and the two of you took it out over the road
on skis, and sixty miles down to town to turn the boy over.
He having no idea that he would be arrested. Thinking he
had done his duty and that you were his friend and he would
be rewarded. He'd helped to haul the old man in so everybody could know how bad the old man had been and how
he'd tried to steal some feed that didn't belong to him, and
when the sheriff put the handcuffs on the boy he couldn't believe it. Then he'd started to cry. That was one story he had
saved to write. He knew at least twenty good stories from out
there and he had never written one. Why?

"You tell them why," he said.

"Why what, dear?"

"Why nothing."

She didn't drink so much, now, since she had him. But if
he lived he would never write about her, he knew that now.
Nor about any of them. The rich were dull and they drank
too much, or they played too much backgammon. They were
dull and they were repetitious. He remembered poor Julian
and his romantic awe of them and how he had started a story
once that began, "The very rich are different from you and
me." And how some one had said to Julian, Yes, they have
more money. But that was not humorous to Julian. He thought
they were a special glamorous race and when he found they

weren't it wrecked him just as much as any other thing that wrecked him.

He had been contemptuous of those who wrecked. You did not have to like it because you understood it. He could beat anything, he thought, because no thing could hurt him if he did not care.

All right. Now he would not care for death. One thing he had always dreaded was the pain. He could stand pain as well as any man, until it went on too long, and wore him out, but here he had something that had hurt frightfully and just when he had felt it breaking him, the pain had stopped.

He remembered long ago when Williamson, the bombing officer, had been hit by a stick bomb some one in a German patrol had thrown as he was coming in through the wire that night and, screaming, had begged every one to kill him. He was a fat man, very brave, and a good officer, although addicted to fantastic shows. But that night he was caught in the wire, with a flare lighting him up and his bowels spilled out into the wire, so when they brought him in, alive, they had to cut him loose. Shoot me, Harry. For Christ sake shoot me. They had had an argument one time about our Lord never sending you anything you could not bear and some one's theory had been that meant that at a certain time the pain passed you out automatically. But he had always remembered Williamson, that night. Nothing passed out Williamson until he gave him all his morphine tablets that he had always saved to use himself and then they did not work right away.

Still this now, that he had, was very easy; and if it was no worse as it went on there was nothing to worry about. Except that he would rather be in better company.

He thought a little about the company that he would like to have.

No, he thought, when everything you do, you do too long, and do too late, you can't expect to find the people still there. The people all are gone. The party's over and you are with your hostess now.

company meaningful
— Part of game in
contrast with
remembered
experiences

I'm getting as bored with dying as with everything else, he thought.

"It's a bore," he said out loud.

"What is, my dear?"

"Anything you do too bloody long."

He looked at her face between him and the fire. She was leaning back in the chair and the firelight shone on her pleasantly lined face and he could see that she was sleepy. He heard the hyena make a noise just outside the range of the fire.

"I've been writing," he said. "But I got tired."

"Do you think you will be able to sleep?"

"Pretty sure. Why don't you turn in?"

"I like to sit here with you."

"Do you feel anything strange?" he asked her.

"No. Just a little sleepy."

"I do," he said.

He had just felt death come by again.

"You know the only thing I've never lost is curiosity," he said to her.

"You've never lost anything. You're the most complete man I've ever known."

"Christ," he said. "How little a woman knows. What is that? Your intuition?"

Because, just then, death had come and rested its head on the foot of the cot and he could smell its breath.

"Never believe any of that about a scythe and a skull," he told her. "It can be two bicycle policemen as easily, or be a bird. Or it can have a wide snout like a hyena."

It had moved up on him now, but it had no shape any more. It simply occupied space.

"Tell it to go away."

It did not go away but moved a little closer.

"You've got a hell of a breath," he told it. "You stinking bastard."

It moved up closer to him still and now he could not speak to it, and when it saw he could not speak it came a little closer, and now he tried to send it away without speaking, but it moved in on him so its weight was all upon his chest, and while it crouched there and he could not move, or speak, he heard the woman say, "Bwana is asleep now. Take the cot up very gently and carry it into the tent."

He could not speak to tell her to make it go away and it crouched now, heavier, so he could not breathe. And then, while they lifted the cot, suddenly it was all right and the weight went from his chest.

It was morning and had been morning for some time and he heard the plane. It showed very tiny and then made a wide circle and the boys ran out and lit the fires, using kerosene, and piled on grass so there were two big smudges at each end of the level place and the morning breeze blew them toward the camp and the plane circled twice more, low this time, and then glided down and levelled off and landed smoothly and, coming walking toward him, was old Compton in slacks, a tweed jacket and a brown felt hat.

"What's the matter, old cock?" Compton said.

"Bad leg," he told him. "Will you have some breakfast?"

"Thanks. I'll just have some tea. It's the Puss Moth you know. I won't be able to take the Memsahib. There's only room for one. Your lorry is on the way."

Helen had taken Compton aside and was speaking to him. Compton came back more cheery than ever.

"We'll get you right in," he said. "I'll be back for the Mem. Now I'm afraid I'll have to stop at Arusha to refuel. We'd better get going."

"What about the tea?"

"I don't really care about it you know."

The boys had picked up the cot and carried it around the green tents and down along the rock and out onto the plain and along past the smudges that were burning brightly now, the grass all consumed, and the wind fanning the fire, to the little plane. It was difficult getting him in, but once in he lay back in the leather seat, and the leg was stuck straight out to one side of the seat, where Compton sat. Compton started the motor and got in. He waved to Helen and to the boys and, as the clatter moved into the old familiar roar, they swung around with Compie watching for wart-hog holes and roared, bumping, along the stretch between the fires and with the last bump rose and he saw them all standing below, waving, and the camp beside the hill, flattening now, and the plain spreading, clumps of trees, and the bush flattening, while the game trails ran now smoothly to the dry waterholes, and there was a new water that he had never known of. The zebra, small rounded backs now, and the wildebeeste, big-headed dots seeming to climb as they moved in long fingers across the plain, now scattering as the shadow came toward them, they were tiny now, and the movement had no gallop, and the plain was as far as you could see, gray-yellow now and ahead old Compie's tweed back and the brown felt hat. Then they were over the first hills and the wildebeeste were trailing up them, and then they were over mountains with sudden depths of green-rising forest and the solid bamboo slopes, and then the heavy forest again, sculptured into peaks and hollows until they crossed, and hills sloped down and then another plain, hot now, and purple brown, bumpy with heat and Compie looking back to see how he was riding. Then there were other mountains dark ahead.

And then instead of going on to Arusha they turned left, he evidently figured that they had the gas, and looking down he saw a pink sifting cloud, moving over the ground, and in the air, like the first snow in a blizzard, that comes from nowhere, and he knew the locusts were coming up from the South. Then they began to climb and they were going to the East it seemed, and then it darkened and they were in a storm, the rain so thick it seemed like flying through a waterfall, and then they were out and Compie turned his head and grinned and pointed and there, ahead, all he could see, as wide as all the world, great, high, unbelievably white in the sun, was the square top of Kilimanjaro. And then he knew that there was where he was going.

Just then the hyena stopped whimpering in the night and started to make a strange, human, almost crying sound. The woman heard it and stirred uneasily. She did not wake. In her dream she was at the house on Long Island and it was the night before her daughter's début. Somehow her father was there and he had been very rude. Then the noise the hyena made was so loud she woke and for a moment she did not know where she was and she was very afraid. Then she took the flashlight and shone it on the other cot that they had carried in after Harry had gone to sleep. She could see his bulk under the mosquito bar but somehow he had gotten his leg out and it hung down alongside the cot. The dressings had all come down and she could not look at it.

"Molo," she called, "Molo! Molo!"

Then she said, "Harry, Harry!" Then her voice rising, "Harry! Please, Oh Harry!"

There was no answer and she could not hear him breathing.

Outside the tent the hyena made the same strange noise that had awakened her. But she did not hear him for the beating of her heart.

The Leader of the People

ON SATURDAY afternoon Billy Buck, the ranch-hand, raked together the last of the old year's haystack and pitched small forkfuls over the wire fence to a few mildly interested cattle. High in the air small clouds like puffs of cannon smoke were driven eastward by the March wind. The wind could be heard whishing in the brush on the ridge crests, but no breath of it penetrated down into the ranch-cup.

The little boy, Jody, emerged from the house eating a thick piece of buttered bread. He saw Billy working on the last of the haystack. Jody tramped down scuffing his shoes in a way he had been told was destructive to good shoe-leather. A flock of white pigeons flew out of the black cypress tree as Jody passed, and circled the tree and landed again. A half-grown tortoise-shell cat leaped from the bunkhouse porch, galloped on stiff legs across the road, whirled and galloped back again. Jody picked up a stone to help the game along, but he was too late, for the cat was under the porch before the stone could be discharged. He threw the stone into the cypress tree and started the white pigeons on another whirling flight.

Arriving at the used-up haystack, the boy leaned against the barbed wire fence. "Will that be all of it, do you think?" he asked.

The middle-aged ranch-hand stopped his careful raking and stuck his fork into the ground. He took off his black hat and smoothed down his hair. "Nothing left of it that isn't soggy from ground moisture," he said. He replaced his hat and rubbed his dry leathery hands together.

"Ought to be plenty mice," Jody suggested.

"Lousy with them," said Billy. "Just crawling with mice."

"Well, maybe, when you get all through, I could call the dogs and hunt the mice."

"Sure, I guess you could," said Billy Buck. He lifted a fork-ful of the damp ground-hay and threw it into the air. Instantly three mice leaped out and burrowed frantically under the hay again.

Jody sighed with satisfaction. Those plump, sleek, arrogant mice were doomed. For eight months they had lived and multiplied in the haystack. They had been immune from cats, from traps, from poison and from Jody. They had grown smug in their security, overbearing and fat. Now the time of disaster had come; they would not survive another day.

Billy looked up at the top of the hills that surrounded the ranch. "Maybe you better ask your father before you do it," he suggested.

"Well, where is he? I'll ask him now."

"He rode up to the ridge ranch after dinner. He'll be back pretty soon."

Jody slumped against the fence post. "I don't think he'd care."

As Billy went back to his work he said ominously, "You'd better ask him anyway. You know how he is."

Jody did know. His father, Carl Tiflin, insisted upon giving permission for anything that was done on the ranch, whether it was important or not. Jody sagged farther against the post until he was sitting on the ground. He looked up at the little puffs of wind-driven cloud. "Is it like to rain, Billy?"

"It might. The wind's good for it, but not strong enough."

"Well, I hope it don't rain until after I kill those damn mice." He looked over his shoulder to see whether Billy had noticed the mature profanity. Billy worked on without comment.

Jody turned back and looked at the side-hill where the road from the outside world came down. The hill was washed with lean March sunshine. Silver thistles, blue lupins and a few poppies bloomed among the sage bushes. Halfway up the hill Jody could see Doubletree Mutt, the black dog, digging in a squirrel hole. He paddled for a while and then paused to kick bursts of dirt out between his hind legs, and he dug with an earnestness which belied the knowledge he must have had that no dog had ever caught a squirrel by digging in a hole.

Suddenly, while Jody watched, the black dog stiffened, and backed out of the hole and looked up the hill toward the cleft in the ridge where the road came through. Jody looked up too. For a moment Carl Tiflin on horseback stood out against the pale sky and then he moved down the road toward the house. He carried something white in his hand.

The boy started to his feet. "He's got a letter," Jody cried. He trotted away toward the ranch house, for the letter would probably be read aloud and he wanted to be there. He reached the house before his father did, and ran in. He heard Carl dismount from his creaking saddle and slap the horse on the side to send it to the barn where Billy would unsaddle it and turn it out.

Jody ran into the kitchen. "We got a letter!" he cried.

His mother looked up from a pan of beans. "Who has?"

"Father has. I saw it in his hand."

Carl strode into the kitchen then, and Jody's mother asked, "Who's the letter from, Carl?"

He frowned quickly. "How did you know there was a letter?"

She nodded her head in the boy's direction. "Big-Britches Jody told me."

Jody was embarrassed.

His father looked down at him contemptuously. "He is getting to be a Big-Britches," Carl said. "He's minding everybody's business but his own. Got his big nose into everything."

Mrs. Tiflin relented a little. "Well, he hasn't enough to keep him busy. Who's the letter from?"

Carl still frowned on Jody. "I'll keep him busy if he isn't careful." He held out a sealed letter. "I guess it's from your father."

Mrs. Tiflin took a hairpin from her head and slit open the

flap. Her lips pursed judiciously. Jody saw her eyes snap back and forth over the lines. "He says," she translated, "he says he's going to drive out Saturday to stay for a little while. Why, this is Saturday. The letter must have been delayed." She looked at the postmark. "This was mailed day before yesterday. It should have been here yesterday." She looked up questioningly at her husband, and then her face darkened angrily. "Now what have you got that look on you for? He doesn't come often."

Carl turned his eyes away from her anger. He could be stern with her most of the time, but when occasionally her temper arose, he could not combat it.

"What's the matter with you?" she demanded again.

In his explanation there was a tone of apology Jody himself might have used. "It's just that he talks," Carl said lamely. "Just talks."

"Well, what of it? You talk yourself."

"Sure I do. But your father only talks about one thing."

"Indians!" Jody broke in excitedly. "Indians and crossing the plains!"

Carl turned fiercely on him. "You get out, Mr. Big-Britches! Go on, now! Get out!"

Jody went miserably out the back door and closed the screen with elaborate quietness. Under the kitchen window his shamed, downcast eyes fell upon a curiously shaped stone, a stone of such fascination that he squatted down and picked it up and turned it over in his hands.

The voices came clearly to him through the open kitchen window. "Jody's damn well right," he heard his father say. "Just Indians and crossing the plains. I've heard that story about how the horses got driven off about a thousand times. He just goes on and on, and he never changes a word in the things he tells."

When Mrs. Tiflin answered her tone was so changed that Jody, outside the window, looked up from his study of the stone. Her voice had become soft and explanatory. Jody knew how her face would have changed to match the tone. She said quietly. "Look at it this way, Carl. That was the big thing in my father's life. He led a wagon train clear across the plains to the coast, and when it was finished, his life was done. It was a big thing to do, but it didn't last long enough. Look!" she continued, "it's as though he was born to do that, and after he finished it, there wasn't anything more for him to do but think about it and talk about it. If there'd been any farther west to go, he'd have gone. He's told me so himself. But at last there was the ocean. He lives right by the ocean where he had to stop."

She had caught Carl, caught him and entangled him in her soft tone.

"I've seen him," he agreed quietly. "He goes down and stares off west over the ocean." His voice sharpened a little. "And then he goes up to the Horseshoe Club in Pacific Grove, and he tells people how the Indians drove off the horses."

She tried to catch him again. "Well, it's everything to him. You might be patient with him and pretend to listen."

Carl turned impatiently away. "Well, if it gets too bad, I can always go down to the bunkhouse and sit with Billy," he said irritably. He walked through the house and slammed the front door after him.

Jody ran to his chores. He dumped the grain to the chickens without chasing any of them. He gathered the eggs from the nests. He trotted into the house with the wood and interlaced it so carefully in the wood-box that two armloads seemed to fill it to overflowing.

His mother had finished the beans by now. She stirred up the fire and brushed off the stove-top with a turkey wing. Jody peered cautiously at her to see whether any rancor toward him remained. "Is he coming today?" Jody asked.

"That's what his letter said."

"Maybe I better walk up the road to meet him."

Mrs. Tiflin clanged the stove-lid shut. "That would be nice," she said. "He'd probably like to be met."

"I guess I'll just do it then."

Outside, Jody whistled shrilly to the dogs. "Come on up

the hill," he commanded. The two dogs waved their tails and ran ahead. Along the roadside the sage had tender new tips. Jody tore off some pieces and rubbed them on his hands until the air was filled with the sharp wild smell. With a rush the dogs leaped from the road and yapped into the brush after a rabbit. That was the last Jody saw of them, for when they failed to catch the rabbit, they went back home.

Jody plodded on up the hill toward the ridge top. When he reached the little cleft where the road came through, the afternoon wind struck him and blew up his hair and ruffled his shirt. He looked down on the little hills and ridges below and then out at the huge green Salinas Valley. He could see the white town of Salinas far out in the flat and the flash of its windows under the waning sun. Directly below him, in an oak tree, a crow congress had convened. The tree was black with crows all cawing at once.

Then Jody's eyes followed the wagon road down from the ridge where he stood, and lost it behind a hill, and picked it up again on the other side. On that distant stretch he saw a cart slowly pulled by a bay horse. It disappeared behind the hill. Jody sat down on the ground and watched the place where the cart would reappear again. The wind sang on the hilltops and the puff-ball cloud hurried eastward.

Then the cart came into sight and stopped. A man dressed in black dismounted from the seat and walked to the horse's head. Although it was so far away, Jody knew he had unhooked the check-rein, for the horse's head dropped forward. The horse moved on, and the man walked slowly up the hill beside it. Jody gave a glad cry and ran down the road toward them. The squirrels bumped along off the road, and a roadrunner flirted its tail and raced over the edge of the hill and sailed out like a glider.

Jody tried to leap into the middle of his shadow at every step. A stone rolled under his foot and he went down. Around a little bend he raced, and there, a short distance ahead, were his grandfather and the cart. The boy dropped from his unseemly running and approached at a dignified walk.

The horse plodded stumble-footedly up the hill and the old man walked beside it. In the lowering sun their giant shadows flickered darkly behind them. The grandfather was dressed in a black broadcloth suit and he wore kid congress gaiters and a black tie on a short, hard collar. He carried his black slouch hat in his hand. His white beard was cropped close and his white eyebrows overhung his eyes like moustaches. The blue eyes were sternly merry. About the whole face and figure there was a granite dignity, so that every motion seemed an impossible thing. Once at rest, it seemed the old man would be stone, would never move again. His steps were slow and certain. Once made, no step could ever be retraced; once headed in a direction, the path would never bend nor the pace increase nor slow.

When Jody appeared around the bend, Grandfather waved his hat slowly in welcome, and he called, "Why, Jody! Come down to meet me, have you?"

Jody sidled near and turned and matched his step to the old man's step and stiffened his body and dragged his heels a little. "Yes, sir," he said. "We got your letter only today."

"Should have been here yesterday," said Grandfather. "It certainly should. How are all the folks?"

"They're fine, sir." He hesitated and then suggested shyly, "Would you like to come on a mouse hunt tomorrow, sir?"

"Mouse hunt, Jody?" Grandfather chuckled. "Have the people of this generation come down to hunting mice? They aren't very strong, the new people, but I hardly thought mice would be game for them."

"No, sir. It's just play. The haystack's gone. I'm going to drive out the mice to the dogs. And you can watch, or even beat the hay a little."

The stern, merry eyes turned down on him. "I see. You don't eat them, then. You haven't come to that yet."

Jody explained, "The dogs eat them, sir. It wouldn't be much like hunting Indians, I guess."

"No, not much—but then later, when the troops were hunting Indians and shooting children and burning teepees, it wasn't much different from your mouse hunt."

They topped the rise and started down into the ranch-cup, and they lost the sun from their shoulders. "You've grown," Grandfather said. "Nearly an inch, I should say."

"More," Jody boasted. "Where they mark me on the door, I'm up more than an inch since Thanksgiving even."

Grandfather's rich throaty voice said, "Maybe you're getting too much water and turning to pith and stalk. Wait until you head out, and then we'll see."

Jody looked quickly into the old man's face to see whether his feelings should be hurt, but there was no will to injure, no punishing nor putting-in-your-place light in the keen blue eyes. "We might kill a pig," Jody suggested.

"Oh, no! I couldn't let you do that. You're just humoring me. It isn't the time and you know it."

"You know Riley, the big boar, sir?"

"Yes. I remember Riley well."

"Well, Riley ate a hole into that same haystack, and it fell down on him and smothered him."

"Pigs do that when they can," said Grandfather.

"Riley was a nice pig, for a boar, sir. I rode him sometimes, and he didn't mind."

A door slammed at the house below them, and they saw Jody's mother standing on the porch waving her apron in welcome. And they saw Carl Tiflin walking up from the barn to be at the house for the arrival.

The sun had disappeared from the hills by now. The blue smoke from the house chimney hung in flat layers in the purpling ranch-cup. The puff-ball clouds, dropped by the falling wind, hung listlessly in the sky.

Billy Buck came out of the bunkhouse and flung a wash basin of soapy water on the ground. He had been shaving in mid-week, for Billy held Grandfather in reverence, and Grandfather said that Billy was one of the few men of the new generation who had not gone soft. Although Billy was in middle age, Grandfather considered him a boy. Now Billy was hurrying toward the house too.

When Jody and Grandfather arrived, the three were waiting for them in front of the yard gate.

Carl said, "Hello, sir. We've been looking for you."

Mrs. Tiflin kissed Grandfather on the side of his beard, and stood still while his big hand patted her shoulder. Billy shook hands solemnly, grinning under his straw moustache. "I'll put up your horse," said Billy, and he led the rig away.

Grandfather watched him go, and then, turning back to the group, he said as he had said a hundred times before, "There's a good boy. I knew his father, old Mule-tail Buck. I never knew why they called him Mule-tail except he packed mules."

Mrs. Tiflin turned and led the way into the house. "How long are you going to stay, Father? Your letter didn't say."

"Well, I don't know. I thought I'd stay about two weeks. But I never stay as long as I think I'm going to."

In a short while they were sitting at the white oilcloth table eating their supper. The lamp with the tin reflector hung over the table. Outside the dining-room windows the big moths battered softly against the glass.

Grandfather cut his steak into tiny pieces and chewed slowly. "I'm hungry," he said. "Driving out here got my appetite up. It's like when we were crossing. We all got so hungry every night we could hardly wait to let the meat get done. I could eat about five pounds of buffalo meat every night."

"It's moving around does it," said Billy. "My father was a government packer. I helped him when I was a kid. Just the two of us could about clean up a deer's ham."

"I knew your father, Billy," said Grandfather. "A fine man he was. They called him Mule-tail Buck. I don't know why except he packed mules."

"That was it," Billy agreed. "He packed mules."

Grandfather put down his knife and fork and looked around the table. "I remember one time we ran out of meat—"

His voice dropped to a curious low sing-song, dropped into a tonal groove the story had worn for itself. "There was no buffalo, no antelope, not even rabbits. The hunters couldn't even shoot a coyote. That was the time for the leader to be on the watch. I was the leader, and I kept my eyes open. Know why? Well, just the minute the people began to get hungry they'd start slaughtering the team oxen. Do you believe that? I've heard of parties that just ate up their draft cattle. Started from the middle and worked toward the ends. Finally they'd eat the lead pair, and then the wheelers. The leader of a party had to keep them from doing that."

In some manner a big moth got into the room and circled the hanging kerosene lamp. Billy got up and tried to clap it between his hands. Carl struck with a cupped palm and caught the moth and broke it. He walked to the window and dropped it out.

"As I was saying," Grandfather began again, but Carl interrupted him. "You'd better eat some more meat. All the rest of us are ready for our pudding."

Jody saw a flash of anger in his mother's eyes. Grandfather picked up his knife and fork. "I'm pretty hungry, all right," he said. "I'll tell you about that later."

When supper was over, when the family and Billy Buck sat in front of the fireplace in the other room, Jody anxiously watched Grandfather. He saw the signs he knew. The bearded head leaned forward; the eyes lost their sternness and looked wonderingly into the fire; the big lean fingers laced themselves on the black knees. "I wonder," he began, "I just wonder whether I ever told you how those thieving Piutes drove off thirty-five of our horses."

"I think you did," Carl interrupted. "Wasn't it just before you went up into the Tahoe country?"

Grandfather turned quickly toward his son-in-law. "That's right. I guess I must have told you that story."

"Lots of times," Carl said cruelly, and he avoided his wife's eyes. But he felt the angry eyes on him, and he said, " 'Course I'd like to hear it again."

Grandfather looked back at the fire. His fingers unlaced and laced again. Jody knew how he felt, how his insides were collapsed and empty. Hadn't Jody been called a Big-Britches that very afternoon? He rose to heroism and opened himself to the term Big-Britches again. "Tell about Indians," he said softly.

Grandfather's eyes grew stern again. "Boys always want to hear about Indians. It was a job for men, but boys want to hear about it. Well, let's see. Did I ever tell you how I wanted each wagon to carry a long iron plate?"

Everyone but Jody remained silent. Jody said, "No. You didn't."

"Well, when the Indians attacked, we always put the wagons in a circle and fought from between the wheels. I thought that if every wagon carried a long plate with rifle holes, the men could stand the plates on the outside of the wheels when the wagons were in the circle and they would be protected. It would save lives and that would make up for the extra weight of the iron. But of course the party wouldn't do it. No party had done it before and they couldn't see why they should go to the expense. They lived to regret it, too."

Jody looked at his mother, and knew from her expression that she was not listening at all. Carl picked at a callus on his thumb and Billy Buck watched a spider crawling up the wall.

Grandfather's tone dropped into its narrative groove again. Jody knew in advance exactly what words would fall. The story droned on, speeded up for the attack, grew sad over the wounds, struck a dirge at the burials on the great plains. Jody sat quietly watching Grandfather. The stern blue eyes were detached. He looked as though he were not very interested in the story himself.

When it was finished, when the pause had been politely respected as the frontier of the story, Billy Buck stood up and stretched and hitched his trousers. "I guess I'll turn in," he said. Then he faced Grandfather. "I've got an old powder horn and a cap and ball pistol down to the bunkhouse. Did I ever show them to you?"

Grandfather nodded slowly. "Yes, I think you did, Billy. Reminds me of a pistol I had when I was leading the people across." Billy stood politely until the little story was done, and then he said, "Good night," and went out of the house.

Carl Tiflin tried to turn the conversation then. "How's the country between here and Monterey? I've heard it's pretty dry."

"It is dry," said Grandfather. "There's not a drop of water in the Laguna Seca. But it's a long pull from '87. The whole country was powder then, and in '61 I believe all the coyotes starved to death. We had fifteen inches of rain this year."

"Yes, but it all came too early. We could do with some now." Carl's eye fell on Jody. "Hadn't you better be getting to bed?"

Jody stood up obediently. "Can I kill the mice in the old haystack, sir?"

"Mice? Oh! Sure, kill them all off. Billy said there isn't any good hay left."

Jody exchanged a secret and satisfying look with Grandfather. "I'll kill every one tomorrow," he promised.

Jody lay in his bed and thought of the impossible world of Indians and buffaloes, a world that had ceased to be forever. He wished he could have been living in the heroic time, but he knew he was not of heroic timber. No one living now, save possibly Billy Buck, was worthy to do the things that had been done. A race of giants had lived then, fearless men, men of a staunchness unknown in this day. Jody thought of the wide plains and of the wagons moving across like centipedes. He thought of Grandfather on a huge white horse, marshaling the people. Across his mind marched the great phantoms, and they marched off the earth and they were gone.

He came back to the ranch for a moment, then. He heard the dull rushing sound that space and silence make. He heard one of the dogs, out in the doghouse, scratching a flea and bumping his elbow against the floor with every stroke. Then the wind arose again and the black cypress groaned and Jody went to sleep.

He was up half an hour before the triangle sounded for breakfast. His mother was rattling the stove to make the flames roar when Jody went through the kitchen. "You're up early," she said. "Where are you going?"

"Out to get a good stick. We're going to kill the mice today."

"Who is 'we'?"

"Why, Grandfather and I."

"So you've got him in it. You always like to have someone in with you in case there's blame to share."

"I'll be right back," said Jody. "I just want to have a good stick ready for after breakfast."

He closed the screen door after him and went out into the cool blue morning. The birds were noisy in the dawn and the ranch cats came down from the hill like blunt snakes. They had been hunting gophers in the dark, and although the four cats were full of gopher meat, they sat in a semi-circle at the back door and mewed piteously for milk. Doubletree Mutt and Smasher moved sniffing along the edge of the brush, performing the duty with rigid ceremony, but when Jody whistled, their heads jerked up and their tails waved. They plunged down to him, wriggling their skins and yawning. Jody patted their heads seriously, and moved on to the weathered scrap pile. He selected an old broom handle and a short piece of inch-square scrap wood. From his pocket he took a shoelace and tied the ends of the sticks loosely together to make a flail. He whistled his new weapon through the air and struck the ground experimentally, while the dogs leaped aside and whined with apprehension.

Jody turned and started down past the house toward the old haystack ground to look over the field of slaughter, but Billy Buck, sitting patiently on the back steps, called to him, "You better come back. It's only a couple of minutes till breakfast."

Jody changed his course and moved toward the house. He leaned his flail against the steps. "That's to drive the mice out," he said. "I'll bet they're fat. I'll bet they don't know what's going to happen to them today."

"No, nor you either," Billy remarked philosophically, "nor me, nor anyone."

Jody was staggered by this thought. He knew it was true. His imagination twitched away from the mouse hunt. Then his mother came out on the back porch and struck the triangle, and all thoughts fell in a heap.

Grandfather hadn't appeared at the table when they sat down. Billy nodded at his empty chair. "He's all right? He isn't sick?"

"He takes a long time to dress," said Mrs. Tiflin. "He combs his whiskers and rubs up his shoes and brushes his clothes."

Carl scattered sugar on his mush. "A man that's led a wagon trail across the plains has got to be pretty careful how he dresses."

Mrs. Tiflin turned on him. "Don't do that, Carl! Please don't!" There was more of threat than of request in her tone. And the threat irritated Carl.

"Well, how many times do I have to listen to the story of the iron plates, and the thirty-five horses? That time's done. Why can't he forget it, now it's done?" He grew angrier while he talked, and his voice rose. "Why does he have to tell them over and over? He came across the plains. All right! Now it's finished. Nobody wants to hear about it over and over."

The door into the kitchen closed softly. The four at the table sat frozen. Carl laid his mush spoon on the table and touched his chin with his fingers.

Then the kitchen door opened and Grandfather walked in. His mouth smiled tightly and his eyes were squinted. "Good morning," he said, and he sat down and looked at his mush dish.

Carl could not leave it there. "Did—did you hear what I said?"

Grandfather jerked a little nod.

"I don't know what got into me, sir. I didn't mean it. I was just being funny."

Jody glanced in shame at his mother, and he saw that she was looking at Carl, and that she wasn't breathing. It was an awful thing that he was doing. He was tearing himself to pieces to talk like that. It was a terrible thing to him to retract a word, but to retract it in shame was infinitely worse.

Grandfather looked sidewise. "I'm trying to get right side up," he said gently. "I'm not being mad. I don't mind what you said, but it might be true, and I would mind that."

"It isn't true," said Carl. "I'm not feeling well this morning. I'm sorry I said it."

"Don't be sorry, Carl. An old man doesn't see things sometimes. Maybe you're right. The crossing is finished. Maybe it should be forgotten, now it's done."

Carl got up from the table. "I've had enough to eat. I'm going to work. Take your time, Billy!" He walked quickly out of the dining-room. Billy gulped the rest of his food and followed soon after. But Jody could not leave his chair.

"Won't you tell any more stories?" Jody asked.

"Why, sure I'll tell them, but only when—I'm sure people want to hear them."

"I like to hear them, sir."

"Oh! Of course you do, but you're a little boy. It was a job for men, but only little boys like to hear about it."

Jody got up from his place. "I'll wait outside for you, sir. I've got a good stick for those mice."

He waited by the gate until the old man came out on the porch. "Let's go down and kill the mice now," Jody called.

"I think I'll just sit in the sun, Jody. You go kill the mice."

"You can use my stick if you like."

"No, I'll just sit here a while."

Jody turned disconsolately away, and walked down toward the old haystack. He tried to whip up his enthusiasm with thoughts of the fat juicy mice. He beat the ground with his flail. The dogs coaxed and whined about him, but he could not go. Back at the house he could see Grandfather sitting on the porch, looking small and thin and black. Jody gave up and went to sit on the steps at the old man's feet.

"Back already? Did you kill the mice?"

"No, sir. I'll kill them some other day."

The morning flies buzzed close to the ground and the ants dashed about in front of the steps. The heavy smell of sage slipped down the hill. The porch boards grew warm in the sunshine.

Jody hardly knew when Grandfather started to talk. "I shouldn't stay here, feeling the way I do." He examined his strong old hands. "I feel as though the crossing wasn't worth doing." His eyes moved up the side-hill and stopped on a motionless hawk perched on a dead limb. "I tell those old stories, but they're not what I want to tell. I only know how I want people to feel when I tell them.

"It wasn't Indians that were important, nor adventures, nor even getting out here. It was a whole bunch of people made into one big crawling beast. And I was the head. It was westering and westering. Every man wanted something for himself, but the big beast that was all of them wanted only westering. I was the leader, but if I hadn't been there, someone else would have been the head. The thing had to have a head.

"Under the little bushes the shadows were black at white noonday. When we saw the mountains at last, we cried—all of us. But it wasn't getting here that mattered, it was movement and westering.

"We carried life out here and set it down the way those ants carry eggs. And I was the leader. The westering was as big as God, and the slow steps that made the movement piled up and piled up until the continent was crossed.

"Then we came down to the sea, and it was done." He stopped and wiped his eyes until the rims were red. "That's what I should be telling instead of stories."

When Jody spoke, Grandfather started and looked down at him. "Maybe I could lead the people some day," Jody said.

The old man smiled. "There's no place to go. There's the

ocean to stop you. There's a line of old men along the shore hating the ocean because it stopped them."

"In boats I might, sir."

"No place to go, Jody. Every place is taken. But that's not the worst—no, not the worst. Westering has died out of the people. Westering isn't a hunger any more. It's all done. Your father is right. It is finished." He laced his fingers on his knee and looked at them.

Jody felt very sad. "If you'd like a glass of lemonade I could make it for you."

Grandfather was about to refuse, and then he saw Jody's face. "That would be nice," he said. "Yes, it would be nice to drink a lemonade."

Jody ran into the kitchen where his mother was wiping the last of the breakfast dishes. "Can I have a lemon to make a lemonade for Grandfather?"

His mother mimicked— "And another lemon to make a lemonade for you."

"No, ma'am. I don't want one."

"Jody! You're sick!" Then she stopped suddenly. "Take a lemon out of the cooler," she said softly. "Here, I'll reach the squeezer down to you."

Champion

MIDGE KELLY scored his first knockout when he was seventeen. The knockee was his brother Connie, three years his junior and a cripple. The purse was a half dollar given to the younger Kelly by a lady whose electric had just missed bumping his soul from his frail little body.

Connie did not know Midge was in the house, else he never would have risked laying the prize on the arm of the least comfortable chair in the room, the better to observe its shining beauty. As Midge entered from the kitchen, the crippled boy covered the coin with his hand, but the movement lacked the speed requisite to escape his brother's quick eye.

"Watcha got there?" demanded Midge.

"Nothin'," said Connie.

"You're a one legged liar!" said Midge.

He strode over to his brother's chair and grasped the hand that concealed the coin.

"Let loose!" he ordered.

Connie began to cry.

"Let loose and shut up your noise," said the elder, and jerked his brother's hand from the chair arm.

The coin fell onto the bare floor. Midge pounced on it. His weak mouth widened in a triumphant smile.

"Nothin', huh?" he said. "All right, if it's nothin' you don't want it."

"Give that back," sobbed the younger.

"I'll give you a red nose, you little sneak! Where'd you steal it?"

"I didn't steal it. It's mine. A lady give it to me after she pretty near hit me with a car."

"It's a crime she missed you," said Midge.

Midge started for the front door. The cripple picked up his crutch, rose from his chair with difficulty, and, still sobbing, came toward Midge. The latter heard him and stopped.

"You better stay where you're at," he said.

"I want my money," cried the boy.

"I know what you want," said Midge.

Doubling up the fist that held the half dollar, he landed with all his strength on his brother's mouth. Connie fell to the floor with a thud, the crutch tumbling on top of him. Midge stood beside the prostrate form.

"Is that enough?" he said. "Or do you want this, too?"

And he kicked him in the crippled leg.

"I guess that'll hold you," he said.

There was no response from the boy on the floor. Midge looked at him a moment, then at the coin in his hand, and then went out into the street, whistling.

An hour later, when Mrs. Kelly came home from her day's work at Faulkner's Steam Laundry, she found Connie on the floor, moaning. Dropping on her knees beside him, she called him by name a score of times. Then she got up and, pale as a ghost, dashed from the house. Dr. Ryan left the Kelly abode about dusk and walked toward Halsted Street. Mrs. Dorgan spied him as he passed her gate.

"Who's sick, Doctor?" she called.

"Poor little Connie," he replied. "He had a bad fall."

"How did it happen?"

"I can't say for sure, Margaret, but I'd almost bet he was knocked down."

"Knocked down!" exclaimed Mrs. Dorgan.

"Why, who—?"

"Have you seen the other one lately?"

"Michael? No, not since mornin'. You can't be thinkin'——"

"I wouldn't put it past him, Margaret," said the doctor gravely. "The lad's mouth is swollen and cut, and his poor, skinny little leg is bruised. He surely didn't do it to himself and I think Ellen suspects the other one."

"Lord save us!" said Mrs. Dorgan. "I'll run over and see if I can help."

"That's a good woman," said Dr. Ryan, and went on down the street.

Near midnight, when Midge came home, his mother was sitting at Connie's bedside. She did not look up.

"Well," said Midge, "what's the matter?"

She remained silent. Midge repeated his question.

"Michael, you know what's the matter," she said at length.

"I don't know nothin'," said Midge.

"Don't lie to me, Michael. What did you do to your brother?"

"Nothin'."

"You hit him."

"Well, then, I hit him. What of it? It ain't the first time."

Her lips pressed tightly together, her face like chalk, Ellen Kelly rose from her chair and made straight for him. Midge backed against the door.

"Lay off'n me, Ma. I don't want to fight no woman."

Still she came on breathing heavily.

"Stop where you're at, Ma," he warned.

There was a brief struggle and Midge's mother lay on the floor before him.

"You ain't hurt, Ma. You're lucky I didn't land good. And I told you to lay off'n me."

"God forgive you, Michael!"

Midge found Hap Collins in the showdown game at the Royal.

"Come on out a minute," he said.

Hap followed him out on the walk.

"I'm leavin' town for a w'ile," said Midge.

"What for?"

"Well, we had a little run-in up to the house. The kid stole a half buck off'n me, and when I went after it he cracked me with his crutch. So I nailed him. And the old lady came at me with a chair and I took it off'n her and she fell down."

"How is Connie hurt?"

"Not bad."

"What are you runnin' away for?"

"Who the hell said I was runnin' away? I'm sick and tired o' gettin' picked on; that's all. So I'm leavin' for a w'ile and I want a piece o' money."

"I ain't only got six bits," said Happy.

"You're in bad shape, ain't you? Well, come through with it."

Happy came through.

"You oughtn't to hit the kid," he said.

"I ain't astin' you who can I hit," snarled Midge. "You try to put somethin' over on me and you'll get the same dose. I'm goin' now."

"Go as far as you like," said Happy, but not until he was sure that Kelly was out of hearing.

Early the following morning, Midge boarded a train for Milwaukee. He had no ticket, but no one knew the difference. The conductor remained in the caboose.

On a night six months later, Midge hurried out of the "stage door" of the Star Boxing Club and made for Duane's saloon, two blocks away. In his pocket were twelve dollars, his reward for having battered up one Demon Dempsey through the six rounds of the first preliminary.

It was Midge's first professional engagement in the manly art. Also it was the first time in weeks that he had earned twelve dollars.

On the way to Duane's he had to pass Niemann's. He pulled his cap over his eyes and increased his pace until he had gone by. Inside Niemann's stood a trusting bartender, who for ten days had staked Midge to drinks and allowed him to ravage the lunch on a promise to come in and settle the moment he was paid for the "prelim."

Midge strode into Duane's and aroused the napping bartender by slapping a silver dollar on the festive board.

"Gimme a shot," said Midge.

The shooting continued until the wind-up at the Star

was over and part of the fight crowd joined Midge in front of Duane's bar. A youth in the early twenties, standing next to young Kelly, finally summoned sufficient courage to address him.

"Wasn't you in the first bout?" he ventured.

"Yeh," Midge replied.

"My name's Hersch," said the other.

Midge received the startling information in silence.

"I don't want to butt in," continued Mr. Hersch, "but I'd like to buy you a drink."

"All right," said Midge, "but don't overstrain yourself."

Mr. Hersch laughed uproariously and beckoned to the bartender.

"You certainly gave that wop a trimmin' tonight," said the buyer of the drink, when they had been served. "I thought you'd kill him."

"I would if I hadn't let up," Midge replied. "I'll kill 'em all."

"You got the wallop all right," the other said admiringly.

"Have I got the wallop?" said Midge. "Say, I can kick like a mule. Did you notice them muscles in my shoulders?"

"Notice 'em? I couldn't help from noticin' 'em," said Hersch. "I says to the fella settin' alongside o' me, I says: 'Look at them shoulders! No wonder he can hit,' I says to him."

"Just let me land and it's good-by, baby," said Midge. "I'll kill 'em all."

The oral manslaughter continued until Duane's closed for the night. At parting, Midge and his new friend shook hands and arranged for a meeting the following evening.

For nearly a week the two were together almost constantly. It was Hersch's pleasant rôle to listen to Midge's modest revelations concerning himself, and to buy every time Midge's glass was empty. But there came an evening when Hersch regretfully announced that he must go home to supper.

"I got a date for eight bells," he confided. "I could stick

till then, only I must clean up and put on the Sunday clo'es, 'cause she's the prettiest little thing in Milwaukee."

"Can't you fix it for two?" asked Midge.

"I don't know who to get," Hersch replied. "Wait, though. I got a sister and if she ain't busy, it'll be O.K. She's no bum for looks herself."

So it came about that Midge and Emma Hersch and Emma's brother and the prettiest little thing in Milwaukee foregathered at Wall's and danced half the night away. And Midge and Emma danced every dance together, for though every little onestep seemed to induce a new thirst of its own, Lou Hersch stayed too sober to dance with his own sister.

The next day, penniless at last in spite of his phenomenal ability to make someone else settle, Midge Kelly sought out Doc Hammon, matchmaker for the Star, and asked to be booked for the next show.

"I could put you on with Tracy for the next bout," said Doc.

"What's they in it?" asked Midge.

"Twenty if you cop," Doc told him.

"Have a heart," protested Midge. "Didn't I look good the other night?"

"You looked all right. But you aren't Freddie Welsh yet by a consid'able margin."

"I ain't scared of Freddie Welsh or none of 'em," said Midge.

"Well, we don't pay our boxers by the size of their chests," Doc said. "I'm offerin' you this Tracy bout. Take it or leave it."

"All right; I'm on," said Midge, and he passed a pleasant afternoon at Duane's on the strength of his booking.

Young Tracy's manager came to Midge the night before the show.

"How do you feel about this go?" he asked.

"Me?" said Midge, "I feel all right. What do you mean, how do I feel?"

"I mean," said Tracy's manager, "that we're mighty anxious to win, 'cause the boy's got a chanct in Philly if he cops this one."

"What's your proposition?" asked Midge.

"Fifty bucks," said Tracy's manager.

"What do you think I am, a crook? Me lay down for fifty bucks. Not me!"

"Seventy-five, then," said Tracy's manager.

The market closed on eighty and the details were agreed on in short order. And the next night Midge was stopped in the second round by a terrific slap on the forearm.

This time Midge passed up both Niemann's and Duane's, having a sizable account at each place, and sought his refreshment at Stein's farther down the street.

When the profits of his deal with Tracy were gone, he learned, by first-hand information from Doc Hammond and the matchmakers at the other "clubs," that he was no longer desired for even the cheapest of preliminaries. There was no danger of his starving or dying of thirst while Emma and Lou Hersch lived. But he made up his mind, four months after his defeat by Young Tracy, that Milwaukee was not the ideal place for him to live.

"I can lick the best of 'em," he reasoned, "but there ain't no more chanct for me here. I can maybe go east and get on somewheres. And besides——"

But just after Midge had purchased a ticket to Chicago with the money he had "borrowed" from Emma Hersch "to buy shoes," a heavy hand was laid on his shoulders and he turned to face two strangers.

"Where are you goin', Kelly?" inquired the owner of the heavy hand.

"Nowheres," said Midge. "What the hell do you care?"

The other stranger spoke:

"Kelly, I'm employed by Emma Hersch's mother to see that you do right by her. And we want you to stay here till you've done it."

"You won't get nothin' but the worst of it, monkeying with me," said Midge.

Nevertheless, he did not depart for Chicago that night. Two days later, Emma Hersch became Mrs. Kelly, and the gift of the groom, when once they were alone, was a crushing blow on the bride's pale cheek.

Next morning, Midge left Milwaukee as he had entered it—by fast freight.

"They's no use kiddin' ourself any more," said Tommy Haley. "He might get down to thirty-seven in a pinch, but if he done below that a mouse could stop him. He's a welter; that's what he is and he knows it as well as I do. He's growed like a weed in the last six mont's. I told him, I says, 'If you don't quit growin' they won't be nobody for you to box, only Willard and them.' He says, 'Well, I wouldn't run away from Willard if I weighed twenty pounds more.'"

"He must hate himself," said Tommy's brother.

"I never seen a good one that didn't," said Tommy. "And Midge is a good one; don't make no mistake about that. I wisht we could of got Welsh before the kid growed so big. But it's too late now. I won't make no holler, though, if we can match him up with the Dutchman."

"Who do you mean?"

"Young Goetz, the welter champ. We mightn't not get so much dough for the bout itself, but it'd roll in afterward. What a drawin' card we'd be, 'cause the people pays their money to see the fella with the wallop, and that's Midge. And we'd keep the title just as long as Midge could make the weight."

"Can't you land no match with Goetz?"

"Sure, 'cause he needs the money. But I've went careful with the kid so far and look at the results I got! So what's the use of takin' a chanct? The kid's comin' every minute and Goetz is goin' back faster'n big Johnson did. I think we could lick him now; I'd bet my life on it. But six mont's from now they won't be no risk. He'll of licked hisself before that time. Then all as we'll have to do is sign up with him and wait for the referee to stop it. But Midge is so crazy to get at him now that I can't hardly hold him back."

The brothers Haley were lunching in a Boston hotel. Dan had come down from Holyoke to visit with Tommy and to watch the latter's protégé go twelve rounds, or less, with Bud Cross. The bout promised little in the way of a contest, for Midge had twice stopped the Baltimore youth and Bud's reputation for gameness was all that had earned him the date. The fans were willing to pay the price to see Midge's hay-making left, but they wanted to see it used on an opponent who would not jump out of the ring the first time he felt its crushing force. Bud Cross was such an opponent, and his willingness to stop boxing-gloves with his eyes, ears, nose and throat had long enabled him to escape the horrors of honest labor. A game boy was Bud, and he showed it in his battered, swollen, discolored face.

"I should think," said Dan Haley, "that the kid'd do whatever you tell him after all you done for him."

"Well," said Tommy, "he's took my dope pretty straight so far, but he's so sure of hisself that he can't see no reason for waitin'. He'll do what I say, though; he'd be a sucker not to."

"You got a contrac' with him?"

"No, I don't need no contrac'. He knows it was me that drug him out o' the gutter and he ain't goin' to turn me down now, when he's got the dough and bound to get more. Where'd he of been at if I hadn't listened to him when he first come to me? That's pretty near two years ago now, but it seems like last week. I was settin' in the s'loon acrost from the Pleasant Club in Philly, waitin' for McCann to count the dough and come over, when this little bum blowed in and tried to stand the house off for a drink. They told him nothin' doin' and to beat it out o' there, and then he seen me and come over to where I was settin' and ast me wasn't I a boxin' man and I told him who I was. Then he ast me for money to buy a shot and I told him to set down and I'd buy it for him. "Then we got talkin' things over and he told me his name and told me about fightin' a couple o' prelims out to Milwaukee. So I says, 'Well, boy, I don't know how good or how rotten you are, but you won't never get nowheres trainin' on that stuff.' So he says he'd cut it out if he could get on in a bout and I says I would give him a chanct if he played square with me and didn't touch no more to drink. So we shook hands and I took him up to the hotel with me and give him a bath and the next day I bought him some clo'es. And I staked him to eats and sleeps for over six weeks. He had a hard time breakin' away from the polish, but finally I thought he was fit and I give him his chanct. He went on with Smiley Sayer and stopped him so quick that Smiley thought sure he was poisoned.

"Well, you know what he's did since. The only beatin' in his record was by Tracy in Milwaukee before I got hold of him, and he's licked Tracy three times in the last year.

"I've gave him all the best of it in a money way and he's got seven thousand bucks in cold storage. How's that for a kid that was in the gutter two years ago? And he'd have still more yet if he wasn't so nuts over clo'es and got to stop at the good hotels and so forth."

"Where's his home at?"

"Well, he ain't really got no home. He came from Chicago and his mother canned him out o' the house for bein' no good. She give him a raw deal, I guess, and he says he won't have nothin' to do with her unlest she comes to him first. She's got a pile o' money, he says, so he ain't worryin' about her."

The gentleman under discussion entered the café and swaggered to Tommy's table, while the whole room turned to look.

Midge was the picture of health despite a slightly colored eye and an ear that seemed to have no opening. But perhaps it was not his healthiness that drew all eyes. His diamond horse-shoe tie pin, his purple cross-striped shirt, his orange shoes and his light blue suit fairly screamed for attention.

"Where you been?" he asked Tommy. "I been lookin' all over for you."

"Set down," said his manager.

"No time," said Midge. "I'm goin' down to the w'arf and see 'em unload the fish."

"Shake hands with my brother Dan," said Tommy.

Midge shook with the Holyoke Haley.

"If you're Tommy's brother, you're O. K. with me," said Midge, and the brothers beamed with pleasure.

Dan moistened his lips and murmured an embarrassed reply, but it was lost on the young gladiator.

"Leave me take twenty," Midge was saying. "I prob'ly won't need it, but I don't like to be caught short."

Tommy parted with a twenty dollar bill and recorded the transaction in a small black book the insurance company had given him for Christmas.

"But," he said, "it won't cost you no twenty to look at them fish. Want me to go along?"

"No," said Midge hastily. "You and your brother here prob'ly got a lot to say to each other."

"Well," said Tommy, "don't take no bad money and don't get lost. And you better be back at four o'clock and lay down a w'ile."

"I don't need no rest to beat this guy," said Midge. "He'll do enough layin' down for the both of us."

And laughing even more than the jest called for, he strode out through the fire of admiring and startled glances.

The corner of Boylston and Tremont was the nearest Midge got to the wharf, but the lady awaiting him was doubtless a more dazzling sight than the catch of the luckiest Massachusetts fisherman. She could talk, too—probably better than the fish.

"O you Kid!" she said, flashing a few silver teeth among the gold. "O you fighting man!"

Midge smiled up at her.

"We'll go somewheres and get a drink," he said. "One won't hurt."

In New Orleans, five months after he had rearranged the

map of Bud Cross for the third time, Midge finished training for his championship bout with the Dutchman.

Back in his hotel after the final workout, Midge stopped to chat with some of the boys from up north, who had made the long trip to see a champion dethroned, for the result of this bout was so nearly a foregone conclusion that even the experts had guessed it.

Tommy Haley secured the key and the mail and ascended to the Kelly suite. He was bathing when Midge came in, half an hour later.

"Any mail?" asked Midge.

"There on the bed," replied Tommy from the tub.

Midge picked up the stack of letters and postcards and glanced them over. From the pile he sorted out three letters and laid them on the table. The rest he tossed into the wastebasket. Then he picked up the three and sat for a few moments holding them, while his eyes gazed off into space. At length he looked again at the three unopened letters in his hand; then he put one in his pocket and tossed the other two at the basket. They missed their target and fell on the floor.

"Hell!" said Midge, and stooping over picked them up.

He opened one postmarked Milwaukee and read:

Dear Husband:

I have wrote to you so manny times and got no anser and I dont know if you ever got them, so I am writeing again in the hopes you will get this letter and anser. I dont like to bother you with my trubles and I would not only for the baby and I am not asking you should write to me but only send a little money and I am not asking for myself but the baby has not been well a day sence last Aug. and the dr. told me she cant live much longer unless I give her better food and thats impossible the way things are. Lou has not been working for a year and what I make dont hardley pay for the rent. I am not asking for you to give me any money, but only you should send what I loaned when convenient and I think it amts. to about $36.00. Please try and send that amt. and it will help me, but if you cant send the whole amt. try and send me something.

Your wife,
Emma.

Midge tore the letter into a hundred pieces and scattered them over the floor.

"Money, money, money!" he said. "They must think I'm made o' money. I s'pose the old woman's after it too."

He opened his mother's letter:

dear Michael Connie wonted me to rite and say you must beet the dutchman and he is sure you will and wonted me to say we wont you to rite and tell us about it, but I gess you havent no time to rite or we herd from you long beffore this but I wish you wuld rite jest a line or 2 boy becaus it wuld be better for Connie than a barl of medisin. It wuld help me to keep things going if you send me money now and then when you can spair it but if you cant send no money try and fine time to rite a letter onley a few lines and it will please Connie. jest think boy he hasent got out of bed in over 3 yrs. Connie says good luck.

Your Mother,
Ellen F. Kelly.

"I thought so," said Midge. "They're all alike."

The third letter was from New York. It read:

Hon:—This is the last letter you will get from me before your champ, but I will send you a telegram Saturday, but I can't say as much in a telegram as in a letter and I am writeing this to let you know I am thinking of you and praying for good luck.

Lick him good hon and don't wait no longer than you have to and don't forget to wire me as soon as its over. Give him that little old left of yours on the nose hon and don't be afraid of spoiling his good looks because he couldn't be no homlier than he is. But don't let him spoil my baby's pretty face. You won't will you hon.

Well hon I would give anything to be there and see it, but I guess you love Haley better than me or you wouldn't let him keep me away. But when your champ hon we can do as we please and tell Haley to go to the devil.

Well hon I will send you a telegram Saturday and I almost forgot to tell you I will need some more money, a couple hundred say and you will have to wire it to me as soon as you get this. You will won't you hon.

I will send you a telegram Saturday and remember hon I am pulling for you.

Well good-by sweetheart and good luck.

                                                            Grace.

"They're all alike," said Midge. "Money, money, money."

Tommy Haley, shining from his ablutions, came in from the adjoining room.

"Thought you'd be layin' down," he said.

"I'm goin' to," said Midge, unbuttoning his orange shoes.

"I'll call you at six and you can eat up here without no bugs to pester you. I got to go down and give them birds their tickets."

"Did you hear from Goldberg?" asked Midge.

"Didn't I tell you? Sure; fifteen weeks at five hundred, if we win. And we can get a guarantee o' twelve thousand, with privileges either in New York or Milwaukee."

"Who with?"

"Anybody that'll stand up in front of you. You don't care who it is, do you?"

"Not me. I'll make 'em all look like a monkey."

"Well you better lay down aw'ile."

"Oh, say, wire two hundred to Grace for me, will you? Right away; the New York address."

"Two hundred! You just sent her three hundred last Sunday."

"Well, what the hell do you care?"

"All right, all right. Don't get sore about it. Anything else?"

"That's all," said Midge, and dropped onto the bed.

"And I want the deed done before I come back," said Grace as she rose from the table. "You won't fall down on me, will you, hon?"

"Leave it to me," said Midge. "And don't spend no more than you have to."

Grace smiled a farewell and left the café. Midge continued to sip his coffee and read his paper.

They were in Chicago and they were in the middle of Midge's first week in vaudeville. He had come straight north to reap the rewards of his glorious victory over the broken down Dutchman. A fortnight had been spent in learning his act, which consisted of a gymnastic exhibition and a ten minutes' monologue on the various excellences of Midge Kelly. And now he was twice daily turning 'em away from the Madison Theater.

His breakfast over and his paper read, Midge sauntered into the lobby and asked for his key. He then beckoned to a bell-boy, who had been hoping for that very honor.

"Find Haley, Tommy Haley," said Midge. "Tell him to come up to my room."

"Yes, sir, Mr. Kelly," said the boy, and proceeded to break all his former records for diligence.

Midge was looking out of his seventh-story window when Tommy answered the summons.

"What'll it be?" inquired his manager.

There was a pause before Midge replied.

"Haley," he said, "twenty-five per cent's a whole lot o' money."

"I guess I got it comin', ain't I?" said Tommy.

"I don't see how you figger it. I don't see where you're worth it to me."

"Well," said Tommy, "I didn't expect nothin' like this. I thought you was satisfied with the bargain. I don't want to beat nobody out o' nothin', but I don't see where you could have got anybody else that would of did all I done for you."

"Sure, that's all right," said the champion. "You done a lot for me in Philly. And you got good money for it, didn't you?"

"I ain't makin' no holler. Still and all, the big money's still ahead of us yet. And if it hadn't been for me, you wouldn't of never got within grabbin' distance."

"Oh, I guess I could of went along all right," said Midge. "Who was it that hung that left on the Dutchman's jaw, me or you?"

"Yes, but you wouldn't been in the ring with the Dutchman if it wasn't for how I handled you."

"Well, this won't get us nowheres. The idear is that you ain't worth no twenty-five per cent now and it don't make no diff'rence what come off a year or two ago."

"Don't it?" said Tommy. "I'd say it made a whole lot of difference."

"Well, I say it don't and I guess that settles it."

"Look here, Midge," Tommy said, "I thought I was fair with you, but if you don't think so, I'm willin' to hear what you think is fair. I don't want nobody callin' me a Sherlock. Let's go down to business and sign up a contrac'. What's your figger?"

"I ain't namin' no figger," Midge replied. "I'm sayin' that twenty-five's too much. Now what are you willin' to take?"

"How about twenty?"

"Twenty's too much," said Kelly.

"What ain't too much?" asked Tommy.

"Well, Haley, I might as well give it to you straight. They ain't nothin' that ain't too much."

"You mean you don't want me at no figger?"

"That's the idear."

There was a minute's silence. Then Tommy Haley walked toward the door.

"Midge," he said, in a choking voice, "you're makin' a big mistake, boy. You can't throw down your best friends and get away with it. That damn woman will ruin you."

Midge sprang from his seat.

"You shut your mouth!" he stormed. "Get out o' here before they have to carry you out. You been spongin' off o' me
long enough. Say one more word about the girl or about anything else and you'll get what the Dutchman got. Now get
out!"

And Tommy Haley, having a very vivid memory of the
Dutchman's face as he fell, got out.

Grace came in later, dropped her numerous bundles on the
lounge and perched herself on the arm of Midge's chair.

"Well?" she said.

"Well," said Midge, "I got rid of him."

"Good boy!" said Grace. "And now I think you might give
me that twenty-five per cent."

"Besides the seventy-five you're already gettin'?" said
Midge.

"Don't be no grouch, hon. You don't look pretty when
you're grouchy."

"It ain't my business to look pretty," Midge replied.

"Wait till you see how I look with the stuff I bought this
mornin'!"

Midge glanced at the bundles on the lounge.

"There's Haley's twenty-five per cent," he said, "and then
some."

The champion did not remain long without a manager.
Haley's successor was none other than Jerome Harris, who
saw in Midge a better meal ticket than his popular-priced
musical show had been.

The contract, giving Mr. Harris twenty-five per cent of
Midge's earnings, was signed in Detroit the week after Tommy Haley had heard his dismissal read. It had taken Midge
just six days to learn that a popular actor cannot get on without the ministrations of a man who thinks, talks and means
business. At first Grace objected to the new member of the
firm, but when Mr. Harris had demanded and secured from
the vaudeville people a one-hundred dollar increase in

Midge's weekly stipend, she was convinced that the champion had acted for the best.

"You and my missus will have some great old times," Harris told Grace. "I'd of wired her to join us here, only I seen the Kid's bookin' takes us to Milwaukee next week, and that's where she is."

But when they were introduced in the Milwaukee hotel, Grace admitted to herself that her feeling for Mrs. Harris could hardly be called love at first sight. Midge, on the contrary, gave his new manager's wife the many times over and seemed loath to end the feast of his eyes.

"Some doll," he said to Grace when they were alone.

"Doll is right," the lady replied, "and sawdust where her brains ought to be."

"I'm li'ble to steal that baby," said Midge, and he smiled as he noted the effect of his words on his audience's face.

On Tuesday of the Milwaukee week the champion successfully defended his title in a bout that the newspapers never reported. Midge was alone in his room that morning when a visitor entered without knocking. The visitor was Lou Hersch.

Midge turned white at sight of him.

"What do you want?" he demanded.

"I guess you know," said Lou Hersch. "Your wife's starvin' to death and your baby's starvin' to death and I'm starvin' to death. And you're dirty with money."

"Listen," said Midge, "if it wasn't for you, I wouldn't never saw your sister. And, if you ain't man enough to hold a job, what's that to me? The best thing you can do is keep away from me."

"You give me a piece o' money and I'll go."

Midge's reply to the ultimatum was a straight right to his brother-in-law's narrow chest.

"Take that home to your sister."

And after Lou Hersch had picked himself up and slunk away, Midge thought: "It's lucky I didn't give him my left or I'd of croaked him. And if I'd hit him in the stomach, I'd of broke his spine."

There was a party after each evening performance during the Milwaukee engagement. The wine flowed freely and Midge had more of it than Tommy Haley ever would have permitted him. Mr. Harris offered no objection, which was possibly just as well for his own physical comfort.

In the dancing between drinks, Midge had his new manager's wife for a partner as often as Grace. The latter's face as she floundered around in the arms of the portly Harris, belied her frequent protestations that she was having the time of her life.

Several times that week, Midge thought Grace was on the point of starting the quarrel he hoped to have. But it was not until Friday night that she accommodated. He and Mrs. Harris had disappeared after the matinee and when Grace saw him again at the close of the night show, she came to the point at once.

"What are you tryin' to pull off?" she demanded.

"It's none o' your business, is it?" said Midge.

"You bet it's my business; mine and Harris's. You cut it short or you'll find out."

"Listen," said Midge, "have you got a mortgage on me or somethin'? You talk like we was married."

"We're goin' to be, too. And to-morrow's as good a time as any."

"Just about," Midge said. "You got as much chanct o' marryin' me to-morrow as the next day or next year and that ain't no chanct at all."

"We'll find out," said Grace.

"You're the one that's got somethin' to find out."

"What do you mean?"

"I mean I'm married already."

"You lie!"

"You think so, do you? Well, s'pose you go to this here address and get acquainted with my missus."

Midge scrawled a number on a piece of paper and handed it to her. She stared at it unseeingly.

"Well," said Midge, "I ain't kiddin' you. You go there and

ask for Mrs. Michael Kelly, and if you don't find her, I'll marry you to-morrow before breakfast."

Still Grace stared at the scrap of paper. To Midge it seemed an age before she spoke again.

"You lied to me all this w'ile."

"You never ast me was I married. What's more, what the hell diff'rence did it make to you? You got a split, didn't you? Better'n fifty-fifty."

He started away.

"Where you goin'?"

"I'm goin' to meet Harris and his wife."

"I'm goin' with you. You're not goin' to shake me now."

"Yes, I am, too," said Midge quietly. "When I leave town to-morrow night, you're going to stay here. And if I see where you're goin' to make a fuss, I'll put you in a hospital where they'll keep you quiet. You can get your stuff to-morrow mornin' and I'll slip you a hundred bucks. And then I don't want to see no more o' you. And don't try and tag along now or I'll have to add another K. O. to the old record."

When Grace returned to the hotel that night, she discovered that Midge and the Harrises had moved to another. And when Midge left town the following night, he was again without a manager, and Mr. Harris was without a wife.

Three days prior to Midge Kelly's ten-round bout with Young Milton in New York City, the sporting editor of *The News* assigned Joe Morgan to write two or three thousand words about the champion to run with a picture layout for Sunday. Joe Morgan dropped in at Midge's training quarters Friday afternoon. Midge, he learned, was doing road work, but Midge's manager, Wallie Adams, stood ready and willing to supply reams of dope about the greatest fighter of the age.

"Let's hear what you've got," said Joe, "and then I'll try to fix up something."

So Wallie stepped on the accelerator of his imagination and shot away.

"Just a kid; that's all he is; a regular boy. Get what I mean?

Don't know the meanin' o' bad habits. Never tasted liquor in his life and would prob'bly get sick if he smelled it. Clean livin' put him up where he's at. Get what I mean? And modest and unassumin' as a school girl. He's so quiet you wouldn't never know he was around. And he'd go to jail before he'd talk about himself.

"No job at all to get him in shape, 'cause he's always that way. The only trouble we have with him is gettin' him to light into these poor bums they match him up with. He's scared he'll hurt somebody. Get what I mean? He's tickled to death over this match with Milton, 'cause everybody says Milton can stand the gaff. Midge'll maybe be able to cut loose a little this time. But the last two bouts he had, the guys hadn't no business in the ring with him, and he was holdin' back all the w'ile for the fear he'd kill somebody. Get what I mean?"

"Is he married?" inquired Joe.

"Say, you'd think he was married to hear him rave about them kiddies he's got. His fam'ly's up in Canada to their summer home and Midge is wild to get up there with 'em. He thinks more o' that wife and them kiddies than all the money in the world. Get what I mean?"

"How many children has he?"

"I don't know, four or five, I guess. All boys and every one of 'em a dead ringer for their dad."

"Is his father living?"

"No, the old man died when he was a kid. But he's got a grand old mother and a kid brother out in Chi. They're the first ones he thinks about after a match, them and his wife and kiddies. And he don't forget to send the old woman a thousand bucks after every bout. He's goin' to buy her a new home as soon as they pay him off for this match."

"How about his brother? Is he going to tackle the game?"

"Sure, and Midge says he'll be a champion before he's twenty years old. They're a fightin' fam'ly and all of 'em honest and straight as a die. Get what I mean? A fella that I can't tell you his name come to Midge in Milwaukee onct and wanted him to throw a fight and Midge gave him such a trimmin' in the street that he couldn't go on that night. That's the kind he is. Get what I mean?"

Joe Morgan hung around the camp until Midge and his trainers returned.

"One o' the boys from *The News*," said Wallie by way of introduction. "I been givin' him your fam'ly hist'ry."

"Did he give you good dope?" he inquired.

"He's some historian," said Joe.

"Don't call me no names," said Wallie smiling. "Call us up if they's anything more you want. And keep your eyes on us Monday night. Get what I mean?"

The story in Sunday's *News* was read by thousands of lovers of the manly art. It was well written and full of human interest. Its slight inaccuracies went unchallenged, though three readers, besides Wallie Adams and Midge Kelly, saw and recognized them. The three were Grace, Tommy Haley and Jerome Harris and the comments they made were not for publication.

Neither the Mrs. Kelly in Chicago nor the Mrs. Kelly in Milwaukee knew that there was such a paper as the New York *News*. And even if they had known of it and that it contained two columns of reading matter about Midge, neither mother nor wife could have bought it. For *The News* on Sunday is a nickel a copy.

Joe Morgan could have written more accurately, no doubt, if instead of Wallie Adams, he had interviewed Ellen Kelly and Connie Kelly and Emma Kelly and Lou Hersch and Grace and Jerome Harris and Tommy Haley and Hap Collins and two or three Milwaukee bartenders.

But a story built on their evidence would never have passed the sporting editor.

"Suppose you can prove it," that gentleman would have said. "It wouldn't get us anything but abuse to print it. The people don't want to see him knocked. He's champion."

Babylon Revisited

"AND WHERE'S Mr. Campbell?" Charlie asked.

"Gone to Switzerland. Mr. Campbell's a pretty sick man, Mr. Wales."

"I'm sorry to hear that. And George Hardt?" Charlie inquired.

"Back in America, gone to work."

"And where is the Snow Bird?"

"He was in here last week. Anyway, his friend, Mr. Schaeffer, is in Paris."

Two familiar names from the long list of a year and a half ago. Charlie scribbled an address in his notebook and tore out the page.

"If you see Mr. Schaeffer, give him this," he said. "It's my brother-in-law's address. I haven't settled on a hotel yet."

He was not really disappointed to find Paris was so empty. But the stillness in the Ritz bar was strange and portentous. It was not an American bar any more—he felt polite in it, and not as if he owned it. It had gone back into France. He felt the stillness from the moment he got out of the taxi and saw the doorman, usually in a frenzy of activity at this hour, gossiping with a *chasseur*[1] by the servants' entrance.

Passing through the corridor, he heard only a single, bored voice in the once-clamorous women's room. When he turned into the bar he travelled the twenty feet of green carpet with his eyes fixed straight ahead by old habit; and then, with his foot firmly on the rail, he turned and surveyed the room, encountering only a single pair of eyes that fluttered up from a

[1] Footman.

newspaper in the corner. Charlie asked for the head barman, Paul, who in the latter days of the bull market had come to work in his own custom-built car—disembarking, however, with due nicety at the nearest corner. But Paul was at his country house today and Alix giving him information.

"No, no more," Charlie said, "I'm going slow these days."

Alix congratulated him: "You were going pretty strong a couple of years ago."

"I'll stick to it all right," Charlie assured him. "I've stuck to it for over a year and a half now."

"How do you find conditions in America?"

"I haven't been to America for months. I'm in business in Prague, representing a couple of concerns there. They don't know about me down there."

Alix smiled.

"Remember the night of George Hardt's bachelor dinner here?" said Charlie. "By the way, what's become of Claude Fessenden?"

Alix lowered his voice confidentially: "He's in Paris, but he doesn't come here any more. Paul doesn't allow it. He ran up a bill of thirty thousand francs, charging all his drinks and his lunches, and usually his dinner, for more than a year. And when Paul finally told him he had to pay, he gave him a bad check."

Alix shook his head sadly.

"I don't understand it, such a dandy fellow. Now he's all bloated up—" He made a plump apple of his hands.

Charlie watched a group of strident queens installing themselves in a corner.

"Nothing affects them," he thought. "Stocks rise and fall, people loaf or work, but they go on forever." The place oppressed him. He called for the dice and shook with Alix for the drink.

"Here for long, Mr. Wales?"

"I'm here for four or five days to see my little girl."

"Oh-h! You have a little girl?"

Outside, the fire-red, gas-blue, ghost-green signs shone

smokily through the tranquil rain. It was late afternoon and the streets were in movement; the *bistros*[2] gleamed. At the corner of the Boulevard des Capucines he took a taxi. The Place de la Concorde moved by in pink majesty; they crossed the logical Seine, and Charlie felt the sudden provincial quality of the Left Bank.

Charlie directed his taxi to the Avenue de l'Opera, which was out of his way. But he wanted to see the blue hour spread over the magnificent façade, and imagine that the cab horns, playing endlessly the first few bars of *Le Plus que Lent*, were the trumpets of the Second Empire. They were closing the iron grill in front of Brentano's Book-store, and people were already at dinner behind the trim little bourgeois hedge of Duval's. He had never eaten at a really cheap restaurant in Paris. Five-course dinner, four francs fifty, eighteen cents, wine included. For some odd reason he wished that he had.

As they rolled on to the Left Bank and he felt its sudden provincialism, he thought, "I spoiled this city for myself. I didn't realize it, but the days came along one after another, and then two years were gone, and everything was gone, and I was gone."

He was thirty-five, and good to look at. The Irish mobility of his face was sobered by a deep wrinkle between his eyes. As he rang his brother-in-law's bell in the Rue Palatine, the wrinkle deepened till it pulled down his brows; he felt a cramping sensation in his belly. From behind the maid who opened the door darted a lovely little girl of nine who shrieked "Daddy!" and flew up, struggling like a fish, into his arms. She pulled his head around by one ear and set her cheek against his.

"My old pie," he said.

"Oh, daddy, daddy, daddy, daddy, dads, dads, dads!"

She drew him into the salon, where the family waited, a boy and girl his daughter's age, his sister-in-law and her husband. He greeted Marion with his voice pitched carefully to

[2] Bars.

avoid either feigned enthusiasm or dislike, but her response was more frankly tepid, though she minimized her expression of unalterable distrust by directing her regard toward his child. The two men clasped hands in a friendly way and Lincoln Peters rested his for a moment on Charlie's shoulder.

The room was warm and comfortably American. The three children moved intimately about, playing through the yellow oblongs that led to other rooms; the cheer of six o'clock spoke in the eager smacks of the fire and the sounds of French activity in the kitchen. But Charlie did not relax; his heart sat up rigidly in his body and he drew confidence from his daughter, who from time to time came close to him, holding in her arms the doll he had brought.

"Really extremely well," he declared in answer to Lincoln's question. "There's a lot of business there that isn't moving at all, but we're doing even better than ever. In fact, damn well. I'm bringing my sister over from America next month to keep house for me. My income last year was bigger than it was when I had money. You see, the Czechs——"

His boasting was for a specific purpose; but after a moment, seeing a faint restiveness in Lincoln's eye, he changed the subject:

"Those are fine children of yours, well brought up, good manners."

"We think Honoria's a great little girl too."

Marion Peters came back from the kitchen. She was a tall woman with worried eyes, who had once possessed a fresh American loveliness. Charlie had never been sensitive to it and was always surprised when people spoke of how pretty she had been. From the first there had been an instinctive antipathy between them.

"Well, how do you find Honoria?" she asked.

"Wonderful. I was astonished how much she's grown in ten months. All the children are looking well."

"We haven't had a doctor for a year. How do you like being back in Paris?"

"It seems very funny to see so few Americans around."

"I'm delighted," Marion said vehemently. "Now at least you can go into a store without their assuming you're a millionaire. We've suffered like everybody, but on the whole it's a good deal pleasanter."

"But it was nice while it lasted," Charlie said. "We were a sort of royalty, almost infallible, with a sort of magic around us. In the bar this afternoon"—he stumbled, seeing his mistake—"there wasn't a man I knew."

She looked at him keenly. "I should think you'd have had enough of bars."

"I only stayed a minute. I take one drink every afternoon, and no more."

"Don't you want a cocktail before dinner?" Lincoln asked.

"I take only one drink every afternoon, and I've had that."

"I hope you keep to it," said Marion.

Her dislike was evident in the coldness with which she spoke, but Charlie only smiled; he had larger plans. Her very aggressiveness gave him an advantage, and he knew enough to wait. He wanted them to initiate the discussion of what they knew had brought him to Paris.

At dinner he couldn't decide whether Honoria was most like him or her mother. Fortunate if she didn't combine the traits of both that had brought them to disaster. A great wave of protectiveness went over him. He thought he knew what to do for her. He believed in character; he wanted to jump back a whole generation and trust in character again as the eternally valuable element. Everything else wore out.

He left soon after dinner, but not to go home. He was curious to see Paris by night with clearer and more judicious eyes than those of other days. He bought a *strapontin*[3] for the Casino and watched Josephine Baker go through her chocolate arabesques.

After an hour he left and strolled toward Montmartre, up the Rue Pigalle into the Place Blanche. The rain had stopped and there were a few people in evening clothes disembarking

[3] Flap seat.

from taxis in front of cabarets, and *cocottes*[4] prowling singly
or in pairs, and many Negroes. He passed a lighted door from
which issued music, and stopped with the sense of familiarity;
it was Bricktop's, where he had parted with so many hours
and so much money. A few doors farther on he found another
ancient rendezvous and incautiously put his head inside. Immediately an eager orchestra burst into sound, a pair of professional dancers leaped to their feet and a maître d'hôtel
swooped toward him, crying, "Crowd just arriving, sir!" But
he withdrew quickly.

"You have to be damn drunk," he thought.

Zelli's was closed, the bleak and sinister cheap hotels sur-
rounding it were dark; up in the Rue Blanche there was more
light and a local, colloquial French crowd. The Poet's Cave
had disappeared, but the two great mouths of the Café of
Heaven and the Café of Hell still yawned—even devoured, as
he watched, the meagre contents of a tourist bus—a German,
a Japanese, and an American couple who glanced at him with
frightened eyes.

So much for the effort and ingenuity of Montmartre. All the
catering to vice and waste was on an utterly childish scale,
and he suddenly realized the meaning of the word "dissipate"
—to dissipate into thin air; to make nothing out of something.
In the little hours of the night every move from place to place
was an enormous human jump, an increase of paying for the
privilege of slower and slower motion.

He remembered thousand-franc notes given to an orchestra
for playing a single number, hundred-franc notes tossed to a
doorman for calling a cab.

But it hadn't been given for nothing.

It had been given, even the most wildly squandered sum,
as an offering to destiny that he might not remember the
things most worth remembering, the things that now he
would always remember—his child taken from his control, his
wife escaped to a grave in Vermont.

4 Prostitutes.

In the glare of a *brasserie*[5] a woman spoke to him. He bought her some eggs and coffee, and then, eluding her encouraging stare, gave her a twenty-franc note and took a taxi to his hotel.

II

He woke up on a fine fall day—football weather. The depression of yesterday was gone and he liked the people on the streets. At noon he sat opposite Honoria at Le Grand Vatel, the only restaurant he could think of not reminiscent of champagne dinners and long luncheons that began at two and ended in a blurred and vague twilight.

"Now, how about vegetables? Oughtn't you to have some vegetables?"

"Well, yes."

"Here's *épinards*[6] and *chou-fleur*[7] and carrots and *haricots*."[8]

"I'd like *chou-fleur*."

"Wouldn't you like to have two vegetables?"

"I usually only have one at lunch."

The waiter was pretending to be inordinately fond of children. *"Qu'elle est mignonne la petite? Elle parle exactement comme une française."*[9]

"How about dessert? Shall we wait and see?"

The waiter disappeared. Honoria looked at her father expectantly.

"What are we going to do?"

"First, we're going to that toy store in the Rue Saint-Honoré and buy you anything you like. And then we're going to the vaudeville at the Empire."

She hesitated. "I like it about the vaudeville, but not the toy store."

[5] Beer parlor.
[6] Spinach.   [7] Cabbage.   [8] Beans.
[9] Isn't the child a darling? She speaks exactly like a French girl.

"Why not?"

"Well, you brought me this doll." She had it with her. "And I've got lots of things. And we're not rich any more, are we?"

"We never were. But today you are to have anything you want."

"All right," she agreed resignedly.

When there had been her mother and a French nurse he had been inclined to be strict; now he extended himself, reached out for a new tolerance; he must be both parents to her and not shut any of her out of communication.

"I want to get to know you," he said gravely. "First let me introduce myself. My name is Charles J. Wales, of Prague."

"Oh, daddy!" her voice cracked with laughter.

"And who are you, please?" he persisted, and she accepted a rôle immediately: "Honoria Wales, Rue Palatine, Paris."

"Married or single?"

"No, not married. Single."

He indicated the doll. "But I see you have a child, madame."

Unwilling to disinherit it, she took it to her heart and thought quickly: "Yes, I've been married, but I'm not married now. My husband is dead."

He went on quickly, "And the child's name?"

"Simone. That's after my best friend at school."

"I'm very pleased that you're doing so well at school."

"I'm third this month," she boasted. "Elsie"—that was her cousin—"is only about eighteenth, and Richard is about at the bottom."

"You like Richard and Elsie, don't you?"

"Oh, yes. I like Richard quite well and I like her all right."

Cautiously and casually he asked: "And Aunt Marion and Uncle Lincoln—which do you like best?"

"Oh, Uncle Lincoln, I guess."

He was increasingly aware of her presence. As they came

in, a murmur of ". . . adorable" followed them, and now the people at the next table bent all their silences upon her, staring as if she were something no more conscious than a flower.

"Why don't I live with you?" she asked suddenly. "Because mamma's dead?"

"You must stay here and learn more French. It would have been hard for daddy to take care of you so well."

"I don't really need much taking care of any more. I do everything for myself."

Going out of the restaurant, a man and a woman unexpectedly hailed him! "Well, the old Wales!"

"Hello there, Lorraine. . . . Dunc."

Sudden ghosts out of the past: Duncan Schaeffer, a friend from college. Lorraine Quarrles, a lovely, pale blonde of thirty; one of a crowd who had helped them make months into days in the lavish times of three years ago.

"My husband couldn't come this year," she said, in answer to his question. "We're poor as hell. So he gave me two hundred a month and told me I could do my worst on that. . . . This your little girl?"

"What about coming back and sitting down?" Duncan asked.

"Can't do it." He was glad for an excuse. As always, he felt Lorraine's passionate, provocative attraction, but his own rhythm was different now.

"Well, how about dinner?" she asked.

"I'm not free. Give me your address and let me call you."

"Charlie, I believe you're sober," she said judicially. "I honestly believe he's sober, Dunc. Pinch him and see if he's sober."

Charlie indicated Honoria with his head. They both laughed.

"What's your address?" said Duncan sceptically.

He hesitated, unwilling to give the name of his hotel.

"I'm not settled yet. I'd better call you. We're going to see the vaudeville at the Empire."

"There! That's what I want to do," Lorraine said. "I want to see some clowns and acrobats and jugglers. That's just what we'll do, Dunc."

"We've got to do an errand first," said Charlie. "Perhaps we'll see you there."

"All right, you snob. . . . Good-by, beautiful little girl."

"Good-by."

Honoria bobbed politely.

Somehow, an unwelcome encounter. They liked him because he was functioning, because he was serious; they wanted to see him, because he was stronger than they were now, because they wanted to draw a certain sustenance from his strength.

At the Empire, Honoria proudly refused to sit upon her father's folded coat. She was already an individual with a code of her own, and Charlie was more and more absorbed by the desire of putting a little of himself into her before she crystallized utterly. It was hopeless to try to know her in so short a time.

Between the acts they came upon Duncan and Lorraine in the lobby where the band was playing.

"Have a drink?"

"All right, but not up at the bar. We'll take a table."

"The perfect father."

Listening abstractedly to Lorraine, Charlie watched Honoria's eyes leave their table, and he followed them wistfully about the room, wondering what they saw. He met her glance and she smiled.

"I liked that lemonade," she said.

What had she said? What had he expected? Going home in a taxi afterward, he pulled her over until her head rested against his chest.

"Darling, do you ever think about your mother?"

"Yes, sometimes," she answered vaguely.

"I don't want you to forget her. Have you got a picture of her?"

"Yes, I think so. Anyhow, Aunt Marion has. Why don't you want me to forget her?"

"She loved you very much."

"I loved her too."

They were silent for a moment.

"Daddy, I want to come and live with you," she said suddenly.

His heart leaped; he had wanted it to come like this.

"Aren't you perfectly happy?"

"Yes, but I love you better than anybody. And you love me better than anybody, don't you, now that mummy's dead?"

"Of course I do. But you won't always like me best, honey. You'll grow up and meet somebody your own age and go marry him and forget you ever had a daddy."

"Yes, that's true," she agreed tranquilly.

He didn't go in. He was coming back at nine o'clock and he wanted to keep himself fresh and new for the thing he must say then.

"When you're safe inside, just show yourself in that window."

"All right. Good-by, dads, dads, dads, dads."

He waited in the dark street until she appeared, all warm and glowing, in the window above and kissed her fingers out into the night.

III

They were waiting. Marion sat behind the coffee service in a dignified black dinner dress that just faintly suggested mourning. Lincoln was walking up and down with the animation of one who had already been talking. They were as anxious as he was to get into the question. He opened it almost immediately:

"I suppose you know what I want to see you about—why I really came to Paris."

Marion played with the black stars on her necklace and frowned.

"I'm awfully anxious to have a home," he continued. "And I'm awfully anxious to have Honoria in it. I appreciate your taking in Honoria for her mother's sake, but things have changed now"—he hesitated and then continued more forcibly —"changed radically with me, and I want to ask you to reconsider the matter. It would be silly for me to deny that about three years ago I was acting badly——"

Marion looked up at him with hard eyes.

"—but all that's over. As I told you, I haven't had more than a drink a day for over a year, and I take that drink deliberately, so that the idea of alcohol won't get too big in my imagination. You see the idea?"

"No," said Marion succinctly.

"It's a sort of stunt I set myself. It keeps the matter in proportion."

"I get you," said Lincoln. "You don't want to admit it's got any attraction for you."

"Something like that. Sometimes I forget and don't take it. But I try to take it. Anyhow, I couldn't afford to drink in my position. The people I represent are more than satisfied with what I've done, and I'm bringing my sister over from Burlington to keep house for me, and I want awfully to have Honoria too. You know that even when her mother and I weren't getting along well we never let anything that happened touch Honoria. I know she's fond of me and I know I'm able to take care of her and—well, there you are. How do you feel about it?"

He knew that now he would have to take a beating. It would last an hour or two hours, and it would be difficult, but if he modulated his inevitable resentment to the chastened attitude of the reformed sinner, he might win his point in the end.

Keep your temper, he told himself. You don't want to be justified. You want Honoria.

Lincoln spoke first: "We've been talking it over ever since

we got your letter last month. We're happy to have Honoria here. She's a dear little thing, and we're glad to be able to help her, but of course that isn't the question——"

Marion interrupted suddenly. "How long are you going to stay sober, Charlie?" she asked.

"Permanently, I hope."

"How can anybody count on that?"

"You know I never did drink heavily until I gave up business and came over here with nothing to do. Then Helen and I began to run around with——"

"Please leave Helen out of it. I can't bear to hear you talk about her like that."

He stared at her grimly; he had never been certain how fond of each other the sisters were in life.

"My drinking only lasted about a year and a half—from the time we came over until I—collapsed."

"It was time enough."

"It was time enough," he agreed.

"My duty is entirely to Helen," she said. "I try to think what she would have wanted me to do. Frankly, from the night you did that terrible thing you haven't really existed for me. I can't help that. She was my sister."

"Yes."

"When she was dying she asked me to look out for Honoria. If you hadn't been in a sanitarium then, it might have helped matters."

He had no answer.

"I'll never in my life be able to forget the morning when Helen knocked at my door, soaked to the skin and shivering, and said you'd locked her out."

Charlie gripped the sides of the chair. This was more difficult than he expected; he wanted to launch out into a long expostulation and explanation, but he only said: "The night I locked her out—" and she interrupted, "I don't feel up to going over that again."

After a moment's silence Lincoln said: "We're getting off the subject. You want Marion to set aside her legal guardianship and give you Honoria. I think the main point for her is whether she has confidence in you or not."

"I don't blame Marion," Charlie said slowly, "but I think she can have entire confidence in me. I had a good record up to three years ago. Of course, it's within human possibilities I might go wrong any time. But if we wait much longer I'll lose Honoria's childhood and my chance for a home." He shook his head, "I'll simply lose her, don't you see?"

"Yes, I see," said Lincoln.

"Why didn't you think of all this before?" Marion asked.

"I suppose I did, from time to time, but Helen and I were getting along badly. When I consented to the guardianship, I was flat on my back in a sanitarium and the market had cleaned me out. I knew I'd acted badly, and I thought if it would bring any peace to Helen, I'd agree to anything. But now it's different. I'm functioning, I'm behaving damn well, so far as——"

"Please don't swear at me," Marion said.

He looked at her, startled. With each remark the force of her dislike became more and more apparent. She had built up all her fear of life into one wall and faced it toward him. This trivial reproof was possibly the result of some trouble with the cook several hours before. Charlie became increasingly alarmed at leaving Honoria in this atmosphere of hostility against himself; sooner or later it would come out, in a word here, a shake of the head there, and some of that distrust would be irrevocably implanted in Honoria. But he pulled his temper down out of his face and shut it up inside him; he had a point, for Lincoln realized the absurdity of Marion's remark and asked her lightly since when she had objected to the word "damn."

"Another thing," Charlie said: "I'm able to give her certain advantages now. I'm going to take a French governess to Prague with me. I've got a lease on a new apartment——"

He stopped, realizing that he was blundering. They

couldn't be expected to accept with equanimity the fact that his income was again twice as large as their own.

"I suppose you can give her more luxuries than we can," said Marion. "When you were throwing away money we were living along watching every ten francs. . . . I suppose you'll start doing it again."

"Oh, no," he said. "I've learned. I worked hard for ten years, you know—until I got lucky in the market, like so many people. Terribly lucky. It didn't seem any use working any more, so I quit. It won't happen again."

There was a long silence. All of them felt their nerves straining, and for the first time in a year Charlie wanted a drink. He was sure now that Lincoln Peters wanted him to have his child.

Marion shuddered suddenly; part of her saw that Charlie's feet were planted on the earth now, and her own maternal feeling recognized the naturalness of his desire; but she had lived for a long time with a prejudice—a prejudice founded on a curious disbelief in her sister's happiness, and which, in the shock of one terrible night, had turned to hatred for him. It had all happened at a point in her life where the discouragement of ill health and adverse circumstances made it necessary for her to believe in tangible villainy and a tangible villain.

"I can't help what I think!" she cried out suddenly. "How much you were responsible for Helen's death, I don't know. It's something you'll have to square with your own conscience."

An electric current of agony surged through him; for a moment he was almost on his feet, an unuttered sound echoing in his throat. He hung on to himself for a moment, another moment.

"Hold on there," said Lincoln uncomfortably. "I never thought you were responsible for that."

"Helen died of heart trouble," Charlie said dully.

"Yes, heart trouble." Marion spoke as if the phrase had another meaning for her.

Then, in the flatness that followed her outburst, she saw him plainly and she knew he had somehow arrived at control over the situation. Glancing at her husband, she found no help from him, and as abruptly as if it were a matter of no importance, she threw up the sponge.

"Do what you like!" she cried, springing up from her chair. "She's your child. I'm not the person to stand in your way. I think if it were my child I'd rather see her—" She managed to check herself. "You two decide it. I can't stand this. I'm sick. I'm going to bed."

She hurried from the room; after a moment Lincoln said:

"This has been a hard day for her. You know how strongly she feels—" His voice was almost apologetic: "When a woman gets an idea in her head."

"Of course."

"It's going to be all right. I think she sees now that you —can provide for the child, and so we can't very well stand in your way or Honoria's way."

"Thank you, Lincoln."

"I'd better go along and see how she is."

"I'm going."

He was still trembling when he reached the street, but a walk down the Rue Bonaparte to the quais set him up, and as he crossed the Seine, fresh and new by the quai lamps, he felt exultant. But back in his room he couldn't sleep. The image of Helen haunted him. Helen whom he had loved so until they had senselessly begun to abuse each other's love, tear it into shreds. On that terrible February night that Marion remembered so vividly, a slow quarrel had gone on for hours. There was a scene at the Florida, and then he attempted to take her home, and then she kissed young Webb at a table; after that there was what she had hysterically said. When he arrived home alone he turned the key in the lock in wild anger. How could he know she would arrive an hour later alone, that there would be a snowstorm in which she wandered about in slippers, too confused to find a taxi. Then the aftermath, her escaping pneumonia by a miracle, and all the attendant horror. They were "reconciled," but that was the beginning of the end, and Marion, who had seen with her own eyes and who imagined it to be one of many scenes from her sister's martyrdom, never forgot.

Going over it again brought Helen nearer, and in the white, soft light that steals upon half sleep near morning he found himself talking to her again. She said that he was perfectly right about Honoria and that she wanted Honoria to be with him. She said she was glad he was being good and doing better. She said a lot of other things—very friendly things—but she was in a swing in a white dress, and swinging faster and faster all the time, so that at the end he could not hear clearly all that she said.

IV

He woke up feeling happy. The door of the world was open again. He made plans, vistas, futures for Honoria and himself, but suddenly he grew sad, remembering all the plans he and Helen had made. She had not planned to die. The present was the thing—work to do and someone to love. But not to love too much, for he knew the injury that a father can do to a daughter or a mother to a son by attaching them too closely: afterward, out in the world, the child would seek in the marriage partner the same blind tenderness and, failing probably to find it, turn against love and life.

It was another bright, crisp day. He called Lincoln Peters at the bank where he worked and asked if he could count on taking Honoria when he left for Prague. Lincoln agreed that there was no reason for delay. One thing—the legal guardianship. Marion wanted to retain that a while longer. She was upset by the whole matter, and it would oil things if she felt that the situation was still in her control for another year. Charlie agreed, wanting only the tangible, visible child.

Then the question of a governess. Charlie sat in a gloomy

agency and talked to a cross Bernaise and to a buxom Breton peasant, neither of whom he could have endured. There were others whom he would see tomorrow.

He lunched with Lincoln Peters at Griffons, trying to keep down his exultation.

"There's nothing quite like your own child," Lincoln said. "But you understand how Marion feels too."

"She's forgotten how hard I worked for seven years there," Charlie said. "She just remembers one night."

"There's another thing." Lincoln hesitated. "While you and Helen were tearing around Europe throwing money away, we were just getting along. I didn't touch any of the prosperity because I never got ahead enough to carry anything but my insurance. I think Marion felt there was some kind of injustice in it—you not even working toward the end, and getting richer and richer."

"It went just as quick as it came," said Charlie.

"Yes, a lot of it stayed in the hands of *chasseurs* and saxophone players and maîtres d'hôtel—well, the big party's over now. I just said that to explain Marion's feeling about those crazy years. If you drop in about six o'clock tonight before Marion's too tired, we'll settle the details on the spot."

Back at his hotel, Charlie found a *pneumatique*[10] that had been redirected from the Ritz bar where Charlie had left his address for the purpose of finding a certain man.

DEAR CHARLIE: You were so strange when we saw you the other day that I wondered if I did something to offend you. If so, I'm not conscious of it. In fact, I have thought about you too much for the last year, and it's always been in the back of my mind that I might see you if I came over here. We *did* have such good times that crazy spring, like the night you and I stole the butcher's tricycle, and the time we tried to call on the president and you had the old derby rim and the wire cane. Everybody seems so old lately, but

[10] Express letter—a kind of telegram.

I don't feel old a bit. Couldn't we get together some time today for old time's sake? I've got a vile hangover for the moment, but will be feeling better this afternoon and will look for you about five in the sweat-shop at the Ritz.

Always devotedly,

LORRAINE.

His first feeling was one of awe that he had actually, in his mature years, stolen a tricycle and pedalled Lorraine all over the Étoile between the small hours and dawn. In retrospect it was a nightmare. Locking out Helen didn't fit in with any other act of his life, but the tricycle incident did—it was one of many. How many weeks or months of dissipation to arrive at that condition of utter irresponsibility?

He tried to picture how Lorraine had appeared to him then—very attractive; Helen was unhappy about it, though she said nothing. Yesterday, in the restaurant, Lorraine had seemed trite, blurred, worn away. He emphatically did not want to see her, and he was glad Alix had not given away his hotel address. It was a relief to think, instead, of Honoria, to think of Sundays spent with her and saying good morning to her and of knowing she was there in his house at night, drawing her breath in the darkness.

At five he took a taxi and bought presents for all the Peters—a piquant cloth doll, a box of Roman soldiers, flowers for Marion, big linen handkerchiefs for Lincoln.

He saw, when he arrived in the apartment, that Marion had accepted the inevitable. She greeted him now as though he were a recalcitrant member of the family rather than a menacing outsider. Honoria had been told she was going; Charlie was glad to see that her tact made her conceal her excessive happiness. Only on his lap did she whisper her delight and the question "When?" before she slipped away with the other children.

He and Marion were alone for a minute in the room, and on an impulse he spoke out boldly:

"Family quarrels are bitter things. They don't go according to any rules. They're not like aches or wounds; they're more like splits in the skin that won't heal because there's not enough material. I wish you and I could be on better terms."

"Some things are hard to forget," she answered. "It's a question of confidence." There was no answer to this and presently she asked, "When do you propose to take her?"

"As soon as I can get a governess. I hoped the day after tomorrow."

"That's impossible. I've got to get her things in shape. Not before Saturday."

He yielded. Coming back into the room, Lincoln offered him a drink.

"I'll take my daily whisky," he said.

It was warm here, it was a home, people together by a fire. The children felt very safe and important; the mother and father were serious, watchful. They had things to do for the children more important than his visit here. A spoonful of medicine was, after all, more important than the strained relations between Marion and himself. They were not dull people, but they were very much in the grip of life and circumstances. He wondered if he couldn't do something to get Lincoln out of his rut at the bank.

A long peal at the door-bell; the *bonne à tout faire*[11] passed through and went down the corridor. The door opened upon another long ring, and then voices, and the three in the salon looked up expectantly; Richard moved to bring the corridor within his range of vision, and Marion rose. Then the maid came back along the corridor, closely followed by the voices, which developed under the light into Duncan Schaeffer and Lorraine Quarrles.

They were gay, they were hilarious, they were roaring with laughter. For a moment Charlie was astounded; unable to understand how they ferreted out the Peters' address.

"Ah-h-h!" Duncan wagged his finger roguishly at Charlie. "Ah-h-h!"

[11] Maid-of-all-work.

They both slid down another cascade of laughter. Anxious and at a loss, Charlie shook hands with them quickly and presented them to Lincoln and Marion. Marion nodded, scarcely speaking. She had drawn back a step toward the fire; her little girl stood beside her, and Marion put an arm about her shoulder.

With growing annoyance at the intrusion, Charlie waited for them to explain themselves. After some concentration Duncan said:

"We came to invite you out to dinner. Lorraine and I insist that all this shishi, cagey business 'bout your address got to stop."

Charlie came closer to them, as if to force them backward down the corridor.

"Sorry, but I can't. Tell me where you'll be and I'll phone you in half an hour."

This made no impression. Lorraine sat down suddenly on the side of a chair, and focusing her eyes on Richard, cried, "Oh, what a nice little boy! Come here, little boy." Richard glanced at his mother, but did not move. With a perceptible shrug of her shoulders, Lorraine turned back to Charlie:

"Come and dine. Sure your cousins won' mine. See you so sel'om. Or solemn."

"I can't," said Charlie sharply. "You two have dinner and I'll phone you."

Her voice became suddenly unpleasant. "All right, we'll go. But I remember once when you hammered on my door at four A.M. I was enough of a good sport to give you a drink. Come on, Dunc."

Still in slow motion, with blurred, angry faces, with uncertain feet, they retired along the corridor.

"Good night," Charlie said.

"Good night!" responded Lorraine emphatically.

When he went back into the salon Marion had not moved, only now her son was standing in the circle of her other arm. Lincoln was still swinging Honoria back and forth like a pendulum from side to side.

"What an outrage!" Charlie broke out. "What an absolute outrage!"

Neither of them answered. Charlie dropped into an armchair, picked up his drink, set it down again and said:

"People I haven't seen for two years having the colossal nerve——"

He broke off. Marion had made the sound "Oh!" in one swift, furious breath, turned her body from him with a jerk and left the room.

Lincoln set down Honoria carefully.

"You children go in and start your soup," he said, and when they obeyed, he said to Charlie:

"Marion's not well and she can't stand shocks. That kind of people make her really physically sick."

"I didn't tell them to come here. They wormed your name out of somebody. They deliberately——"

"Well, it's too bad. It doesn't help matters. Excuse me a minute."

Left alone, Charlie sat tense in his chair. In the next room he could hear the children eating, talking in monosyllables, already oblivious to the scene between their elders. He heard a murmur of conversation from a farther room and then the ticking bell of a telephone receiver picked up, and in a panic he moved to the other side of the room and out of earshot.

In a minute Lincoln came back. "Look here, Charlie. I think we'd better call off dinner for tonight. Marion's in bad shape."

"Is she angry with me?"

"Sort of," he said, almost roughly. "She's not strong and—"

"You mean she's changed her mind about Honoria?"

"She's pretty bitter right now. I don't know. You phone me at the bank tomorrow."

"I wish you'd explain to her I never dreamed these people would come here. I'm just as sore as you are."

"I couldn't explain anything to her now."

Charlie got up. He took his coat and hat and started down the corridor. Then he opened the door of the dining room and said in a strange voice, "Good night, children."

Honoria rose and ran around the table to hug him.

"Good night, sweetheart," he said vaguely, and then trying to make his voice more tender, trying to conciliate something, "Good night, dear children."

v

Charlie went directly to the Ritz bar with the furious idea of finding Lorraine and Duncan, but they were not there, and he realized that in any case there was nothing he could do. He had not touched his drink at the Peters', and now he ordered a whisky-and-soda. Paul came over to say hello.

"It's a great change," he said sadly. "We do about half the business we did. So many fellows I hear about back in the States lost everything, maybe not in the first crash, but then in the second. Your friend George Hardt lost every cent, I hear. Are you back in the States?"

"No, I'm in business in Prague."

"I heard that you lost a lot in the crash."

"I did," and he added grimly, "but I lost everything I wanted in the boom."

"Selling short."

"Something like that."

Again the memory of those days swept over him like a nightmare—the people they had met travelling; then people who couldn't add a row of figures or speak a coherent sentence. The little man Helen had consented to dance with at the ship's party, who had insulted her ten feet from the table; the women and girls carried screaming with drink or drugs out of public places——

—The men who locked their wives out in the snow, because the snow of twenty-nine wasn't real snow. If you didn't want it to be snow, you just paid some money.

He went to the phone and called the Peters' apartment; Lincoln answered.

"I called up because this thing is on my mind. Has Marion said anything definite?"

"Marion's sick," Lincoln answered shortly. "I know this thing isn't altogether your fault, but I can't have her go to pieces about it. I'm afraid we'll have to let it slide for six months; I can't take the chance of working her up to this state again."

"I see."

"I'm sorry, Charlie."

He went back to his table. His whisky glass was empty, but he shook his head when Alix looked at it questioningly. There wasn't much he could do now except send Honoria some things; he would send her a lot of things tomorrow. He thought rather angrily that this was just money—he had given so many people money. . . .

"No, no more," he said to another waiter. "What do I owe you?"

He would come back some day; they couldn't make him pay forever. But he wanted his child, and nothing was much good now, beside that fact. He wasn't young any more, with a lot of nice thoughts and dreams to have by himself. He was absolutely sure Helen wouldn't have wanted him to be so alone.

Silent Snow, Secret Snow

JUST why it should have happened, or why it should have happened just when it did, he could not, of course, possibly have said; nor perhaps could it even have occurred to him to ask. The thing was above all a secret, something to be preciously concealed from Mother and Father; and to that very fact it owed an enormous part of its deliciousness. It was like a peculiarly beautiful trinket to be carried unmentioned in one's trouser-pocket—a rare stamp, an old coin, a few tiny gold links found trodden out of shape on the path in the park, a pebble of carnelian, a sea shell distinguishable from all others by an unusual spot or stripe—and, as if it were anyone of these, he carried around with him everywhere a warm and persistent and increasingly beautiful sense of possession. Nor was it only a sense of possession—it was also a sense of protection. It was as if, in some delightful way, his secret gave him a fortress, a wall behind which he could retreat into heavenly seclusion. This was almost the first thing he had noticed about it—apart from the oddness of the thing itself—and it was this that now again, for the fiftieth time, occurred to him, as he sat in the little schoolroom. It was the half hour for geography. Miss Buell was revolving with one finger, slowly, a huge terrestrial globe which had been placed on her desk. The green and yellow continents passed and repassed, questions were asked and answered, and now the little girl in front of him, Deirdre, who had a funny little constellation of freckles on the back of her neck, exactly like the Big Dipper, was standing up and telling Miss Buell that the equator was the line that ran round the middle.

Miss Buell's face, which was old and grayish and kindly,

with gray stiff curls beside the cheeks, and eyes that swam very brightly, like little minnows, behind thick glasses, wrinkled itself into a complication of amusements.

"Ah! I see. The earth is wearing a belt, or a sash. Or some-one drew a line round it!"

"Oh, no—not that—I mean—"

In the general laughter, he did not share, or only a very little. He was thinking about the Arctic and Antarctic regions, which of course, on the globe, were white. Miss Buell was now telling them about the tropics, the jungles, the steamy heat of equatorial swamps, where the birds and butterflies, and even the snakes, were like living jewels. As he listened to these things, he was already, with a pleasant sense of half-effort, putting his secret between himself and the words. Was it really an effort at all? For effort implied something voluntary, and perhaps even something one did not especially want; whereas this was distinctly pleasant, and came almost of its own accord. All he needed to do was to think of that morning, the first one, and then of all the others—

But it was all so absurdly simple! It had amounted to so little. It was nothing, just an idea—and just why it should have become so wonderful, so permanent, was a mystery—a very pleasant one, to be sure, but also, in an amusing way, foolish. However, without ceasing to listen to Miss Buell, who had now moved up to the north temperate zones, he deliber-ately invited his memory of the first morning. It was only a moment or two after he had waked up—or perhaps the mo-ment itself. But was there, to be exact, an exact moment? Was one awake all at once? or was it gradual? Anyway, it was after he had stretched a lazy hand up towards the headrail, and yawned, and then relaxed again among his warm covers, all the more grateful on a December morning, that the thing had happened. Suddenly, for no reason, he had thought of the postman, he remembered the postman. Perhaps there was nothing so odd in that. After all, he heard the postman almost every morning in his life—his heavy boots could be heard clumping round the corner at the top of the little cobbled hill-street, and then, progressively nearer, progressively louder, the double knock at each door, the crossings and re-crossings of the street, till finally the clumsy steps came stumbling across to the very door, and the tremendous knock came which shook the house itself.

(Miss Buell was saying "Vast wheat-growing areas in North America and Siberia."

Deirdre had for the moment placed her left hand across the back of her neck.)

But on this particular morning, the first morning, as he lay there with his eyes closed, he had for some reason *waited* for the postman. He wanted to hear him come round the corner. And that was precisely the joke—he never did. He never came. He never had come—*round the corner*—again. For when at last the steps *were* heard, they had already, he was quite sure, come a little down the hill, to the first house; and even so, the steps were curiously different—they were softer, they had a new secrecy about them, they were muffled and indistinct; and while the rhythm of them was the same, it now said a new thing—it said peace, it said remoteness, it said cold, it said sleep. And he had understood the situation at once—nothing could have seemed simpler—there had been snow in the night, such as all winter he had been longing for; and it was this which had rendered the postman's first footsteps inaudible, and the later ones faint. Of course! How lovely! And even now it must be snowing—it was going to be a snowy day—the long white ragged lines were drifting and sifting across the street, across the faces of the old houses, whispering and hushing, making little triangles of white in the corners between cobblestones, seething a little when the wind blew them over the ground to a drifted corner; and so it would be all day, getting deeper and deeper and silenter and silenter.

(Miss Buell was saying "Land of perpetual snow.")

All this time, of course (while he lay in bed), he had kept his eyes closed, listening to the nearer progress of the postman, the muffled footsteps thumping and slipping on the

snow-sheathed cobbles; and all the other sounds—the double
knocks, a frosty far-off voice or two, a bell ringing thinly and
softly as if under a sheet of ice—had the same slightly ab-
stracted quality, as if removed by one degree from actuality—
as if everything in the world had been insulated by snow.
But when at last, pleased, he opened his eyes, and turned
them towards the window, to see for himself this long-desired
and now so clearly imagined miracle—what he saw instead
was brilliant sunlight on a roof; and when, astonished, he
jumped out of bed and stared down into the street, expecting to see the cobbles obliterated by the snow, he saw nothing but the bare bright cobbles themselves.

Queer, the effect this extraordinary surprise had had upon
him—all the following morning he had kept with him a sense
as of snow falling about him, a secret screen of new snow between himself and the world. If he had not dreamed such a
thing—and how could he have dreamed it while awake?—how
else could one explain it? In any case, the delusion had been
so vivid as to affect his entire behavior. He could not now
remember whether it was on the first or the second morning
—or was it even the third?—that his mother had drawn attention to some oddness in his manner.

"But my darling—" she had said at the breakfast table—
"what has come over you? You don't seem to be listening. . . ."

And how often that very thing had happened since!

(Miss Buell was now asking if anyone knew the difference
between the North Pole and the Magnetic Pole. Deirdre was
holding up her flickering brown hand, and he could see the
four white dimples that marked the knuckles.)

Perhaps it hadn't been either the second or third morning
—or even the fourth or fifth. How could he be sure? How
could he be sure just when the delicious *progress* had become clear? Just when it had really *begun*? The intervals
weren't very precise. . . . All he now knew was, that at some
point or other—perhaps the second day, perhaps the sixth—he
had noticed that the presence of the snow was a little more
insistent, the sound of it clearer; and, conversely, the sound of

the postman's footsteps more indistinct. Not only could he not hear the steps come round the corner, he could not even hear them at the first house. It was below the first house that he heard them; and then, a few days later, it was below the second house that he heard them; and a few days later again, below the third. Gradually, gradually, the snow was becoming heavier, the sound of its seething louder, the cobblestones more and more muffled. When he found, each morning, on going to the window, after the ritual of listening, that the roofs and cobbles were as bare as ever, it made no difference. This was, after all, only what he had expected. It was even what pleased him, what rewarded him: the thing was his own, belonged to no one else. No one else knew about it, not even his mother and father. There, outside, were the bare cobbles; and here, inside, was the snow. Snow growing heavier each day, muffling the world, hiding the ugly, and deadening increasingly—above all—the steps of the postman.

"But my darling—" she had said at the luncheon table— "what has come over you? You don't seem to listen when people speak to you. That's the third time I've asked you to pass your plate. . . ."

How was one to explain this to Mother? or to Father? There was, of course, nothing to be done about it: nothing. All one could do was to laugh embarrassedly, pretend to be a little ashamed, apologize, and take a sudden and somewhat disingenuous interest in what was being done or said. The cat had stayed out all night. He had a curious swelling on his left cheek—perhaps somebody had kicked him, or a stone had struck him. Mrs. Kempton was or was not coming to tea. The house was going to be house cleaned, or "turned out," on Wednesday instead of Friday. A new lamp was provided for his evening work—perhaps it was eye-strain which accounted for this new and so peculiar vagueness of his— Mother was looking at him with amusement as she said this, but with something else as well. A new lamp? A new lamp. Yes Mother, No Mother, Yes Mother. School is going very well. The geometry is very easy. The history is very dull. The

geography is very interesting—particularly when it takes one
to the North Pole. Why the North Pole? Oh, well, it would be
fun to be an explorer. Another Peary or Scott or Shackleton.
And then abruptly he found his interest in the talk at an end,
stared at the pudding on his plate, listened, waited, and began once more—ah how heavenly, too, the first beginnings—
to hear or feel—for could he actually hear it?—the silent snow,
the secret snow.

(Miss Buell was telling them about the search for the Northwest Passage, about Hendrick Hudson, the Half Moon.)

This had been, indeed, the only distressing feature of the
new experience: the fact that it so increasingly had brought
him into a kind of mute misunderstanding, or even conflict,
with his father and mother. It was as if he were trying to lead
a double life. On the one hand he had to be Paul Hasleman,
and keep up the appearance of being that person—dress,
wash, and answer intelligently when spoken to—; on the
other, he had to explore this new world which had been
opened to him. Nor could there be the slightest doubt—not
the slightest—that the new world was the profounder and
more wonderful of the two. It was irresistible. It was miraculous. Its beauty was simply beyond anything—beyond speech
as beyond thought—utterly incommunicable. But how then,
between the two worlds, of which he was thus constantly
aware, was he to keep a balance? One must get up, one must
go to breakfast, one must talk with Mother, go to school, do
one's lessons—and, in all this, try not to appear too much of a
fool. But if all the while one was also trying to extract the full
deliciousness of another and quite separate existence, one
which could not easily (if at all) be spoken of—how was one
to manage? How was one to explain? Would it be safe to explain? Would it be absurd? Would it merely mean that he
would get into some obscure kind of trouble?

These thoughts came and went, came and went, as softly
and secretly as the snow; they were not precisely a disturbance, perhaps they were even a pleasure; he liked to have
them; their presence was something almost palpable, some-

thing he could stroke with his hand, without closing his eyes, and without ceasing to see Miss Buell and the school-room and the globe and the freckles on Deirdre's neck; nevertheless he did in a sense cease to see, or to see the obvious external world, and substituted for this vision the vision of snow, the sound of snow, and the slow, almost soundless, approach of the postman. Yesterday, it had been only at the sixth house that the postman had become audible; the snow was much deeper now, it was falling more swiftly and heavily, the sound of its seething was more distinct, more soothing, more persistent. And this morning, it had been—as nearly as he could figure—just above the seventh house—perhaps only a step or two above: at most, he had heard two or three footsteps before the knock had sounded. . . . And with each such narrowing of the sphere, each nearer approach of the limit at which the postman was first audible, it was odd how sharply was increased the amount of illusion which had to be carried into the ordinary business of daily life. Each day, it was harder to get out of bed, to go to the window, to look out at the—as always—perfectly empty and snowless street. Each day it was more difficult to go through the perfunctory motions of greeting Mother and Father at breakfast, to reply to their questions, to put his books together and go to school. And at school, how extraordinarily hard to conduct with success simultaneously the public life and the life that was secret. There were times when he longed—positively ached—to tell everyone about it—to burst out with it—only to be checked almost at once by a far-off feeling as of some faint absurdity which was inherent in it—but *was* it absurd?—and more importantly by a sense of mysterious power in his very secrecy. Yes: it must be kept secret. That, more and more, became clear. At whatever cost to himself, whatever pain to others—

(Miss Buell looked straight at him, smiling, and said, "Perhaps we'll ask Paul. I'm sure Paul will come out of his daydream long enough to be able to tell us. Won't you, Paul." He rose slowly from his chair, resting one hand on the brightly varnished desk, and deliberately stared through the snow towards the blackboard. It was an effort, but it was amusing to make it. "Yes," he said slowly, "it was what we now call the Hudson River. This he thought to be the Northwest Passage. He was disappointed." He sat down again, and as he did so Deirdre half turned in her chair and gave him a shy smile, of approval and admiration.)

At whatever pain to others.

This part of it was very puzzling, very puzzling. Mother was very nice, and so was Father. Yes, that was all true enough. He wanted to be nice to them, to tell them everything—and yet, was it really wrong of him to want to have a secret place of his own?

At bedtime, the night before, Mother had said, "If this goes on, my lad, we'll have to see a doctor, we will! We can't have our boy—." But what was it she had said? "Live in another world"? "Live so far away"? The word "far" had been in it, he was sure, and then Mother had taken up a magazine again and laughed a little, but with an expression which wasn't mirthful. He had felt sorry for her. . . .

The bell rang for dismissal. The sound came to him through long curved parallels of falling snow. He saw Deirdre rise, and had himself risen almost as soon—but not quite as soon—as she.

II

On the walk homeward, which was timeless, it pleased him to see through the accompaniment, or counterpoint, of snow, the items of mere externality on his way. There were many kinds of bricks in the sidewalks, and laid in many kinds of patterns. The garden walls too were various, some of wooden palings, some of plaster, some of stone. Twigs of bushes leaned over the walls; the little hard green winter-buds of lilac, on gray stems, sheathed and fat; other branches very thin and fine and black and desiccated. Dirty sparrows huddled in the bushes, as dull in color as dead fruit left in leafless trees. A single starling creaked on a weather vane. In the gutter, beside a drain, was a scrap of torn and dirty newspaper, caught in a little delta of filth: the word ECZEMA appeared in large capitals, and below it was a letter from Mrs. Amelia D. Cravath, 2100 Pine Street, Fort Worth, Texas, to the effect that after being a sufferer for years she had been cured by Caley's Ointment. In the little delta, beside the fan-shaped and deeply runneled continent of brown mud, were lost twigs, descended from their parent trees, dead matches, a rusty horse-chestnut burr, a small concentration of sparkling gravel on the lip of the sewer, a fragment of eggshell, a streak of yellow sawdust which had been wet and was now dry and congealed, a brown pebble, and a broken feather. Further on was a cement sidewalk, ruled into geometrical parallelograms, with a brass inlay at one end commemorating the contractors who had laid it, and, halfway across, an irregular and random series of dog-tracks, immortalized in synthetic stone. He knew these well, and always stepped on them; to cover the little hollows with his own foot had always been a queer pleasure; today he did it once more, but perfunctorily and detachedly, all the while thinking of something else. That was a dog, a long time ago, who had made a mistake and walked on the cement while it was still wet. He had probably wagged his tail, but that hadn't been recorded. Now, Paul Hasleman, aged twelve, on his way home from school, crossed the same river, which in the meantime had frozen into rock. Homeward through the snow, the snow falling in bright sunshine. Homeward?

Then came the gateway with the two posts surmounted by egg-shaped stones which had been cunningly balanced on their ends, as if by Columbus, and mortared in the very act of balance: a source of perpetual wonder. On the brick wall just beyond, the letter H had been stenciled, presumably for some purpose. H? H.

The green hydrant, with a little green-painted chain attached to the brass screw-cap.

The elm tree, with the great gray wound in the bark, kidney-shaped, into which he always put his hand—to feel the

cold but living wood. The injury, he had been sure, was due
to the gnawings of a tethered horse. But now it deserved only
a passing palm, a merely tolerant eye. There were more important things. Miracles. Beyond the thoughts of trees, mere
elms. Beyond the thoughts of sidewalks, mere stone, mere
brick, mere cement. Beyond the thoughts even of his own
shoes, which trod these sidewalks obediently, bearing a bur-
den—far above—of elaborate mystery. He watched them. They
were not very well polished; he had neglected them, for a
very good reason: they were one of the many parts of the in-
creasing difficulty of the daily return to daily life, the morning struggle. To get up, having at last opened one's eyes, to
go to the window, and discover no snow, to wash, to dress,
to descend the curving stairs to breakfast—

At whatever pain to others, nevertheless, one must per-
severe in severance, since the incommunicability of the experience demanded it. It was desirable of course to be kind
to Mother and Father, especially as they seemed to be worried, but it was also desirable to be resolute. If they should
decide—as appeared likely—to consult the doctor, Doctor
Howells, and have Paul inspected, his heart listened to
through a kind of dictaphone, his lungs, his stomach—well,
that was all right. He would go through with it. He would
give them answer for question, too—perhaps such answers as
they hadn't expected? No. That would never do. For the
secret world must, at all costs, be preserved.

The bird-house in the apple-tree was empty—it was the
wrong time of year for wrens. The little round black door had
lost its pleasure. The wrens were enjoying other houses, other
nests, remoter trees. But this too was a notion which he only
vaguely and grazingly entertained—as if, for the moment, he
merely touched an edge of it; there was something further on,
which was already assuming a sharper importance; something
which already teased at the corners of his eyes, teasing also
at the corner of his mind. It was funny to think that he so
wanted this, so awaited it—and yet found himself enjoying
this momentary dalliance with the bird-house, as if for a quite

deliberate postponement and enhancement of the approaching pleasure. He was aware of his delay, of his smiling and detached and now almost uncomprehending gaze at the little bird-house: he knew what he was going to look at next: it was his own little cobbled hill-street, his own house, the little river at the bottom of the hill, the grocer's shop with the cardboard man in the window—and now, thinking of all this, he turned his head, still smiling, and looking quickly right and left through the snow-laden sunlight.

And the mist of snow, as he had foreseen, was still on it— a ghost of snow falling in the bright sunlight, softly and steadily floating and turning and pausing, soundlessly meeting the snow that covered, as with a transparent mirage, the bare bright cobbles. He loved it—he stood still and loved it. Its beauty was paralyzing—beyond all words, all experience, all dream. No fairy-story he had ever read could be compared with it—none had ever given him this extraordinary combination of ethereal loveliness with a something else, unnameable, which was just faintly and deliciously terrifying. What was this thing? As he thought of it, he looked upward toward his own bedroom window, which was open—and it was as if he looked straight into the room and saw himself lying half awake in his bed. There he was—at this very instant he was still perhaps actually there—more truly there than standing here at the edge of the cobbled hill-street, with one hand lifted to shade his eyes against the snow-sun. Had he indeed ever left his room, in all this time? since that very first morning? Was the whole progress still being enacted there, was it still the same morning, and himself not yet wholly awake? And even now, had the postman not yet come round the corner? . . .

This idea amused him, and automatically, as he thought of it, he turned his head and looked toward the top of the hill. There was, of course, nothing there—nothing and no one. The street was empty and quiet. And all the more because of its emptiness it occurred to him to count the houses—a thing which, oddly enough, he hadn't before thought of doing. Of course, he had known there weren't many—many, that is, on his own side of the street, which were the ones that figured in the postman's progress—but nevertheless it came to him as something of a shock to find that there were precisely *six*, above his own house—his own house was the seventh.

Six!

Astonished, he looked at his own house—looked at the door, on which was the number thirteen—and then realized that the whole thing was exactly and logically and absurdly what he ought to have known. Just the same, the realization gave him abruptly, and even a little frighteningly, a sense of hurry. He was being hurried—he was being rushed. For—he knit his brows—he couldn't be mistaken—it was just above the *seventh* house, his *own* house, that the postman had first been audible this very morning. But in that case—in that case—did it mean that tomorrow he would hear nothing? The knock he had heard must have been the knock of their own door. Did it mean—and this was an idea which gave him a really extraordinary feeling of surprise—that he would never hear the postman again?—that tomorrow morning the postman would already have passed the house, in a snow by then so deep as to render his footsteps completely inaudible? That he would have made his approach down the snow-filled street so soundlessly, so secretly, that he, Paul Hasleman, there lying in bed, would not have waked in time, or, waking, would have heard nothing?

But how could that be? Unless even the knocker should be muffled in the snow—frozen tight, perhaps? . . . But in that case—

A vague feeling of disappointment came over him; a vague sadness, as if he felt himself deprived of something which he had long looked forward to, something much prized. After all this, all this beautiful progress, the slow delicious advance of the postman through the silent and secret snow, the knock creeping closer each day, and the footsteps nearer, the audible compass of the world thus daily narrowed, narrowed, narrowed, as the snow soothingly and beautifully encroached and deepened, after all this, was he to be defrauded of the one thing he had so wanted—to be able to count, as it were, the last two or three solemn footsteps, as they finally approached his own door? Was it all going to happen, at the end, so suddenly? or indeed, had it already happened? with no slow and subtle gradations of menace, in which he could luxuriate?

He gazed upward again, toward his own window which flashed in the sun: and this time almost with a feeling that it would be better if he *were* still in bed, in that room; for in that case this must still be the first morning, and there would be six more mornings to come—or, for that matter, seven or eight or nine—how could he be sure?—or even more.

III

After supper, the inquisition began. He stood before the doctor, under the lamp, and submitted silently to the usual thumpings and tappings.

"Now will you please say 'Ah!'?"

"Ah!"

"Now again please, if you don't mind."

"Ah."

"Say it slowly, and hold it if you can—"

"Ah-h-h-h-h-h—"

"Good."

How silly all this was. As if it had anything to do with his throat! Or his heart or lungs!

Relaxing his mouth, of which the corners, after all this absurd stretching, felt uncomfortable, he avoided the doctor's eyes, and stared towards the fireplace, past his mother's feet (in gray slippers) which projected from the green chair, and his father's feet (in brown slippers) which stood neatly side by side on the hearth rug.

"Hm. There is certainly nothing wrong there . . ."

He felt the doctor's eyes fixed upon him, and, as if merely to be polite, returned the look, but with a feeling of justifiable evasiveness.

"Now, young man, tell me,—do you feel all right?"

"Yes, sir, quite all right."

"No headaches? No dizziness?"

"No, I don't think so."

"Let me see. Let's get a book, if you don't mind—yes, thank you, that will do splendidly—and now, Paul, if you'll just read it, holding it as you would normally hold it—"

He took the book and read:

"And another praise have I to tell for this the city our mother, the gift of a great god, a glory of the land most high; the might of horses, the might of young horses, the might of the sea. . . . For thou, son of Cronus, our lord Poseidon, hast throned herein this pride, since in these roads first thou didst show forth the curb that cures the rage of steeds. And the shapely oar, apt to men's hands, hath a wondrous speed on the brine, following the hundred-footed Nereids. . . . O land that art praised above all lands, now is it for thee to make those bright praises seen in deeds."

He stopped, tentatively, and lowered the heavy book.

"No—as I thought—there is certainly no superficial sign of eye-strain."

Silence thronged the room, and he was aware of the focused scrutiny of the three people who confronted him. . . .

"We could have his eyes examined—but I believe it is something else."

"What could it be?" This was his father's voice.

"It's only this curious absent-minded—" This was his mother's voice.

In the presence of the doctor, they both seemed irritatingly apologetic.

"I believe it is something else. Now Paul—I would like very much to ask you a question or two. You will answer them, won't you—you know I'm an old, old friend of yours, eh? That's right! . . ."

His back was thumped twice by the doctor's fat fist,—then the doctor was grinning at him with false amiability, while with one finger-nail he was scratching the top button of his waistcoat. Beyond the doctor's shoulder was the fire, the fingers of flame making light prestidigitation against the sooty fireback, the soft sound of their random flutter the only sound.

"I would like to know—is there anything that worries you?"

The doctor was again smiling, his eyelids low against the little black pupils, in each of which was a tiny white bead of light. Why answer him? why answer him at all? "At whatever pain to others"—but it was all a nuisance, this necessity for resistance, this necessity for attention: it was as if one had been stood up on a brilliantly lighted stage, under a great round blaze of spotlight; as if one were merely a trained seal, or a performing dog, or a fish, dipped out of an aquarium and held up by the tail. It would serve them right if he were merely to bark or growl. And meanwhile, to miss these last few precious hours, these hours of which every minute was more beautiful than the last, more menacing—? He still looked, as if from a great distance, at the beads of light in the doctor's eyes, at the fixed false smile, and then, beyond, once more at his mother's slippers, his father's slippers, the soft flutter of the fire. Even here, even amongst these hostile presences, and in this arranged light, he could see the snow, he could hear it—it was in the corners of the room, where the shadow was deepest, under the sofa, behind the half-opened door which led to the dining room. It was gentler here, softer, its seethe the quietest of whispers, as if, in deference to a drawing room, it had quite deliberately put on its "manners"; it kept itself out of sight, obliterated itself, but distinctly with an air of saying, "Ah, but just wait! Wait till we are alone together! Then I will begin to tell you something new! Something white! something cold! something sleepy! something of cease, and peace, and the long bright curve of space! Tell them to go away. Banish them. Refuse to speak. Leave them, go upstairs to your room, turn out the light and get into bed— I will go with you, I will be waiting for you, I will tell you a better story than Little Kay of the Skates, or The Snow Ghost —I will surround your bed, I will close the windows, pile a deep drift against the door, so that none will ever again be able to enter. Speak to them! . . ." It seemed as if the little hissing voice came from a slow white spiral of falling flakes in the corner by the front window—but he could not be sure. He felt himself smiling, then, and said to the doctor, but without looking at him, looking beyond him still—

"Oh, no, I think not—"

"But are you sure, my boy?"

His father's voice came softly and coldly then—the familiar voice of silken warning. . . .

"You needn't answer at once, Paul—remember we're trying to help you—think it over and be quite sure, won't you?"

He felt himself smiling again, at the notion of being quite sure. What a joke! As if he weren't so sure that reassurance was no longer necessary, and all this cross-examination a ridiculous farce, a grotesque parody! What could they know about it? These gross intelligences, these humdrum minds so bound to the usual, the ordinary? Impossible to tell them about it! Why, even now, even now, with the proof so abundant, so formidable, so imminent, so appallingly present here in this very room, could they believe it?—could even his mother believe it? No—it was only too plain that if anything were said about it, the merest hint given, they would be incredulous—they would laugh—they would say "Absurd!"— think things about him which weren't true. . . .

"Why no, I'm not worried—why should I be?"

He looked then straight at the doctor's low-lidded eyes, looked from one of them to the other, from one bead of light to the other, and gave a little laugh.

The doctor seemed to be disconcerted by this. He drew back in his chair, resting a fat white hand on either knee. The smile faded slowly from his face.

"Well, Paul!" he said, and paused gravely, "I'm afraid you don't take this quite seriously enough. I think you perhaps don't quite realize—don't quite realize—" He took a deep quick breath, and turned, as if helplessly, at a loss for words, to the others. But Mother and Father were both silent—no help was forthcoming.

"You must surely know, be aware, that you have not been quite yourself of late? don't you know that? . . ."

It was amusing to watch the doctor's renewed attempt at a smile, a queer disorganized look, as of confidential embarrassment.

"I feel all right, sir," he said, and again gave the little laugh.

"And we're trying to help you." The doctor's tone sharpened.

"Yes sir, I know. But why? I'm all right. I'm just *thinking*, that's all."

His mother made a quick movement forward, resting a hand on the back of the doctor's chair.

"Thinking?" she said. "But my dear, about what?"

This was a direct challenge—and would have to be directly met. But before he met it, he looked again into the corner by the door, as if for reassurance. He smiled again at what he saw, at what he heard. The little spiral was still there, still softly whirling, like the ghost of a white kitten chasing the ghost of a white tail and making as it did so the faintest of whispers. It was all right! If only he could remain firm, everything was going to be all right.

"Oh, about anything, about nothing,—*you* know the way you do!"

"You mean—day-dreaming?"

"Oh, no—thinking!"

"But thinking about *what*?"

"Anything."

He laughed a third time—but this time, happening to glance upward towards his mother's face, he was appalled at the effect his laughter seemed to have upon her. Her mouth had opened in an expression of horror. . . . This was too bad! Unfortunate! He had known it would cause pain, of course—but he hadn't expected it to be quite so bad as this. Perhaps perhaps if he just gave them a tiny gleaming hint—?

"About the snow," he said.

"What on earth!" This was his father's voice. The brown slippers came a step nearer on the hearth-rug.

"But my dear, what do you mean!" This was his mother's voice.

The doctor merely stared.

"Just *snow,* that's all. I like to think about it."

"Tell us about it, my boy."

"But that's all it is. There's nothing to tell. *You* know what snow is?"

This he said almost angrily, for he felt that they were trying to corner him. He turned sideways so as no longer to face the doctor, and the better to see the inch of blackness between the window-sill and the lowered curtain,—the cold inch of beckoning and delicious night. At once he felt better, more assured.

"Mother—can I go to bed, now, please? I've got a headache."

"But I thought you said—"

"It's just come. It's all these questions—! Can I, mother?"

"You can go as soon as the doctor has finished."

"Don't you think this thing ought to be gone into thoroughly, and *now?*" This was Father's voice. The brown slippers again came a step nearer, the voice was the well-known "punishment" voice, resonant and cruel.

"Oh, what's the use, Norman—"

Quite suddenly, everyone was silent. And without precisely facing them, nevertheless he was aware that all three of them were watching him with an extraordinary intensity—staring hard at him—as if he had done something monstrous, or was himself some kind of monster. He could hear the soft irregular flutter of the flames; the cluck-click-cluck-click of the clock; far and faint, two sudden spurts of laughter from the kitchen, as quickly cut off as begun; a murmur of water in the pipes; and then, the silence seemed to deepen, to spread out, to become world-long and worldwide, to become timeless and shapeless, and to center inevitably and rightly, with a slow and sleepy but enormous concentration of all power, on the beginning of a new sound. What this new sound was going to be, he knew perfectly well. It might begin with a hiss, but it would end with a roar—there was no time to lose—he must escape. It mustn't happen here—

Without another word, he turned and ran up the stairs.

IV

Not a moment too soon. The darkness was coming in long white waves. A prolonged sibilance filled the night—a great seamless seethe of wild influence went abruptly across it—a cold low humming shook the windows. He shut the door and flung off his clothes in the dark. The bare black floor was like a little raft tossed in waves of snow, almost overwhelmed, washed under whitely, up again, smothered in curled billows of feather. The snow was laughing: it spoke from all sides at once: it pressed closer to him as he ran and jumped exulting into his bed.

"Listen to us!" it said. "Listen! We have come to tell you the story we told you about. You remember? Lie down. Shut your eyes, now—you will no longer see much—in this white darkness who could see, or want to see? We will take the place of everything. . . . Listen—"

A beautiful varying dance of snow began at the front of the room, came forward and then retreated, flattened out toward the floor, then rose fountain-like to the ceiling, swayed, recruited itself from a new stream of flakes which poured laughing in through the humming window, advanced again, lifted long white arms. It said peace, it said remoteness, it said cold —it said—

But then a gash of horrible light fell brutally across the room from the opening door—the snow drew back hissing— something alien had come into the room—something hostile. This thing rushed at him, clutched at him, shook him—and he was not merely horrified, he was filled with such a loathing as he had never known. What was this? this cruel disturbance? this act of anger and hate? It was as if he had to reach

up a hand toward another world for any understanding of it,
—an effort of which he was only barely capable. But of that
other world he still remembered just enough to know the
exorcising words. They tore themselves from his other life
suddenly—

"Mother! Mother! Go away! I hate you!"

And with that effort, everything was solved, everything became all right: the seamless hiss advanced once more, the
long white wavering lines rose and fell like enormous whispering sea-waves, the whisper becoming louder, the laughter
more numerous.

"Listen!" it said. "We'll tell you the last, the most beautiful
and secret story—shut your eyes—it is a very small story—a
story that gets smaller and smaller—it comes inward instead
of opening like a flower—it is a flower becoming a seed—a little cold seed—do you hear? we are leaning closer to you—"

The hiss was now becoming a roar—the whole world was
a vast moving screen of snow—but even now it said peace, it
said remoteness, it said cold, it said sleep.

ERSKINE CALDWELL

Country Full of Swedes

THERE I was, standing in the middle of the chamber, trembling like I was coming down with the flu, and still not knowing what god-awful something had happened. In all my days in the Back Kingdom, I never heard such noises so early in the forenoon.

It was about half an hour after sun-rise, and a gun went off like a coffer-dam breaking up under ice at twenty below, and I'd swear it sounded like it wasn't any farther away than my feet are from my head. That gun shot off, pitching me six-seven inches off the bed, and, before I could come down out of the air, there was another roar like somebody coughing through a megaphone, with a two weeks' cold, right in my ear. God-helping, I hope I never get waked up like that again until I can get myself home to the Back Kingdom where I rightfully belong to stay.

I must have stood there ten-fifteen minutes shivering in my night-shirt, my heart pounding inside of me like a ramrod working on a plugged-up bore, and listening for that gun again, if it was going to shoot some more. A man never knows what's going to happen next in the State of Maine; that's why I wish sometimes I'd never left the Back Kingdom to begin with. I was making sixty a month, with the best of bed and board, back there in the intervale; but like a God damn fool I had to jerk loose and come down here near the Bay. I'm going back where I came from, God-helping; I've never had a purely calm and peaceful day since I got here three-four years ago. This is the damnedest country for the unexpected raising of all kinds of unlooked-for hell a man is apt to run across in a lifetime of traveling. If a man's born and raised in

the Back Kingdom, he ought to stay there where he belongs;
that's what I'd done if I'd had the sense to stay out of this
down-country near the Bay, where you don't ever know, God-
helping, what's going to happen next, where, or when.

But there I was, standing in the middle of the upstairs
chamber, shaking like a rag weed in an August windstorm,
and not knowing what minute, maybe right at me, that gun
was going to shoot off again, for all I knew. Just then, though,
I heard Jim and Mrs. Frost trip-trapping around downstairs
in their bare feet. Even if I didn't know what god-awful
something had happened, I knew things around the place
weren't calm and peaceful, like they generally were of a Sunday morning in May, because it took a stiff mixture of heaven
and hell to get Jim and Mrs. Frost up and out of a warm bed
before six of a forenoon, any of the days of the week.

I ran to the window and stuck my head out as far as I
could get it, to hear what the trouble was. Everything out
there was as quiet and peaceful as midnight on a backroad in
middlemost winter. But I knew something was up, because
Jim and Mrs. Frost didn't make a practice of getting up and
out of a warm bed that time of forenoon in the chillish May-
time.

There wasn't any sense in me standing there in the cold air
shivering in my night-shirt, so I put on my clothes, whistling
all the time through my teeth to drive away the chill, and trying to figure out what God damn fool was around so early
shooting off a gun of a Sunday morning. Just then I heard the
downstairs door open, and up the steps, two at a time, came
Jim in his breeches and his shirt-tail flying out behind him.

He wasn't long in coming up the stairs, for a man sixty-
seven, but before he reached the door to my room, that gun
went off again: BOOM! Just like that; and the echo came rolling back through the open window from the hills: *Boom!*
Boom! Like fireworks going off with your eyes shut. Jim had
busted through the door already, but when he heard that
Boom! sound he sort of spun around, like a cock-eyed
weathervane, five-six times, and ran out the door again like

he had been shot in the hind parts with a moose gun. That *Boom!* so early in the forenoon was enough to scare the day-lights out of any man, and Jim wasn't any different from me or anybody else in the town of East Joloppi. He just turned around and jumped through the door to the first tread on the stairway like his mind was made up to go somewhere else in a hurry, and no fooling around at the start.

I'd been hired to Jim and Mrs. Frost for all of three-four years, and I was near about as much of a Frost, excepting name, as Jim himself was. Jim and me got along first-rate to-gether, doing chores and haying and farm work in general, be-cause neither one of us was ever trying to make the other do more of the work. We were hitched to make a fine team, and I never had a kick coming, and Jim said he didn't either. Jim had the name of Frost, to be sure, but I wouldn't ever hold that against a man.

The echo of that gun-shot was still rolling around in the hills and coming in through the window, when all at once that god-awful cough-like whoop through a megaphone sounded again right there in the room and everywhere else, like it might have been, in the whole town of East Joloppi. The man or beast or whatever animal he was who hollered like that ought to be locked up to keep him from scaring all the women and children to death, and it wasn't any stomach-comforting sound for a grown man who's used to the peaceful calm of the Back Kingdom all his life to hear so early of a Sunday forenoon, either.

I jumped to the door where Jim, just a minute before, leaped through. He didn't stop till he got clear to the bottom of the stairs. He stood there, looking up at me like a wild-eyed cow moose surprised in the sheriff's corn field.

"Who fired that god-awful shot, Jim?" I yelled at him, leap-ing down the stairs quicker than a man of my years ought to let himself do.

"Good God!" Jim said, his voice hoarse, and falling all to pieces like a stump of punk-wood. "The Swedes! The Swedes are shooting, Stan!"

"What Swedes, Jim—those Swedes who own the farm and buildings across the road over there?" I said, trying to find the buttonholes in my shirt. "Have they come back here to live on that farm?"

"Good God, yes!" he said, his voice croaking deep down in his throat, like he had swallowed too much water. "The Swedes are all over the place. They're everywhere you can see, there's that many of them."

"What's their name, Jim?" I asked him. "You and Mrs. Frost never told me what their name is."

"Good God, I don't know. I never heard them called anything but Swedes, and that's what it is, I guess. It ought to be that, if it ain't."

I ran across the hall to look out a window, but it was on the wrong side of the house, and I couldn't see a thing. Mrs. Frost was stepping around in the downstairs chamber, locking things up in the drawers and closet and forgetting where she was hiding the keys. I could see her through the open door, and she was more scared-looking than Jim was. She was so scared of the Swedes she didn't know what she was doing, none of the time.

"What made those Swedes come back for, Jim?" I said to him. "I thought you said they were gone for good this time."

"Good God, Stan," he said, "I don't know what they came back for. I guess hard times are bringing everybody back to the land, and the Swedes are always in the front rush of everything. I don't know what brought them back, but they're all over the place, shooting and yelling and raising hell. There are thirty-forty of them, looks like to me, counting everything with heads."

"What are they doing now, Jim, except yelling and shooting?"

"Good God," Jim said, looking behind him to see what Mrs. Frost was doing with his things in the downstairs chamber. "I don't know what they're not doing. But I can hear them, Stan! You hurry out right now and lock up all the tools in the barn and bring in the cows and tie them up in the stalls. I've got to hurry out now and bring in all of those new cedar fence posts across the front of the yard before they start pulling them up and carrying them off. Good God, Stan, the Swedes are everywhere you look outdoors. We've got to make haste, Stan!"

Jim ran to the side door and out the back of the house, but I took my time about going. I wasn't scared of the Swedes, like Jim and Mrs. Frost were, and I didn't aim to have Jim putting me to doing tasks and chores, or anything else, before breakfast and the proper time. I wasn't any more scared of the Swedes than I was of the Finns and Portuguese, anyway. It's a god-awful shame for Americans to let Swedes and Finns and Portuguese scare the daylights out of them. God-helping, they are no different than us, and you never see a Finn or a Swede scared of an American. But people like Jim and Mrs. Frost are scared to death of Swedes and other people from the old countries; Jim and Mrs. Frost and people like that never stop to think that all of us Americans came over from the old countries, one time or another, to begin with.

But there wasn't any sense in trying to argue with Jim and Mrs. Frost right then, when the Swedes, like a fired nest of yellow-headed bumble bees, were swarming all over the place as far as the eye could see, and when Mrs. Frost was scared to death that they were coming into the house and carry out all of her and Jim's furniture and household goods. So while Mrs. Frost was tying her and Jim's shoes in pillow cases and putting them out of sight in closets and behind beds, I went to the kitchen window and looked out to see what was going on around that tall yellow house across the road.

Jim and Mrs. Frost both were right about there being Swedes all over the place. God-helping, there were Swedes all over the country, near about all over the whole town of East Joloppi, for what I could see out the window. They were as thick around the barn and pump and the woodpile as if they had been a nest of yellow-headed bumble bees strewn over the countryside. There were Swedes everywhere a man could see, and the ones that couldn't be seen, could be heard yelling their heads off inside the yellow clapboarded house across the road. There wasn't any mistake about their being Swedes there, either; because I've never yet seen a man who mistakes a Swede or a Finn for an American. Once you see a Finn or a Swede you know, God-helping, that he is a Swede or a Finn, and not a Portugee or an American.

There was a Swede everywhere a man could look. Some of them were little Swedes, and women Swedes, to be sure; but little Swedes, in the end, and women Swedes too, near about, grow up as big as any of them. When you come right down to it, there's no sense in counting out the little Swedes and the women Swedes.

Out in the road in front of their house were seven-eight autos and trucks loaded down with furniture and household goods. All around, everything was Swedes. The Swedes were yelling and shouting at one another, the little Swedes and the women Swedes just as loud as the big Swedes, and it looked like none of them knew what all the shouting and yelling was for, and when they found out, they didn't give a damn about it. That was because all of them were Swedes. It didn't make any difference what a Swede was yelling about; just as long as he had leave to open his mouth, he was tickled to death about it.

I have never seen the like of so much yelling and shouting anywhere else before; but down here in the State of Maine, in the down-country on the Bay, there's no sense in being taken-back at the sights to be seen, because anything on God's green earth is likely and liable to happen between day and night, and the other way around, too.

Now, you take the Finns; there's any God's number of them in the woods, where you least expect to see them, logging and such. When a Finn crew breaks a woods camp, it looks like there's a Finn for every tree in the whole State, but you don't see them going around making the noise that

Swedes do, with all their yelling and shouting and shooting off guns. Finns are quiet about their hell-raising. The Portuguese are quiet, too; you see them tramping around, minding their own business, and working hard on the river dam or something, but you never hear them shouting and yelling and shooting off guns at five-six of a Sunday morning. There's no known likeness to the noise that a houseful of Swedes can make when they get to yelling and shouting at one another early in the forenoon.

I was standing there all that time, looking out the window at the Swedes across the road, when Jim came into the kitchen with an armful of wood and threw it into the woodbox behind the range.

"Good God, Stan," Jim said, "the Swedes are everywhere you can look out-doors. They're not going to get that armful of wood, anyway, though."

Mrs. Frost came to the door and stood looking like she didn't know it was her business to cook breakfast for Jim and me. I made a fire in the range and put on a pan of water to boil for the coffee. Jim kept running to the window to look out, and there wasn't much use in expecting Mrs. Frost to start cooking unless somebody set her to it, in the shape she was in, with all the Swedes around the place. She was so up-set, it was a downright pity to look at her. But Jim and me had to eat, and I went and took her by the arm and brought her to the range and left her standing there so close she would get burned if she didn't stir around and make breakfast.

"Good God, Stan," Jim said, "those Swedes are into everything. They're in the barn, and in the pasture running the cows, and I don't know what else they've been into since I looked last. They'll take the tools and the horses and cows, and the cedar posts, too, if we don't get out there and put everything under lock and key."

"Now, hold on, Jim," I said, looking out the window. "Them you see are little Swedes out there, and they're not going to make off with anything of yours and Mrs. Frost's.

The big Swedes are busy carrying in furniture and household goods. Those Swedes aren't going to tamper with anything of yours and Mrs. Frost's. They're people just like us. They don't go around stealing everything in sight. Now, let's just sit here by the window and watch them while Mrs. Frost is getting breakfast ready."

"Good God, Stan, they're Swedes," Jim said, "and they're moving into the house across the road. I've got to put everything under lock and key before——"

"Hold on, Jim," I told him. "It's their house they're moving into. God-helping, they're not moving into your and Jim's house, are they, Mrs. Frost?"

"Jim," Mrs. Frost said, shaking her finger at him and looking at me wild-eyed and sort of flustered-like, "Jim, don't you sit there and let Stanley stop you from saving the stock and tools. Stanley doesn't know the Swedes like we do. Stanley came down here from the Back Kingdom, and he doesn't know anything about Swedes."

Mrs. Frost was partly right, because I've never seen the things in my whole life that I've seen down here near the Bay; but there wasn't any sense in Americans like Jim and Mrs. Frost being scared of Swedes. I've seen enough Finns and Portuguese in my time in the Back Kingdom, up in the intervale, to know that Americans are no different from the others.

"Now, you hold on a while, Jim," I said. "Swedes are no different than Finns. Finns don't go around stealing another man's stock and tools. Up in the Back Kingdom the Finns are the finest kind of neighbors."

"That may be so up in the Back Kingdom, Stan," Jim said, "but Swedes down here near the Bay are nothing like anything that's ever been before or since. Those Swedes over there across the road work in a pulp mill over to Waterville three-four years, and when they've got enough money saved up, or when they lose it all, as the case may be, they all move back here to East Joloppi on this farm of theirs for two-three years at a time. That's what they do. And they've been doing it for the past thirty-forty years, ever since I can remember, and they haven't changed none in all that time. I can recall the first time they came to East Joloppi; they built that house across the road then, and if you've ever seen a sight like Swedes building a house in a hurry, you haven't got much else to live for. Why! Stan, those Swedes built that house in four-five days—just like that! I've never seen the equal to it. Of course now, Stan, it's the damnedest-looking house a man ever saw, because it's not a farmhouse, and it's not a city house, and it's no kind of a house an American would erect. Why! those Swedes threw that house together in four-five days—just like that! But whoever saw a house like that before, with three storeys to it, and only six rooms in the whole building! And painted yellow, too; Good God, Stan, white is the only color to paint a house, and those Swedes went and painted it yellow. Then on top of that, they went and painted the barn red. And of all of the shouting and yelling, at all times of the day and night, a man never saw or heard before. Those Swedes acted like they were purely crazy for the whole of four-five days, and they were, and they still are. But what gets me is the painting of it yellow, and the making of it three storeys high, with only six rooms in the whole building. Nobody but Swedes would go and do a thing like that; an American would have built a farmhouse, here in the country, resting square on the ground, with one storey, maybe a storey and a half, and then painted it lead-white. But Good God, Stan, those fool Swedes had to put up three storeys, to hold six rooms, and then went and painted the building yellow."

"Swedes are a little queer, sometimes," I said. "But Finns and Portuguese are too, Jim. And Americans sometimes——"

"A little queer!" Jim said. "Why! Good God, Stan, the Swedes are the queerest people on the earth, if that's the right word for them. You don't know Swedes, Stan. This is the first time you've ever seen those Swedes across the road, and that's why you don't know what they're like after being shut up in a pulpwood mill over to Waterville for four-five

years. They're purely wild, I tell you, Stan. They don't stop
for anything they set their heads on. If you was to walk out
there now and tell them to move their autos and trucks off
of the town road so the travelers could get past without
having to drive through the brush, they'd tear you apart,
they're that wild, after being shut up in the pulp mill over to
Waterville, these three-four, maybe four-five years."

"Finns get that way, too," I tried to tell Jim. "After Finns
have been shut up in a woods camp all winter, they make a
lot of noise when they get out. Everybody who has to stay
close to the job for three-four years likes to act free when he
gets out from under the job. Now, Jim, you take the Portuguese——"

"Don't you sit there, Jim, and let Stanley keep you from
putting the tools away," Mrs. Frost said. "Stanley doesn't
know the Swedes like we do. He's lived up in the Back
Kingdom most of his life, tucked away in the intervale, and
he's never seen Swedes——"

"Good God, Stan," Jim said, standing up, he was that
nervous and up-set, "the Swedes are over-running the whole
country. I'll bet there are more Swedes in the town of East
Joloppi than there are in the rest of the country. Everybody
knows there's more Swedes in the State of Maine than there
are in the old country. Why! Jim, they take to this State like
potato bugs take to——"

"Don't you sit there and let Stanley keep you back, Jim,"
Mrs. Frost put in again. "Stanley doesn't know the Swedes
like we do. Stanley's lived up there in the Back Kingdom
most of his life."

Just then one of the big Swedes started yelling at some
of the little Swedes and women Swedes. I'll swear, those big
Swedes sounded like a pastureful of hoarse bulls, near the
end of May, mad about the black-flies. God-helping, they
yelled like they were fixing to kill all the little Swedes and
women Swedes they could get their hands on. It didn't
amount to anything, though; because the little Swedes and
the women Swedes yelled right back at them just like they

had been big Swedes too. The little Swedes and women Swedes couldn't yell hoarse bull bass, but it was close enough to it to make a man who's lived most of his life up in the Back Kingdom, in the intervale, think that the whole town of East Joloppi was full of big Swedes.

Jim was all for getting out after the tools and stock right away, but I pulled him back to the table. I wasn't going to let Jim and Mrs. Frost set me to doing tasks and chores before breakfast and the regular time. Forty dollars a month isn't much to pay a man for ten-eleven hours' work a day, including Sundays, when the stock has to be attended to like any other day, and I set myself that I wasn't going to work twelve-thirteen hours a day for them, even if I was practically one of the Frosts myself, except in name, by that time.

"Now, hold on a while, Jim," I said. "Let's just sit here by the window and watch them carry their furniture and household goods inside while Mrs. Frost's getting the cooking ready to eat. If they start taking off any of your and Mrs. Frost's things, we can see them just as good from here by the window as we could out there in the yard and road."

"Now, Jim, I'm telling you," Mrs. Frost said, shaking all over, and not even trying to cook us a meal, "don't you sit there and let Stanley keep you from saving the stock and tools. Stanley doesn't know the Swedes like we do. He thinks they're like everybody else."

Jim wasn't for staying in the house when all of his tools were lying around in the yard, and while his cows were in the pasture unprotected, but he saw how it would be better to wait where we could hurry up Mrs. Frost with the cooking, if we were ever going to eat breakfast that forenoon. She was so excited and nervous about the Swedes moving back to East Joloppi from the pulp mill in Waterville that she hadn't got the beans and brown bread fully heated from the night before, and we had to sit and eat them cold.

We were sitting there by the window eating the cold beans and brown bread, and watching the Swedes, when two of the little Swedes started running across Jim and Mrs. Frost's lawn. They were chasing one of their big yellow tom cats they had brought with them from Waterville. The yellow tom was as large as an eight-months collie puppy, and he ran like he was on fire and didn't know how to put it out. His great bushy tail stuck straight up in the air behind him, like a flag, and he was leaping over the lawn like a devilish calf, new-born.

Jim and Mrs. Frost saw the little Swedes and the big yellow tom cat at the same time I did.

"Good God," Jim shouted, raising himself part out of the chair. "Here they come now!"

"Hold on now, Jim," I said, pulling him back to the table. "They're only chasing one of their tom cats. They're not after taking anything that belongs to you and Mrs. Frost. Let's just sit here and finish eating the beans, and watch them out the window."

"My crown in heaven!" Mrs. Frost cried out, running to the window, and looking through. "Those Swedes are going to kill every plant on the place. They'll dig up all the bulbs and pull up all the vines in the flower bed."

"Now you just sit and calm yourself, Mrs. Frost," I told her. "Those little Swedes are just chasing a tom cat. They're not after doing hurt to your flowers."

The big Swedes were unloading the autos and trucks and carrying the furniture and household goods into their three storey, yellow clapboarded house. None of them was paying any attention to the little Swedes chasing the yellow tom over Jim and Mrs. Frost's lawn.

Just then the kitchen door burst open, and the two little Swedes stood there looking at us, panting and blowing their heads off.

Mrs. Frost took one look at them, and then she let out a yell, but the kids didn't notice her at all.

"Hey," one of them shouted, "come out here and help us get the cat. He climbed up in one of your trees."

By that time, Mrs. Frost was all for slamming the door in their faces, but I pushed in front of her and went out into the yard with them. Jim came right behind me, after he had finished calming Mrs. Frost, and telling her we wouldn't let the Swedes come and carry out her furniture and household goods.

The yellow tom was all the way up in one of Jim's young maple shade trees. The maple wasn't strong enough to support even the smallest of the little Swedes, if he should take it into his head to climb to the top after the cat, and neither Jim nor me was hurting ourselves trying to think of a way to get the feline down. We were all for letting the cat stay where he was, till he got ready to come down of his own free will, but the little Swedes couldn't wait for anything. They wanted the tom right away, then and there, and no wasting of time in getting him.

"You boys go home and wait for the cat to come down," Jim told them. "There's no way to make him come down now, till he gets ready to come down of his own mind."

But no, those two boys were little Swedes. They weren't thinking of going back home till they got the yellow tom down from the maple. One of them ran to the tree, before Jim or me could head him off, and started shinnying up it like a pop-eyed squirrel. In no time, it seemed to me like, he was up amongst the limbs jumping up there from one limb to another like he had been brought up in just such a tree.

"Good Cod, Stan," Jim said, "can't you keep them out of the trees?"

There was no answer for that, and Jim knew there wasn't. There's no way of stopping a Swede from doing what he has set his head on doing.

The boy got almost to the top branch, where the yellow tom was clinging and spitting, when the tree began to bend towards the house. I knew what was coming, if something wasn't done about it pretty quick, and so did Jim. Jim saw his young maple shade tree begin to bend, and he almost had a fit looking at it. He ran to the lumber stack and came back dragging two lengths of two-by-fours. He got them set up against the tree before it had time to do any splitting, and then we stood there, like two damn fools, shoring up the tree and yelling at the little Swede to come down out of there before we broke his neck for being up in it.

The big Swedes across the road heard the fuss we were making, and they came running out of that three storey, six room house like it had been on fire inside.

"Good God, Stan," Jim shouted at me, "here comes the Swedes!"

"Don't turn and run off, Jim," I cautioned him, yanking him back by his coat-tail. "They're not wild beasts; we're not scared of them. Hold on where you are, Jim."

I could see Mrs. Frost's head almost breaking through the window-glass in the kitchen. She was all for coming out and driving the Swedes off her lawn and out of her flowers, but she was too scared to unlock the kitchen door and open it.

Jim was getting ready to run again, when he saw the Swedes coming toward us like a nest of yellow-headed bumble bees, but I wasn't scared of them, and I held on to Jim's coat-tail and told him I wasn't. Jim and me were shoring up the young maple, and I knew if one of us let go, the tree would bend to the ground away and split wide open right up the middle. There was no sense in ruining a young maple shade tree like that, and I told Jim there wasn't.

"Hey," one of the big Swedes shouted at the little Swede up in the top of the maple, "come down out of that tree and go home to your mother."

"Ah, to hell with the old lady," the little Swede shouted down. "I'm getting the cat by the tail."

The big Swede looked at Jim and me. Jim was almost ready to run again by that time, but I wasn't, and I held him and told him I wasn't. There was no sense in letting the Swedes scare the day-lights out of us.

"What in the hell can you do with kids when they get that age?" he asked Jim and me.

Jim was all for telling him to make the boy come down out of the maple before it bent over and split wide open, but

I knew there was no sense in trying to make him come down out of there until he got good and ready to come, or else got the yellow tom by the tail.

Just then another big Swede came running out of that three storey, six room house across the road, holding a double-bladed ax out in front of him, like it was a red-hot poker, and yelling for all he was worth at the other Swedes.

"Good God, Stan," Jim said, "don't let those Swedes cut down my young maple!"

I had lots better sense than to try to make the Swedes stop doing what they had set their heads on doing. A man would be purely a fool to try to stop it from raining from above when it got ready to, even if he was trying to get his corn crop planted.

I looked around again, and there was Mrs. Frost all but popping through the window-glass. I could see what she was thinking, but I couldn't hear a word she was saying. It was good and plenty though, whatever it was.

"Come down out of that tree!" the Swede yelled at the boy up in Jim's maple.

Instead of starting to climb down, the little Swede reached up for the big yellow tom cat's tail. The tom reached out a big fat paw and harried the boy five-six times, just like that, quicker than the eye could follow. The kid let out a yell and a shout that must have been heard all the way to the other side of town, sounding like a whole houseful of Swedes up in the maple.

The big Swede covered the distance to the tree in one stride, pushing everything behind him.

"Good God, Stan," Jim shouted at me, "we've got to do something!"

There wasn't anything a man could do, unless he was either a Swede himself, or a man of prayer. Americans like Jim and me had no business getting in a Swede's way, especially when he was swinging a big double-bladed ax, and he just out of a pulp mill after being shut up making paper four-five years.

The big Swede grabbed the ax and let go at the trunk of the maple with it. There was no stopping him then, because he had the ax going, and it was whipping around his shoulders like a cow's tail in a swarm of black-flies. The little maple shook all over every time the ax-blade struck it, like wind blowing a corn stalk, and then it began to bend on the other side from Jim and me where we were shoring it up with the two-by-fours. Chips as big as dinner plates were flying across the lawn and pelting the house like a gang of boys stoning telephone insulators. One of those big dinner-plate chips crashed through the window where Mrs. Frost was, about that time. Both Jim and me thought at first she had fallen through the window, but when we looked again, we could see that she was still on the inside, and madder than ever at the Swedes.

The two-by-fours weren't any good any longer, because it was too late to get the other side of the maple in time to keep it from bending in that direction. The Swede with the double-bladed ax took one more swing, and the tree began to bend towards the ground.

The tree came down, the little Swede came down, and the big yellow tom came down on top of everything, holding for all he was worth to the top of the little Swede's head. Long before the tree and the boy struck the ground, the big yellow tom had sprung what looked like thirty feet, and landed in the middle of Mrs. Frost's flowers and bulbs. The little Swede let out a yell and a whoop when he hit the ground that brought out six-seven more Swedes from that three storey, six room house, piling out into the road like it was the first time they had ever heard a kid bawl. The women Swedes and the little Swedes and the big Swedes piled out on Jim and Mrs. Frost's front lawn like they had been dropped out of a dump-truck and didn't know which was straight up from straight down.

I thought Mrs. Frost was going to have a fit right then and there in the kitchen window. When she saw that swarm of Swedes coming across her lawn, and the big yellow tom cat in her flower bed among the tender plants and bulbs, digging up the things she had planted, and the Swedes with their No. 12 heels squashing the green shoots she had been nursing along—well, I guess she just sort of caved in, and fell out of sight for the time being. I didn't have time to run to see what was wrong with her, because Jim and me had to tear out behind the tom and the Swedes to try to save as much as we could.

"Good God, Stan," Jim shouted at me, "go run in the house and ring up all the neighbors on the line, and tell them to hurry over here and help us before the Swedes wreck my farm and buildings. There's no telling what they'll do next. They'll be setting fire to the house and barn the next thing, maybe. Hurry, Stan!"

I didn't have time to waste talking to the neighbors on the telephone line. I was right behind Jim and the Swedes to see what they were going to do next.

"I pay you good pay, Stan," Jim said, "and I want my money's worth. Now, you go ring up the neighbors and tell them to hurry."

The big yellow tom made one more spring when he hit the flower bed, and that leap landed him over the stone-wall. He struck out for the deep woods with every Swede on the place behind him. When Jim and me got to the stone-wall, I pulled up short and held Jim back.

"Well, Jim," I said, "if you want me to, I'll go down in the woods and raise hell with every Swede on the place for cutting down your young maple and tearing up Mrs. Frost's flower-bed."

We turned around and there was Mrs. Frost, right behind us. There was no knowing how she got there so quick after the Swedes had left for the woods.

"My crown in heaven," Mrs. Frost said, running up to Jim and holding on to him. "Jim, don't let Stanley make the Swedes mad. This is the only place we have got to live in, and they'll be here a year now this time, maybe two-three, if the hard times don't get better soon."

"That's right, Stan," he said. "You don't know the Swedes like we do. You would have to be a Swede yourself to know what to tell them. Don't go over there doing anything like that."

"God-helping, Jim," I said, "you and Mrs. Frost aren't scared of the Swedes, are you?"

"Good God, no," he said, his eyes popping out; "but don't go making them mad."

You Were Perfectly Fine

THE PALE young man eased himself carefully into the low chair, and rolled his head to the side, so that the cool chintz comforted his cheek and temple.

"Oh, dear," he said. "Oh, dear, oh, dear, oh, dear. Oh."

The clear-eyed girl, sitting light and erect on the couch, smiled brightly at him.

"Not feeling so well today?" she said.

"Oh, I'm great," he said. "Corking, I am. Know what time I got up? Four o'clock this afternoon, sharp. I kept trying to make it, and every time I took my head off the pillow, it would roll under the bed. This isn't my head I've got on now. I think this is something that used to belong to Walt Whitman. Oh, dear, oh, dear, oh, dear."

"Do you think maybe a drink would make you feel better?" she said.

"The hair of the mastiff that bit me?" he said. "Oh, no, thank you. Please never speak of anything like that again. I'm through. I'm all, all through. Look at that hand; steady as a humming-bird. Tell me, was I very terrible last night?"

"Oh, goodness," she said, "everybody was feeling pretty high. You were all right."

"Yeah," he said. "I must have been dandy. Is everybody sore at me?"

"Good heavens, no," she said. "Everyone thought you were terribly funny. Of course, Jim Pierson was a little stuffy, there for a minute at dinner. But people sort of held him back in his chair, and got him calmed down. I don't think anybody at the other tables noticed it at all. Hardly anybody."

"He was going to sock me?" he said. "Oh, Lord. What did I do to him?"

"Why, you didn't do a thing," she said. "You were perfectly fine. But you know how silly Jim gets, when he thinks anybody is making too much fuss over Elinor."

"Was I making a pass at Elinor?" he said. "Did I do that?"

"Of course you didn't," she said. "You were only fooling, that's all. She thought you were awfully amusing. She was having a marvelous time. She only got a little tiny bit annoyed just once, when you poured the clam-juice down her back."

"My God," he said. "Clam-juice down that back. And every vertebra a little Cabot. Dear God. What'll I ever do?"

"Oh, she'll be all right," she said. "Just send her some flowers, or something. Don't worry about it. It isn't anything."

"No, I won't worry," he said. "I haven't got a care in the world. I'm sitting pretty. Oh, dear, oh, dear. Did I do any other fascinating tricks at dinner?"

"You were fine," she said. "Don't be so foolish about it. Everybody was crazy about you. The maître d'hôtel was a little worried because you wouldn't stop singing, but he really didn't mind. All he said was, he was afraid they'd close the place again, if there was so much noise. But he didn't care a bit, himself. I think he loved seeing you have such a good time. Oh, you were just singing away, there, for about an hour. It wasn't so terribly loud, at all."

"So I sang," he said. "That must have been a treat. I sang."

"Don't you remember?" she said. "You just sang one song after another. Everybody in the place was listening. They loved it. Only you kept insisting that you wanted to sing some song about some kind of fusiliers or other, and everybody kept shushing you, and you'd keep trying to start it again. You were wonderful. We were all trying to make you stop singing for a minute, and eat something, but you wouldn't hear of it. My, you were funny."

"Didn't I eat any dinner?" he said.

"Oh, not a thing," she said. "Every time the waiter would

offer you something, you'd give it right back to him, because you said that he was your long-lost brother, changed in the cradle by a gypsy band, and that anything you had was his. You had him simply roaring at you."

"I bet I did," he said. "I bet I was comical. Society's Pet, I must have been. And what happened then, after my overwhelming success with the waiter?"

"Why, nothing much," she said. "You took a sort of dislike to some old man with white hair, sitting across the room, because you didn't like his necktie and you wanted to tell him about it. But we got you out, before he got really mad."

"Oh, we got out," he said. "Did I walk?"

"Walk! Of course you did," she said. "You were absolutely all right. There was that nasty stretch of ice on the sidewalk, and you did sit down awfully hard, you poor dear. But good heavens, that might have happened to anybody."

"Oh, sure," he said. "Louisa Alcott or anybody. So I fell down on the sidewalk. That would explain what's the matter with my— Yes. I see. And then what, if you don't mind?"

"Ah, now, Peter!" she said. "You can't sit there and say you don't remember what happened after that! I did think that maybe you were just a little tight at dinner—oh, you were perfectly all right, and all that, but I did know you were feeling pretty gay. But you were so serious, from the time you fell down—I never knew you to be that way. Don't you know, how you told me I had never seen your real self before? Oh, Peter, I just couldn't bear it, if you didn't remember that lovely long ride we took together in the taxi! Please, you do remember that, don't you? I think it would simply kill me, if you didn't."

"Oh, yes," he said. "Riding in the taxi. Oh, yes, sure. Pretty long ride, hmm?"

"Round and round and round the park," she said. "Oh, and the trees were shining so in the moonlight. And you said you never knew before that you really had a soul."

"Yes," he said. "I said that. That was me."

"You said such lovely, lovely things," she said. "And I'd

never known, all this time, how you had been feeling about me, and I'd never dared to let you see how I felt about you. And then last night—oh, Peter dear, I think that taxi ride was the most important thing that ever happened to us in our lives."

"Yes," he said. "I guess it must have been."

"And we're going to be so happy," she said. "Oh, I just want to tell everybody! But I don't know—I think maybe it would be sweeter to keep it all to ourselves."

"I think it would be," he said.

"Isn't it lovely?" she said.

"Yes," he said. "Great."

"Lovely!" she said.

"Look here," he said, "do you mind if I have a drink? I mean, just medicinally, you know. I'm off the stuff for life, so help me. But I think I feel a collapse coming on."

"Oh, I think it would do you good," she said. "You poor boy, it's a shame you feel so awful. I'll go make you a whisky and soda."

"Honestly," he said, "I don't see how you could ever want to speak to me again, after I made such a fool of myself, last night. I think I'd better go join a monastery in Tibet."

"You crazy idiot!" she said. "As if I could ever let you go away now! Stop talking like that. You were perfectly fine."

She jumped up from the couch, kissed him quickly on the forehead, and ran out of the room.

The pale young man looked after her and shook his head long and slowly, then dropped it in his damp and trembling hands.

"Oh, dear," he said. "Oh, dear, oh, dear, oh, dear."

JAMES THURBER

The Night the Ghost Got In

THE GHOST that got into our house on the night of November 17, 1915, raised such a hullabaloo of misunderstandings that I am sorry I didn't just let it keep on walking, and go to bed. Its advent caused my mother to throw a shoe through a window of the house next door and ended up with my grandfather shooting a patrolman. I am sorry, therefore, that I ever paid any attention to the footsteps.

They began about a quarter past one o'clock in the morning, a rhythmic, quick-cadenced walking around the dining-room table. My mother was asleep in one room upstairs, my brother Herman in another; grandfather was in the attic, in the old walnut bed, which, as you will remember, once fell on my father. I had just stepped out of the bathtub and was busily rubbing myself with a towel when I heard the steps. They were the steps of a man walking rapidly around the dining-room table downstairs. The light from the bathroom shone down the back steps, which dropped directly into the dining-room; I could see the faint shine of plates on the plate-rail; I couldn't see the table. The steps kept going round and round the table; at regular intervals a board creaked, when it was trod upon. I supposed at first that it was my father or my brother Roy, who had gone to Indianapolis but were expected home at any time. I suspected next that it was a burglar. It did not enter my mind until later that it was a ghost.

After the walking had gone on for perhaps three minutes, I tiptoed to Herman's room. "Psst!" I hissed, in the dark, shaking him. "Awp," he said, in the low, hopeless tone of a despondent beagle—he always half suspected that something would "get him" in the night. I told him who I was. "There's

183

something downstairs!" I said. He got up and followed me to the head of the back staircase. We listened together. There was no sound. The steps had ceased. Herman looked at me in some alarm: I had only the bath towel around my waist. He wanted to go back to bed, but I gripped his arm. "There's something down there!" I said. Instantly the steps began again, circled the dining-room table like a man running, and started up the stairs toward us, heavily, two at a time. The light still shone palely down the stairs; we saw nothing coming; we only heard the steps. Herman rushed to his room and slammed the door. I slammed shut the door at the stairs top and held my knee against it. After a long minute, I slowly opened it again. There was nothing there. There was no sound. None of us ever heard the ghost again.

The slamming of the doors had aroused mother: she peered out of her room. "What on earth are you boys doing?" she demanded. Herman ventured out of his room. "Nothing," he said gruffly, but he was, in color, a light green. "What was all that running around downstairs?" said mother. So she had heard the steps, too! We just looked at her. "Burglars!" she shouted, intuitively. I tried to quiet her by starting lightly downstairs.

"Come on, Herman," I said.

"I'll stay with mother," he said. "She's all excited."

I stepped back onto the landing.

"Don't either of you go a step," said mother. "We'll call the police." Since the phone was downstairs, I didn't see how we were going to call the police—nor did I want the police—but mother made one of her quick, incomparable decisions. She flung up a window of her bedroom which faced the bedroom windows of the house of a neighbor, picked up a shoe, and whammed it through a pane of glass across the narrow space that separated the two houses. Glass tinkled into the bedroom occupied by a retired engraver named Bodwell and his wife. Bodwell had been for some years in rather a bad way and was subject to mild "attacks." Most everybody we knew or lived near had *some* kind of attacks.

It was now about two o'clock of a moonless night; clouds hung black and low. Bodwell was at the window in a minute, shouting, frothing a little, shaking his fist. "We'll sell the house and go back to Peoria," we could hear Mrs. Bodwell saying. It was some time before mother "got through" to Bodwell. "Burglars!" she shouted. "Burglars in the house!" Herman and I hadn't dared to tell her that it was not burglars but ghosts, for she was even more afraid of ghosts than of burglars. Bodwell at first thought that she meant there were burglars in his house, but finally he quieted down and called the police for us over an extension phone by his bed. After he had disappeared from the window, mother suddenly made as if to throw another shoe, not because there was further need of it but, as she later explained, because the thrill of heaving a shoe through a window glass had enormously taken her fancy. I prevented her.

The police were on hand in a commendably short time: a Ford sedan full of them, two on motorcycles, and a patrol wagon with about eight in it and a few reporters. They began banging at our front door. Flashlights shot streaks of gleam up and down the walls, across the yard, down the walk between our house and Bodwell's. "Open up!" cried a hoarse voice. "We're men from Headquarters!" I wanted to go down and let them in, since there they were, but mother wouldn't hear of it. "You haven't a stitch on," she pointed out. "You'd catch your death." I wound the towel around me again. Finally the cops put their shoulders to our big heavy front door with its thick beveled glass and broke it in: I could hear a rending of wood and a splash of glass on the floor of the hall. Their lights played all over the living-room and criss-crossed nervously in the dining-room, stabbed into hallways, shot up the front stairs and finally up the back. They caught me standing in my towel at the top. A heavy policeman bounded up the steps. "Who are you?" he demanded. "I live here," I said. "Well, whattsa matta, ya hot?" he asked. It was, as a matter of fact, cold; I went to my room and pulled on some trousers. On my way out, a cop stuck a gun into my ribs.

"Whatta you doin' here?" he demanded. "I live here," I said.

The officer in charge reported to mother. "No sign of no-body, lady," he said. "Musta got away—what'd he look like?" "There were two or three of them," mother said, "whooping and carrying on and slamming doors." "Funny," said the cop. "All ya windows and doors was locked on the inside tight as a tick."

Downstairs, we could hear the tromping of the other police. Police were all over the place; doors were yanked open, draw-ers were yanked open, windows were shot up and pulled down, furniture fell with dull thumps. A half-dozen police-men emerged out of the darkness of the front hallway up-stairs. They began to ransack the floor: pulled beds away from walls, tore clothes off hooks in the closets, pulled suitcases and boxes off shelves. One of them found an old zither that Roy had won in a pool tournament. "Looky here, Joe," he said, strumming it with a big paw. The cop named Joe took it and turned it over. "What is it?" he asked me. "It's an old zither our guinea pig used to sleep on," I said. It was true that a pet guinea pig we once had would never sleep any-where except on the zither, but I should never have said so. Joe and the other cop looked at me a long time. They put the zither back on a shelf.

"No sign o' nuthin'," said the cop who had first spoken to mother. "This guy," he explained to the others, jerking a thumb at me, "was nekked. The lady seems historical." They all nodded, but said nothing; just looked at me. In the small silence we all heard a creaking in the attic. Grandfather was turning over in bed. "What's 'at?" snapped Joe. Five or six cops sprang for the attic door before I could intervene or ex-plain. I realized that it would be bad if they burst in on grandfather unannounced, or even announced. He was going through a phase in which he believed that General Meade's men, under steady hammering by Stonewall Jackson, were beginning to retreat and even desert.

When I got to the attic, things were pretty confused. Grandfather had evidently jumped to the conclusion that the police were deserters from Meade's army, trying to hide away in his attic. He bounded out of bed wearing a long flannel nightgown over long woolen underwear, a nightcap, and a leather jacket around his chest. The cops must have realized at once that the indignant white-haired old man belonged in the house, but they had no chance to say so. "Back, ye cowardly dogs!" roared grandfather. "Back t' the lines, ye goddam lily-livered cattle!" With that, he fetched the officer who found the zither a flat-handed smack alongside his head that sent him sprawling. The others beat a retreat, but not fast enough; grandfather grabbed Zither's gun from its holster and let fly. The report seemed to crack the rafters; smoke filled the attic. A cop cursed and shot his hand to his shoulder. Somehow, we all finally got downstairs again and locked the door against the old gentleman. He fired once or twice more in the darkness and then went back to bed. "That was grandfather," I explained to Joe, out of breath. "He thinks you're deserters." "I'll say he does," said Joe.

The cops were reluctant to leave without getting their hands on somebody besides grandfather; the night had been distinctly a defeat for them. Furthermore, they obviously didn't like the "layout"; something looked—and I can see their viewpoint—phony. They began to poke into things again. A reporter, a thin-faced, wispy man, came up to me. I had put on one of mother's blouses, not being able to find anything else. The reporter looked at me with mingled suspicion and interest. "Just what the hell is the real low-down here, Bud?" he asked. I decided to be frank with him. "We had ghosts," I said. He gazed at me a long time as if I were a slot machine into which he had, without results, dropped a nickel. Then he walked away. The cops followed him, the one grandfather shot holding his now-bandaged arm, cursing and blaspheming. "I'm gonna get my gun back from that old bird," said the zither-cop. "Yeh," said Joe. "You—and who else?" I told them I would bring it to the station house the next day.

"What was the matter with that one policeman?" mother asked, after they had gone. "Grandfather shot him," I said.

"What for?" she demanded. I told her he was a deserter. "Of all things!" said mother. "He was such a nice-looking young man."

Grandfather was fresh as a daisy and full of jokes at breakfast next morning. We thought at first he had forgotten all about what had happened, but he hadn't. Over his third cup of coffee, he glared at Herman and me. "What was the idee of all them cops tarryhootin' round the house last night?" he demanded. He had us there.

Young Man Axelbrod

THE COTTONWOOD is a tree of a slovenly and plebeian habit. Its woolly wisps turn gray the lawns and engender neighborhood hostilities about our town. Yet it is a mighty tree, a refuge and an inspiration; the sun flickers in its towering foliage, whence the tattoo of locusts enlivens our dusty summer afternoons. From the wheat country out to the sagebrush plains between the buttes and the Yellowstone it is the cottonwood that keeps a little grateful shade for sweating homesteaders.

In Joralemon we call Knute Axelbrod "Old Cottonwood." As a matter of fact, the name was derived not so much from the quality of the man as from the wide grove about his gaunt white house and red barn. He made a comely row of trees on each side of the country road, so that a humble, daily sort of a man, driving beneath them in his lumber wagon, might fancy himself lord of a private avenue.

And at sixty-five Knute was like one of his own cottonwoods, his roots deep in the soil, his trunk weathered by rain and blizzard and baking August noons, his crown spread to the wide horizon of day and the enormous sky of a prairie night.

This immigrant was an American even in speech. Save for a weakness about his j's and w's, he spoke the twangy Yankee English of the land. He was the more American because in his native Scandinavia he had dreamed of America as a land of light. Always through disillusion and weariness he beheld America as the world's nursery for justice, for broad, fair towns, and eager talk; and always he kept a young soul that dared to desire beauty.

As a lad Knute Axelbrod had wished to be a famous scholar, to learn the ease of foreign tongues, the romance of history, to unfold in the graciousness of wise books. When he first came to America he worked in a sawmill all day and studied all evening. He mastered enough book-learning to teach district school for two terms; then, when he was only eighteen, a great-hearted pity for faded little Lena Wesselius moved him to marry her. Gay enough, doubtless, was their hike by prairie schooner to new farmlands, but Knute was promptly caught in a net of poverty and family. From eighteen to fifty-eight he was always snatching children away from death or the farm away from mortgages.

He had to be content—and generously content he was— with the second-hand glory of his children's success and, for himself, with pilfered hours of reading—that reading of big, thick dismal volumes of history and economics which the lone mature learner chooses. Without ever losing his desire for strange cities and the dignity of towers he stuck to his farm. He acquired a half-section, free from debt, fertile, well-stocked, adorned with a cement silo, a chicken-run, a new windmill. He became comfortable, secure, and then he was ready, it seemed, to die; for at sixty-three his work was done, and he was unneeded and alone.

His wife was dead. His sons had scattered afar, one a dentist in Fargo, another a farmer in the Golden Valley. He had turned over his farm to his daughter and son-in-law. They had begged him to live with them, but Knute refused.

"No," he said, "you must learn to stand on your own feet. I vill not give you the farm. You pay me four hundred dollars a year rent, and I live on that and vatch you from my hill."

On a rise beside the lone cottonwood which he loved best of all his trees Knute built a tar-paper shack, and here he "bached it"; cooked his meals, made his bed, sometimes sat in the sun, read many books from the Joralemon library, and began to feel that he was free of the yoke of citizenship which he had borne all his life.

For hours at a time he sat on a backless kitchen chair before the shack, a wide-shouldered man, white-bearded, motionless; a seer despite his grotesquely baggy trousers, his collarless shirt. He looked across the miles of stubble to the steeple of the Jackrabbit Forks church and meditated upon the uses of life. At first he could not break the rigidity of habit. He rose at five, found work in cleaning his cabin and cultivating his garden, had dinner exactly at twelve, and went to bed by afterglow. But little by little he discovered that he could be irregular without being arrested. He stayed abed till seven or even eight. He got a large, deliberate, tortoise-shell cat, and played games with it; let it lap milk upon the table, called it the Princess, and confided to it that he had a "sneaking idee" that men were fools to work so hard. Around this coatless old man, his stained waistcoat flapping about a huge torso, in a shanty of rumpled bed and pine table covered with sheets of food-daubed newspaper, hovered all the passionate aspiration of youth and the dreams of ancient beauty.

He began to take long walks by night. In his necessitous life night had ever been a period of heavy slumber in close rooms. Now he discovered the mystery of the dark; saw the prairies wide-flung and misty beneath the moon, heard the voices of grass and cottonwoods and drowsy birds. He tramped for miles. His boots were dew-soaked, but he did not heed. He stopped upon hillocks, shyly threw wide his arms, and stood worshiping the naked, slumbering land.

These excursions he tried to keep secret, but they were bruited abroad. Neighbors, good, decent fellows with no sense about walking in the dew at night, when they were returning late from town, drunk, lashing their horses and flinging whisky bottles from racing democrat wagons, saw him, and they spread the tidings that Old Cottonwood was "getting nutty since he give up his farm to that son-in-law of his and retired. Seen the old codger wandering around at midnight. Wish I had his chance to sleep. Wouldn't catch me out in the night air."

Any rural community from Todd Center to Seringapatam

is resentful of any person who varies from its standard, and is morbidly fascinated by any hint of madness. The countryside began to spy on Knute Axelbrod, to ask him questions, and to stare from the road at his shack. He was sensitively aware of it, and inclined to be surly to inquisitive acquaintances. Doubtless that was the beginning of his great pilgrimage.

As a part of the general wild license of his new life—really, he once roared at that startled cat, the Princess: "By gollies! I ain't going to brush my teeth tonight. All my life I've brushed 'em, and alvays vanted to skip a time vunce"—Knute took considerable pleasure in degenerating in his taste in scholarship. He wilfully declined to finish *The Conquest of Mexico,* and began to read light novels borrowed from the Joralemon library. So he rediscovered the lands of dancing and light wines, which all his life he had desired. Some economics and history he did read, but every evening he would stretch out in his buffalo-horn chair, his feet on the cot and the Princess in his lap, and invade Zenda or fall in love with Trilby.

Among the novels he chanced upon a highly optimistic story of Yale in which a worthy young man "earned his way through" college, stroked the crew, won Phi Beta Kappa, and had the most entertaining, yet moral, conversations on or adjacent to "the dear old fence."

As a result of this chronicle, at about three o'clock one morning, when Knute Axelbrod was sixty-four years of age, he decided that he would go to college. All his life he had wanted to. Why not do it?

When he awoke he was not so sure about it as when he had gone to sleep. He saw himself as ridiculous, a ponderous, oldish man among clean-limbed youths, like a dusty cottonwood among silver birches. But for months he wrestled and played with that idea of a great pilgrimage to the Mount of Muses; for he really supposed college to be that sort of place. He believed that all college students, except for the wealthy idlers, burned to acquire learning. He pictured Harvard and Yale and Princeton as ancient groves set with marble temples, before which large groups of Grecian youths talked gently about astronomy and good government. In his picture they never cut classes or ate.

With a longing for music and books and graciousness such as the most ambitious boy could never comprehend, this thick-faced farmer dedicated himself to beauty, and defied the unconquerable power of approaching old age. He sent for college catalogues and school books, and diligently began to prepare himself for college.

He found Latin irregular verbs and the whimsicalities of algebra fiendish. They had nothing to do with actual life as he had lived it. But he mastered them; he studied twelve hours a day, as once he had plodded through eighteen hours a day in the hayfield. With history and English literature he had comparatively little trouble; already he knew much of them from his recreative reading. From German neighbors he had picked up enough Plattdeutsch to make German easy. The trick of study began to come back to him from his small school teaching of forty-five years before. He began to believe that he could really put it through. He kept assuring himself that in college, with rare and sympathetic instructors to help him, there would not be this baffling search, this nervous strain.

But the unreality of the things he studied did disillusion him, and he tired of his new game. He kept it up chiefly because all his life he had kept up onerous labor without any taste for it. Toward the autumn of the second year of his eccentric life he no longer believed that he would ever go to college.

Then a busy little grocer stopped him on the street in Joralemon and quizzed him about his studies, to the delight of the informal club which always loafs at the corner of the hotel.

Knute was silent, but dangerously angry. He remembered just in time how he had once laid wrathful hands upon a hired man, and somehow the man's collar bone had been broken. He turned away and walked home, seven miles, still boiling. He picked up the Princess, and, with her mewing on his shoulder, tramped out again to enjoy the sunset.

He stopped at a reedy slough. He gazed at a hopping plover without seeing it. Suddenly he cried:

"I am going to college. It opens next veek. I t'ink that I can pass the examinations."

Two days later he had moved the Princess and his sticks of furniture to his son-in-law's house, had bought a new slouch hat, a celluloid collar and a solemn suit of black, had wrestled with God in prayer through all of a star-clad night, and had taken the train for Minneapolis, on the way to New Haven.

While he stared out of the car window Knute was warning himself that the millionaires' sons would make fun of him. Perhaps they would haze him. He bade himself avoid all these sons of Belial and cleave to his own people, those who "earned their way through."

At Chicago he was afraid with a great fear of the lightning flashes that the swift crowds made on his retina, the batteries of ranked motor cars that charged at him. He prayed, and ran for his train to New York. He came at last to New Haven.

Not with gibing rudeness, but with politely quizzical eyebrows, Yale received him, led him through entrance examinations, which, after sweaty plowing with the pen, he barely passed, and found for him a roommate. The roommate was a large-browed soft white grub named Ray Gribble, who had been teaching school in New England and seemed chiefly to desire college training so that he might make more money as a teacher. Ray Gribble was a hustler; he instantly got work tutoring the awkward son of a steel man, and for board he waited on table.

He was Knute's chief acquaintance. Knute tried to fool himself into thinking he liked the grub, but Ray couldn't keep his damp hands off the old man's soul. He had the skill of a professional exhorter of young men in finding out Knute's motives, and when he discovered that Knute had a hidden desire to sip at gay, polite literature, Ray said in a shocked way:

"Strikes me a man like you, that's getting old, ought to be thinking more about saving your soul than about all these frills. You leave this poetry and stuff to these foreigners and artists, and you stick to Latin and math. and the Bible. I tell you, I've taught school, and I've learned by experience."

With Ray Gribble, Knute lived grubbily, an existence of torn comforters and smelly lamp, of lexicons and logarithm tables. No leisurely loafing by fireplaces was theirs. They roomed in West Divinity, where gather the theologues, the lesser sort of law students, a whimsical genius or two, and a horde of unplaced freshmen and "scrub seniors."

Knute was shockingly disappointed, but he stuck to his room because outside of it he was afraid. He was a grotesque figure, and he knew it, a white-polled giant squeezed into a small seat in a classroom, listening to instructors younger than his own sons. Once he tried to sit on the fence. No one but "ringers" sat on the fence any more, and at the sight of him trying to look athletic and young, two upper-class men snickered, and he sneaked away.

He came to hate Ray Gribble and his voluble companions of the submerged tenth of the class, the hewers of tutorial wood. It is doubtless safer to mock the flag than to question that best-established tradition of our democracy—that those who "earn their way through" college are necessarily stronger, braver, and more assured of success than the weaklings who talk by the fire. Every college story presents such a moral. But tremblingly the historian submits that Knute discovered that waiting on table did not make lads more heroic than did football or happy loafing. Fine fellows, cheerful and fearless, were many of the boys who "earned their way," and able to talk to richer classmates without fawning; but just as many of them assumed an abject respectability as the most convenient pose. They were pickers up of unconsidered trifles; they toadied to the classmates whom they tutored; they wriggled before the faculty committee on scholarships; they looked pious at Dwight Hall prayer-meetings to make an impression on the

serious minded; and they drank one glass of beer at Jake's
to show the light minded that they meant nothing offensive
by their piety. In revenge for cringing to the insolent athletes
whom they tutored, they would, when safe among their own
kind, yammer about the "lack of democracy of college today."
Not that they were so indiscreet as to do anything about it.
They lacked the stuff of really rebellious souls. Knute listened
to them and marveled. They sounded like young hired men
talking behind his barn at harvest time.

This submerged tenth hated the dilettantes of the class
even more than they hated the bloods. Against one Gilbert
Washburn, a rich esthete with more manner than any freshman ought to have, they raged righteously. They spoke of
seriousness and industry till Knute, who might once have
desired to know lads like Washburn, felt ashamed of himself as a wicked, wasteful old man.

Humbly though he sought, he found no inspiration and
no comradeship. He was the freak of the class, and aside
from the submerged tenth, his classmates were afraid of
being "queered" by being seen with him.

As he was still powerful, one who could take up a barrel
of pork on his knees, he tried to find friendship among the
athletes. He sat at Yale Field, watching the football tryouts,
and tried to get acquainted with the candidates. They stared
at him and answered his questions grudgingly—beefy youths
who in their simple-hearted way showed that they considered
him plain crazy.

The place itself began to lose the haze of magic through
which he had first seen it. Earth is earth, whether one sees
it in Camelot or Joralemon or on the Yale campus—or possibly even in the Harvard yard! The buildings ceased to be
temples to Knute; they became structures of brick or stone,
filled with young men who lounged at windows and watched
him amusedly as he tried to slip by.

The Gargantuan hall of Commons became a tri-daily
horror because at the table where he dined were two youths
who, having uncommonly penetrating minds, discerned that

Knute had a beard, and courageously told the world about it. One of them, named Atchison, was a superior person, very industrious and scholarly, glib in mathematics and manners. He despised Knute's lack of definite purpose in coming to college. The other was a play-boy, a wit and a stealer of street signs, who had a wonderful sense for a subtle jest; and his references to Knute's beard shook the table with jocund mirth three times a day. So these youths of gentle birth drove the shambling, wistful old man away from Commons, and thereafter he ate at the lunch counter at the Black Cat.

Lacking the stimulus of friendship, it was the harder for Knute to keep up the strain of studying the long assignments. What had been a week's pleasant reading in his shack was now thrown at him as a day's task. But he would not have minded the toil if he could have found one as young as himself. They were all so dreadfully old, the money-earners, the serious laborers at athletics, the instructors who worried over their life work of putting marks in class-record books.

Then, on a sore, bruised day, Knute did meet one who was young.

Knute had heard that the professor who was the idol of the college had berated the too-earnest lads in his Browning class, and insisted that they read *Alice in Wonderland*. Knute floundered dustily about in a second-hand bookshop till he found an "Alice," and he brought it home to read over his lunch of a hot-dog sandwich. Something in the grave absurdity of the book appealed to him, and he was chuckling over it when Ray Gribble came into the room and glanced at the reader.

"Huh!" said Mr. Gribble.

"That's a fine, funny book," said Knute.

"Huh! *Alice in Wonderland!* I've heard of it. Silly nonsense. Why don't you read something really fine, like Shakespeare or *Paradise Lost?*"

"Vell——" said Knute, all he could find to say.

With Ray Gribble's glassy eye on him, he could no longer

roll and roar with the book. He wondered if indeed he ought not to be reading Milton's pompous anthropological misconceptions. He went unhappily out to an early history class, ably conducted by Blevins, Ph.D.

Knute admired Blevins, Ph.D. He was so tubbed and eyeglassed and terribly right. But most of Blevins' lambs did not like Blevins. They said he was a "crank." They read newspapers in his class and covertly kicked one another.

In the smug, plastered classroom, his arm leaning heavily on the board tablet-arm of his chair, Knute tried not to miss one of Blevins' sardonic proofs that the correct date of the second marriage of Themistocles was two years and seven days later than the date assigned by that illiterate ass, Frutari of Padua. Knute admired young Blevins' performance, and he felt virtuous in application to these hard, unnonsensical facts.

He became aware that certain lewd fellows of the lesser sort were playing poker just behind him. His prairie-trained ear caught whispers of "Two to dole," and "Raise you two beans." Knute revolved, and frowned upon these mockers of sound learning. As he turned back he was aware that the offenders were chuckling, and continuing their game. He saw that Blevins, Ph.D., perceived that something was wrong; he frowned, but he said nothing. Knute sat in meditation. He saw Blevins as merely a boy. He was sorry for him. He would do the boy a good turn.

When class was over he hung about Blevins' desk till the other students had clattered out. He rumbled:

"Say, Professor, you're a fine fellow. I do something for you. If any of the boys make themselves a nuisance, you yust call on me, and I spank the son of a guns."

Blevins, Ph.D., spake in a manner of culture and nastiness:

"Thanks so much, Axelbrod, but I don't fancy that will ever be necessary. I am supposed to be a reasonably good disciplinarian. Good day. Oh, one moment. There's something I've been wishing to speak to you about. I do wish you wouldn't try quite so hard to show off whenever I call on you during quizzes. You answer at such needless length, and you smile as though there were something highly amusing about me. I'm quite willing to have you regard me as a humorous figure, privately, but there are certain classroom conventions, you know, certain little conventions."

"Why, Professor!" wailed Knute, "I never make fun of you! I didn't know I smile. If I do, I guess it's yust because I am so glad when my stupid old head gets the lesson good."

"Well, well, that's very gratifying, I'm sure. And if you will be a little more careful——"

Blevins, Ph.D., smiled a toothy, frozen smile, and trotted off to the Graduates' Club, to be witty about old Knute and his way of saying "yust," while in the deserted classroom Knute sat chill, an old man and doomed. Through the windows came the light of Indian summer; clean, boyish cries rose from the campus. But the lover of autumn smoothed his baggy sleeve, stared at the blackboard, and there saw only the gray of October stubble about his distant shack. As he pictured the college watching him, secretly making fun of him and his smile, he was now faint and ashamed, now bull-angry. He was lonely for his cat, his fine chair of buffalo horns, the sunny doorstep of his shack, and the understanding land. He had been in college for about one month.

Before he left the classroom he stepped behind the instructor's desk and looked at an imaginary class.

"I might have stood there as a prof if I could have come earlier," he said softly to himself.

Calmed by the liquid autumn gold that flowed through the streets, he walked out Whitney Avenue toward the butte-like hill of East Rock. He observed the caress of the light upon the scarped rock, heard the delicate music of leaves, breathed in air pregnant with tales of old New England. He exulted: " 'Could write poetry now if I yust—if I yust could write poetry!"

He climbed to the top of East Rock, whence he could see the Yale buildings like the towers of Oxford, and see Long Island Sound, and the white glare of Long Island beyond the water. He marveled that Axelbrod of the cottonwood country was looking across an arm of the Atlantic to New York state. He noticed a freshman on a bench at the edge of the rock, and he became irritated. The freshman was Gilbert Washburn, the snob, the dilettante, of whom Ray Gribble had once said: "That guy is the disgrace of the class. He doesn't go out for anything, high stand or Dwight Hall or anything else. Thinks he's so doggone much better than the rest of the fellows that he doesn't associate with anybody. Thinks he's literary, they say, and yet he doesn't even heel the 'Lit,' like the regular literary fellows! Got no time for a loafing, mooning snob like that."

As Knute stared at the unaware Gil, whose profile was fine in outline against the sky, he was terrifically public-spirited and disapproving and that sort of moral thing. Though Gil was much too well dressed, he seemed moodily discontented.

"What he needs is to vork in a threshing crew and sleep in the hay," grumbled Knute almost in the virtuous manner of Gribble. "Then he vould know when he vas vell off, and not look like he had the earache. Pff!" Gil Washburn rose, trailed toward Knute, glanced at him, sat down on Knute's bench.

"Great view!" he said. His smile was eager.

That smile symbolized to Knute all the art of life he had come to college to find. He tumbled out of his moral attitude with ludicrous haste, and every wrinkle of his weathered face creased deep as he answered:

"Yes: I t'ink the Acropolis must be like this here."

"Say, look here, Axelbrod; I've been thinking about you."

"Yas?"

"We ought to know each other. We two are the class scandal. We came here to dream, and these busy little goats like Atchison and Giblets, or whatever your roommate's name is, think we're fools not to go out for marks. You may not agree with me, but I've decided that you and I are precisely alike."

"What makes you t'ink I come here to dream?" bristled Knute.

"Oh, I used to sit near you at Commons and hear you try to quell old Atchison whenever he got busy discussing the reasons for coming to college. That old, moth-eaten topic! I wonder if Cain and Abel didn't discuss it at the Eden Agricultural College. You know, Abel the mark-grabber, very pious and high stand, and Cain wanting to read poetry."

"Yes," said Knute, "and I guess Prof. Adam say, 'Cain, don't you read this poetry; it von't help you in algebry.'"

"Of course. Say, wonder if you'd like to look at this volume of Musset I was sentimental enough to lug up here today. Picked it up when I was abroad last year."

From his pocket Gil drew such a book as Knute had never seen before, a slender volume, in a strange language, bound in hand-tooled crushed levant, an effeminate bibelot over which the prairie farmer gasped with luxurious pleasure. The book almost vanished in his big hands. With a timid forefinger he stroked the levant, ran through the leaves.

"I can't read it, but that's the kind of book I alvays t'ought there must be some like it," he sighed.

"Listen!" cried Gil. "Ysaÿe is playing up at Hartford tonight. Let's go hear him. We'll trolley up. Tried to get some of the fellows to come, but they thought I was a nut."

What an Ysaÿe was, Knute Axelbrod had no notion; but "Sure!" he boomed.

When they got to Hartford they found that between them they had just enough money to get dinner, hear Ysaÿe from gallery seats, and return only as far as Meriden. At Meriden Gil suggested:

"Let's walk back to New Haven, then. Can you make it?"

Knute had no knowledge as to whether it was four miles or forty back to the campus, but "Sure!" he said. For the last few months he had been noticing that, despite his bulk, he had to be careful, but tonight he could have flown.

In the music of Ysaÿe, the first real musician he had ever heard, Knute had found all the incredible things of which he had slowly been reading in William Morris and "Idylls of the King." Tall knights he had beheld, and slim princesses in white samite, the misty gates of forlorn towns, and the glory of the chivalry that never was.

They did walk, roaring down the road beneath the October moon, stopping to steal apples and to exclaim over silvered hills, taking a puerile and very natural joy in chasing a profane dog. It was Gil who talked, and Knute who listened, for the most part; but Knute was lured into tales of the pioneer days, of blizzards, of harvesting, and of the first flame of the green wheat. Regarding the Atchisons and Gribbles of the class both of them were youthfully bitter and supercilious. But they were not bitter long, for they were atavisms tonight. They were wandering minstrels, Gilbert the troubadour with his man-at-arms.

They reached the campus at about five in the morning. Fumbling for words that would express his feeling, Knute stammered:

"Vell, it vas fine. I go to bed now and I dream about——"

"Bed? Rats! Never believe in winding up a party when it's going strong. Too few good parties. Besides, it's only the shank of the evening. Besides, we're hungry. Besides—oh, besides! Wait here a second. I'm going up to my room to get some money, and we'll have some eats. Wait! Please do!"

Knute would have waited all night. He had lived almost seventy years and traveled fifteen hundred miles and endured Ray Gribble to find Gil Washburn.

Policemen wondered to see the celluloid-collared old man and the expensive-looking boy rolling arm in arm down Chapel Street in search of a restaurant suitable to poets. They were all closed.

"The Ghetto will be awake by now," said Gil. "We'll go buy some eats and take 'em up to my room. I've got some tea there."

Knute shouldered through dark streets beside him as naturally as though he had always been a nighthawk, with an aversion to anything as rustic as beds. Down on Oak Street, a place of low shops, smoky lights and alley mouths, they found the slum already astir. Gil contrived to purchase boxed biscuits, cream cheese, chicken-loaf, a bottle of cream. While Gil was chaffering, Knute stared out into the street milkily lighted by wavering gas and the first feebleness of coming day; he gazed upon Kosher signs and advertisements in Russian letters, shawled women and bearded rabbis; and as he looked he gathered contentment which he could never lose. He had traveled abroad tonight.

The room of Gil Washburn was all the useless, pleasant things Knute wanted it to be. There was more of Gil's Paris days in it than of his freshmanhood: Persian rugs, a silver tea service, etchings, and books. Knute Axelbrod of the tar-paper shack and piggy farmyards gazed in satisfaction. Vast bearded, sunk in an easy chair, he clucked amiably while Gil lighted a fire.

Over supper they spoke of great men and heroic ideals. It was good talk, and not unspiced with lively references to Gribble and Atchison and Blevins, all asleep now in their correct beds. Gil read snatches of Stevenson and Anatole France; then at last he read his own poetry.

It does not matter whether that poetry was good or bad. To Knute it was a miracle to find one who actually wrote it.

The talk grew slow, and they began to yawn. Knute was sensitive to the lowered key of their Indian-summer madness, and he hastily rose. As he said good-by he felt as though he had but to sleep a little while and return to this unending night of romance.

But he came out of the dormitory upon day. It was six-thirty of the morning, with a still, hard light upon red-brick walls.

"I can go to his room plenty times now; I find my friend," Knute said. He held tight the volume of Musset, which Gil had begged him to take.

As he started to walk the few steps to West Divinity Knute

felt very tired. By daylight the adventure seemed more and more incredible.

As he entered the dormitory he sighed heavily:

"Age and youth, I guess they can't team together long." As he mounted the stairs he said: "If I saw the boy again, he vould get tired of me. I tell him all I got to say." And as he opened his door, he added: "This is what I come to college for—this one night. I go avay before I spoil it."

He wrote a note to Gil, and began to pack his telescope. He did not even wake Ray Gribble, sonorously sleeping in the stale air.

At five that afternoon, on the day coach of a westbound train, an old man sat smiling. A lasting content was in his eyes, and in his hands a small book in French.

WILLIAM FAULKNER

That Evening Sun Go Down

MONDAY is no different from any other week day in Jefferson now. The streets are paved now, and the telephone and the electric companies are cutting down more and more of the shade trees—the water oaks, the maples and locusts and elms —to make room for iron poles bearing clusters of bloated and ghostly and bloodless grapes, and we have a city laundry which makes the rounds on Monday morning, gathering the bundles of clothes into bright-colored, specially made motor-cars: the soiled wearing of a whole week now flees apparition-like behind alert and irritable electric horns, with a long diminishing noise of rubber and asphalt like a tearing of silk, and even the Negro women who still take in white people's washing after the old custom, fetch and deliver it in automobiles.

But fifteen years ago, on Monday morning the quiet, dusty, shady streets would be full of Negro women with, balanced on their steady turbaned heads, bundles of clothes tied up in sheets, almost as large as cotton bales, carried so without touch of hand between the kitchen door of the white house and the blackened wash-pot beside a cabin door in Negro Hollow.

Nancy would set her bundle on the top of her head, then upon the bundle in turn she would set the black straw sailor hat which she wore Winter and Summer. She was tall, with a high, sad face sunken a little where her teeth were missing. Sometimes we would go a part of the way down the lane and across the pasture with her, to watch the balanced bundle and the hat that never bobbed nor wavered, even when she walked down into the ditch and climbed out again and stooped through the fence. She would go down on her hands and knees and crawl through the gap, her head rigid, up-tilted, the bundle steady as a rock or a balloon, and rise to her feet and go on.

Sometimes the husbands of the washing women would fetch and deliver the clothes, but Jubah never did that for Nancy, even before father told him to stay away from our house, even when Dilsey was sick and Nancy would come to cook for us.

And then about half the time we'd have to go down the lane to Nancy's house and tell her to come on and get breakfast. We would stop at the ditch, because father told us not to have anything to do with Jubah—he was a short black man, with a razor scar down his face—and we would throw rocks at Nancy's house until she came to the door, leaning her head around it without any clothes on.

"What yawl mean, chunking my house?" Nancy said. "What you little devils mean?"

"Father says for you to come and get breakfast," Caddy said. "Father says it's over a half an hour now, and you've got to come this minute."

"I ain't studying no breakfast," Nancy said. "I going to get my sleep out."

"I bet you're drunk," Jason said. "Father says you're drunk. Are you drunk, Nancy?"

"Who says I is?" Nancy said. "I got to get my sleep out. I ain't studying no breakfast."

So after a while we quit chunking the house and went back home. When she finally came, it was too late for me to go to school. So we thought it was whiskey until that day when they arrested her again, and they were taking her to jail and they passed Mr. Stovall. He was the cashier in the bank and a deacon in the Baptist church, and Nancy began to say:

"When you going to pay me, white man? When you going to pay me, white man? It's been three times now since you paid me a cent——" Mr. Stovall knocked her down, but she kept on saying, "When you going to pay me, white man? It's been three times now since——" until Mr. Stovall kicked her in the mouth with his heel and the marshal caught Mr. Stovall back, and Nancy lying in the street, laughing. She turned her head and spat out some blood and teeth and said, "It's been three times now since he paid me a cent."

That was how she lost her teeth, and all that day they told about Nancy and Mr. Stovall, and all that night the ones that passed the jail could hear Nancy singing and yelling. They could see her hands holding to the window bars, and a lot of them stopped along the fence, listening to her and to the jailer trying to make her shut up. She didn't shut up until just before daylight, when the jailer began to hear a bumping and scraping upstairs and he went up there and found Nancy hanging from the window bar. He said that it was cocaine and not whiskey, because no nigger would try to commit suicide unless he was full of cocaine, because a nigger full of cocaine was not a nigger any longer.

The jailer cut her down and revived her; then he beat her, whipped her. She had hung herself with her dress. She had fixed it all right, but when they arrested her she didn't have on anything except a dress and so she didn't have anything to tie her hands with and she couldn't make her hands let go of the window ledge. So the jailer heard the noise and ran up there and found Nancy hanging from the window, stark naked.

When Dilsey was sick in her cabin and Nancy was cooking for us, we could see her apron swelling out; that was before father told Jubah to stay away from the house. Jubah was in the kitchen, sitting behind the stove, with his razor scar on his black face like a piece of dirty string. He said it was a watermelon that Nancy had under her dress. And it was Winter, too.

"Where did you get a watermelon in the Winter?" Caddy said.

"I didn't," Jubah said. "It wasn't me that give it to her. But I can cut it down, same as if it was."

"What makes you want to talk that way before these chillen?" Nancy said. "Whyn't you go on to work? You done et. You want Mr. Jason to catch you hanging around his kitchen, talking that way before these chillen?"

"Talking what way, Nancy?" Caddy said.

"I can't hang around white man's kitchen," Jubah said. "But white man can hang around mine. White man can come in my house, but I can't stop him. When white man want to come in my house, I ain't got no house. I can't stop him, but he can't kick me outen it. He can't do that."

Dilsey was still sick in her cabin. Father told Jubah to stay off our place. Dilsey was still sick. It was a long time. We were in the library after supper.

"Isn't Nancy through yet?" mother said. "It seems to me that she has had plenty of time to have finished the dishes."

"Let Quentin go and see," father said. "Go and see if Nancy is through, Quentin. Tell her she can go on home."

I went to the kitchen. Nancy was through. The dishes were put away and the fire was out. Nancy was sitting in a chair, close to the cold stove. She looked at me.

"Mother wants to know if you are through," I said.

"Yes," Nancy said. She looked at me. "I done finished." She looked at me.

"What is it?" I said. "What is it?"

"I ain't nothing but a nigger," Nancy said. "It ain't none of my fault."

She looked at me, sitting in the chair before the cold stove, the sailor hat on her head. I went back to the library. It was the cold stove and all, when you think of a kitchen being warm and busy and cheerful. And with a cold stove and the dishes all put away, and nobody wanting to eat at that hour.

"Is she through?" mother said.

"Yessum," I said.

"What is she doing?" mother said.

"She's not doing anything. She's through."

"I'll go and see," father said.

"Maybe she's waiting for Jubah to come and take her home," Caddy said.

"Jubah is gone," I said. Nancy told us how one morning she woke up and Jubah was gone.

"He quit me," Nancy said. "Done gone to Memphis, I reckon. Dodging them city *po*-lice for a while, I reckon."

"And a good riddance," father said. "I hope he stays there."

"Nancy's scaired of the dark," Jason said.

"So are you," Caddy said.

"I'm not," Jason said.

"Scairy cat," Caddy said.

"I'm not," Jason said.

"You, Candace!" mother said. Father came back.

"I am going to walk down the lane with Nancy," he said. "She says Jubah is back."

"Has she seen him?" mother said.

"No. Some Negro sent her word that he was back in town. I won't be long."

"You'll leave me alone, to take Nancy home?" mother said. "Is her safety more precious to you than mine?"

"I won't be long," father said.

"You'll leave these children unprotected, with that Negro about?"

"I'm going too," Caddy said. "Let me go, father."

"What would he do with them, if he were unfortunate enough to have them?" father said.

"I want to go, too," Jason said.

"Jason!" mother said. She was speaking to father. You could tell that by the way she said it. Like she believed that all day father had been trying to think of doing the thing that she wouldn't like the most, and that she knew all the time that after a while he would think of it. I stayed quiet, because father and I both knew that mother would want him to make me stay with her, if she just thought of it in time. So father didn't look at me. I was the oldest. I was nine and Caddy was seven and Jason was five.

"Nonsense," Father said. "We won't be long."

Nancy had her hat on. We came to the lane. "Jubah always been good to me," Nancy said. "Whenever he had two dollars, one of them was mine." We walked in the lane. "If I can just get through the lane," Nancy said, "I be all right then."

The lane was always dark. "This is where Jason got scared on Hallowe'en," Caddy said.

" I didn't," Jason said.

"Can't Aunt Rachel do anything with him?" father said. Aunt Rachel was old. She lived in a cabin beyond Nancy's, by herself. She had white hair and she smoked a pipe in the door, all day long; she didn't work any more. They said she was Jubah's mother. Sometimes she said she was and sometimes she said she wasn't any kin to Jubah.

"Yes you did," Caddy said. "You were scairder than Frony. You were scairder than T. P. even. Scairder than niggers."

"Can't nobody do nothing with him," Nancy said. "He say I done woke up the devil in him, and ain't but one thing going to lay it again."

"Well, he's gone now," father said. "There's nothing for you to be afraid of now. And if you'd just let white men alone."

"Let what white men alone?" Caddy said. "How let them alone?"

"He ain't gone nowhere," Nancy said. "I can feel him. I can feel him now, in this lane. He hearing us talk, every word, hid somewhere, waiting. I ain't seen him, and I ain't going to see him again, but once more, with that razor. That razor on that string down his back, inside his shirt. And then I ain't going to be even surprised."

"I wasn't scaired," Jason said.

"If you'd behave yourself, you'd have kept out of this," father said. "But it's all right now. He's probably in St. Louis now. Probably got another wife by now and forgot all about you."

"If he has, I better not find out about it," Nancy said.

"I'd stand there and every time he wropped her, I'd cut that arm off. I'd cut his head off and I'd slit her belly and I'd shove——"

"Hush," father said.

"Slit whose belly, Nancy?" Caddy said.

"I wasn't scared," Jason said. "I'd walk right down this lane by myself."

"Yah," Caddy said. "You wouldn't dare to put your foot in it if we were not with you."

Dilsey was still sick, and so we took Nancy home every night until mother said, "How much longer is this going to go on? I to be left alone in this big house while you take home a frightened Negro?"

We fixed a pallet in the kitchen for Nancy. One night we waked up, hearing the sound. It was not singing and it was not crying, coming up the dark stairs. There was a light in mother's room and we heard father going down the hall, down the back stairs, and Caddy and I went into the hall. The floor was cold. Our toes curled away from the floor while we listened to the sound. It was like singing and it wasn't like singing, like the sounds that Negroes make.

Then it stopped and we heard father going down the back stairs, and we went to the head of the stairs. Then the sound began again, in the stairway, not loud, and we could see Nancy's eyes half way up the stairs, against the wall. They looked like cat's eyes do, like a big cat against the wall, watching us. When we come down the steps to where she was she quit making the sound again, and we stood there until father came back up from the kitchen, with his pistol in his hand. He went back down with Nancy and they came back with Nancy's pallet.

We spread the pallet in our room. After the light in mother's room went off, we could see Nancy's eyes again. "Nancy," Caddy whispered, "are you asleep, Nancy?"

Nancy whispered something. It was oh or no, I don't know which. Like nobody had made it, like it came from nowhere and went nowhere, until it was like Nancy was not there at all; that I had looked so hard at her eyes on the stair that they had got printed on my eyelids, like the sun does when you have closed your eyes and there is no sun. "Jesus," Nancy whispered. "Jesus."

"Was it Jubah?" Caddy whispered. "Did he try to come into the kitchen?"

"Jesus," Nancy said. Like this: Jeeeeeeeeeeeeeeesus, until the sound went out like a match or a candle does.

"Can you see us, Nancy?" Caddy whispered. "Can you see our eyes too?"

"I ain't nothing but a nigger," Nancy said. "God knows. God knows."

"What did you see down there in the kitchen?" Caddy whispered. "What tried to get in?"

"God knows," Nancy said. We could see her eyes. "God knows."

Dilsey got well. She cooked dinner. "You'd better stay in bed a day or two longer," father said.

"What for?" Dilsey said. "If I had been a day later, this place would be to rack and ruin. Get on out of here, now, and let me get my kitchen straight again."

Dilsey cooked supper, too. And that night, just before dark, Nancy came into the kitchen.

"How do you know's he's back?" Dilsey said. "You ain't seen him."

"Jubah is a nigger," Jason said.

"I can feel him," Nancy said. "I can feel him laying yonder in the ditch."

"Tonight?" Dilsey said. "Is he there tonight?"

"Dilsey's a nigger too," Jason said.

"You try to eat something," Dilsey said.

"I don't want nothing," Nancy said.

"I ain't a nigger," Jason said.

"Drink some coffee," Dilsey said. She poured a cup of coffee for Nancy. "Do you know he's out there tonight? How come you know it's tonight?"

"I know," Nancy said. "He's there, waiting. I know. I done lived with him too long. I know what he fixing to do fore he knows it himself."

"Drink some coffee," Dilsey said. Nancy held the cup to her mouth and blew into the cup. Her mouth pursed out like a spreading adder's, like a rubber mouth, like she had blown all the color out of her lips with blowing the coffee.

"I ain't a nigger," Jason said. "Are you a nigger, Nancy?"

"I hell-born, child," Nancy said. "I won't be nothing soon. I going back where I come from soon."

She began to drink the coffee. While she was drinking, holding the cup in both hands, she began to make the sound again. She made the sound into the cup and the coffee sploshed out on to her hands and her dress. Her eyes looked at us and she sat there, her elbows on her knees, holding the cup in both hands, looking at us across the wet cup, making the sound.

"Look at Nancy," Jason said. "Nancy can't cook for us now. Dilsey's got well now."

"You hush up," Dilsey said. Nancy held the cup in both hands, looking at us, making the sound like there were two of them; one looking at us and the other making the sound. "Whyn't you let Mr. Jason telefoam the marshal?" Dilsey said. Nancy stopped then, holding the cup in her long brown hands. She tried to drink some coffee again, but it sploshed out of the cup, on to her hands and her dress, and she put the cup down. Jason watched her.

"I can't swallow it," Nancy said. "I swallows but it won't go down me."

"You go down to the cabin," Dilsey said. "Frony will fix you a pallet and I'll be there soon."

"Won't no nigger stop him," Nancy said.

"I ain't a nigger," Jason said. "Am I, Dilsey?"

"I reckon not," Dilsey said. She looked at Nancy. "I don't reckon so. What you going to do, then?"

Nancy looked at us. Her eyes went fast, like she was

afraid there wasn't time to look, without hardly moving at all. She looked at us, at all three of us at one time. "You member that night I stayed in yawls' room?" she said. She told about how we waked up early the next morning, and played. We had to play quiet, on her pallet, until father woke and it was time for her to go down and get breakfast. "Go and ask you maw to let me stay here tonight," Nancy said. "I won't need no pallet. We can play some more," she said.

Caddy asked mother. Jason went too. "I can't have Negroes sleeping in the house," mother said. Jason cried. He cried until mother said he couldn't have any dessert for three days if he didn't stop. Then Jason said he would stop if Dilsey would make a chocolate cake. Father was there.

"Why don't you do something about it?" mother said. "What do we have officers for?"

"Why is Nancy afraid of Jubah?" Caddy said. "Are you afraid of father, mother?"

"What could they do?" father said. "If Nancy hasn't seen him, how could the officers find him?"

"Then why is she afraid?" mother said.

"She says he is there. She says she knows he is there tonight."

"Yet we pay taxes," mother said. "I must wait here alone in this big house while you take a Negro woman home."

"You know that I am not lying outside with a razor," father said.

"I'll stop if Dilsey will make a chocolate cake," Jason said. Mother told us to go out and father said he didn't know if Jason would get a chocolate cake or not, but he knew what Jason was going to get in about a minute. We went back to the kitchen and told Nancy.

"Father said for you to go home and lock the door, and you'll be all right," Caddy said. "All right from what, Nancy? Is Jubah mad at you?" Nancy was holding the coffee cup in her hands, her elbows on her knees and her hands holding the cup between her knees. She was looking into the cup.

"What have you done that made Jubah mad?" Caddy said. Nancy let the cup go. It didn't break on the floor, but the coffee spilled out, and Nancy sat there with her hands making the shape of the cup. She began to make the sound again, not loud. Not singing and not un-singing. We watched her.

"Here," Dilsey said. "You quit that, now. You get a-holt of yourself. You wait here. I going to get Versh to walk home with you." Dilsey went out.

We looked at Nancy. Her shoulders kept shaking, but she had quit making the sound. We watched her. "What's Jubah going to do to you?" Caddy said. "He went away."

Nancy looked at us. "We had fun that night I stayed in yawls' room, didn't we?"

"I didn't," Jason said. "I didn't have any fun."

"You were asleep," Caddy said. "You were not there."

"Let's go down to my house and have some more fun," Nancy said.

"Mother won't let us," I said. "It's too late now."

"Don't bother her," Nancy said. "We can tell her in the morning. She won't mind."

"She wouldn't let us," I said.

"Don't ask her now," Nancy said. "Don't bother her now."

"They didn't say we couldn't go," Caddy said.

"We didn't ask," I said.

"If you go, I'll tell," Jason said.

"We'll have fun," Nancy said. "They won't mind, just to my house. I been working for yawl a long time. They won't mind."

"I'm not afraid to go," Caddy said. "Jason is the one that's afraid. He'll tell."

"I'm not," Jason said.

"Yes you are," Caddy said. "You'll tell."

"I won't tell," Jason said. "I'm not afraid."

"Jason ain't afraid to go with me," Nancy said. "Is you, Jason?"

"Jason is going to tell," Caddy said. The lane was dark.

We passed the pasture gate. "I bet if something was to jump out from behind that gate, Jason would holler."

"I wouldn't," Jason said. We walked down the lane. Nancy was talking loud.

"What are you talking so loud for, Nancy?" Caddy said.

"Who; me?" Nancy said. "Listen at Quentin and Caddy and Jason saying I'm talking loud."

"You talk like there was four of us here," Caddy said. "You talk like father was here too."

"Who; me talking loud, Mr. Jason?" Nancy said.

"Nancy called Jason 'Mister,'" Caddy said.

"Listen how Caddy and Quentin and Jason talk," Nancy said.

"We're not talking loud," Caddy said. "You're the one that's talking like father——"

"Hush," Nancy said; "hush, Mr. Jason."

"Nancy called Jason 'Mister' aguh——"

"Hush," Nancy said. She was talking loud when we crossed the ditch and stooped through the fence where she used to stoop through with the clothes on her head. Then we came to her house. We were going fast then. She opened the door. The smell of the house was like the lamp and the smell of Nancy was like the wick, like they were waiting for one another to smell. She lit the lamp and closed the door and put the bar up. Then she quit talking loud, looking at us.

"What're we going to do?" Caddy said.

"What you all want to do?" Nancy said.

"You said we would have some fun," Caddy said.

There was something about Nancy's house; something you could smell. Jason smelled it, even. "I don't want to stay here," he said. "I want to go home."

"Go home, then," Caddy said.

"I don't want to go by myself," Jason said.

"We're going to have some fun," Nancy said.

"How?" Caddy said.

Nancy stood by the door. She was looking at us, only

it was like she had emptied her eyes, like she had quit using them.

"What do you want to do?" she said.

"Tell us a story," Caddy said. "Can you tell a story?"

"Yes," Nancy said.

"Tell it," Caddy said. We looked at Nancy. "You don't know any stories," Caddy said.

"Yes," Nancy said. "Yes I do."

She came and sat down in a chair before the hearth. There was some fire there; she built it up; it was already hot. You didn't need a fire. She built a good blaze. She told a story. She talked like her eyes looked, like her eyes watching us and her voice talking to us did not belong to her. Like she was living somewhere else, waiting somewhere else. She was outside the house. Her voice was there and the shape of her, the Nancy that could stoop under the fence with the bundle of clothes balanced as though without weight, like a balloon, on her head, was there. But that was all. "And so this here queen come walking up to the ditch, where that bad man was hiding. She was walking up the ditch, and she say, 'If I can just get past this here ditch,' was what she say. . . ."

"What ditch?" Caddy said. "A ditch like that one out there? Why did the queen go into the ditch?"

"To get to her house," Nancy said. She looked at us. "She had to cross that ditch to get home."

"Why did she want to go home?" Caddy said.

Nancy looked at us. She quit talking. She looked at us. Jason's legs stuck straight out of his pants, because he was little. "I don't think that's a good story," he said. "I want to go home."

"Maybe we had better," Caddy said. She got up from the floor. "I bet they are looking for us right now." She went toward the door.

"No," Nancy said. "Don't open it." She got up quick and passed Caddy. She didn't touch the door, the wooden bar.

"Why not?" Caddy said.

"Come back to the lamp," Nancy said. "We'll have fun. You don't have to go."

"We ought to go," Caddy said. "Unless we have a lot of fun." She and Nancy came back to the fire, the lamp.

"I want to go home," Jason said. "I'm going to tell."

"I know another story," Nancy said. She stood close to the lamp. She looked at Caddy, like when your eyes look up at a stick balanced on your nose. She had to look down to see Caddy, but her eyes looked like that, like when you are balancing a stick.

"I won't listen to it," Jason said. "I'll bang on the floor."

"It's a good one," Nancy said. "It's better than the other one."

"What's it about?" Caddy said. Nancy was standing by the lamp. Her hand was on the lamp, against the light, long and brown.

"Your hand is on that hot globe," Caddy said. "Don't it feel hot to your hand?"

Nancy looked at her hand on the lamp chimney. She took her hand away, slow. She stood there, looking at Caddy, wringing her long hand as though it were tied to her wrist with a string.

"Let's do something else," Caddy said.

"I want to go home," Jason said.

"I got some popcorn," Nancy said. She looked at Caddy and then at Jason and then at me and then at Caddy again. "I got some popcorn."

"I don't like popcorn," Jason said. "I'd rather have candy."

Nancy looked at Jason. "You can hold the popper." She was still wringing her hand; it was long and limp and brown.

"All right," Jason said. "I'll stay a while if I can do that. Caddy can't hold it. I'll want to go home, if Caddy holds the popper."

Nancy built up the fire. "Look at Nancy putting her hands in the fire," Caddy said. "What's the matter with you, Nancy?"

"I got popcorn," Nancy said. "I got some." She took the

popper from under the bed. It was broken. Jason began to cry.

"We can't have any popcorn," he said.

"We ought to go home, anyway," Caddy said. "Come on, Quentin."

"Wait," Nancy said; "wait. I can fix it. Don't you want to help me fix it?"

"I don't think I want any," Caddy said. "It's too late now."

"You help me, Jason," Nancy said. "Don't you want to help me?"

"No," Jason said. "I want to go home."

"Hush," Nancy said; "hush. Watch. Watch me. I can fix it so Jason can hold it and pop the corn." She got a piece of wire and fixed the popper.

"It won't hold good," Caddy said.

"Yes it will," Nancy said. "Yawl watch. Yawl help me shell the corn."

The corn was under the bed too. We shelled it in to the popper and Nancy helped Jason hold the popper over the fire.

"It's not popping," Jason said. "I want to go home."

"You wait," Nancy said. "It'll begin to pop. We'll have fun then." She was sitting close to the fire. The lamp was turned up so high it was beginning to smoke.

"Why don't you turn it down some?" I said.

"It's all right," Nancy said. "I'll clean it. Yawl wait. The popcorn will start in a minute."

"I don't believe it's going to start," Caddy said. "We ought to go home, anyway. They'll be worried."

"No," Nancy said. "It's going to pop. Dilsey will tell um yawl with me. I been working for yawl long time. They won't mind if you at my house. You wait, now. It'll start popping in a minute."

Then Jason got some smoke in his eyes and he began to cry. He dropped the popper into the fire. Nancy got a wet rag and wiped Jason's face, but he didn't stop crying.

"Hush," she said. "Hush." He didn't hush. Caddy took the popper out of the fire.

"It's burned up," she said. "You'll have to get some more popcorn, Nancy."

"Did you put all of it in?" Nancy said.

"Yes," Caddy said. Nancy looked at Caddy. Then she took the popper and opened it and poured the blackened popcorn into her apron and began to sort the grains, her hands long and brown, and we watching her.

"Haven't you got any more?" Caddy said.

"Yes," Nancy said; "yes. Look. This here ain't burnt. All we need to do is——"

"I want to go home," Jason said. "I'm going to tell."

"Hush," Caddy said. We all listened. Nancy's head was already turned toward the barred door, her eyes filled with red lamplight. "Somebody is coming," Caddy said.

Then Nancy began to make that sound again, not loud, sitting there above the fire, her long hands dangling between her knees; all of a sudden water began to come out on her face in big drops, running down her face, carrying in each one a little turning ball of firelight until it dropped off her chin.

"She's not crying," I said.

"I ain't crying," Nancy said. Her eyes were closed. "I ain't crying. Who is it?"

"I don't know," Caddy said. She went to the door and looked out. "We've got to go home now," she said. "Here comes father."

"I'm going to tell," Jason said. "You all made me come."

The water still ran down Nancy's face. She turned in her chair. "Listen. Tell him. Tell him we going to have fun. Tell him I take good care of yawl until in the morning. Tell him to let me come home with yawl and sleep on the floor. Tell him I won't need no pallet. We'll have fun. You remember last time how we had so much fun?"

"I didn't have any fun," Jason said. "You hurt me. You put smoke in my eyes."

Father came in. He looked at us. Nancy did not get up.

"Tell him," she said.

"Caddy made us come down here," Jason said. "I didn't want to."

Father came to the fire. Nancy looked up at him. "Can't you go to Aunt Rachel's and stay?" he said. Nancy looked up at father, her hands between her knees. "He's not here," father said. "I would have seen. There wasn't a soul in sight."

"He in the ditch," Nancy said. "He waiting in the ditch yonder."

"Nonsense," father said. He looked at Nancy. "Do you know he's there?"

"I got the sign," Nancy said.

"What sign?"

"I got it. It was on the table when I come in. It was a hog bone, with blood meat still on it, laying by the lamp. He's out there. When yawl walk out that door, I gone."

"Who's gone, Nancy?" Caddy said.

"I'm not a tattletale," Jason said.

"Nonsense," father said.

"He out there," Nancy said. "He looking through that window this minute, waiting for yawl to go. Then I gone."

"Nonsense," father said. "Lock up your house and we'll take you on to Aunt Rachel's."

" 'Twon't do no good," Nancy said. She didn't look at father now, but he looked down at her, at her long, limp, moving hands.

"Putting it off won't do no good."

"Then what do you want to do?" father said.

"I don't know," Nancy said. "I can't do nothing. Just put it off. And that don't do no good. I reckon it belong to me. I reckon what I going to get ain't no more than mine."

"Get what?" Caddy said. "What's yours?"

"Nothing," father said. "You all must get to bed."

"Caddy made me come," Jason said.

"Go on to Aunt Rachel's," father said.

"It won't do no good," Nancy said. She sat before the fire, her elbows on her knees, her long hands between her knees. "When even your own kitchen wouldn't do no good. When even if I was sleeping on the floor in the room with your own children, and the next morning there I am, and blood all——"

"Hush," father said. "Lock the door and put the lamp out and go to bed."

"I scared of the dark," Nancy said. "I scared for it to happen in the dark."

"You mean you're going to sit right here, with the lamp lighted?" father said. Then Nancy began to make the sound again, sitting before the fire, her long hands between her knees. "Ah, damnation," father said. "Come along, chillen. It's bedtime."

"When yawl go, I gone," Nancy said. "I be dead tomorrow. I done had saved up the coffin money with Mr. Lovelady——"

Mr. Lovelady was a short, dirty man who collected the Negro insurance, coming around to the cabins and the kitchen every Saturday morning, to collect fifteen cents. He and his wife lived in the hotel. One morning his wife committed suicide. They had a child, a little girl. After his wife committed suicide Mr. Lovelady and the child went away. After a while Mr. Lovelady came back. We could see him going down the lanes on Saturday morning. He went to the Baptist church.

Father carried Jason on his back. We went out Nancy's door; she was sitting before the fire. "Come and put the bar up," father said. Nancy didn't move. She didn't look at us again. We left her there, sitting before the fire with the door opened, so that it wouldn't happen in the dark.

"What, father?" Caddy said. "Why is Nancy scared of Jubah? What is Jubah going to do to her?"

"Jubah wasn't there," Jason said.

"No," father said. "He's not there. He's gone away."

"Who is it that's waiting in the ditch?" Caddy said. We looked at the ditch. We came to it, where the path went down into the thick vines and went up again.

"Nobody," father said. There was just enough moon to see by. The ditch was vague, thick, quiet. "If he's there, he can see us, can't he?" Caddy said.

"You made me come," Jason said on father's back. "I didn't want to."

The ditch was quite still, quite empty, massed with honeysuckle. We couldn't see Jubah, any more than we could see Nancy sitting there in her house, with the door open and the lamp burning, because she didn't want it to happen in the dark. "I just done got tired," Nancy said. "I just a nigger. It ain't no fault of mine."

But we could still hear her. She began as soon as we were out of the house, sitting there above the fire, her long brown hands between her knees. We could still hear her when we had crossed the ditch, Jason high and close and little about father's head.

Then we had crossed the ditch, walking out of Nancy's life. Then her life was sitting there with the door open and the lamp lit, waiting, and the ditch between us and us going on, the white people going on, dividing the impinged lives of us and Nancy.

"Who will do our washing now, father?" I said.

"I'm not a nigger," Jason said on father's shoulders.

"You're worse," Caddy said, "you are a tattletale. If something was to jump out, you'd be scairder than a nigger."

"I wouldn't," Jason said.

"You'd cry," Caddy said.

"Caddy!" father said.

"I wouldn't," Jason said.

"Scairy cat," Caddy said.

"Candace!" father said.

The Explorers

IT WAS a warm day, too warm for that time of year, and the lake in the park had a couple of dozen rowboats on it. The freshly painted benches had been brought out on the asphalt apron between the boathouse and the water. Here and there people sat on them, reading newspapers or straining their faces to the sun, their eyes closed, trying to catch a bit of sunburn to carry home proudly. The weather was of the sort that, had it come on a Sunday, would have permitted the newspapers to report record-breaking crowds in the park. But it was an ordinary Wednesday morning and there weren't any crowds.

Just that handful of unexciting people, spread about as though by arrangement, one to a bench. They seemed to have no interest in one another beyond a sharp glance or two when a newcomer arrived and began to hunt for a seat. Nobody chose a bench with someone on it already, even though the man or woman might be sitting all the way over at one end. Everybody wanted a bench to himself.

The boathouse was a gray imitation-stone affair, with a huge clock on it that faced the lake so that the people who had rented boats and were out on the water would know when their time was up. The benches were arranged in front of it in two rows. This left a lane down the middle, four or five feet wide, that led from the cashier's window of the boathouse to the water's edge, where the boats were tied.

The three young men came down this lane at a curious gait, walking a shade faster than the ordinary bench hunter and yet too slowly to indicate any other purpose. They were very well dressed, much better than most of the people on the benches. But their coats were taken in a trifle too much at the waist and the brims of their hats snapped a bit too sharply. They advanced to the water's edge and looked at the lake.

They did it as though somebody had told them recently that a lake was a fascinating thing but they didn't believe it and had come to look for themselves. They didn't seem to be impressed. Their faces, which had started out with identical looks of faint incredulity, were soon reflecting definite contempt. After a few moments they turned their backs on the lake abruptly and lit cigarettes. All three of them. They smoked slowly, inhaling huge quantities of smoke, and sent their eyes over the people on the benches. They were quick little eyes that moved in darts. For a while they saw nothing, apparently, that merited changing the expression on their faces, which continued to reflect their uncomplimentary opinion of the lake. Then the roving eyes stopped on the last bench to the left.

A young girl, a pretty girl, was sitting in the exact center of the bench, reading the *Times*. She, too, seemed to be much better dressed than the other people on the benches. She held the *Times*, which was folded lengthwise down the middle, in her left hand and her left elbow rested on the back of the bench. This brought her shoulders at almost right angles to the bench. Sitting like that, with her legs crossed and her right hand resting in her lap and touching the bottom of the *Times* lightly, she made a very attractive picture.

The three young men at the water's edge looked at her for a moment. Then the one in the middle nudged the other two and winked. He was carrying a copy of the *Daily News* folded under one arm. He dropped his cigarette and walked up the lane swiftly. The others followed and they all stopped next to the girl's bench. The first young man leaned toward the girl and held out his folded newspaper.

"Pardon me, Miss," he said, "but you through with that paper? I'm through with this one. I figured you give me the *Times*, I give you the *News?*"

The girl looked up quickly, startled and confused. But

somehow she didn't seem to be startled or confused enough. Her elbow, for instance, which appeared to be perched so precariously on the back of the bench, didn't slip from its resting place, even though she had jumped visibly. She looked up at the young man for a moment and then swung herself forward on the bench and buried her eyes in the paper. The young man looked at his two friends. His face was expressionless.

"You think it's possible she don't read the *News?*" he said aloud. "Only the *Times?*"

"You ask me?" one of the others said. "Ask her."

"A nice girl like that reading only the *Times?*" The young man with the folded paper shook his head as though he couldn't quite believe that. "She doesn't read the *Daily Worker*—all right, a thing like that I could understand. But the *News?*" He leaned toward the girl again. "Pardon me, Miss. You got a grudge against the *News?*"

The girl's face took on a look of exaggerated disdain, but she did not raise her head from the *Times.*

"That's how life is," one of the other young men said. They all spoke alike, in loud, clear voices, as though they were accustomed to addressing slightly deaf people. "A pretty girl like that, she's got nice clothes, so three gorillas come along and bother her. She didn't have such nice clothes, she didn't look so pretty, so no three gorillas wouldn't bother her." He shook his head sorrowfully.

"It's not a question of bothering," the first young man said. "A pretty girl like that, she don't read the *News,* that's something must be looked into. You can't leave things like that without looking into it."

"You wanna look into it, Flassy?" the second young man asked.

"We *must* look into it, Lou," said Flassy.

He sat down quickly, about two feet to the right of the girl. At the same time Lou sat down at her left, the same distance away. The third man took up his post in back of the bench, about two feet behind her, so that she was completely surrounded. For a moment, while this was happening, the girl looked genuinely frightened. Then she recovered, turned a page of the *Times* defiantly, and continued reading. She continued looking at the paper, anyway.

"We gotta study this calmly," Flassy said.

"Calmly, I don't care," said Lou, on the left. "Intelligently we gotta study it."

"All right," the one in the rear said. "But let's study it."

They talked across the girl and over her head. They leaned toward each other and peered closely at the paper she was holding. But they were scrupulously careful not to touch her or even brush her clothes. They never touched her once.

"Books maybe," Flassy said. The girl was looking at the book page of the paper. "Ask her she likes books."

"That's an idea." Lou leaned toward the girl. "You like books, Miss?"

The girl read on stonily.

"Tell her I read a book once," Flassy said. "Very good, too."

"I don't think she likes us, Flassy," Lou said.

"No, no. That's too hasty. It's only books she don't like." Flassy peered at the paper in the girl's hands. It was open at the theatrical page. "I know what she likes. She likes Ethel Barrymore. Ask her."

Lou leaned toward the girl. "There's a rumor going around you like Ethel Barrymore. You like Ethel Barrymore, Miss?"

The girl turned the page calmly. She had recovered from her original surprise.

"She don't like Ethel Barrymore," Lou said.

"John, maybe. Ask her she likes John."

"Pardon me, Miss. You like John? John Barrymore?"

No answer.

"She don't like John, either."

"Maybe because he's married. *You* ask her this time, Gus," said Lou to the man in the rear.

Gus leaned forward to look down on the girl. "You don't like John because he's married, Miss?" he asked.

Flassy nudged his arm. "Tell her we can fix that," he said.

"Miss, you don't like John because he's married, we can fix that," said Gus. "You want us to fix that?"

The girl turned a page carefully.

"Maybe we wouldn't have to fix that," Lou said. "You know John."

"That's right. The way John is, maybe by this time we won't have to fix that," said Flassy.

Gus shook his head. "I'm afraid it's not John, fellas."

"Who then? Bob?"

"Bob? Yeah, well, maybe. It could be Bob."

"Bob who? Which Bob?" asked Flassy.

Lou seemed surprised. "That's a question to ask? A pretty girl like this, a pretty girl with such a nice clothes, which Bob would it be? Use your head."

"All right with my head. But it could be two Bobs. It could be Taylor. It could be Montgomery."

Gus shook his head at him. "Flassy," he said, "you surprise me. Honest. A girl like this you say Taylor? With a girl like this Taylor hasn't got a chance. A Chinaman's chance. This is a Montgomery girl, Flassy."

Flassy shrugged. "Maybe," he said. "I could be wrong. I was wrong once. But how I could be wrong with a girl like this, I don't know. Montgomery? Better ask her."

Lou leaned over. "Pardon me, Miss. There is an argument here. We decided with you it's a Bob. But question: Are you a Taylor or a Montgomery? Which?"

The girl turned another page and rustled the paper into comfortable reading position.

"You know what I think, fellas?" Gus said. He was looking across her shoulder at the paper.

"What?"

"I think we're getting no place very fast."

Flassy looked shocked. "I can't believe that," he said. "That's impossible. Why should you say a thing like that?"

Lou pointed at the paper. "She's reading the editorials," he said.

Flassy was impressed. "Editorials," he said. He shook his head. "I'll admit it looks bad. Editorials. My God!"

He turned to look out across the benches toward the lake. A small Negro boy of seven or eight was walking idly down the lane toward the water.

"Hey!" Flassy called. "Hey, Joe Louis!"

The small boy turned quickly.

"C'm 'ere, kid," Flassy said. He motioned toward the bench with his hand. "Something I wanna ask you."

The boy came up shyly. He seemed a little frightened, but not much. He was wearing a half-sleeved light-blue jumper that fastened to the top of his short pants with large white buttons. His knees were bare and looked startlingly thin and fragile.

"Yes, suh?" he said timidly.

"You wanna make a nickel?" Flassy asked.

"Yes, suh," the boy said eagerly.

"Find out first he's got working papers," Gus said.

"Flassy wants him only for a small job," Lou said. "For what Flassy wants him, he don't need no working papers."

"That's right," Flassy said. "What I want you for, it'll take a minute. Easiest nickel you ever made, Joe Louis."

"I don't think his name is Joe Louis," Gus said.

The girl rustled the paper as she turned a page.

"Better work fast, Flassy," Lou said. "She's getting impatient."

"A pretty girl like that," Gus said, "she's got a right to be impatient." He leaned toward the girl. "You go ahead and be impatient, Miss. You got a right."

The girl's lip curled slightly as she read through the *Times* obituaries.

"I'm working fast us I can," Flassy said. "This is a delicate situation. Has to be handled with kid gloves. I gotta work through a third party. I gotta work through Joe Louis here."

"I still don't think his name is Joe Louis," Gus said.

"Better get his right name, Flassy," said Lou. "Always get the right name."

Flassy turned back to the small boy. "What's your right name, Joe Louis?"

"Johnson," the boy said.

"Johnson?" Gus said, looking at the sky. "Johnson? Johnson? Johnson? Never heard that name before."

"The first name," Lou said. "Get the first name, Flassy."

"What's your first name, Johnson?"

"Martin, suh," the small boy said.

"Martin Johnson?"

"Yes, suh."

"That's an explorer," Flassy said. "Martin Johnson is an explorer."

"No," Gus said. "He goes to Africa with a camera. He takes pictures."

"But he goes to Africa. No?"

"Sure."

"Then he's an explorer. Anybody goes to Africa, he's an explorer."

"He's no explorer. He's married," said Gus.

"Him, too? Everybody's married. It's the new thing."

"Not Martin Johnson," Lou said. "He got killed in an airplane crash."

"That's right," said Flassy. "My God. First he was married. Now he's dead. My God."

"You gotta work fast here, Flassy."

"That's right." Flassy spoke to the small boy. "Here's what I want you to do, Johnson. You see this very pretty girl here?" He nodded toward the girl beside him, and the small boy looked at her.

"Yes, suh," he said, but the eagerness for the promised nickel was gone from his voice. It sounded troubled and his eyes began to look vaguely frightened again.

"You go up to this here pretty girl," Flassy said, "and you ask her why she don't like us. That's all. Just you say to her, 'Miss, why don't you like these three very handsome gentlemen?' For that you get a nickel. Think you can handle the job, Johnson?"

The small boy mumbled something in a scared voice and began to back away. Flassy's hand shot out and clamped down on the boy's wrist.

"Johnson," he said, "you shock me. You yellow, Johnson?"

"Flassy," Gus said, "you're color-blind. He's not yellow. He's—"

"Quiet," Flassy said. "I'm handling this."

"O.K.," Gus said. "Handle it."

Flassy turned to the boy again and pulled on his arm slowly until he was back where he had been.

"Johnson," he said, "three friends ask you to do them a favor. Three of the best friends you ever had, Johnson. A little thing they ask you to do, and they want to give you a nickel to do it. You going to turn them down, Johnson?"

The terror in the small boy's eyes spread to the rest of his face and to his body. He strained away from Flassy and tried to free his hand, but the hold on his wrist did not relax.

"He's not talking," Lou said.

"He'll talk," Flassy said. He drew the small, frightened boy to him and held him between his knees. Then he lowered his face to look into the boy's eyes. "Johnson," he said, "I am very much annoyed. I am disturbed. I am disappointed. I am all these things. But mostly I am annoyed. The way things are going, Johnson, I may even get sore. I hate to get sore, because it makes my collar wilt. It is not gentlemanly. Johnson, don't make my collar wilt. Now, once more." He held up his forefinger in front of the terrified boy. "You will go up to this very pretty young girl here and you will say, 'Miss, why don't you like these three gentlemen?' That's all. For that you will get a nickel. O.K., Johnson?"

The girl didn't raise her head from the paper, but her eyes were watching the scene. The small Negro boy's chin began to quiver. The girl bit her lip and dropped her eyes to the paper again.

"Johnson isn't talking," Gus said.

"True," Flassy said. "Johnson isn't talking." He sighed and pulled a small leather notebook from his pocket. He flipped it open and held up his hand. "Pencil," he said. Gus took out a pencil and put it into the upraised hand. Flassy lowered the pencil to the notebook. "Johnson," he said, "what are you doing in the park this time of day? Why aren't you in school?"

The small boy scowled and dug his fist into his eye.

"I—I—" he began.

"Too bad, Johnson," Flassy said. "Hooky. I thought so." He sighed again. "You know who I am, Johnson?"

"Tell him, Flassy," Lou said.

"I will," Flassy said. "I'm a truant officer, Johnson."

The small boy started to cry violently. His shoulders shook with his sobs and the tears rolled down his face like water from a dripping faucet. Flassy pushed him a little further away, but still held him clamped between his knees.

"Careful of the suit, Johnson," he said. He dug the pencil into the paper of the notebook. "Martin Johnson," he said as he wrote, "I asked you a simple favor, but you wouldn't do it." He shook his head sadly. "Too bad, Johnson. Now I must report you. What class, Johnson?"

"Two B," the boy said through his tears.

Flassy wrote.

"Teacher's name?" he asked.

"M— M— Miss Goldberg," the boy said, sobbing.

"Miss Goldberg?" Flassy said. He looked up at the other young men. "You hear that? Playing hooky from Miss Goldberg!"

"One of the nicest teachers I ever saw," Gus said.

"Playing hooky from Miss Goldberg," Lou said. "My God!" Flassy shook his head.

"This is bad, Johnson. Bad." He started to write the name, and stopped. "You got one more chance, Johnson. You talk to this pretty girl here like I asked you, you do what I tell you, I won't report you. What do you say, Johnson?"

The small boy stopped crying for a moment and looked at the girl, sniffing. Then he was off again, blubbering wildly, his thin body shaking, and hiding his face in the end of his elbow.

"Tchk! Tchk! Tchk!" Flassy said, beginning to write. "I'm afraid it's curtains, Johnson. This is too—"

Suddenly the girl smacked the *Times* onto her lap angrily.

"Oh, why don't you let the boy alone!" she snapped. "You —you—you great big overgrown—"

The three young men stared at her and then at each other in pleased surprise.

"Say!" Gus said. "She's talking!"

"I told you to let me handle this," Flassy said. He swung himself around to face the girl and the pressure of his knees was released. The small boy darted out and began to run. Flassy reached for him quickly, but missed. "C'm 'ere, you dirty little—"

"I'll get him," Gus said.

"Never mind," Flassy said. "We don't need him any more. Let him go. We save a nickel. We got her talking."

The girl rustled the paper in her lap and glared at him. She was breathing quickly and her lips were pressed thin.

"A poor little kid like that," she said.

"Girlie," Flassy said, "a girl with eyes like yours, you shouldn't never—"

Lou reached over and touched Flassy's knee. He pointed to the clock on the boathouse. "Flassy," he said, "it's late. We better get going. Johnny'll be waiting."

All three of them looked at the clock.

"That's right," Flassy said.

He stood up at once and the three of them walked away briskly. They buttoned their tight coats and adjusted their hats as they went, but they did not look back at the girl on the bench.

ALBERT MALTZ

The Happiest Man on Earth

JESSE felt ready to weep. He had been sitting in the shanty waiting for Tom to appear, grateful for the chance to rest his injured foot, quietly, joyously anticipating the moment when Tom would say, "Why of course, Jesse, you can start whenever you're ready!"

For two weeks he had been pushing himself, from Kansas City, Missouri, to Tulsa, Oklahoma, through nights of rain and a week of scorching sun, without sleep or a decent meal, sustained by the vision of that one moment. And then Tom had come into the office. He had come in quickly, holding a sheaf of papers in his hand; he had glanced at Jesse only casually, it was true—but long enough. He had not known him. He had turned away. . . . And Tom Brackett was his brother-in-law.

Was it his clothes? Jesse knew he looked terrible. He had tried to spruce up at a drinking fountain in the park, but even that had gone badly; in his excitement he had cut himself shaving, an ugly gash down the side of his cheek. And nothing could get the red gumbo dust out of his suit even though he had slapped himself till both arms were worn out. . . . Or was it just that he *had* changed so much?

True, they hadn't seen each other for five years; but Tom looked five years older, that was all. He was still Tom. God! was *he* so different?

Brackett finished his telephone call. He leaned back in his swivel chair and glanced over at Jesse with small, clear blue eyes that were suspicious and unfriendly. He was a heavy, paunchy man of forty-five, auburn-haired, rather dour looking; his face was meaty, his features pronounced and forceful, his nose somewhat bulbous and reddish-hued at the tip. He looked like a solid, decent, capable business man who was commander of his local branch of the American Legion—which he was. He surveyed Jesse with cold indifference, manifestly unwilling to spend time on him. Even the way he chewed his toothpick seemed contemptuous to Jesse.

"Yes?" Brackett said suddenly. "What do you want?"

His voice was decent enough, Jesse admitted. He had expected it to be worse. He moved up to the wooden counter that partitioned the shanty. He thrust a hand nervously through his tangled hair.

"I guess you don't recognize me, Tom," he said falteringly, "I'm Jesse Fulton."

"Huh?" Brackett said. That was all.

"Yes, I am, and Ella sends you her love."

Brackett rose and walked over to the counter until they were face to face. He surveyed Fulton incredulously, trying to measure the resemblance to his brother-in-law as he remembered him. This man was tall, about thirty. That fitted! He had straight good features and a lank erect body. That was right too. But the face was too gaunt, the body too spiny under the baggy clothes for him to be sure. His brother-in-law had been a solid, strong young man with muscle and beef to him. It was like looking at a faded, badly taken photograph and trying to recognize the subject: the resemblance was there but the difference was tremendous. He searched the eyes. They at least seemed definitely familiar, gray, with a curiously shy but decent look in them. He had liked that about Fulton.

Jesse stood quiet. Inside he was seething. Brackett was like a man examining a piece of broken-down horse flesh; there was a look of pure pity in his eyes. It made Jesse furious. He knew he wasn't as far gone as all that.

"Yes, I believe you are," Brackett said finally, "but you sure have changed."

"By God, it's five years, ain't it?" Jesse said resentfully. "You only saw me a couple of times anyway." Then, to himself, with his lips locked together, in mingled vehemence and shame, What if I have changed? Don't everybody? I ain't no corpse.

"You was solid looking," Brackett continued softly, in the same tone of incredulous wonder. "You lost weight, I guess?"

Jesse kept silent. He needed Brackett too much to risk antagonizing him. But it was only by deliberate effort that he could keep from boiling over. The pause lengthened, became painful. Brackett flushed. "Jiminy Christmas, excuse me," he burst out in apology. He jerked the counter up. "Come in. Take a seat. Good God, boy"—he grasped Jesse's hand and shook it—"I *am* glad to see you; don't think anything else! You just looked so peaked."

"It's all right," Jesse murmured. He sat down, thrusting his hand through his curly, tangled hair.

"Why are you limping?"

"I stepped on a stone; it jagged a hole through my shoe." Jesse pulled his feet back under the chair. He was ashamed of his shoes. They had come from the Relief originally, and two weeks on the road had about finished them. All morning, with a kind of delicious, foolish solemnity, he had been vowing to himself that before anything else, before even a suit of clothes, he was going to buy himself a brand new strong pair of shoes.

Brackett kept his eyes off Jesse's feet. He knew what was bothering the boy and it filled his heart with pity. The whole thing was appalling. He had never seen anyone who looked more down and out. His sister had been writing to him every week, but she hadn't told him they were as badly off as this.

"Well now, listen," Brackett began, "tell me things. How's Ella?"

"Oh, she's pretty good," Jesse replied absently. He had a soft, pleasing, rather shy voice that went with his soft gray eyes. He was worrying over how to get started.

"And the kids?"

"Oh, they're fine. . . . Well, you know," Jesse added, becoming more attentive, "the young one has to wear a brace.

He can't run around, you know. But he's smart. He draws pictures and he does things, you know."

"Yes," Brackett said. "That's good." He hesitated. There was a moment's silence. Jesse fidgeted in his chair. Now that the time had arrived, he felt awkward. Brackett leaned forward and put his hand on Jesse's knee. "Ella didn't tell me things were so bad for you, Jesse. I might have helped."

"Well, goodness," Jesse returned softly, "you been having your own troubles, ain't you?"

"Yes." Brackett leaned back. His ruddy face became mournful and darkly bitter. "You know I lost my hardware shop?"

"Well sure, of course," Jesse answered, surprised. "You wrote us. That's what I mean."

"I forgot," Brackett said. "I keep on being surprised over it myself. Not that it was worth much," he added bitterly. "It was running down hill for three years. I guess I just wanted it because it was mine." He laughed pointlessly, without mirth. "Well tell me about yourself," he asked. "What happened to the job you had?"

Jesse burst out abruptly, with agitation, "Let it wait, Tom, I got something on my mind."

"It ain't you and Ella?" Brackett interrupted anxiously.

"Why no!" Jesse sat back. "Why however did you come to think that? Why Ella and me—" he stopped, laughing. "Why, Tom, I'm just crazy about Ella. Why she's just wonderful. She's just my whole life, Tom."

"Excuse me. Forget it." Brackett chuckled uncomfortably, turned away. The naked intensity of the youth's burst of love had upset him. It made him wish savagely that he could do something for them. They were both too decent to have had it so hard. Ella was like this boy too, shy and a little soft.

"Tom, listen," Jesse said, "I come here on purpose." He thrust his hand through his hair. "I want you to help me."

"Damn it, boy," Brackett groaned. He had been expecting this. "I can't much. I only get thirty-five a week and I'm damn grateful for it."

"Sure, I know," Jesse emphasized excitedly. He was feeling once again the wild, delicious agitation that had possessed him in the early hours of the morning. "I know you can't help us with money! But we met a man who works for you! He was in our city! He said you could give me a job!"

"Who said?"

"Oh, why didn't you tell me?" Jesse burst out reproachfully. "Why as soon as I heard it I started out. For two weeks now I been pushing ahead like crazy."

Brackett groaned aloud. "You come walking from Kansas City in two weeks so I could give you a job?"

"Sure, Tom, of course. What else could I do?"

"God Almighty, there ain't no jobs, Jesse! It's a slack season. And you don't know this oil business. It's special. I got my Legion friends here but they couldn't do nothing now. Don't you think I'd ask for you as soon as there was a chance?"

Jesse felt stunned. The hope of the last two weeks seemed rolling up into a ball of agony in his stomach. Then, frantically, he cried, "But listen, this man said *you* could hire! He *told* me! He drives trucks for you! He said you *always* need men!"

"Oh! . . . You mean *my* department?" Brackett said in a low voice.

"*Yes,* Tom. That's it!"

"Oh, no, you don't want to work in my department," Brackett told him in the same low voice. "You don't know what it is."

"Yes, I do," Jesse insisted. "He told me all about it, Tom. You're a dispatcher, ain't you? You send the dynamite trucks out?"

"Who was the man, Jesse?"

"Everett, Everett, I think."

"Egbert? Man about my size?" Brackett asked slowly.

"Yes, Egbert. He wasn't a phony, was he?"

Brackett laughed. For the second time his laughter was curiously without mirth. "No, he wasn't a phony." Then, in a changed voice: "Jiminy, boy, you should have asked me before you trekked all the way down here."

"Oh, I didn't want to," Jesse explained with naïve cunning. "I knew you'd say 'no.' He told me it was risky work, Tom. But I don't care."

Brackett locked his fingers together. His solid, meaty face became very hard. "I'm going to say 'no' anyway, Jesse."

Jesse cried out. It had not occurred to him that Brackett would not agree. It had seemed as though reaching Tulsa were the only problem he had to face. "Oh, no," he begged, "you can't. Ain't there any jobs, Tom?"

"Sure, there's jobs. There's even Egbert's job if you want it."

"He's quit?"

"He's dead!"

"Oh!"

"On the job, Jesse. Last night if you want to know."

"Oh!" . . . Then, "I don't care!"

"Now you listen to me," Brackett said. "I'll tell you a few things that you should have asked before you started out. It ain't dynamite you drive. They don't use anything as safe as dynamite in drilling oil wells. They wish they could, but they can't. It's nitroglycerin! Soup!"

"But I know," Jesse told him reassuringly. "He advised me, Tom. You don't have to think I don't know."

"Shut up a minute," Brackett ordered angrily. "Listen! You just have to *look* at this soup, see? You just *cough* loud and it blows! You know how they transport it? In a can that's shaped like this, see, like a fan? That's to give room for compartments, because each compartment has to be lined with rubber. That's the only way you can even *think* of handling it."

"Listen, Tom—"

"Now wait a minute, Jesse. For God's sake just put your mind to this. I know you had your heart set on a job, but you've got to understand. This stuff goes only in special trucks! At night! They got to follow a special route! They can't go through any city! If they lay over, it's got to be in a special garage! Don't you see what that means? Don't that tell you how dangerous it is?"

"I'll drive careful," Jesse said. "I know how to handle a truck. I'll drive slow."

Brackett groaned. "Do you think Egbert didn't drive careful or know how to handle a truck?"

"Tom," Jesse said earnestly, "you can't scare me. I got my mind fixed on only one thing: Egbert said he was getting a dollar a mile. He was making five to six hundred dollars a month for a half a month's work, he said. Can I get the same?"

"Sure, you can get the same," Brackett told him savagely. "A dollar a mile. It's easy. But why do you think the company has to pay so much? It's easy—until you run over a stone that your headlights didn't pick out, like Egbert did. Or get a blowout! Or get something in your eye, so the wheel twists and you jar the truck! Or any other God damn thing that nobody ever knows! We can't ask Egbert what happened to him. There's no truck to give any evidence. There's no corpse. There's nothing! Maybe tomorrow somebody'll find a piece of twisted steel way off in a cornfield. But we never find the driver. Not even a finger nail. All we know is that he don't come in on schedule. Then we wait for the police to call us. You know what happened last night? Something went wrong on the bridge. Maybe Egbert was nervous. Maybe he brushed the side with his fender. Only there's no bridge any more. No truck. No Egbert. Do you understand now? That's what you get for your God damn dollar a mile!"

There was a moment of silence. Jesse sat twisting his long thin hands. His mouth was sagging open, his face was agonized. Then he shut his eyes and spoke softly. "I don't care about that, Tom. You told me. Now you got to be good to me and give me the job."

Brackett slapped the palm of his hand down on his desk. "No!"

"Listen, Tom," Jesse said softly, "you just don't understand." He opened his eyes. They were filled with tears.

They made Brackett turn away. "Just look at me, Tom. Don't that tell you enough? What did you think of me when you first saw me? You thought: 'Why don't that bum go away and stop panhandling?' Didn't you, Tom? Tom, I just can't live like this any more. I got to be able to walk down the street with my head up."

"You're crazy," Brackett muttered. "Every year there's one out of five drivers gets killed. That's the average. What's worth that?"

"Is my life worth anything now? We're just starving at home, Tom. They ain't put us back on relief yet."

"Then you should have told me," Brackett exclaimed harshly. "It's your own damn fault. A man has no right to have false pride when his family ain't eating. I'll borrow some money and we'll telegraph it to Ella. Then you go home and get back on relief."

"And then what?"

"And then wait, God damn it! You're no old man. You got no right to throw your life away. Sometime you'll get a job."

"No!" Jesse jumped up. "No. I believed that too. But I don't now," he cried passionately. "I ain't getting a job no more than you're getting your hardware store back. I lost my skill, Tom. Linotyping is skilled work. I'm rusty now. I've been six years on relief. The only work I've had is pick and shovel. When I got that job this spring I was supposed to be an A-1 man. But I wasn't. And they got new machines now. As soon as the slack started they let me out."

"So what?" Brackett said harshly. "Ain't there other jobs?"

"How do I know?" Jesse replied. "There ain't been one for six years. I'd even be afraid to take one now. It's been too hard waiting so many weeks to get back on relief."

"Well you got to have some courage," Brackett shouted. "You've got to keep up hope."

"I got all the courage you want," Jesse retorted vehemently, "but no, I ain't got no hope. The hope has dried up in me in six years' waiting. You're the only hope I got."

"You're crazy," Brackett muttered. "I won't do it. For God's sake think of Ella for a minute."

"Don't you *know* I'm thinking about her?" Jesse asked softly. He plucked at Brackett's sleeve. "That's what decided me, Tom." His voice became muted into a hushed, pained whisper. "The night Egbert was at our house I looked at Ella like I'd seen her for the first time. *She ain't pretty any more, Tom!*" Brackett jerked his head and moved away. Jesse followed him, taking a deep, sobbing breath. "Don't that tell you, Tom? Ella was like a little doll or something, you remember. I couldn't walk down the street without somebody turning to look at her. She ain't twenty-nine yet, Tom, and she ain't pretty no more."

Brackett sat down with his shoulders hunched up wearily. He gripped his hands together and sat leaning forward, staring at the floor.

Jesse stood over him, his gaunt face flushed with emotion, almost unpleasant in its look of pleading and bitter humility. "I ain't done right for Ella, Tom. Ella deserved better. This is the only chance I see in my whole life to do something for her. I've just been a failure."

"Don't talk nonsense," Brackett commented, without rancor. "You ain't a failure. No more than me. There's millions of men in the identical situation. It's just the depression, or the recession, or the God damn New Deal, or . . . !" He swore and lapsed into silence.

"Oh, no," Jesse corrected him, in a knowing, sorrowful tone, "those things maybe excuse other men. But not me. It was up to me to do better. This is my own fault!"

"Oh, beans!" Brackett said. "It's more sun spots than it's you!"

Jesse's face turned an unhealthy mottled red. It looked swollen. "Well, I don't care," he cried wildly. "I don't care! You got to give me this! I got to lift my head up. I went through one stretch of hell but I can't go through another. You want me to keep looking at my little boy's legs and tell myself if I had a job he wouldn't be like that? Every time he walks he says to me, 'I got soft bones from the rickets and you give it to me because you didn't feed me right.' Jesus Christ, Tom, you think I'm going to sit there and watch him like that another six years?"

Brackett leaped to his feet. "So what if you do?" he shouted. "You say you're thinking about Ella. How's she going to like it when you get killed?"

"Maybe I won't," Jesse pleaded. "I've got to have some luck sometime."

"That's what they all think," Brackett replied scornfully. "When you take this job your luck is a question mark. The only thing certain is that sooner or later you get killed."

"Okay then," Jesse shouted back. "Then I do! But meanwhile I got something, don't I? I can buy a pair of shoes. Look at me! I can buy a suit that don't say 'Relief' by the way it fits. I can smoke cigarettes. I can buy some candy for the kids. I can eat some myself. Yes, by God, I want to eat some candy. I want a glass of beer once a day. I want Ella dressed up. I want her to eat meat three times a week, four times maybe. I want to take my family to the movies."

Brackett sat down. "Oh, shut up," he said wearily.

"No," Jesse told him softly, passionately, "you can't get rid of me. Listen, Tom," he pleaded, "I got it all figured out. On six hundred a month look how much I can save! If I last only three months, look how much it is—a thousand dollars—more! And maybe I'll last longer. Maybe a couple years. I can fix Ella up for life!"

"You said it," Brackett interposed. "I suppose you think she'll enjoy living when you're on a job like that?"

"I got it all figured out," Jesse answered excitedly. "She don't know, see? I tell her I make only forty. You put the rest in a bank account for her, Tom."

"Oh, shut up," Brackett said. "You think you'll be happy? Every minute, waking and sleeping, you'll be wondering if to-morrow you'll be dead. And the worst days will be your days off, when you're not driving. They have to give you every other day free to get your nerve back. And you lay around the house eating your heart out. That's how happy you'll be."

Jesse laughed. "I'll be happy! Don't you worry, I'll be so happy, I'll be singing. Lord God, Tom, I'm going to feel *proud* of myself for the first time in seven years!"

"Oh, shut up, shut up," Brackett said.

The little shanty became silent. After a moment Jesse whispered: "You got to, Tom. You got to. You got to."

Again there was silence. Brackett raised both hands to his head, pressing the palms against his temples.

"Tom, Tom—" Jesse said.

Brackett sighed. "Oh God damn it," he said finally, "all right, I'll take you on, God help me." His voice was low, hoarse, infinitely weary. "If you're ready to drive to-night, you can drive to-night."

Jesse didn't answer. He couldn't. Brackett looked up. The tears were running down Jesse's face. He was swallowing and trying to speak, but only making an absurd, gasping noise.

"I'll send a wire to Ella," Brackett said in the same hoarse, weary voice. "I'll tell her you got a job, and you'll send her fare in a couple of days. You'll have some money then—that is, if you last the week out, you jackass!"

Jesse only nodded. His heart felt so close to bursting that he pressed both hands against it, as though to hold it locked within his breast.

"Come back here at six o'clock," Brackett said. "Here's some money. Eat a good meal."

"Thanks," Jesse whispered.

"Wait a minute," Brackett said. "Here's my address." He wrote it on a piece of paper. "Take any car going that way. Ask the conductor where to get off. Take a bath and get some sleep."

"Thanks," Jesse said. "Thanks, Tom."

"Oh, get out of here," Brackett said.

"Tom."

"What?"

"I just—" Jesse stopped. Brackett saw his face. The eyes were still glistening with tears, but the gaunt face was shining now, with a kind of fierce radiance.

Brackett turned away. "I'm busy," he said.

Jesse went out. The wet film blinded him but the whole world seemed to have turned golden. He limped slowly, with the blood pounding his temples and a wild, incommunicable joy in his heart. "I'm the happiest man in the world," he whispered to himself. "I'm the happiest man on the whole earth."

Brackett sat watching till finally Jesse turned the corner of the alley and disappeared. Then he hunched himself over, with his head in his hands. His heart was beating painfully, like something old and clogged. He listened to it as it beat. He sat in desperate tranquillity, gripping his head in his hands.

That Tree

HE HAD really wanted to be a cheerful bum lying under a tree in a good climate, writing poetry. He wrote bushel basketsful of poetry and it was all no good and he knew it, even while he was writing it. Knowing his poetry was no good did not take away much from his pleasure in it. He would have enjoyed just that kind of life: no respectability, no responsibility, no money to speak of, wearing wornout sandals and a becoming, if probably ragged, blue shirt, lying under a tree writing poetry. That was why he had come to Mexico in the first place. He had felt in his bones that it was the country for him. Long after he had become quite an important journalist, an authority on Latin-American revolutions and a best seller, he confessed to any friends and acquaintances who would listen to him— he enjoyed this confession, it gave him a chance to talk about the thing he believed he loved best, the idle free romantic life of a poet—that the day Miriam kicked him out was the luckiest day of his life. She had left him, really, packing up suddenly in a cold quiet fury, stabbing him with her elbows when he tried to get his arms around her, now and again cutting him to the bone with a short sentence expelled through her clenched teeth; but he felt that he had been, as he always explained, kicked out. She had kicked him out and it had served him right.

The shock had brought him to himself as if he had been surprised out of a long sleep. He had sat quite benumbed in the bare clean room, among the straw mats and the painted Indian chairs Miriam hated, in the sudden cold silence, his head in his hands, nearly all night. It hadn't even occurred to him to lie down. It must have been almost daylight when he got up stiff in every joint from sitting still so long, and though he could not say he had been thinking yet he had formed a new resolution. He had started out, you might almost say that very day, to make a career for himself in journalism. He couldn't say why he had hit on that, except that the word would impress his wife, the work was just intellectual enough to save his self-respect, such as it was, and even to him it seemed a suitable occupation for a man such as he had suddenly become, bent on getting on in the world of affairs. Nothing ever happens suddenly to anyone, he observed, as if the thought had just occurred to him; it had been coming on probably for a long time, sneaking up on him when he wasn't looking. His wife had called him "Parasite!" She had said "Ne'er-do-well!" and as she repeated these things for what proved to be the last time, it struck him she had said them often before, when he had not listened to her with the ear of his mind. He translated these relatively harmless epithets instantly into their proper synonyms of Loafer! and Bum! Miriam had been a schoolteacher, and no matter what her disappointments and provocations may have been, you could not expect her easily to forget such discipline. She had got into a professional habit of primness; besides, she was a properly brought-up girl, not a prissy bore, not at all, but a —well, there you are, a nicely brought-up Middle-Western girl, who took life seriously. And what can you do about that? She was sweet and gay and full of little crazy notions, but she never gave way to them honestly, or at least never at the moment when they might have meant something. She was never able to see the amusing side of a threatening situation which, taken solemnly, would ruin everything. No, her sense of humor never worked for salvation. It was just an extra frill on what would have been a good time anyhow.

He wondered if anybody had ever thought—oh, well, of course everybody else had, he was always making marvelous discoveries that other people had known all along—how impossible it is to explain or to make other eyes see the special qualities in the person you love. There was such a special kind of beauty in Miriam. In certain lights and moods he simply got a clutch in the pit of his stomach when he looked at her. It was something that could happen any hour of the day, in the midst of the most ordinary occupations. He thought there was something to be said for living with one person day and night the year round. It brings out the worst, but it brings out the best, too, and Miriam's best was pretty damn swell. He couldn't describe it. It was easy to talk about her faults. He remembered all of them, he could add them up against her like rows of figures in a vast unpaid debt. He had lived with her for four years, and even now sometimes he woke out of a sound sleep in a sweating rage with himself, asking himself again why he had ever wasted a minute on her. She wasn't beautiful in his style. He confessed to a weakness for the kind that knocks your eye out. Her notion of daytime dress was a tailored suit with a round-collared blouse and a little felt hat like a bent shovel pulled down over her eyes. In the evening she put on a black dinner dress, positively disappeared into it. But she did her hair well and had the most becoming nightgowns he ever saw. You could have put her mind in a peanut shell. She hadn't temperament of the kind he had got used to in the Mexican girls. She did not approve of his use of the word temperament, either. She thought it was a kind of occupational disease among artists, or a trick they practiced to make themselves interesting. In any case, she distrusted artists and she distrusted temperament. But there was something about her. In cold blood he could size her up to himself, but it made him furious if any-one even hinted a criticism against her. His second wife had made a point of being catty about Miriam. In the end he could almost be willing to say this had led to his second divorce. He could not bear hearing Miriam called a mousy little nit-wit—at least not by *that* woman. . . .

They both jumped nervously at an explosion in the street, the backfire of an automobile.

"Another revolution," said the fat scarlet young man in

the tight purplish suit, at the next table. He looked like a parboiled sausage ready to burst from its skin. It was the oldest joke since the Mexican Independence, but he was trying to look as if he had invented it. The journalist glanced back at him over a sloping shoulder. "Another of those smart-cracking newspaper guys," he said in a tough voice, too loudly on purpose, "sitting around the Hotel Regis lobby wearing out the spittoons."

The smart-cracker swelled visibly and turned a darker red. "Who do you think you're talking about, you banjo-eyed chinless wonder, you?" he asked explicitly, spreading his chest across the table.

"Somebody way up, no doubt," said the journalist, in his natural voice, "somebody in with the government, I'll bet."

"Dyuhwana fight?" asked the newspaper man, trying to unwedge himself from between the table and his chair, which sat against the wall.

"Oh, I don't mind," said the journalist, "if you don't."

The newspaper man's friends laid soothing paws all over him and held him down. "Don't start anything with that shrimp," said one of them, his wet pink eyes trying to look sober and responsible. "For crisesake, Joe, can't you see he's about half your size and a feeb to boot? You wouldn't hit a feeb, now, Joe, would you?"

"I'll feeb him," said the newspaper man, wiggling faintly under restraint.

"*Señores'n, señores'n,*" urged the little Mexican waiter, "there are respectable ladies and gentlemen present. Please, a little silence and correct behavior, please."

"Who the hell are *you,* anyhow?" the newspaper man asked the journalist, from under his shelter of hands, around the thin form of the waiter.

"Nobody you'd wanta know, Joe," said another of his pawing friends. "Pipe down now before these greasers turn in a general alarm. You know how liable they are to go off when you least expect it. Pipe down, now, Joe, now you just remember what happened the last time, Joe. Whaddayah *care*, anyhow?"

"*Señores'n,*" said the little waiter, working his thin out-spread mahogany-colored hands up and down alternately as if they were on sticks, "it is necessary it must cease or the *señores'n* must remove themselves."

It did cease. It seemed to evaporate. The four newspaper men at the next table subsided, cluttered in a circle with their heads together, muttering into their highballs. The journalist turned back, ordered another round of drinks, and went on talking, in a low voice.

He had never liked this café, never had any luck in it. Something always happened here to spoil his evening. If there was one brand of bum on earth he despised, it was a newspaper bum. Or anyhow the drunken illiterates the United Press and Associated Press seemed to think were good enough for Mexico and South America. They were always getting mixed up in affairs that were none of their business, and they spent their time trying to work up trouble somewhere so they could get a story out of it. They were always having to be thrown out on their ears by the government. He just happened to know that the bum at the next table was about due to be deported. It had been pretty safe to make that crack about how he was no doubt way up in Mexican official esteem. . . . He thought that would remind him of something, all right.

One evening he had come here with Miriam for dinner and dancing, and at the very next table sat four fat generals from the North, with oxhorn mustaches and big bellies and big belts full of cartridges and pistols. It was in the old days just after Obregón had taken the city, and the town was crawling with generals. They infested the steam baths, where they took off their soiled campaign harness and sweated away the fumes of tequila and fornication, and they infested the cafés to get drunk again on champagne, and pick up the French whores who had been imported for the festivities of the presidential inauguration. These four were having an argument very quietly, their mean little eyes boring into each other's faces. He and his wife were dancing within arm's length of the table when one of the generals got up suddenly, tugging at his pistol, which stuck, and the other three jumped and grabbed him, all without a word; everybody in the place saw it at once. So far there was nothing unusual. The point was, every right-minded Mexican girl just seized her man firmly by the waist and spun him around until his back was to the generals, holding him before her like a shield, and there the whole roomful had stood frozen for a second, the music dead. His wife Miriam had broken from him and hidden under a table. He had to drag her out by the arm before everybody. "Let's have another drink," he said, and paused, looking around him as if he saw again the place as it had been on that night nearly ten years before. He blinked, and went on. It had been the most utterly humiliating moment of his whole blighted life. He had thought he couldn't survive to pick up their things and get her out of there. The generals had all sat down again and everybody went on dancing as though nothing had happened. . . . Indeed, nothing had happened to anyone except himself.

He tried, for hours that night and on and on for nearly a year, to explain to her how he felt about it. She could not understand at all. Sometimes she said it was all perfect nonsense. Or she remarked complacently that it had never occurred to her to save her life at his expense. She thought such tricks were all very well for the Mexican girls who had only one idea in their heads, and any excuse would do to hold a man closer than they should, but she could not, could *not*, see why he should expect her to imitate them. Besides, she had felt safer under the table. It was her first and only thought. He told her a bullet might very well have gone through the wood; a plank was no protection at all, a human torso was as good as a feather pillow to stop a bullet. She kept saying it simply had not occurred to her to do anything else, and that it really had nothing at all to do with him. He could never make her see his point of view for one moment. It should have had something to do with him. All those Mexican girls were born knowing what they should do and they did it instantly, and Miriam had merely proved once for all that her instincts were out of tune. When she tightened her mouth to bite her lip and say "Instincts!" she could make it sound like the most obscene word in any language. It was a shocking word. And she didn't stop there. At last she said, she hadn't the faintest interest in what Mexican girls were born for, but she had no intention of wasting her life flattering male vanity. "Why should I trust you in anything?" she asked. "What reason have you given me to trust you?"

He was surprised at the change in her since he had first met her in Minneapolis. He chose to believe this change had been caused by her teaching school. He told her he thought it the most deadly occupation there was and a law should be passed prohibiting pretty women under thirty-five years of age from taking it up. She reminded him they were living on the money she had earned at it. They had been engaged for three years, a chaste long-distance engagement which he considered morbid and unnatural. Of course he had to do something to wear away the time, so while she was in Minneapolis saving her money and filling a huge trunk with household linen, he had been living in Mexico City with an Indian girl who posed for a set of painters he knew. He had a job teaching English in one of the technical schools—damned odd, he had been a schoolteacher too, but he never thought of it just that way until this minute—and he lived very comfortably with the Indian girl on his wages, for naturally the painters did not pay her for posing. The Indian girl divided her time cheerfully between the painters, the cooking pot, and his bed, and she managed to have a baby without interrupting any of these occupations for more than a few days. Later on she was taken up by one of the more famous and successful painters, and grew very sophisticated and a "character," but at that time she was still simple and nice. She took, later on, to wearing native art-jewelry and doing native dances in costume, and learned to paint almost as well as a seven-year-old child; "you know," he said, "the primitive style." Well, by that time, he was having troubles of his own. When the time came for Miriam to come out and marry him—the whole delay, he realized afterward, was caused by Miriam's expansive notions of what a bride's outfit should be—the Indian girl had gone away very cheerfully, too cheerfully, in fact, with a new man. She had come back in three days to say she was at last going to get married honestly, and she felt he should give her the furniture for a dowry. He had helped her pile the stuff on the backs of two Indian carriers, and the girl had walked away with the baby's head dangling out of her shawl. For just a moment when he saw the baby's face, he had an odd feeling. "That's mine," he said to himself, and added at once, "perhaps." There was no way of knowing, and it certainly looked like any other little shock-haired Indian baby. Of course the girl had not got married; she had never even thought of it.

When Miriam arrived, the place was almost empty, because he had not been able to save a peso. He had a bed and a stove, and the walls were decorated with drawings and paintings by his Mexican friends, and there was a litter of painted gourds and carved wood and pottery in beautiful colors. It didn't seem so bad to him, but Miriam's face, when she stepped into the first room, was, he had to admit, pretty much of a study. She said very little, but she began to be unhappy about a number of things. She cried intermittently for the first few weeks, for the most mysterious and far-fetched causes. He would wake in the night and find her crying hopelessly. When she sat down to coffee in the morning she would lean her head on her hands and cry. "It's nothing, nothing really," she would tell him. "I don't know what is the matter. I just want to cry." He knew now what was the matter. She had come all that way to marry after three years' planning, and she couldn't see herself going back and facing the music at home. This mood had not lasted, but it made a fairly dreary failure of their honeymoon. She knew nothing about the Indian girl, and believed, or professed to believe, that he was a virgin as she was at their marriage. She hadn't much curiosity and her moral standards were severe, so it was impossible for him ever to take her into his confidence about his past. She simply took it for granted in the most irritating way that he hadn't any past worth mentioning except the three years they were engaged, and that, of course, they shared already. He had believed that all virgins, however austere their behavior, were palpitating to learn about life, were you might say hanging on by an eyelash until they arrived safely at initiation within the secure yet libertine advantages of marriage. Miriam upset this theory as in time she upset most of his theories. His intention to play the rôle of a man of the world educating an innocent but interestingly teachable bride was nipped in the bud. She was not at all teachable and she took no trouble to make herself interesting. In their most intimate hours her mind seemed elsewhere, gone into some darkness of its own, as if a prior and greater shock of knowledge had forestalled her attention. She was not to be won, for reasons of her own which she would not or could not give. He could not even play the rôle of poet. She was not interested in his poetry. She preferred Milton, and she let him know it. She let him know also that she believed their mutual sacrifice of virginity was the most important act of their marriage, and this sacred rite once achieved, the whole affair had descended to a pretty low plane. She had a terrible phrase about "walking the chalk line" which she applied to all sorts of situations. One walked, as never before, the chalk line in marriage; there seemed to be a chalk line drawn between them as they lay together. . . .

The thing that finally got him down was Miriam's devilish inconsistency. She spent three mortal years writing him how dull and dreadful and commonplace her life was, how sick and tired she was of petty little conventions and amusements, how narrow-minded everybody around her was, how she longed to live in a beautiful dangerous place among interesting people who painted and wrote poetry, and how his letters came into her stuffy little world like a breath of free mountain air, and all that. "For God's sake," he said to his guest, "let's have another drink." Well, he had something of a notion he was freeing a sweet bird from a cage. Once freed, she would perch gratefully on his hand. He wrote a poem about a caged bird set free, dedicated it to her and sent her a copy. She forgot to mention it in her next letter. Then she came out with a two-hundred-pound trunk of linen and enough silk underwear to last her a lifetime, you might have supposed, expecting to settle down in a modern steam-heated flat and have nice artistic young couples from the American colony in for dinner Wednesday evenings. No wonder her face had changed at the first glimpse of her new home. His Mexican friends had scattered flowers all over the place, tied bunches of carnations on the door knobs, almost carpeted the floor with red roses, pinned posies of small bright blooms on the sagging cotton curtains, spread a coverlet of gardenias on the lumpy bed, and had disappeared discreetly, leaving gay reassuring messages scribbled here and there, even on the white plastered walls. . . . She had walked through with a vague look of terror in her eyes, pushing back the wilting flowers with her advancing feet. She swept the gardenias aside to sit on the edge of the bed, and she had said not a word. Hail, Hymen! What next?

He had lost his teaching job almost immediately. The Minister of Education, who was a patron of the school superintendent, was put out of office suddenly, and naturally every soul in his party down to the school janitors went out with him, and there you were. After a while you learn to take such things calmly. You wait until your man gets back in the saddle or you work up an alliance with the new one. . . . Whichever. . . . Meanwhile the change and movement made such a good show you almost forgot the effect it had on your food supply. Miriam was not interested in politics or the movement of local history. She could see nothing but that he had lost his job. They lived on Miriam's savings eked out with birthday checks and Christmas checks from her father, who threatened constantly to come for a visit, in spite of Miriam's desperate letters warning him that the country was appalling, and the climate would most certainly ruin his health. Miriam went on holding her nose when she went to the markets, trying to cook wholesome civilized American food over a charcoal brasier, and doing the washing in the patio over a stone tub with a cold water tap; and everything that had seemed so jolly and natural and inexpensive with the Indian girl was too damnifying and costly for words with Miriam. Her money melted away and they got nothing for it.

She would not have an Indian servant near her: they were dirty and besides how could she afford it? He could not see why she despised and resented housework so, especially since he offered to help. He had thought it rather a picnic to wash a lot of gayly colored Indian crockery outdoors in the sunshine, with the bougainvillea climbing up the wall and the heaven tree in full bloom. Not Miriam. She despised him for thinking it a picnic. He remembered for the first time his mother doing the housework when he was a child. There were half a dozen assorted children, her work was hard and endless, but she went about it with a quiet certainty, a happy absorbed look on her face, as if her hands were working automatically while her imagination was away playing somewhere. "Ah, your mother," said his wife, without any particular emphasis. He felt horribly injured, as if she were insulting his mother and calling down a curse on her head for bringing such a son into the world. No doubt about it, Miriam had force. She could make her personality, which no one need really respect, felt in a bitter, sinister way. She had a background, and solid earth under her feet, and a point of view and a strong spine: even when she danced with him he could feel her tense controlled hips and her locked knees, which gave her dancing a most attractive strength and lightness without any yielding at all. She had her points, all right, like a good horse, but she had missed being beautiful. It wasn't in her. He began to cringe when she reminded him that if he were an invalid she would cheerfully work for him and take care of him, but he appeared to be in the best of health, he was not even looking for a job, and he was still writing that poetry, which was the last straw. She called him a failure. She called him worthless and shiftless and trifling and faithless. She showed him her ruined hands and asked him what she had to look forward to, and told him again, and again, that she was not used to associating with the simply indescribably savage and awful persons who kept streaming through the place. Moreover, she had no intention of getting used to it. He tried to tell her that these persons were the best painters and poets and what-alls in Mexico, that she should try to appreciate them; these were the artists he had told her about in his letters. She wanted to know why Carlos never changed his shirt. "I told her," said the journalist, "it was because probably he hadn't got any other shirt." And why was Jaime such a glutton, leaning over his plate and wolfing his food? Because he was famished, no doubt. It was precisely that she could not understand. Why didn't they go to work and make a living? It was no good trying to explain to her his Franciscan notions of holy Poverty as being the natural companion for the artist. She said, "So you think they're being poor on purpose? Nobody but you would be such a fool." Really, the things that girl said. And his general impression of her was that she was silent as a cat. He went on in his pawky way trying to make clear to her his mystical faith in these men who went ragged and hungry because they had chosen once for all between what he called in all seriousness their souls, and this world. Miriam knew better. She knew they were looking for the main chance. "She was abominably, obscenely right. How I hate that woman, I hate her as I hate no one else. She assured me they were not so stupid as I thought; and I lived to see Jaime take up with a rich old woman, and Ricardo decide to turn film actor, and Carlos sitting easy with a government job, painting revolutionary frescoes to order, and I asked myself, Why shouldn't a man survive in any way he can?" But some fixed point of feeling in him refused to be convinced, he had a sackful of romantic notions about artists and their destiny and he was left holding it. Miriam had seen through them with half an eye, and how he wished he might have thought of a trick to play on her that would have finished her for life. But he had not. They all in turn ran out on him and in the end he had run out too. "So you see, I don't feel any better about doing what I did finally do, but I can say I am not unusual. That I can say. The trouble was that Miriam was right, damn her. I am not a poet, my poetry is filthy, and I had notions about artists that I must have got out of books. . . . You know, a race apart, dedicated men much superior to common human needs and ambitions. . . . I mean I thought art was a religion. . . . I mean that when Miriam kept saying . . ."

What he meant was that all this conflict began to damage him seriously. Miriam had become an avenging fury, yet he could not condemn her. Hate her, yes, that was almost too simple. His old-fashioned respectable middle-class hard-working American ancestry and training rose up in him and fought on Miriam's side. He felt he had broken about every bone in him to get away from them and live them down, and here he had been overtaken at last and beaten into resignation that had nothing to do with his mind or heart. It was as if his blood stream had betrayed him. The prospect of taking a job and being a decent little clerk with shiny pants and elbows—for he couldn't think of a job in any other terms—seemed like a kind of premature death which would not even compensate him with loss of memory. He didn't do anything about it at all. He did odd jobs and picked up a little money, but never enough. He could see her side of it, at least he tried hard to see it. When it came to a showdown, he hadn't a single argument in favor of his way of life that would hold water. He had been trying to live and think in a way that he hoped would end by making a poet of him, but it hadn't worked. That was the long and short of it. So he might have just gone on to some unimaginably sordid end if Miriam, after four years: four years? yes, good God, four years and one month and eleven days, had not written home for money, packed up what was left of her belongings, called him a few farewell names, and left. She had been shabby and thin and wild-looking for so long he could not remember ever having seen her any other way, yet all at once her profile in the doorway was unrecognizable to him.

So she went, and she did him a great favor without knowing it. He had fallen into the cowardly habit of thinking their marriage was permanent, no matter how evil it might be, that they loved each other, and so it did not matter what cruelties they committed against each other, and he had developed a real deafness to her words. He was unable, towards the end, either to see her or hear her. He realized this afterward, when remembered phrases and expressions of her eyes and mouth began to eat into his marrow. He was grateful to her. If she had not gone, he might have loitered on, wasting his time trying to write poetry, hanging around dirty picturesque little cafés with a fresh set of clever talkative poverty-stricken young Mexicans who were painting or writing or talking about getting ready to paint or write. His faith had renewed itself; these fellows were pure artists—they would never sell out. They were not bums, either. They worked all the time at something to do with Art. "Sacred Art," he said, "our glasses are empty again."

But try telling anything of the kind to Miriam. Somehow he had never got to that tree he meant to lie down under. If he had, somebody would certainly have come around and collected rent for it, anyhow. He had spent a good deal of time lying under tables at Dinty Moore's or the Black Cat with a gang of Americans like himself who were living a free life and studying the native customs. He was rehearsing, he explained to Miriam, hoping for once she would take a joke, for lying under a tree later on. It didn't go over. She would have died with her boots on before she would have cracked a smile at that. So then. . . . He had gone in for a career in the hugest sort of way. It had been easy. He hardly could say now just what his first steps were, but it had been easy. Except for Miriam, he would have been a lousy failure, like those bums at Dinty Moore's, still rolling under the tables, studying the native customs. He had gone in for a career in journalism and he had made a good thing of it. He was a recognized authority on revolutions in twenty-odd Latin-American countries, and his sympathies happened to fall in exactly right with the high-priced magazines of a liberal humanitarian slant which paid him well for telling the world about the oppressed peoples. He could really write, too; if he did say so, he had a prose style of his own. He had made the kind of success you can clip out of newspapers and paste in a book, you can count it and put it in the bank, you can eat and drink and wear it, and you can see it in other people's eyes at tea and dinner parties. Fine, and now what? On the strength of all this he had got married again. Twice, in fact, and divorced twice. That made three times, didn't it? That was plenty. He had spent a good deal of time and energy doing all sorts of things he didn't care for in the least to prove to his first wife, who had been a twenty-three-year-old schoolteacher in Minneapolis, Minnesota, that he was not just merely a bum, fit for nothing but lying under a tree—if he had ever been able to locate that ideal tree he had in his mind's eye—writing poetry and enjoying his life.

Now he had done it. He smoothed out the letter he had been turning in his hands and stroked it as if it were a cat. He said, "I've been working up to the climax all this time. You know, good old surprise technique. Now then, get ready."

Miriam had written to him, after these five years, asking him to take her back. And would you believe it, he was going to break down and do that very thing. Her father was dead, she was terribly lonely, she had had time to think everything over, she believed herself to blame for a great many things, she loved him truly and she always had, truly; she regretted, oh, everything, and hoped it was not too late for them to make a happy life together once more. . . . She had read everything she could find of his in print, and she loved all of it. He had that very morning sent by cable the money for her to travel on, and he was going to take her back. She was going to live again in a Mexican house without any conveniences and she was not going to have a modern flat. She was going to take whatever he chose to hand her, and like it. And he wasn't going to marry her again, either. Not he. If she wanted to live with him on these terms, well and good. If not, she could just go back once more to that school of hers in Minneapolis. If she stayed, she would walk a chalk line, all right, one she hadn't drawn for herself. He picked up a cheese knife and drew a long sharp line in the checkered table-cloth. She would, believe him, walk *that*.

The hands of the clock pointed half past two. The journalist swallowed the last of his drink and went on drawing more cross-hatches on the table-cloth with a relaxed hand. His guest wished to say, "Don't forget to invite me to your wedding," but thought better of it. The journalist raised his twitching lids and swung his half-focused eyes upon the shadow opposite and said, "I suppose you think I don't know—"

His guest moved to the chair edge and watched the orchestra folding up for the night. The café was almost empty. The journalist paused, not for an answer, but to give weight to the important statement he was about to make.

"I don't know what's happening, this time," he said, "don't deceive yourself. This time, I know." He seemed to be admonishing himself before a mirror.

WILLIAM SAROYAN

Going Home

THIS valley, he thought, all this country between the mountains, is mine, home to me, the place I dream about, and
everything is the same, not a thing is changed, water sprin-
klers still splash in circles over lawns of Bermuda grass, good
old home town, simplicity, reality.

Walking along Alvin Street he felt glad to be home again.
Everything was fine, common and good, the smell of earth,
cooking suppers, smoke, the rich summer air of the valley full
of plant growth, grapes growing, peaches ripening, and the
oleander bush swooning with sweetness, the same as ever. He
breathed deeply, drawing the smell of home deep into his
lungs, smiling inwardly. It was hot. He hadn't felt his senses
reacting to the earth so cleanly and clearly for years; now it
was a pleasure even to breathe. The cleanliness of the air
sharpened the moment so that, walking, he felt the magnifi-
cence of being, glory of possessing substance, of having form
and motion and intellect, the piety of merely being alive on
the earth.

Water, he thought, hearing the soft splash of a lawn sprin-
kler; to taste the water of home, the full cool water of the
valley, to have that simple thirst and that solid water with
which to quench it, fulfilment, the clarity of life. He saw an
old man holding a hose over some geranium plants, and his
thirst sent him to the man.

Good evening, he said quietly; may I have a drink?

The old man turned slowly, his shadow large against the
house, to look into the young man's face, amazed and pleased.
You bet, he said; here, and he placed the hose into the young
man's hands. Mighty fine water, said the old man, this water

262

of the San Joaquin valley; best yet, I guess. That water up in Frisco makes me sick, ain't got no taste. And down in Los Angeles, why, the water tastes like castor oil; I can't understand how so many people go on living there year after year.

While the old man talked he listened to the water falling from the hose to the earth, leaping thickly, cleanly, sinking swiftly into the earth. You said it, he said to the old man; you said it, our water is the finest water on earth.

He curved his head over the spouting water and began to drink. The sweet rich taste of the water amazed him, and as he drank he thought, God, this is splendid. He could feel the cool water splashing into his being, refreshing and cooling him. Losing his breath, he lifted his head, saying to the old man, We're mighty lucky, us folks in the valley.

He bent his head over the water again and began again to swallow the splashing liquid, laughing to himself with delight. It seemed as if he couldn't get enough of it into his system; the more he drank, the finer the water tasted to him and the more he wanted to drink.

The old man was amazed. You drunk about two quarts, he said.

Still swallowing the water, he could hear the old man talking, and he lifted his head again, replying, I guess so. It sure tastes fine. He wiped his mouth with a handkerchief, still holding the hose, still wanting to drink more. The whole valley was in that water, all the clarity, all the genuineness, all the goodness and simplicity and reality.

Man alive, said the old man. You sure was thirsty. How long since you had a drink, anyway?

Two years, he replied. I mean two years since I had a drink of *this* water. I been away, traveling around. I just got back. I was born here, over on G Street in Russian town; you know, across the Southern Pacific tracks; been away two years and I just got back. Mighty fine too, let me tell you, to be back. I like this place. I'm going to get a job and settle down.

He hung his head over the water again and took several more swallows; then he handed the hose to the old man.

You sure was thirsty, said the old man. I ain't never seen anybody anywhere drink so much water at one time. It sure looked good seeing you swallow all that water.

He went on walking down Alvin Street, humming to himself, the old man staring at him.

Nice to be back, the young man thought; greatest mistake I ever made, coming back this way.

Everything he had ever done had been a mistake, and this was one of the good mistakes. He had come south from San Francisco without even thinking of going home; he had thought of going as far south as Merced, stopping there awhile, and then going back, but once he had got into the country, it had been too much. It had been great fun standing on the highway in his city clothes, hitchhiking.

One little city after another, and here he was walking through the streets of his home town, at seven in the evening. It was great, very amusing; and the water; splendid.

He wasn't far from town, the city itself, and he could see one or two of the taller buildings, the Pacific Gas & Electric Building, all lit up with colored lights, and another, a taller one, that he hadn't seen before. That's a new one, he thought; they put up that one while I was away; things must be booming.

He turned down Fulton Street and began walking into town. It looked great from where he was, far away and nice and small, very genuine, a real quiet little town, the kind of place to live in, settle down in, marry in, have a home, kids, a job, and all the rest of it. It was all he wanted. The air of the valley and the water and the reality of the whole place, the cleanliness of life in the valley, the simplicity of the people.

In the city everything was the same: the names of the stores, the people walking in the streets, and the slow passing of automobiles; boys in cars trying to pick up girls; same as ever; not a thing changed. He saw faces he had known as a boy, people he did not know by name, and then he saw Tony Rocca, his old pal, walking up the street toward him, and he saw that Tony recognized him. He stopped walking, waiting for Tony to come into his presence. It was like a meeting in a dream, strange, almost incredible. He had dreamed of the two of them playing hookey from school to go swimming, to go out to the county fair, to sneak into a moving-picture theatre; and now here he was again, a big fellow with a lazy, easy-going walk, and a genial Italian grin. It was good, and he was glad he had made the mistake and come back.

He stopped walking, waiting for Tony to come into his presence, smiling at him, unable to speak. The two boys shook hands and then began to strike one another with affection, laughing loudly, swearing at one another. You old bastard, Tony said; where the hell have you been? and he punched his friend in the stomach, laughing loudly.

Old Tony, he said; good old punchdrunk Tony. God, it's good to see you. I thought maybe you'd be dead by this time. What the hell have you been doing? He dodged another punch, and struck his friend in the chest. He swore in Italian at Tony, using words Tony had taught him years ago, and Tony swore back at him in Russian.

I've got to go out to the house, he said at last. The folks don't know I'm here. I've got to go out and see them. I'm dying to see my brother Paul.

He went on down the street, smiling about Tony. They would be having a lot of good times together again; they might even go swimming again the way they did as kids. It was great to be back.

Walking by stores, he thought of buying his mother a small gift. A little gift would please the old lady. But he had little money, and all the decent things were expensive. I'll get her something later, he thought.

He turned west on Tulare Street, crossing the Southern Pacific tracks, reached G Street, then turned south. In a few minutes he would be home again, at the door of the little old house; the same as ever; the old woman, the old man, his three sisters, and his kid brother, all of them in the house, living simple lives.

He saw the house from a distance of about a block, and his heart began to jump. He felt suddenly ill and afraid, something he had forgotten about the place, about that life which he had always hated, something ugly and mean. But he walked on, moving slower as he came closer to the house. The fence had fallen and no one had fixed it. The house suddenly appeared to be very ugly, and he wondered why in hell the old man didn't move to a better house in a better neighborhood. Seeing the house again, feeling all its old reality, all his hatred for it returned, and he began to feel again the longing to be away from it, where he could not see it. He began to feel, as he had felt as a boy, the deep inarticulate hatred he had for the whole city, its falseness, its meanness, the stupidity of its people, the emptiness of their minds, and it seemed to him that he would never be able to return to such a place. The water; yes, it was good, it was splendid; but there were other things.

He walked slowly before the house, looking at it as if he might be a stranger, feeling alien and unrelated to it, yet feeling that it was home, the place he dreamed about, the place that tormented him wherever he went. He was afraid someone might come out of the house and see him, because he knew that if he was seen, he might find himself running away. Still, he wanted to see them, all of them, have them before his eyes, feel the full presence of their bodies, even smell them, that old strong Russian smell. But it was too much. He began to feel hatred for everything in the city, and he walked on, going to the corner. There he stood beneath the street lamp, bewildered and disgusted, wanting to see his brother Paul, to talk to the boy, find out what was going on in his mind, how he was taking it, being in such a place, living such a life. He knew how it had been with him when he had been his brother's age, and he hoped he might be able to give his brother a little advice, how to keep from feeling the monotony and the ugliness by reading.

He forgot that he hadn't eaten since breakfast, and that he had been dreaming for months of eating another of his mother's meals, sitting at the old table in the kitchen, seeing her, large and red-faced and serious and angry toward him, loving him, but he had lost his appetite. He thought he might wait at the corner; perhaps his brother would leave the house to take a walk and he would see the boy and talk to him. Paul, he would say, and he would talk to the boy in Russian.

The stillness of the valley began to oppress him, losing its piety, becoming merely a form of the valley's monotony.

Still, he couldn't go away from the house. From the corner he could see it, and he knew that he wanted to go in and be among his people, a part of their lives; he knew this was what he had wanted to do for months, to knock at the door, embrace his mother and his sisters, walk across the floors of the house, sit in the old chairs, sleep in his bed, talk with his old man, eat at the table.

And now something he had forgotten while he had been away, something real but ugly in that life, had come up swiftly, changing everything, changing the appearance and meaning of the house, the city, the whole valley, making it all ugly and unreal, making him wish to go away and never return. He could never come back. He could never enter the house again and go on with his life where he had left off.

Suddenly he was in the alley, climbing over the fence, walking through the yard. His mother had planted tomatoes, and peppers, and the smell of the growing plants was thick and acrid and very melancholy to him. There was a light in the kitchen, and he moved quietly toward it, hoping to see some of them without being seen. He walked close to the house, to the kitchen window, and looking in saw his youngest sister Martha washing dishes. He saw the old table, the old stove, and Martha, with her back turned to him; and all these things seemed so sad and so pathetic that tears came to his eyes, and he began to need a cigarette. He struck a match quietly on the bottom of his shoe and inhaled the smoke, looking at his little sister in the old house, a part of the monotony. Everything seemed very still, very clear, terribly sad; but he hoped his mother would enter the kitchen; he wanted to have another look at her. He wanted to see if his being away had changed her much. How would she look? Would she have that old angry look? He felt angry with himself for not being a good son, for not trying to make his mother happy, but he knew it was impossible.

He saw his brother Paul enter the kitchen for a drink of water, and for a moment he wanted to cry out the boy's name, everything that was good in him, all his love, rushing to the face and form of the boy; but he restrained himself, inhaling deeply, tightening his lips. In the kitchen, the boy seemed lost, bewildered, imprisoned. Looking at his brother, be began to cry softly, saying, Jesus, O Jesus, Jesus.

He no longer wished to see his mother. He would become so angry that he would do something crazy. He walked quietly through the yard, hoisted himself over the fence, and jumped to the alley. He began to walk away, his grief mounting in him. When he was far enough away not to be heard, he began to sob, loving them passionately and hating the ugliness and monotony of their lives. He felt himself hurrying away from home, from his people, crying bitterly in the darkness of the clear night, weeping because there was nothing he could do, not one confounded thing.

Profession: Housewife

ALTHOUGH the window by the breakfast nook was open, it was very warm. The yellow-and-white gingham curtains hung still and the blue oilcloth showed beads of moisture. Even the painted table top felt damp and sticky, and Joe Grannis was conscious of the discomfort of the hard bench on which he sat. He heard Dorothy tear open the letter and, leaning back as far as he could, he shook out his paper and held it before his face.

In a few minutes she slapped the letter down on the table so hard that the coffee in her cup spilled over into the saucer. "I might have known," she said. "They can't come. At least, she *says* they can't come."

Although it was what he had expected, Joe Grannis lowered his paper and managed to look surprised. "That's funny," he answered. "Maybe some other time."

"Some other time," his wife repeated. "Don't be dumb. The point is they don't want to come, now or any other time."

"I wouldn't say that," he said. "There's no reason why they shouldn't want to come."

Dorothy Grannis lifted her saucer and poured the coffee that had spilled back into the cup. Her face, normally a solid pink, had turned a bright cerise and her hair lay against her forehead with the metallic fixity of a doll's wig. "I'm sorry I asked them in the first place," she told him.

Joe Grannis made a mistake. "Well, you can't say I didn't warn you," he said. "You can't expect to make friends with people who were friends of Louise's. Those things never work out. People feel funny, sort of."

269

She pushed the sleeves of her chintz house coat further up on her arms with a hard, deliberate gesture and rested her elbows on the table. "Why?" she asked. "From the way you used to talk, I got the impression they were friends of yours. I got the impression that they didn't think so much of *Louise*, that you were the fair-haired boy with them. I got the impression that they couldn't wait until the divorce and everything was over so they could come here again."

She looked around the bright, shiny kitchen and laughed. "My God!" she went on. "If they saw this place now it might be too much for them. They might drop dead. Digging this place out was like excavating. It might be too much for them to see it clean for a change."

Joe Grannis took his watch from his pocket and looked at it. He edged from behind the table and stood up. "Time to go," he said.

"I suppose so," she told him. "You never know the answers to anything. Well, what are we going to do tonight? Sit here and listen to the radio?"

"Now, don't be sarcastic," he answered. "You've got friends of your own. Why don't you call Ruth and Van up and ask them out?"

"And have them wondering why nobody else ever drops in?" she asked indignantly. "That was all right at first. They didn't think anything of it the first few times. But the last time she acted plenty funny about it. Wanting to know if I didn't get lonesome here all day and everything. I'd rather rot."

He looked at her and his face grew set. "Suit yourself," he said. "And since you're speaking of impressions, I got some myself. I got the impression that all you needed to make you happy was a home of your own and to be able to quit work. God knows you sang that tune long enough. Three years, wasn't it? Well, you got what you wanted. You've spent money like a drunken sailor on this place and if you can't make friends for yourself, I can't help you."

"Well, really!" she exclaimed, her voice politely formal. "Really!"

She remained seated at the table until she heard the front door slam behind him, and then she got up and with brisk, efficient movements carried the breakfast dishes to the sink. The sink was of glaring yellow porcelain and the faucets were shiny and new. The hot water on her hands made her feel warmer and she pulled down the zipper of her house coat. Her grasp on the dishes was rough, but she arranged them almost gently in the wire rack to drain.

Pretty soon now the girls would come straggling into the office where she used to work, cool and neat in their new summer dresses. Because the day was warm, the atmosphere about the place would relax and Mannie, the office boy, would be sent to the drugstore for double cokes. There would be gossip and cigarettes in the washroom and speculation as to whether Mr. Ackerman would leave early for a round of golf.

She opened the drawer of the kitchen cabinet and took out a towel, yellow, with blue featherstitching, and dried the dishes hurriedly. Glancing at the clock and seeing that it was not yet nine, she tried to slow her movements. She wiped the breakfast table with a damp cloth and put away the oilcloth doilies.

The dining room was cool and bare. In the centre of the shiny mahogany table was placed an etched silver bowl around which huddled four thin silver candlesticks. Going to the sideboard, she opened the drawers one by one, looking with satisfaction at the rows of silver-plated knives, forks, and spoons lying on their squares of felt. In each drawer was a lump of camphor to prevent tarnishing.

The stairs led out of the dining room and she walked up them to the upstairs hall. Four doors opened out into the hall, but only two of them stood ajar—the door to the bathroom and the one to their bedroom. She liked to keep the extra bedrooms shut off until she felt she could do them over decently. There was little disorder in their own room. Joe's striped silk pajamas lay folded on his bed and her pale-green satin nightgown lay on a chair by the window. She hung these in the closet and then spread the beds, fitting their lavender taffeta covers smoothly.

As she finished, the front-door bell rang briefly, and looking out the window, she saw a man standing there, a leather briefcase under his arm. She loosened her hair slightly about her face and pulled the zipper up on her house coat.

The man who stood at the door was very young and very thin. His light-gray suit was shabby and the coat hung limply from his shoulders. He wore no hat and his fine, light hair was too long and fell untidily over his forehead. He had been looking down when she opened the door, his whole figure drooping, but hearing the sound of the latch, he straightened up to face her, jerking his head up alertly, smiling pleasantly.

"Good morning, Madam," he said.

She stood looking at him for so long without speaking that he shifted his feet in embarrassment, the smile growing fixed on his face.

"Yes?" she asked finally. "Yes?"

He took the briefcase from under his arm, and after struggling with the catch, opened it and drew forth a book, which he held toward her. Its bright, flowered cover looked worn and dirty, as though it had been often handled. She made no motion to take it from him, but he stood bravely facing her, the book in his hand.

"I'm not interested in buying any books," she told him. "Nor anything else."

The young man laughed brightly. "This book, Madam," he said, "is not for sale. It is a gift to you from the company I represent."

"Yes, I know," she answered. "A gift if I subscribe to what?"

The young man lowered his arm, slightly abashed.

"Well?" she asked, raising her eyebrows and putting her head to one side. "Am I right?"

The young man gave another slight laugh. "I can see that you've learned, Madam, that we don't get anything in this world for nothing. A lot of people haven't learned that, and I guess you must be cleverer than average." For a minute he combed his mind to gather up the first rules of salesmanship, which lay scattered there. Then he went on with more assurance. "No, this book is not exactly free, and yet it is free in the sense that you will not actually be paying for this book. What you will be paying for is a three-year subscription to *Good Homes Magazine*. And you will be paying the exact price you would pay if you went to your local dealer. But by taking a subscription now from me, you also will receive this book of five hundred tested recipes, how to set your table for any occasion, and other helpful household hints. So, you see, in a manner of speaking, this book *is* absolutely free. And what is more, Madam, you are permitted to take it now, look it over, and return it to me if you decide you do not care to take a subscription to *Good Homes*."

He smiled triumphantly at her. "Could anything be fairer than that?"

Mrs. Grannis had heard his speech coldly, but now suddenly she opened the door wider and extended her hand for the book. "How long can I keep it before I decide?" she asked.

"For five days, Madam," he told her. Then he dropped his professional manner, and his voice changed. "To tell you the truth, we are supposed to leave them five days. And that's all right for guys that have a car and can come back for them. But I got to figure differently. It's like this—I go to one of these suburbs and spend a day there. I leave a book, if that's what the lady of the house wants, and then I stop by later in the day and pick it up. You see, we're responsible for the books we hand out, and if you don't take a subscription you can't keep the book. The company couldn't afford it. Why, these books cost three dollars to buy."

She stepped back and laid the book on the hall table. "I see," she said. "Well, I'll let you know."

There was something in her gesture that caused the young man to clear his throat anxiously before he spoke again. "May I ask what time will be most convenient for you?"

"Oh, any time," she answered. "I'll be in, all right."

His face cleared. "Well, let's see," he said. "It isn't ten yet and I'll come back about three. That'll give me plenty of time to cover this neighborhood, come back and write out your subscription, and grab a train back to New York. Now, don't think I am too confident, Madam, but I can safely say it will be worth your while to retain the book *plus* receiving *Good Homes* for three entire years."

He refastened the catch of his briefcase and tucked it under his arm. There was a dark spot where the moisture from his hand had stained the leather. He felt very thirsty and wondered if he dared ask for a drink of water. But the lady acted strange. To be sure, she had taken the book, but you never could tell how people were going to act if you asked for a favor. She might think he was trying to get fresh.

So with the sun beating on his head, he stepped back from the door, smiling. "Good day, Madam," he said. "I will be back later."

Halfway down the path, he turned and called to her. "You're the first lady that's taken a book today. It must be good luck or something."

Mrs. Grannis closed the door and walked into the living room. The glare of the sun hurt her eyes and she lowered the shades. Even then, because of the newness of the light, shiny maple furniture, the room had a sort of glint. She lay down on the couch and closed her eyes, trying to decide whether or not to put on her things and run in to see the girls at the office. She could tell them about the house, she thought, and might even ask them out to see it sometime, although she had almost decided to drop them gradually. Still, you had to see somebody, and with Joe's friends acting the way they did, there didn't seem to be much to look forward to in that direction. The dimness of the room soothed her and she fell asleep.

It was after twelve when she woke up, and her head felt stuffy. She made herself a glass of iced tea, heavily sugared, and toasted a cheese sandwich on the electric grill. Then she dressed leisurely and started for the centre of the village. It was almost three when she arrived back home, her hair freshly washed and waved, her face flushed from sitting under the drier. Remembering the young man, she glanced anxiously up and down the street, but he was not in sight. Upstairs, she took off her street things and slipped once more into her house coat. Then, carefully turning back the taffeta spread from her bed, she lay down and lit a cigarette. She heard the bell ring in the kitchen and, propping herself up on one elbow, she peered cautiously out the window. On the steps below stood the young man, who had come for his book. His clothes were even limper than they had been in the morning and he leaned against the side of the door ready to spring into alert attention at the sound of footsteps. She let the curtain drop and lay back on the bed, smoking and staring at the ceiling. The bell rang again, and then, after a few minutes, more urgently.

For a long while she lay there listening to the bell and then she got up and walked silently down the stairs. She picked up the book from the hall table and carried it back to her room. In a few minutes she heard steps once more on the outside walk and the bell began, persistently now. She sat up on the edge of the bed and, taking the book, deliberately and slowly ripped the pages out. When they all lay scattered on the bed beside her, she began tearing them across. With some difficulty she bent the cover. Then, gathering the pieces together, she went to the window and opened it.

The young man looked up at her and the expression on his face changed. He began to smile. "Wake you up?" he asked pleasantly.

She fumbled with the screen and slowly let the torn pages of the book fall to the grass below.

For a minute the young man stared at them, dazed. Without a word he stooped to pick them up, but realizing the hopelessness of his task, he straightened and stood staring up at the window. For a dreadful moment they looked at one another. Then he turned and walked away.

She fastened the screen, lit a cigarette, and lay down again on the bed, smoking and staring at the ceiling.

A Visit of Charity

IT WAS mid-morning—a very cold, bright day. Holding a potted plant before her, a girl of fourteen jumped off the bus in front of the Old Ladies' Home, on the outskirts of town. She wore a red coat, and her straight yellow hair was hanging down loose from the pointed white cap all the little girls were wearing that year. She stopped for a moment beside one of the prickly dark shrubs with which the city had beautified the Home, and then proceeded slowly toward the building, which was of whitewashed brick and reflected the winter sunlight like a block of ice. As she walked vaguely up the steps she shifted the small pot from hand to hand; then she had to set it down and remove her mittens before she could open the heavy door.

"I'm a Campfire Girl. . . . I have to pay a visit to some old lady," she told the nurse at the desk. This was a woman in a white uniform who looked as if she were cold; she had close-cut hair which stood up on the very top of her head exactly like a sea wave. Marian, the little girl, did not tell her that this visit would give her a minimum of only three points in her score.

"Acquainted with any of our residents?" asked the nurse. She lifted one eyebrow and spoke like a man.

"With any old ladies? No—but—that is, any of them will do," Marian stammered. With her free hand she pushed her hair behind her ears, as she did when it was time to study Science.

The nurse shrugged and rose. "You have a nice *multiflora cineraria* there," she remarked as she walked ahead down the hall of closed doors to pick out an old lady.

There was loose, bulging linoleum on the floor. Marian felt as if she were walking on the waves, but the nurse paid no attention to it. There was a smell in the hall like the interior of a clock. Everything was silent until, behind one of the doors, an old lady of some kind cleared her throat like a sheep bleating. This decided the nurse. Stopping in her tracks, she first extended her arm, bent her elbow, and leaned forward from the hips—all to examine the watch strapped to her wrist; then she gave a loud double-rap on the door.

"There are two in each room," the nurse remarked over her shoulder.

"Two what?" asked Marian without thinking. The sound like a sheep's bleating almost made her turn around and run back.

One old woman was pulling the door open in short, gradual jerks, and when she saw the nurse a strange smile forced her old face dangerously awry. Marian, suddenly propelled by the strong, impatient arm of the nurse, saw next the side-face of another old woman, even older, who was lying flat in bed with a cap on and a counterpane drawn up to her chin.

"Visitor," said the nurse, and after one more shove she was off up the hall.

Marian stood tongue-tied; both hands held the potted plant. The old woman, still with that terrible, square smile (which was a smile of welcome) stamped on her bony face, was waiting. . . . Perhaps she said something. The old woman in bed said nothing at all, and she did not look around.

Suddenly Marian saw a hand, quick as a bird claw, reach up in the air and pluck the white cap off her head. At the same time, another claw to match drew her all the way into the room, and the next moment the door closed behind her.

"My, my, my," said the old lady at her side.

Marian stood enclosed by a bed, a washstand and a chair; the tiny room had altogether too much furniture. Everything smelled wet—even the bare floor. She held onto the back of the chair, which was wicker and felt soft and damp. Her heart beat more and more slowly, her hands got colder and colder, and she could not hear whether the old women were saying anything or not. She could not see them very clearly. How dark it was! The window shade was down, and the only door was shut. Marian looked at the ceiling. . . . It was like being caught in a robber's cave, just before one was murdered.

"Did you come to be our little girl for a while?" the first robber asked.

Then something was snatched from Marian's hand—the little potted plant.

"Flowers!" screamed the old woman. She stood holding the pot in an undecided way. "Pretty flowers," she added.

Then the old woman in bed cleared her throat and spoke. "They are not pretty," she said, still without looking around, but very distinctly.

Marian suddenly pitched against the chair and sat down in it.

"Pretty flowers," the first old woman insisted. "Pretty—pretty. . . ."

Marian wished she had the little pot back for just a moment—she had forgotten to look at the plant herself before giving it away. What did it look like?

"Stinkweeds," said the other old woman sharply. She had a bunchy white forehead and red eyes like a sheep. Now she turned them toward Marian. The fogginess seemed to rise in her throat again, and she bleated, "Who—are—you?"

To her surprise, Marian could not remember her name. "I'm a Campfire Girl," she said finally.

"Watch out for the germs," said the old woman like a sheep, not addressing anyone.

"One came out last month to see us," said the first old woman.

A sheep or a germ? wondered Marian dreamily, holding onto the chair.

"Did not!" cried the other old woman.

"Did so! Read to us out of the Bible, and we enjoyed it!" screamed the first.

"Who enjoyed it!" said the woman in bed. Her mouth was unexpectedly small and sorrowful, like a pet's.

"We enjoyed it," insisted the other. "You enjoyed it—I enjoyed it."

"We all enjoyed it," said Marian, without realizing that she had said a word.

The first old woman had just finished putting the potted plant high, high on the top of the wardrobe, where it could hardly be seen from below. Marian wondered how she had ever succeeded in placing it there, how she could ever have reached so high.

"You mustn't pay any attention to old Addie," she now said to the little girl. "She's ailing today."

"Will you shut your mouth?" said the woman in bed. "I am not."

"You're a story."

"I can't stay but a minute—really, I can't," said Marian suddenly. She looked down at the wet floor and thought that if she were sick in here they would have to let her go.

With much to-do the first old woman sat down in a rocking chair—still another piece of furniture!—and began to rock. With the fingers of one hand she touched a very dirty cameo pin on her chest. "What do you do at school?" she asked.

"I don't know . . ." said Marian. She tried to think but she could not.

"Oh, but the flowers are beautiful," the old woman whispered. She seemed to rock faster and faster; Marian did not see how anyone could rock so fast.

"Ugly," said the woman in bed.

"If we bring flowers—" Marian began, and then fell silent. She had almost said that if Campfire Girls brought flowers to the Old Ladies' Home, the visit would count one extra point, and if they took a Bible with them on the bus and read it to the old ladies, it counted double. But the old woman had not listened, anyway; she was rocking and watching the other one, who watched back from the bed.

"Poor Addie is ailing. She has to take medicine—see?" she

said, pointing a horny finger at a row of bottles on the table, and rocking so high that her black comfort shoes lifted off the floor like a little child's.

"I am no more sick than you are," said the woman in bed.

"Oh yes you are!"

"I just got more sense than you have, that's all," said the other old woman, nodding her head.

"That's only the contrary way she talks when *you all* come," said the first old lady with sudden intimacy. She stopped the rocker with a neat pat of her feet and leaned toward Marian. Her hand reached over—it felt like a petunia leaf, clinging and just a little sticky.

"Will you hush! Will you hush!" cried the other one.

Marian leaned back rigidly in her chair.

"When I was a little girl like you, I went to school and all," said the old woman in the same intimate, menacing voice. "Not here—another town. . . ."

"Hush!" said the sick woman. "You never went to school. You never came and you never went. You never were anywhere—only here. You never were born! You don't know anything. Your head is empty, your heart and hands and your old black purse are all empty, even that little old box that you brought with you you brought empty—you showed it to me. And yet you talk, talk, talk, talk, talk all the time until I think I'm losing my mind. Who are you? You're a stranger—a perfect stranger! Don't you know you're a stranger? Is it possible that they have actually done a thing like this to anyone—sent them in a stranger to talk, and rock, and tell away her whole long rigmarole? Do they seriously suppose that I'll be able to keep it up, day in, day out, night in, night out, living in the same room with a terrible old woman—forever?"

Marian saw the old woman's eyes grow bright and turn toward her. This old woman was looking at her with despair and calculation in her face. Her small lips suddenly dropped apart, and exposed a half circle of false teeth with tan gums.

"Come here, I want to tell you something," she whispered. "Come here!"

Marian was trembling, and her heart nearly stopped beating altogether for a moment.

"Now, now, Addie," said the first old woman. "That's not polite. Do you know what's really the matter with old Addie today?" She, too, looked at Marion; one of her eyelids drooped low.

"The matter?" the child repeated stupidly. "What's the matter with her?"

"Why, she's mad because it's her birthday!" said the first old woman, beginning to rock again and giving a little crow as though she had answered her own riddle.

"It is not, it is not!" screamed the old woman in bed. "It is not my birthday, no one knows when that is but myself, and will you please be quiet and say nothing more, or I'll go straight out of my mind!" She turned her eyes toward Marian again, and presently she said in the soft, foggy voice, "When the worst comes to the worst, I ring this bell, and the nurse comes." One of her hands was drawn out from under the patched counterpane—a thin little hand with enormous black freckles. With a finger which would not hold still she pointed to a little bell on the table among the bottles.

"How old are you?" Marian breathed. Now she could see the old woman in bed very closely and plainly, and very abruptly, from all sides, as in dreams. She wondered about her—she wondered for a moment as though there was nothing else in the world to wonder about. It was the first time such a thing had happened to Marian.

"I won't tell!"

The old face on the pillow, where Marian was bending over it, slowly gathered and collapsed. Soft whimpers came out of the small open mouth. It was a sheep that she sounded like—a little lamb. Marian's face drew very close, the yellow hair hung forward.

"She's crying!" She turned a bright, burning face up to the first old woman.

"That's Addie for you," the old woman said spitefully.

Marian jumped up and moved toward the door. For the

second time, the claw almost touched her hair, but it was not quick enough. The little girl put her cap on.

"Well, it was a real visit," said the old woman, following Marian through the doorway and all the way out into the hall. Then from behind she suddenly clutched the child with her sharp little fingers. In an affected, high-pitched whine she cried, "Oh, little girl, have you a penny to spare for a poor old woman that's not got anything of her own? We don't have a thing in the world—not a penny for candy—not a thing! Little girl, just a nickel—a penny—"

Marian pulled violently against the old hands for a moment before she was free. Then she ran down the hall, without looking behind her and without looking at the nurse, who was reading *Field & Stream* at her desk. The nurse, after another triple motion to consult her wrist watch, asked automatically the question put to visitors in all institutions: "Won't you stay and have dinner with *us?*"

Marian never replied. She pushed the heavy door open into the cold air and ran down the steps.

Under the prickly shrub she stopped and quickly, without being seen, retrieved a red apple she had hidden there.

Her yellow hair under the white cap, her scarlet coat, her bare knees all flashed in the sunlight as she ran to meet the big bus rocketing through the street.

"Wait for me!" she shouted. As though at an imperial command, the bus ground to a stop.

She jumped on and took a big bite out of the apple.

A Tree. A Rock. A Cloud

IT WAS RAINING that morning, and still very dark. When the boy reached the streetcar café he had almost finished his route and he went in for a cup of coffee. The place was an all-night café owned by a bitter and stingy man called Leo. After the raw, empty street the café seemed friendly and bright: along the counter there were a couple of soldiers, three spinners from the cotton mill, and in a corner a man who sat hunched over with his nose and half his face down in a beer mug. The boy wore a helmet such as aviators wear. When he went into the café he unbuckled the chin strap and raised the right flap up over his pink little ear; often as he drank his coffee someone would speak to him in a friendly way. But this morning Leo did not look into his face and none of the men were talking. He paid and was leaving the café when a voice called out to him:

"Son! Hey, son!"

He turned back and the man in the corner was crooking his finger and nodding to him. He had brought his face out of the beer mug and he seemed suddenly very happy. The man was long and pale, with a big nose and faded orange hair.

"Hey, son!"

The boy went toward him. He was an undersized boy of about twelve, with one shoulder drawn higher than the other because of the weight of the paper sack. His face was shallow, freckled, and his eyes were round child eyes.

"Yeah, mister?"

The man laid one hand on the paper boy's shoulder, then grasped the boy's chin and turned his face slowly from one side to the other. The boy shrank back uneasily.

284

"Say! What's the big idea?"

The boy's voice was shrill; inside the café it was suddenly very quiet.

The man said slowly: "I love you."

All along the counter the men laughed. The boy, who had scowled and sidled away, did not know what to do. He looked over the counter at Leo, and Leo watched him with a weary, brittle jeer. The boy tried to laugh also. But the man was serious and sad.

"I did not mean to tease you, son," he said. "Sit down and have a beer with me. There is something I have to explain."

Cautiously, out of the corner of his eye, the paper boy questioned the men along the counter to see what he should do. But they had gone back to their beer or their breakfast and did not notice him. Leo put a cup of coffee on the counter and a little jug of cream.

"He is a minor," Leo said.

The paper boy slid himself up onto the stool. His ear beneath the upturned flap of the helmet was very small and red. The man was nodding at him soberly. "It is important," he said. Then he reached in his hip pocket and brought out something which he held up in the palm of his hand for the boy to see.

"Look very carefully," he said.

The boy stared, but there was nothing to look at very carefully. The man held in his big, grimy palm a photograph. It was the face of a woman, but blurred, so that only the hat and the dress she was wearing stood out clearly.

"See?" the man asked.

The boy nodded and the man placed another picture in his palm. The woman was standing on a beach in a bathing suit. The suit made her stomach very big, and that was the main thing you noticed.

"Got a good look?" He leaned over closer and finally asked: "You ever seen her before?"

The boy sat motionless, staring slantwise at the man. "Not so I know of."

"Very well." The man blew on the photographs and put them back into his pocket. "That was my wife."

"Dead?" the boy asked.

Slowly the man shook his head. He pursed his lips as though about to whistle and answered in a longdrawn way: "Nuuu——" he said, "I will explain."

The beer on the counter before the man was in a large brown mug. He did not pick it up to drink. Instead he bent down and, putting his face over the rim, he rested there for a moment. Then with both hands he tilted the mug and sipped.

"Some night you'll go to sleep with your big nose in a mug and drown," said Leo. "Prominent transient drowns in beer. That would be a cute death."

The paper boy tried to signal to Leo. While the man was not looking he screwed up his face and worked his mouth to question soundlessly: "Drunk?" But Leo only raised his eyebrows and turned away to put some pink strips of bacon on the grill. The man pushed the mug away from him, straightened himself, and folded his loose crooked hands on the counter. His face was sad as he looked at the paper boy. He did not blink, but from time to time the lids closed down with delicate gravity over his pale green eyes. It was nearing dawn and the boy shifted the weight of the paper sack.

"I am talking about love," the man said. "With me it is a science."

The boy half slid down from the stool. But the man raised his forefinger, and there was something about him that held the boy and would not let him go away.

"Twelve years ago I married the woman in the photograph. She was my wife for one year, nine months, three days, and two nights. I loved her. Yes . . .'" He tightened his blurred, rambling voice and said again: "I loved her. I thought also that she loved me. I was a railroad engineer. She had all home comforts and luxuries. It never crept into my brain that she was not satisfied. But do you know what happened?"

"Mgneeow!" said Leo.

The man did not take his eyes from the boy's face. "She left me. I came in one night and the house was empty and she was gone. She left me."

"With a fellow?" the boy asked.

Gently the man placed his palm down on the counter. "Why naturally, son. A woman does not run off like that alone."

The café was quiet, the soft rain black and endless in the street outside. Leo pressed down the frying bacon with the prongs of his long fork: "So you have been chasing the floozy for eleven years. You frazzled old rascal!"

For the first time the man glanced at Leo. "Please don't be vulgar. Besides, I was not speaking to you." He turned back to the boy and said in a trusting and secretive undertone: "Let's not pay any attention to him. O.K.?"

The paper boy nodded doubtfully.

"It was like this," the man continued. "I am a person who feels many things. All my life one thing after another has impressed me. Moonlight. The leg of a pretty girl. One thing after another. But the point is that when I had enjoyed anything there was a peculiar sensation as though it was laying around loose in me. Nothing seemed to finish itself up or fit in with the other things. Women? I had my portion of them. The same. Afterward laying around loose in me. I was a man who had never loved."

Very slowly he closed his eyelids, and the gesture was like a curtain drawn at the end of a scene in a play. When he spoke again his voice was excited and the words came fast—the lobes of his large, loose ears seemed to tremble.

"Then I met this woman. I was fifty-one years old and she always said she was thirty. I met her at a filling station and we were married within three days. And do you know what it was like? I just can't tell you. All I had ever felt was gathered together around this woman. Nothing lay around loose in me any more but was finished up by her."

The man stopped suddenly and stroked his long nose. His

voice sank down to a steady and reproachful undertone: "I'm not explaining this right. What happened was this. There were these beautiful feelings and loose little pleasures inside me. And this woman was something like an assembly line for my soul. I run these little pieces of myself through her and I come out complete. Now do you follow me?"

"What was her name?" the boy asked.

"Oh," he said. "I called her Dodo. But that is immaterial."

"Did you try to make her come back?"

The man did not seem to hear. "Under the circumstances you can imagine how I felt when she left me."

Leo took the bacon from the grill and folded two strips of it between a bun. He had a gray face, with slitted eyes, and a pinched nose saddled by faint blue shadows. One of the mill workers signaled for more coffee and Leo poured it. He did not give refills on coffee free. The spinner ate breakfast there every morning, but the better Leo knew his customers the stingier he treated them. He nibbled his own bun as though he grudged it to himself.

"And you never got hold of her again?"

The boy did not know what to think of the man, and his child's face was uncertain with mingled curiosity and doubt. He was new on the paper route; it was still strange to him to be out in the town in the black, queer early morning.

"Yes," the man said. "I took a number of steps to get her back. I went around trying to locate her. I went to Tulsa where she had folks. And to Mobile. I went to every town she had ever mentioned to me, and I hunted down every man she had formerly been connected with. Tulsa, Atlanta, Chicago, Cheehaw, Memphis . . . For the better part of two years I chased around the country trying to lay hold of her."

"But the pair of them had vanished from the face of the earth!" said Leo.

"Don't listen to him," the man said confidentially. "And also just forget those two years. They are not important. What matters is that around the third year a curious thing begun to happen to me."

"What?" the boy asked.

The man leaned down and tilted his mug to take a sip of beer. But as he hovered over the mug his nostrils fluttered slightly; he sniffed the staleness of the beer and did not drink. "Love is a curious thing to begin with. At first I thought only of getting her back. It was a kind of mania. But then as time went on I tried to remember her. But do you know what happened?"

"No," the boy said.

"When I laid myself down on a bed and tried to think about her my mind became a blank. I couldn't see her. I would take out her pictures and look. No good. Nothing doing. A blank. Can you imagine it?"

"Say, Mack!" Leo called down the counter. "Can you imagine this bozo's mind a blank!"

Slowly, as though fanning away flies, the man waved his hand. His green eyes were concentrated and fixed on the shallow little face of the paper boy.

"But a sudden piece of glass on a sidewalk. Or a nickel tune in a music box. A shadow on a wall at night. And I would remember. It might happen in a street and I would cry or bang my head against a lamppost. You follow me?"

"A piece of glass . . ." the boy said.

"Anything. I would walk around and I had no power of how and when to remember her. You think you can put up a kind of shield. But remembering don't come to a man face forward—it corners around sideways. I was at the mercy of everything I saw and heard. Suddenly instead of me combing the countryside to find her she begun to chase me around in my very soul. *She* chasing *me*, mind you! And in my soul!"

The boy asked finally: "What part of the country were you in then?"

"Ooh," the man groaned. "I was a sick mortal. It was like smallpox. I confess, son, that I boozed. I fornicated. I committed any sin that suddenly appealed to me. I am loath to confess it but I will do so. When I recall that period it is all curdled in my mind, it was so terrible."

The man leaned his head down and tapped his forehead on the counter. For a few seconds he stayed bowed over in this position, the back of his stringy neck covered with orange furze, his hands with their long warped fingers held palm to palm in an attitude of prayer. Then the man straightened himself; he was smiling and suddenly his face was bright and tremulous and old.

"It was in the fifth year that it happened," he said. "And with it I started my science."

Leo's mouth jerked with a pale, quick grin. "Well, none of we boys are getting any younger," he said. Then with sudden anger he balled up a dishcloth he was holding and threw it down hard on the floor. "You draggle-tailed old Romeo!"

"What happened?" the boy asked.

The old man's voice was high and clear: "Peace," he answered.

"Huh?"

"It is hard to explain scientifically, son," he said. "I guess the logical explanation is that she and I had fled around from each other for so long that finally we just got tangled up together and lay down and quit. Peace. A queer and beautiful blankness. It was spring in Portland and the rain came every afternoon. All evening I just stayed there on my bed in the dark. And that is how the science come to me."

The windows in the streetcar were pale blue with light. The two soldiers paid for their beers and opened the door —one of the soldiers combed his hair and wiped off his muddy puttees before they went outside. The three mill workers bent silently over their breakfasts. Leo's clock was ticking on the wall.

"It is this. And listen carefully. I meditated on love and reasoned it out. I realized what is wrong with us. Men fall in love for the first time. And what do they fall in love with?"

The boy's soft mouth was partly open and he did not answer.

"A woman," the old man said. "Without science, with

nothing to go by, they undertake the most dangerous and sacred experience in God's earth. They fall in love with a woman. Is that correct, son?"

"Yeah," the boy said faintly.

"They start at the wrong end of love. They begin at the climax. Can you wonder it is so miserable? Do you know how men should love?"

The old man reached over and grasped the boy by the collar of his leather jacket. He gave him a gentle little shake and his green eyes gazed down unblinking and grave.

"Son, do you know how love should be begun?"

The boy sat small and listening and still. Slowly he shook his head. The old man leaned closer and whispered:

"A tree. A rock. A cloud."

It was still raining outside in the street: a mild, gray, endless rain. The mill whistle blew for the six-o'clock shift and the three spinners paid and went away. There was no one in the café but Leo, the old man, and the little paper boy.

"The weather was like this in Portland," he said. "At the time my science was begun. I meditated and I started very cautious. I would pick up something from the street and take it home with me. I bought a goldfish and I concentrated on the goldfish and I loved it. I graduated from one thing to another. Day by day I was getting this technique. On the road from Portland to San Diego——"

"Aw shut up!" screamed Leo suddenly. "Shut up! Shut up!"

The old man still held the collar of the boy's jacket; he was trembling and his face was earnest and bright and wild. "For six years now I have gone around by myself and built up my science. And now I am a master, son. I can love anything. No longer do I have to think about it even. I see a street full of people and a beautiful light comes in me. I watch a bird in the sky. Or I meet a traveler on the road. Everything, son. And anybody. All strangers and all loved! Do you realize what a science like mine can mean?"

The boy held himself stiffly, his hands curled tight around the counter edge. Finally he asked: "Did you ever really find that lady?"

"What? What say, son?"

"I mean," the boy asked timidly, "have you fallen in love with a woman again?"

The old man loosened his grasp on the boy's collar. He turned away and for the first time his green eyes had a vague and scattered look. He lifted the mug from the counter, drank down the yellow beer. His head was shaking slowly from side to side. Then finally he answered: "No, son. You see, that is the last step in my science. I go cautious. And I am not quite ready yet."

"Well!" said Leo. "Well well well!"

The old man stood in the open doorway. "Remember," he said. Framed there in the gray damp light of the early morning, he looked shrunken and seedy and frail. But his smile was bright. "Remember I love you," he said with a last nod. And the door closed quietly behind him.

The boy did not speak for a long time. He pulled down the bangs on his forehead and slid his grimy little forefinger around the rim of his empty cup. Then without looking at Leo he finally asked:

"Was he drunk?"

"No," said Leo shortly.

The boy raised his clear voice higher. "Then was he a dope fiend?"

"No."

The boy looked up at Leo, and his flat little face was desperate, his voice urgent and shrill. "Was he crazy? Do you think he was a lunatic?" The paper boy's voice dropped suddenly with doubt. "Leo? Or not?"

But Leo would not answer him. Leo had run a night café for fourteen years, and he held himself to be a critic of craziness. There were the town characters and also the transients who roamed in from the night. He knew the manias of all of them. But he did not want to satisfy the questions of the waiting child. He tightened his pale face and was silent.

So the boy pulled down the right flap of his helmet and as he turned to leave he made the only comment that seemed safe to him, the only remark that could not be laughed down and despised:

"He sure has done a lot of traveling."

American Literature

Edited by:
Carl Bode—Professor of English, University of Maryland
Leon Howard—Professor of English, University of California at Los Angeles
Louis B. Wright—Director, Folger Shakespeare Library

Volume I—The 17th and 18th Centuries   47601/90¢

Including works of the Colonial and Revolutionary periods, selections by Bradstreet, Taylor, Edwards, Franklin, Bryant, Irving, Cooper, and many others.

Volume II—The First Part of the 19th Century   47602/90¢

Selections fom the works of Poe, Hawthorne, Emerson, Thoreau, Dana, Parkman, Melville, Longfellow, Stowe, Whittier, Simms, and the works of minor writers.

Volume III—The Last Part of the 19th Century   47603/90¢

Civil War verse, and selections by Timrod, Lanier, Jackson, Howells, Whitman, Dickinson, Harte, Ward, Twain, Crane, and others.

Each volume contains critical introductory essays preceding each section as well as biographical information and up-to-date annotated bibliographies for each author.   *Three volume boxed set—$2.70 (#59351)*

Other Distinguished Anthologies of American Literature

THE NEW POCKET ANTHOLOGY OF AMERICAN VERSE. Edited by Oscar Williams. A noted collection spanning the last 300 years, with special emphasis on the writers of the twentieth century.   47592/90¢

A POCKET BOOK OF MODERN AMERICAN SHORT STORIES. Edited by Phillip Van Doren Stern. Stories written during the twenties and thirties by such renowned writers as Hemingway, Fitzgerald, Caldwell, Faulkner, Steinbeck, and Lardner.   46442/60¢

MIDCENTURY. Edited by Orville Prescott. Twenty American short stories written since the end of World War II by such authors as E. B. White, Jean Stafford, Shirley Jackson, and John P. Marquand.
          46441/60¢

THIS IS AMERICA. Edited by Max J. Herzberg. An exciting and diversified collection of stories, lyrics, essays, biographies, papers, orations, and sayings revealing the spirit of America from the Mayflower Compact to FDR.   50083/50¢

LIVING DOCUMENTS IN AMERICAN HISTORY. Edited by John Anthony Scott. A unique collection of over 60 of the most significant political, literary, and folk documents from earliest colonial times to the Civil War—with introductions, bibliography, and songs.   W • 1040/90¢